Peter Bayne, America Project Making of

The Life and Letters of Hugh Miller

Peter Bayne, America Project Making of

The Life and Letters of Hugh Miller

ISBN/EAN: 9783744687515

Printed in Europe, USA, Canada, Australia, Japan

Cover: Foto ©Raphael Reischuk / pixelio.de

More available books at **www.hansebooks.com**

LIFE AND LETTERS

OF

HUGH MILLER.

THE
𝕷𝖎𝖋𝖊 𝖆𝖓𝖉 𝕷𝖊𝖙𝖙𝖊𝖗𝖘
OF
HUGH MILLER.

By PETER BAYNE, M. A.,
AUTHOR OF "THE CHRISTIAN LIFE," ETC.

The Cottage in which Hugh Miller was born.

IN TWO VOLUMES.

VOL. I.

BOSTON:
GOULD AND LINCOLN,
59 WASHINGTON STREET.
NEW YORK: SHELDON AND COMPANY.
CINCINNATI: GEO. S. BLANCHARD & CO.
1871.

PUBLISHERS' PREFATORY NOTE

AMERICAN EDITION.

Y special arrangement with the family of Mr. Miller, the publishers are gratified in being able to present to the American reader Mr. Bayne's very interesting Life and Letters of Hugh Miller, whose works they have previously published.

The works of Hugh Miller have had quite as large a circle of readers in America as in Great Britain, and nowhere has his genius been more admired, or his sudden death more sincerely deplored. It was known soon after his decease that to Peter Bayne, Esq., was entrusted the duty of preparing his biography. The work could have fallen to no better hands; for Mr. Bayne, in the biographic sketches of his "Christian Life," had proved himself to be a master in this department of literature. He had also succeeded to the editorial chair of the "Witness," and was thus brought into intimate sympathy with Hugh Miller's public life and labors.

The volumes, long expected, are at length completed, and will form an enduring monument to the genius of the Cromarty geologist. In them the *man* is seen to have been far greater than the *author*, and to have built up a character grander than his works. Hugh Miller was one of the true heroes of our age, lifting himself from obscurity to eminence by force of genius, and by uncomplaining toil. Since Benjamin Franklin, there has been no finer example of a self-made man, with character fully rounded, and free alike from vanity and from dogmatism. Since John Knox, there has been no Scotchman, combining in grander proportion the genius and religion of his country. He was a greater man than Robert Burns; for while both

7

rose from the people, and had a sore struggle with poverty and social obstacles, Burns fretted and succumbed and wrecked himself, while Miller endured without a murmur, and conquered, and enjoyed the fruits of victory.

These volumes throw light on an important period in Hugh Miller's life. The American people are tolerably familiar with his early years, whose story has been told by his own pen in his " My Schools and Schoolmasters," with a wonderful charm. They are acquainted also with those geological writings ' which made him the most popular scientific writer of his day. But they have known little of that editorial career, during which the " Witness" became the most influential paper in Scotland, and its editor wielded a power over the Scottish nation second only to that of Chalmers. This part of his life is brought out with great fulness by his biographer, and will awaken general interest.

Hugh Miller was a lover of truth, and scorned all evasions and tricks in argument. As one reads the record of his candor, his thoroughness in scientific study, and his unfaltering faith in the harmony of science and revelation, the longing finds utterance that he were living to take part in present conflicts. The theories of Darwin and Huxley and Spencer are more seductive and dangerous than those of Owen or Chambers. As Dr. McCosh well says, in his interesting reminiscences, "Had Hugh Miller lived, he would certainly have grappled with the 'Positive Philosophy,' as he did with the 'Vestiges of Creation.'" But he passed away ere this conflict was fairly begun, leaving to others both the labor and the honor of vindicating the truth.

These volumes may be the last relating to Hugh Miller which the publishers will have the pleasure of presenting to the American public; and they are a fitting close to the series of his works, which have nurtured a love for science and strengthened religious faith in so many American homes.

BOSTON, April 10, 1871.

CONTENTS OF VOL. I.

BOOK ONE.

THE BOY.

BOOK TWO.

THE APPRENTICE.

CHAPTER II.

CHAPTER III.

CHAPTER IV.

BOOK THREE.

THE JOURNEYMAN.

CHAPTER I.

CHAPTER II.

CHAPTER III.

CHAPTER IV.

CHAPTER V.

CHAPTER VI.

CHAPTER VII.

CHAPTER VIII.

CHAPTER IX.

CHAPTER X.

CHAPTER XI.

CHAPTER XII.

CHAPTER XIII.

CHAPTER XIV.

CHAPTER XV.

CHAPTER XVI.

CHAPTER XVII.

BOOK I.

THE BOY.

———◆———

" Hardy, bold, and wild,
As best befits the mountain-child."

LIFE AND LETTERS

OF

HUGH MILLER.

⚬⚬⦂⚭⦂⚬⚬

CHAPTER I.

BIRTH, PARENTAGE, AND FIRST IMPRESSIONS.

AS the voyager passes from the blue expanse of the
Moray Frith into the land-locked bay of Cromarty,
he sees on the left, crowning a swell of green upland which runs crescent-like along the coast, a
pillar of red sandstone, rising fifty feet into the air, and
surmounted by a statue. The few white houses, embow-
ered in garden foliage, which form the better part of the
village of Cromarty, cluster beneath; and the sea, faced by
a row of thatched fishermen's cottages, comes rippling, at
every flow of the tide, to within a bow-shot of its base.
The statue represents a grave, strong-built man, of massive
head and thoughtful face, who seems to look out steadfastly
upon the waves. Statue and pillar constitute the monument reared by his countrymen to Hugh Miller.

Almost at the foot of the pillar stands a humble cottage,
and on the sward from which it rises is placed the village
church-yard. In that cottage Hugh Miller was born; and
during his boyhood and early youth he was dependent on a

17

widowed mother who maintained herself and her family by the " sedulously plied but indifferently remunerated labor " of her needle. In that church-yard are several headstones chiselled by his hand when he earned his bread as a journeyman mason.

Hugh Miller broke suddenly upon the public of Scotland in the prime of his years. He was already a man of ripe thought and confirmed intellectual habits, betraying none of the extravagance of opinion and spasmodic vehemence of language, usually characteristic of self-trained genius. Solidity and sobriety of judgment, sensitive dislike of paradox, contempt for the catch-words of political sciolism and free-thinking conceit, purity, vigor, and elegance of style, which reminded critics of Goldsmith and of Addison, were the results of his self-education. Possessed of large stores of literary information, an original explorer in science, with definite and firmly held opinions on religious, political, and social questions, thoroughly understanding the character of his countrymen, and ardently sympathizing with its nobler elements, he no sooner found a medium for the communication of his ideas than he became a most influential guide of opinion, and continued to be so to the hour of his death. Adopting literature and science henceforward as the business of his life, he produced a series of unique and remarkable works, in which were intermingled racy and sagacious observations on men and manners, with delineations, exquisitely fresh and vivid, of nature's facts and beauties. They were at once pronounced by eminent critics to belong to a high and rare order of literary productions ; they became popular, and have retained their popularity with the best class of readers in Britain and America ; and they have been translated into most European languages. It will be admitted that they bear the impress of an original, determinate, and admirable mind ;

noble in all its ground-tones, richly endowed in respect both
of intellect and of imagination, penetrated with reverence
for God and for the revelation which God has made of himself in nature, providence, and Christ, full of brotherly
sympathy, of candor, intelligence, and affection. A reputation thus founded is not likely to prove ephemeral ; and
the name of Hugh Miller, we may safely presume, will be
his most enduring monument. How the son of a sailor's
widow came to address and retain an audience as wide as
the world of culture, — how the Cromarty stone-mason
qualified himself for achieving a European reputation, — is
a question fitted to interest wise curiosity, and deserving an
explicit and careful reply.

Hugh Miller, as all the world knows, was the author of
an autobiographic work entitled " My Schools and Schoolmasters," and it may have occurred to some that he thus
anticipated and superseded biography. But there are no
good grounds for this opinion. The book which has been
named, recognized by all judges as one of the most captivating and able of the author's performances, has a place
in English literature from which it cannot be moved ; but
it is no substitute for the biography of Hugh Miller. In
the first place, it deals with but one portion of its author's
career, and that the portion which preceded his emergence
into public life. In the second place, a considerable amount
of biographic material relating to Hugh Miller, unen-
croached upon in the " Schools and Schoolmasters," is in
existence. From early boyhood he was fond of jotting
down particulars connected with his personal history, and
for many years previously to his being harnessed to steady
literary toil, he took great delight in letter-writing. In the
third place, it will hardly be disputed by any one who
reflects upon the subject, that biography is necessarily a
different matter from autobiography, and that the latter is

to be regarded simply as one of the sources from which the biographer constructs his narrative.   Mr. Lewes, whose Life of Goethe has a place of honor not only among biographies, but among the select masterpieces of biography, may be held to have settled this point.   He had before him Goethe's celebrated autobiography, in three volumes, a work which its author declares to have been composed in a spirit of austere veracity, and yet Mr. Lewes finds it characterized by " abiding inaccuracy of *tone.*"   Goethe, looking from the distance of half a century, beheld his own face through a medium which softened, brightened, or obliterated the features.   Hugh Miller, when he wrote the " Schools and Schoolmasters," was not so old as Goethe when he wrote "Poetry and Truth from my Life ; " nor am I prepared to say that the former departs from literal accuracy to the same extent as the latter ; but in the case of Hugh Miller, also, the impression made by an event or spectacle, as set down at the moment by the boy or lad, and the account of that impression given by the man of fifty, prove often to be two different things.   " It is possible," says Hugh Miller himself, " for two histories of the same period and individual to be at once true to fact, and unlike each other in the scenes which they describe and the events which they record."

Hugh Miller was born in the town of Cromarty on the 10th of October, 1802.   The occurrence appears to have acted on the imagination of his father, as he had a " singular dream," respecting his first-born.   The midwife remarked that the conformation of the head was unusual, and indicated, in her sage opinion, that the child would turn out an idiot.*

Cromarty was a more important place seventy years ago

---

* Letter of Miller to Mr. Isaac Forsyth, Feb. 30, 1830.

than it is now, but its dimensions never exceeded those of a considerable village. It is one of several miniature towns which stud the shores of the Maolbuie or Black Isle, a peninsular block of land, washed on the north by the Frith of Cromarty, on the south by the Frith of Beauly, and abutting on the German Ocean in a green headland, fringed with pine, known to mariners as the Southern Sutor of Cromarty. On the landward side of this headland nestles the little town. The Maolbuie, stretching westward, rises from encircling sea, occasionally in abrupt crags, generally in gradual undulation. Here and there, along the water-courses and in the hollows, are glimpses of green field and leafy wood, but the general impression is that of a huge swell of brown moorland, overblown by sea-winds, traversed by chill fogs, and constituting, on the whole, one of the most bleak and ungenial districts in Scotland. The natives of Cromarty have always been a hardy, long-lived race. The climate, though salubrious, is severe. The town is exposed at all seasons to high gales from the North Sea, laden with mist or sleet, and even at midsummer keen blasts from the Atlantic make their way through the western hill-gorges, send the spray of the frith whistling through the air, and pierce to every nook and cranny of the shivering town. But there are fertile spots in its immediate neighborhood, and in sheltered nooks the elm and poplar flourish; the air, except when darkened by sea-fog, is clear and bracing; a chain of hills, running along the frith on the north, leads the eye to the heights of Ben Wyvis sleeping in the pearl-blue of distance; there are brooks rippling through wooded dells, and caves hollowed in the rock; and at all times, and from almost every point of view, there is a gleaming of green or purple waters, wreathed with snowy foam. In favorable weather Cromarty is a pleasant place; one who had passed in it a kindly childhood and youth might love it well. Nature, as seen in its vicinity, if not clad in Alpine grandeur, has many aspects of beauty and tenderness, and at least one aspect, that of ocean in calm or in storm, of utmost sublimity.

Like all towns on the eastern coast of Scotland, Cromarty is inhabited principally by an English-speaking race, substantially identical with that found in the lowlands of Scotland. Hugh Miller never spoke the language of the Scottish Highlanders, and was apt in conversation to lay emphasis on the fact of his being a Teuton. But there was a dash of good Celtic blood in his veins. Donald Ross, called also Donald Roy, or the Red, the grandfather of his grandmother, was of the best Gaelic type, with the vivacity, courage, and religious susceptibility of his race. The history and character of Donald, as portrayed in the revering narratives of his descendants, were among the sacred influences of Hugh Miller's childhood. The figure of his gray-haired sire, standing up in the Church of Nigg, and defying the Presbytery, in the Name of God, to join a minister, not called by its people, to its stone-walls; the ring which Miller's grandmother had received, at the time of her marriage, from Donald, as her spousal ring to her *other* husband, the Head of the Church; the mysterious hints which would pass round the fireside circle in the evening, that this patriarch, like the men of God of old, had been privileged with visions of the unseen world, with whisperings out of the abysmal deeps of futurity, — all this was stamped upon the child's imagination, predisposing him, in the dawn of his sympathies, to look with reverence on the religious character, and preparing him to become, one day, a leader among the evangelical religionists of Scotland.

Strong, however, as the influence of his Celtic ancestry may have been on Hugh Miller, it was not so powerful as that derived from his Lowland fathers. He was descended on that side from a long line of seafaring men, whose intrepid and adventurous spirit had led them from their native Cromarty, to sail, in the earliest times of Scottish history, with Sir Andrew Wood or the "bold Bartons," and at a later period to voyage and fight under Anson, or to engage in buccaneering enterprises on the Spanish Main. For more than a hundred years before the birth of Hugh Miller, not one of his paternal ancestors had been laid in the churchyard of Cromarty. To the latest hour of his life, he cherished the profoundest enthusiasm for his father, the hardy and resolute seaman whose name he bore. He was only five years old when Hugh Miller, the elder, perished at sea; but he had already learned to love his father with an affection stronger than is common in childhood, and " long after every one else had ceased to hope," he might be seen on the grassy knoll behind his mother's house, looking wistfully out upon the Moray Frith for " the sloop with the two stripes of white and the two square topsails."

Miller has left us, in the " Schools and Schoolmasters," a powerful and vivid sketch of his father, and the lineaments are those of a remarkable man. Very gentle, very brave, serenely invincible in every change of fortune, patient to endure individual wrong, but with a flash of keenest fire in him to avenge the cruelty or injustice which he saw practised on others, he was great without knowing it, and, what is also perhaps an advantage, without its being known. Miller says finely that there was a " bit of picture " in all his recollections of his father, and most picturesquely has he arranged the pieces in the mosaic of his narrative. We see the bold seaman, bronzed by the southern sun, asleep in his open boat on the Ganges, and mark him start on awaking as he meets the glare of a tiger's eye, its paws resting on the gunwale. We behold him afloat for three days in the open sea on the bottom of an upturned boat, sharks glancing around him on the crests of the waves. He bears meekly the oppressions of a cruel captain, until his kind-hearted Irish comrade is being chained down to the deck beneath a tropical sun; then, the genial warmth in his bosom kindling into electric flame, he faces the tyrant. "The captain drew a loaded pistol from his belt; the sailor struck up his hand; and, as the bullet whistled through the rigging above, he grappled with him and disarmed him in a trice." At the action off the Dogger Bank he does the work of two men, and, when the action seems over, is utterly prostrate; but no sooner does the sign of battle fly again along the line, than he springs to his feet, fresh as if he had awakened from morning slumber. Not less characteristic is the steadfastness of his manly ambition to realize a competence. As wave after wave of adversity meets him, he rises through the swell, his brow showing clear and proud in the light of victory.

It was the deliberate conviction of Hugh Miller that his father was an abler man than he. To this opinion few will subscribe; but the more we study the character of the son, the deeper will be our conviction that it is essentially the character of the father, developed, on the intellectual side, with more of symmetry and completeness, and seen at last under softer lights. Physiologists would probably have something to say on this point. Modern science tends to show that there was more in Mr. Shandy's philosophy of character than Sterne's humor gives account of, and that, if we can rightly estimate the effect of local circumstance and other influences to modify or to transmute, the ground-plan of a man's character may be found written in his bones. Hugh Miller's father was at the time of his birth a man of forty-four; mature in every faculty; of marked individuality and iron will. His mother was a girl of eighteen, who had been brought up at her husband's knee, and had learned to revere him as a father before she accepted him as a lover. Throughout life she displayed no special force of mind or character. The first child of such a marriage was likely to bear the indelible stamp of his father's manhood.

Fancy delights to construct oracles from the earliest recollections of men who have become famous. We must guard against attaching too much importance to the infantile reminiscences of Miller. Those he mentions are graceful in themselves, and form a singularly appropriate introduction to the life of a man of science. He remembered going into the garden one day before completing his third year, and seeing there " a minute duckling, covered with soft, yellow hair, growing out of the soil by its feet, and beside it a plant that bore as its flowers a crop of little musselshells, of a deep, red color." The "duckling," he tells us, belonged to the vegetable kingdom, though he could no longer identify it; the mussel-bearing plant was, he believed, a scarlet-runner. If there is in this incident anything unusual, it is the circumstance that natural phenomena of form and color, so simple and common, should have powerfully affected the imagination of a child not three years old. The incidents first stored in memory are generally those of change or excitement, — a storm, a removal, a journey, a visit to a puppet show or waxwork. The forms of those natural objects by which a child is surrounded, leaves, trees, flowers, fall faintly on the mental tablets: probably not one man in a thousand retains a more vivid recollection of them than of the curtains round his cradle. During Hugh Miller's life, the observation of a new fact in nature afforded him a thrill of pleasure which never lost its freshness, and it seems probable that the first consciousness of this pleasure arose in the breast of small, toddling, large-headed Hugh, when he opened wide his eyes to take the bearings of the mysterious duckling and the vegetable mussels.

More definitely important, in a biographic point of view, are those incidents of Miller's childhood which formed what he calls a "machinery of the supernatural." About the time when the incomprehensible duckling grew out of the earth before his eyes, he thought that he beheld the apparition of his buccaneering ancestor, John Feddes, "in the form of a large, tall, very old man, attired in a light-blue great-coat," who stood on the landing-place at the top of the stairs and regarded him with apparent complacency. He was much frightened, and for years dreaded a reappearance of the phantom.

Still more circumstantial is his account of what he saw on that night when, far away on the North Sea, his father's ship went down. "There were no forebodings," he is careful to tell us, in the Cromarty cottage. No storm agitated the air, and though the billows of a deep ground-swell broke heavily under leaden skies, the weather occasioned no alarm. A hopeful letter had been received from his father, written at Peterhead, and his mother sat "beside the household fire, plying the cheerful needle." Suddenly the door fell open and little Hugh was sent to shut it. "Day," he proceeds, "had not wholly disappeared, but it was fast posting on to night, and a gray haze spread a neutral tint of dimness over every more distant object, but left the nearer ones comparatively distinct, when I saw at the open door, within less than a yard of my breast, as plainly as I ever saw anything, a dissevered hand and arm stretched towards me. Hand and arm were apparently those of a female; they bore a livid and sodden appearance; and directly fronting me, where the body ought to have been, there was only blank, transparent space, through which I could see the dim forms of the objects beyond. I was fearfully startled and ran shrieking to my mother, telling what I had seen; and the house-girl, whom she next sent to shut the door, apparently affected by my terror, also returned frightened, and said that she, too, had seen the woman's hand; which, however, did not seem to be the case. And finally my mother, going to the door, saw nothing, though she appeared much impressed by the extremeness of my terror, and the minuteness of my description. I communicate the story as it lies fixed in my memory, without attempting to explain it. The supposed apparition may have been merely a momentary affection of the eye, of the nature described by Sir Walter Scott, in his 'Demonology,' and Sir David Brewster, in his 'Natural Magic.' But if so, the affection was one of which I experienced no after return; and its coincidence, in the case, with the probable time of my father's death, seems at least curious."

Men who believe in a ghost-story seldom favor us with unqualified avowals of the fact. Hugh Miller seems to have been persuaded at fifty that the livid hand he saw at five was preternatural. The incident is thus invested with interest in a biographic point of view. It affords us a glimpse into the subtlest workings of Hugh Miller's mind. We must, therefore, consider it carefully.

The appearance, to begin with, is to be classed among the more easily explicable phenomena of optical delusion. The child, from the day his mind began to receive impressions of any kind, had been encompassed with an atmosphere of superstition. In days of steamships and telegraphs, sailors and fishermen continue a superstitious race; but it is only by the strongest effort of imagination that we can realize the extent to which the natural and the supernatural were confounded in remote fishing-towns like Cromarty at the commencement of this century. Teach a child to look for ghosts, and he will be sure to see them. Hugh had learned to associate the idea of his father with a special manifestation of the awful and the supernatural. Often while the embers were burning low on winter evenings, and every inmate of the cottage listened in awe-struck silence, had he hung upon the lips of "Jack Grant, the mate," as he told how his father had sailed from Peterhead beneath a gloomy twilight; how a woman and child who begged a passage were taken on board; how the wind rose and the snow-storm lashed the vessel; how a dead-light gleamed out on the cross-trees; how a ghostly woman, with a child in her arms, flitted round the master at the helm; how, when dawn glimmered over the sea, the ship struck and rolled over amid the breakers on " the terrible bar of Findhorn!" and how the corpse of the woman, still clasping the babe in her arms, was floated out through a hole in the side of the wreck.

Turn now to the passage quoted. His father being away at sea, the child is sent, as the dusk thickens, to close the cottage door. The night-mist is creeping up from the sea. I have seen that mist, seen it through the eyes of childhood, on the moorland of the Maolbuie, a few miles west of Cromarty; and no one who has seen it can wonder that a vivid imagination should evoke spectral forms from its twilight imagery. The same power of fantasy which called up the ghost of old John Feddes, to stand upon the top of the stair, revealed to the eye of the boy, as he peered into the mist on that melancholy evening, a dissevered hand and arm. There is one little circumstance which renders it matter of demonstration that his mind was preoccupied by expectation of the marvellous. "Hand and arm," he informs us, "were apparently those of a female." How did he know this? A child of five could not distinguish between the " livid and sodden " hand and arm of a man and the "livid and sodden" hand and arm of a woman. His imagination, haunted by the woman of Jack Grant's narrative, created her.

The whole affair, then, resolves itself into a strong mental impression of little Hugh's throwing itself out in bodiless form on the mist of the night. And as was the boy so was the man. A sustained intensity of mental vision, a creative power of fantasy, characterized Miller to the last. Not powerful enough to overbear or to pervert the scientific instinct with which it was associated, it had a pervasive influence on his mental operations; the feeling, belief, impression, on his mind had for him a substantive reality; and there was an antecedent probability that, if the steadiness of his intellectual nerve were shaken by disease, or by excess of mental toil, some fixed idea might obtain the mastery over him and hurl his reason from her throne.

It has been said that his mother was not remarkable for mental power or for strength of character. She had, however, one intellectual faculty in extraordinary vigor, to wit, memory, and she loaded it with knowledge of a peculiarly unprofitable kind. Her belief in fairies, witches, dreams, presentiments, ghosts, was unbounded, and she was restrained by no modern scruples from communicating either her fairy lore, or the faith with which she received it, to her son. Her faith in her legendary personages was inextricably involved with her belief in the angels and spirits of Scripture, and to betray scepticism as to apparitions and fairies was in her view to take part with the Sadducee or the infidel. "Such was the powerful influence," says Mrs. Miller, "to which little Hugh was subjected for the first six years of his life, — a kind of education the force of which he himself could scarcely estimate. Add to everything else that much of his mother's sewing was making garments for the dead. Fancy that little, low room in the winter evenings, its atmosphere at all times murky from the dark earthern floor, the small windows, the fire on the hearth which, though furnished with a regular chimney, allowed much smoke to escape before it found passage. Fancy little Hugh sitting on a low stool by that hearth-fire, his mother engaged at a large chest, which serves her for a table on which stands a single candle. Her work is dressing the shroud and the winding-sheet, the dead irons click incessantly, and her conversation as she passes to and fro to heat her irons at the fire is of the departed, and of mysterious warnings and spectres. Suddenly, as the hour grows late, distinct raps are heard on this chest, — the forerunners, she says, of another dissolution. Her tall, thin figure is drawn up in an attitude of intense listening for these signs from the unseen world. The child has been surrounded and permeated with the weird atmosphere. Then a paroxysm of terror supervenes and he is put to bed, to that bed in the corner, in a recess in the wall, where he can still see the work proceed, and hear the monotonous click-click of those irons, till his little eyes close, and the world of dreams mingles with that of reality. I have no doubt that the overpowering terror of those early times, the inability to distinguish between waking and sleeping visions, returned in his last days, stimulating the action of a diseased brain. The peculiarity of his mother's character told against him. There was plenty of affection, but no counterbalancing grain of anything which could in the least qualify these tremendous doses of the supernatural. He did not learn to read so early as most children, — though, as he has told me, he learned his letters first when almost in arms, off the signboards above the shop-doors, — so that, until after six, the marvellous in its lighter and more harmless forms, as in 'Jack and the Bean-stalk,' etc., did not mingle with its darker and stronger shadows. From his mother Hugh undoubtedly drew almost all the materials for his 'Scenes and Legends' and 'Lykewake,' etc., and every minutest touch I have given you has been gathered from his lips and hers."

Hugh Miller's mother was evidently one who, in the jargon of the spirit-rapping fraternity, would be called a good medium. Interpreted into the language of persons who are neither knaves nor fools, this will mean that she was one who, having long permitted fantasy to be sole regent of her mind, had fallen into the habit of mistaking the pale shapes and flitting shadows of its ghostly moonlight for the substantial forms of noonday. Mrs. Miller closes her account of this singular woman with the following anecdote: " She told me that, on the night of Hugh's death, suspecting no evil and anticipating no bad tidings, about midnight she saw a wonderfully bright light, like a ball of electric fire, flit about the room, and linger first on one object of furniture and then on another. She *sat up in bed* to watch its progress. At last it alighted, when, just as she wondered, with her eyes fixed on it, what it might portend, it was suddenly quenched, — did not die out, but, as it were, extinguished itself in a moment, leaving utter blackness behind, and on her frame the thrilling effect of a sudden and awful calamity." The power of distinguishing between visions seen when the eyes were shut and actual phenomena, seen when the eyes were open, had manifestly been impaired in this woman; and we cannot believe that the influence of so superstitious a mother upon Hugh Miller was not powerful, merely because he has refrained from saying much about her in the " Schools and Schoolmasters." Had he completely emancipated himself from that influence, we might have had a full statement of its nature and extent; but, though he evidently believed some of the ghostly sights of his childhood to have been preternatural, he would instinctively shrink from the confession that his notions of the night-side of nature, and

of the boundary line between the visible and the invisible
world, were to the last modified by what he had learned at
his mother's knee.   It is fair to her to add that her power
of enchaining the attention of listeners, while she told her
tales, was quite extraordinary, and that her son assuredly
owed to her, in part at least, his genius for narrative.

CHAPTER II.

THE brave, kind father, then, is dead; and the boy, gaze he never so long across the waves, will not again clap his hands and run to tell his mother that the sloop is in the offing. The girlish widow, with her son of five, and her two daughters just emerging from infancy, must face the world alone. Of fixed yearly income she has about twelve pounds, but she is skilled as a seamstress, and applies herself industriously to her needle. By way of substitute for a father's authority over her children, and for a husband's counsels to herself, she has the vigilant, superintending friendliness of her two brothers, known to readers of the "Schools and Schoolmasters" as Uncle James and Uncle Sandy. These occupied a single dwelling, into which they took one of the little girls, and in which Hugh lived as much as at home. He could hardly have been more happy in fireside guides and instructors. James, the elder, was a saddler; Alexander, a carpenter. In any rank of society they would have been exceptional men. Thoughtful, sagacious, modest, independent; ardent in their love of knowledge, and with no inconsiderable stock of information; reverent towards God; mindful of duty, — they were such as the best Scottish peasants and mechanics of the olden time used to be. "I never knew a man," says Miller, "more rigidly just in his dealings than

33

Uncle James, or who regarded every species of meanness with a more thorough contempt." What a grand contribution to the education of Hugh Miller was made by Uncle James in leaving *that* impression on his memory and his heart! When Miller first heard Dr. M'Crie preach, he wrote to his Uncle James: "In age and figure I know not where to point out any one who more resembles him than yourself." Collating this with his description of the military bearing and combined modesty and dignity of demeanor of Dr. M'Crie, we are led to form a favorable idea of Uncle James' outer man. Uncle Sandy had been in the navy, had fought in many engagements in the great French war, and had settled down in his native place to a life of happy industry, digging his sawyer's pit in summer in some protected nook of the green wood, and finding entertainment at eventide in the wonders of the field or the shore. He fought his battles over again and yet again for the benefit of little Hugh; but it was from others, not from himself, that the boy heard of his personal exploits; and his estimate of military splendors was not extravagant. " Prophecy, I find," he said, "gives to all our glories but a single verse, and it is a verse of judgment." In after life Miller thought of writing a life of Alexander Wright.

Such were Hugh Miller's instructors from the end of his fifth year, instructors to whom, as he justly testifies, he owed more than to any of the teachers whose schools he afterwards attended. The tales with which they charmed him called intellect and imagination into genial and healthful exercise. "I remember," he says, in an account of his early years, composed for Principal Baird when he was twenty-seven, and largely drawn upon in the " Schools and Schoolmasters." "I remember that, from my fourth to my sixth year, I derived much pleasure from oral narrative, and that my imagination, even at this early period, had acquired strength enough to present me with vividly-colored pictures of all the scenes described to me, and of all the incidents related." His eye had not yet opened on the world of books.

Hugh had been sent to a dame's school before his father's death, and in the course of his sixth year, after much labor and small apparent profit, he made the discovery that "the art of reading is the art of finding stories in books." Did ever child in Eastern romance light on so wonderful a talisman? The gates flew open and the gardens of knowledge stretched before him, the trees drooping with golden fruit, the earth radiant with flowers. Hugh Miller had made what he calls the grand acquirement of his life; he could hold converse with books.

Now at last, like all children of talent, he revelled in the traditionary literature of the nursery: "Jack the Giant Killer" "Blue Beard," "Aladdin and the Wonderful Lamp." Two other books gave him equal or greater delight: the "Pilgrim's Progress," and Pope's "Homer." "I saw," says Miller, "even at this immature period, that no writer could cast a javelin with half the force of Homer." Pope's transmutations of the "Iliad" and "Odyssey" have often been favorite reading with children. One of the choice sports of Arnold's early boyhood was to act the battles of the Homeric heroes, and recite their several speeches according to Pope.

Hugh was now promoted from the dame's school to the parish school, and introduced into the society of one hundred and twenty boys. These, with a class of girls, bringing the whole number up to one hundred and fifty, were under the superintendence of a single master; and, when it is added that the competence of that master's acquirements and the excellence of his character were qualified by sluggishness and associated with no force, fineness, or sympathetic richness of mind, it will be evident that little deserving the name of education could be had in the place. A boy of six, however strong his intellectual bent, requires a certain amount of well-applied compulsion to induce him to prefer his lessons to his play. Hugh, left to do as he chose, preferred the latter; but if, in his lessons, he was " an egregious trifler," he was intellectual enough in his sports. In addition to the nursery treasures already mentioned, the narratives of Cook, Anson, and Woods Rogers afforded him inexhaustible delight, and inflamed him with a passionate desire to be a sailor. He spent much of his time sauntering about the harbor, or peering and prying aboard the ships. One of his amusements was to trace on the maps of an old geographical grammar the path of vessels to and from the countries visited by his father or by Uncle Sandy. He began to compose before he could write. " I was in the habit," he says, in the account of his life previously referred to, " of quitting my school companions for the sea-shore, where I would saunter for whole hours, pouring out long blank verse effusions (rhyme was a discovery of after date) about sea-fights, storms, ghosts, and desert islands. These effusions were no sooner brought to a close than forgotten; and no one knew anything of them but myself; for I had not yet attained the art of writing, and I could compose only when alone." That passion for linguistic expression, — that rapture in fitting thought and emotion to words, — by which nature seems to point out the born literary man, was already characteristic of Miller.

Following this child, whose very amusements are intellectual, into the school-room, we perceive that he is in a fair way to earn the reputation of dunce. Accustomed to learn by the eye, — to stray down vistas of picture constructed for him by his imagination from the materials of his favorite books, — he takes no interest in the mechanical operations of memory. The Latin Rudiments in particular prove incapable of imaginative illumination. The sluggard schoolmaster never tells him that, if he be but brave enough to grope for a time as through a dark passage, the classic wonderland will open on his sight. An intelligent and spirited boy, to work heartily at his tasks, must know what he is about, and have some conception of the guerdon which is to reward his toil. It never occurs to this schoolmaster that *he* may.be the dunce, stolidly inapprehensive of the requirements of the case, and of the nature of his duty towards his peculiar pupil. He takes the more obvious, comfortable, and human-natural course of deciding that Hugh's uncles have overrated his abilities, and that he is a mere ordinary dullard.

Miller's trifling proved infectious. He had one day, on some impulse of the moment, taken to relating, to the boy who sat next him, the adventures of Sir William Wallace. A group of fascinated listeners soon hung round the interesting dunce. To narratives from blind Harry succeeded tales from Cook and Anson; and when these were exhausted imagination was called upon to supply the article in request. The improvising practice he had enjoyed in his solitary walks now stood him in good stead, and he regaled his auditors with

> boyish histories,
> Of battle, bold adventure, dungeon, wreck,
> Flights, terrors, sudden rescues.

" In a short time,"—these are his own words,—"my narratives had charmed the very shadow of discipline out of the class." In his English reading lessons he appeared to some advantage, the master contriving to make out that he could distinguish between good and bad in style; but on the whole he looked upon school attendance as a mere curtailment of his freedom, made no progress whatever in spelling or parsing, and in Latin failed utterly.

In some respects, — always excepting those for which it was specially intended, — the school was not amiss. In the company of one hundred and fifty boys and girls, there is likely to be not a little that will contribute to mental and physical development. From the windows could be seen at all hours ships and boats, entering or leaving the harbor; at certain seasons the turf before the door glittered with myriads of herrings, the air became alive with bustle of curing operations; a pig-slaughtering establishment was at hand, where Hugh, turning characteristically from the slaying processes, could look inquiringly into the mysteries of porcine anatomy; and there was a chance, at any moment, of taking part in a glorious expedition sent forth to exact, *arte vel Marte*, the tribute of peats which the boatmen of Ross, as they arrived with their cargoes, were bound to pay to the school. An annual cock-fight was celebrated by the boys and their teacher; but in this he took no more interest than in the killing of the pigs; the tenderness he had derived from his father forbade him.

In his tenth year the spell cast over his imagination by the narratives of the sea-captains had been broken. He had read "The Adventures of Sir William Wallace," by the Scottish Homer of the fifteenth century, of whom we know only that his name was Harry, that he was blind, that he earned his bread by repeating his poetry in the laird's hall and by the farmer's ingle, and that he professed to base his narrative on a history of Wallace, written in Latin by his chaplain, named Blair. The poem is Homerically crowded with incident, and its hero-worship of Wallace is as fervent as Homer's of Odysseus. There is no trace of that sentimental delicacy which glows in the chivalrous romances of the nineteenth century; no cosmopolitan sympathy; not the faintest surmise that anything can be said on the *other* side of the question. National bards are ruthless partisans, from "the Ionian father of the rest," downwards. Homer does not apologize for Ulysses when he lays waste the town of the harmless Cyconians, and distributes their goods, wives, and children among his followers. Homer has not one tear of pity for the tortured Melanthius, tortured for no fault but his courage, or for the female slaves, cruelly murdered for not having been inconceivably faithful to their master and mistress; and it never occurs to him as possible that any one can think the slaughter of the suitors themselves, for the sole fault of continuing to pay their addresses to a woman who would not frankly say No, and whose husband, they reasonably trusted, was at the bottom of the sea, rather startling in its sternness. Compare the return of Odysseus with the return of Enoch Arden, who, by Homeric law, ought to have cut down his Annie with one blow, and her Philip Ray with another, and you will perceive the difference, in what may be called emotional atmosphere, between the time of Tennyson and those periods of national life in which poems like Homer's " Odyssey," and Blind Harry's " Wallace," come into existence. In general poetical capacity the Scottish minstrel is incomparably inferior to Homer; but it was owing doubtless to the entireness and intensity of his patriotic devotion to Scotland and to Wallace, that his book was for centuries " the Bible of the Scottish people," and that it profoundly affected the boyish imaginations of Robert Burns, of Walter Scott, and of Hugh Miller. The fiery patriotism of this book inspired those national songs of Burns, and those magical tones occurring at intervals in all his poems, which will thrill readers to their inmost hearts so long as love of country endures. Its effect on Hugh Miller was to make him a Scottish patriot to the finger-tips. Affection for his country was from that time a ruling passion in his breast, and his ideal of a great man was a great Scotchman.

No wise critic will dispute that this was an important and an auspicious advance in the development of the boy. It appears to be a law of the feelings that, to be sound, strong, and healthful, they must proceed from the particular to the general, philanthropy rooting itself in household kindness, cosmopolitan interest in the human race growing out of undistinguishing ardor of affection for one's countrymen. He who, as a boy, is indifferent to his own country, will, as a man, be indifferent to all countries. Hugh Miller, we need not doubt, owed much of that home-bred vigor, that genial strength, racy picturesqueness and idiomatic pith, which characterize his writings, to the early influence of Blind Harry.

Meanwhile he has been learning to read in a book whose lessons he could not outgrow, and whose illuminated lettering, of gem and flower and shell, has a charm for eye and heart, which had been absent from the Latin Rudiments. Upon the sands at ebb-tide, when the slant sunlight strikes ruddy from the west, the boy may be seen trotting by the side of Uncle Sandy, hunting for lump-fish in the weeded pools, hanging in ecstasy over the sea-mosses, that glance through the lucid wave with more delicate splendor of rubied flush and scarlet gleam, of golden tress and silken fringe, of tender pearl and beaming silver, than graced the jewelled princesses of his fairy-books, and drinking in with eager attention every word uttered by his guide. We can picture him a kilted urchin, probably barefooted, with bright auburn hair, glowing blue eyes, cheek touched with the crimson of health, the face marked by quiet thoughtfulness and incipient power. His uncles were doubtless perplexed with their nephew; but, on the whole, despite the head-shaking of the schoolmaster, and Hugh's manifest lack of interest in the Rudiments, they could not believe that the boy who, since the dawn of his faculties, had been a good listener, a voracious reader, a quick and intelligent observer, was the dunce his pedagogue pronounced him.

CHAPTER III.

HE was twelve years old when the notable adventure of the Doocot Cave afforded him the subject of his first verses. The incident, slight in itself, happens to possess extraordinary interest in a biographical point of view. "Man in immediate presence," says Goethe, " still more in remembrance, fashions and models the external world according to his own peculiarities." An event which impresses the mind strongly in boyhood becomes entwined, as we proceed in our life-journey, with innumerable associations, and when at successive stages in our path we attempt to recall its precise circumstances, we fail to place them in their original bareness before the mind's eye. Suppose, then, that in endeavoring to know a man, to realize what, in the stages of his growth, he was and what he could do, we met with successive accounts from his pen of one and the same incident, — would we not feel that a curiously instructive opportunity was afforded us of taking the observations necessary for our purpose? How glad would the biographer of a great painter be to light upon a series of pictures from his hand, the subject the same in all, but the occasions when they were painted falling at different dates in his history, from the morning of life until its afternoon! It is this advantage we possess in connection with Hugh Miller's boyish adventure in the Doocot Cave. There exist at least four accounts of the incident drawn up by himself, —

42

four successive paintings of the same scene by the boy, the stripling, the man of twenty-seven, and the man of fifty.

The first is that referred to in the "Schools and School-masters," as executed in " enormously bad verse," a day or two after the occurrence. The copy before me is the identical one which excited the admiring wonder of Miss Bond, mistress of the Cromarty Boarding School. Attached to it is that pictorial representation of the scene which Miller describes as consisting of " horrid crags of burnt umber, perforated by yawning caverns of India ink, and crested by a dense forest of sap-green." You can see what is intended; the sea is below the cavern, and the sward and wood are above; but the whole is not superior to the ordinary daubing of child-artists. The verses exhibit internal evidence of having been written within a day or two of the event they record. The agony of distress and terror experienced by the boy of twelve when he and his companion — a lad still younger — found themselves, as night came on, with the sea before, impassable rocks on either hand, and a dark cavern behind, — this, and their contrasted rapture when the boats hailed them at midnight, supersede all reflection on the beauties of the landscape or the wonders of the cave. The grammar and spelling are about as bad as possible. Here are the first two lines : —

> " When I to you unfolds my simple tale,
> And paints the horrors of a rocky vail."

He forgets to say what will happen when the dreadful revelation takes place, and strikes presently into description of the cave. We need not retain the childish misspelling : —

> " There stands a cavern on the sea-beat shore,
> Which stood for ages since the days of yore,

> Whose open mouth stands forth awfully wide,
> And oft takes in the roaring, swelling tide.
> Out through the cavern water oozes fast,
> Which ends in nothing but white stones at last.
> Two boys, the author one, away did stray,
> Being on a beauteous and a sunshine day."

The contemptuous "nothing but white stones" hardly betrays the future geologist, and the *naïveté* of "the author one" is charming. The three last stanzas relate, in very flat prose fitted with rhyme, that the boys went to the cavern "for some stones," found that the water had filled in round them, tried to get out but could not, were doubly pained when "the night came on, down poured the heavy rain," and "ran so very fast" to the boats when they came to rescue them. Nothing here but the sternest historical realism. Fancy has not gilded the clouds, nor enthusiasm softened the colors; the fact stands simply out as an experience of unromantic misery.

For several years this version seems to have contented Hugh, the revision it underwent extending only to verbal alterations. The lad of nineteen, however, discards the whole, and produces a more polished and melodious ditty. The friend who shared the adventure is dismissed, and the interest centres in the "author," or, as he is now more poetically styled, "the Muses' youngest child," or, with a touch, of remorseful pathos, "the Muses' rude, untoward child." He has learned to sketch in Scott's lighter manner, and there is something of gracefulness and vivacity in his handling:

> " Well may fond memory love to trace
> The semblance of that lonely place,
> Much may she joy to picture fair
> Each cliff that frowns in darkness there;
> For when alone in youth I strayed
> To haunted cave or forest glade,

Each rock, each lonely dell, I knew,
Where flow'rets bloomed or berries grew;
Knew where, to shelf of whitened rock,
At eve the sable cormorants flock;
Could point the little arm to where
Deep the wild fox had dug his lair;
Had marked with curious eye the cell
Where the rock-pigeon loved to dwell;
Had watched the seal with silent ken,
And, venturous, stormed the badger's den."

In the following lines there seems to be an echo from Byron's tales : —

" Oft had our poet wished to brave
The giddy height and foaming wave,
That wildly dashed and darkly frowned
The Doocot's yawning caves around.
For many a tale of wondrous kind
With wild impatience fired his mind;
Tales of dark caves where never ray
Of summer's sun was seen to play;
Tales of a spring whose ceaseless wave
Nor gurgling sound nor murmur gave,
But like that queen who, in her pride,
Latona's ruthless twins defied,
To meltless marble, as it flows
Through stiffening moss and lichens, grows.
Before he deem these marvels true
The caves must meet his curious view."

Considerable progress here from the " water oozing fast "
and " nothing but white stones," of the first edition. In
that performance the arrival of the boat had been emphatically chronicled, " the author " dwelling with manifest satisfaction on the event. It would not, however, have been
poetical enough for " the Muses' youngest child " to be taken
off at midnight by mere terrestrial fishermen. In the new

edition, accordingly, he remains until "Aurora" makes her appearance : —

> "And clear and calm the billow rolled,
> With shade of green and crest of gold."

The second of these lines is finely colored.

A moral now *coronat opus* in the tone of Scott's introductions to his cantos. It turns on "art and guile," "vice attired in beauty's smile," and other matters which the reader may imagine.

In the vigor of early manhood, Miller described the adventure of the cave in his letter to Principal Baird. He writes in prose, having estimated his talents with the coolest judgment, and decided that, for the present, he will quit poetry. The picture has become full in detail, and glowing in tint : "The cave proved a mine of wonders. We found it of great depth, and, when at its farthest extremity, the sea and opposite land appeared to us as they would if viewed through the tube of a telescope. We discovered that its sides and roof were crusted over with a white stone resembling marble, and that it contained a petrifying spring. The pigeons which we disturbed were whizzing by us through the gloom, reminding us of the hags of our story-books, when on their night voyage through the air. A shoal of porpoises were tempesting the water in their unwieldy gambols, scarcely an hundred yards from the cavern's mouth, and a flock of sea-gulls were screaming around them, like harpies round the viands of the Trojan. To add to the interest of the place, we had learned from tradition that, *in the lang syne*, this cave had furnished Wallace with a hiding-place, and that more recently it had been haunted by smugglers. In the midst of our engagements, however, the evening began to darken, and we discovered that our very fine cave was neither more nor less than a prison. We attempted climbing round, but in vain; for the shelf from whence we had leaped was unattainable, and there was no other path. 'What will my mother think?' said the poor little fellow, whom I had brought into this predicament, as he burst into tears. 'I would care nothing for myself, — but my mother.' The appeal was powerful, and, had he not cried, I probably would; but the sight of his tears roused my pride, and, with a feeling which Rochefoucault would have at once recognized as springing from the master principle, I attempted to comfort him; and for the time completely forgot my own sorrow in exulting, with all due sympathy, over his. Night came on both dark and rainy, and we lay down together in a corner of the cave. A few weeks prior, the corpse of a fisherman, who had been drowned early in the preceding winter, had been found on the beach below. It was much gashed by the sharp rocks, and the head was beaten to pieces. I had seen it at the time it was carried through the streets of Cromarty to the church, where in this part of the country the bodies of drowned persons are commonly put until the coffin and grave be prepared; and all this night long, sleeping or waking, the image of this corpse was continually before me. As often as I slumbered, a mangled, headless thing would come stalking into the cave and attempt striking me, when I would awaken with a start, cling to my companion, and hide my face in his breast. About one o'clock in the morning we were relieved by two boats, which our friends, who had spent the early part of the night in searching for us in the woods above, had fitted out to try along the shore for our bodies; they having at length concluded that we had fallen over the cliffs, and were killed."

Last of all, written when he was turned of fifty, we have

the narrative of the occurrence as it appears in the
" Schools and Schoolmasters." The passage, too long to
quote in its completeness, is one of the most rich and elaborate in the works of Hugh Miller. The " nothing but
white stones" of the first description, and the " meltless
marble" of the second, have become the blended poetry
and science of the following sentences: " There were
little pools at the side of the cave, where we could see the
work of congelation going on, as at the commencement of
an October frost, when the cold north wind ruffles, and but
barely ruffles, the surface of some mountain lochan or sluggish mountain stream, and shows the newly formed needles
of ice projecting mole-like from the shores into the water.
So rapid was the course of deposition, that there were cases
in which the sides of the hollows seemed growing almost
in proportion as the water rose in them; the springs, lip-
ping over, deposited their minute crystals on the edges;
and the reservoirs deepened and became more capacious as
their mounds were built up by this curious masonry." The
idea of the telescope, which occurs first in the third description, is finely worked out in the fourth: " The long, tele-
scopic prospect of the sparkling sea, as viewed from the
inner extremity of the cavern, while all around was dark
as midnight; the sudden gleam of the sea-gull, seen for
a moment from the recess, as it flitted past in the sunshine; the black, heaving bulk of the grampus, as it threw
up its slender jets of spray, and then, turning downwards,
displayed its glossy back and vast angular fin; even the
pigeons, as they shot whizzing by, one moment scarce visible in the gloom, the next radiant in the light. — all acquired a new interest, from the peculiarity of the setting in
which we saw them. They formed a series of sun-gilt
vignettes, framed in jet; and it was long ere we tired of

seeing and admiring in them much of the strange and the beautiful."

The scenery of the heavens is hardly referred to in the first sketch. The fact of a rain-storm having aggravated the horrors of the situation is mentioned, but the boy thinks of nothing except the additional pain it occasioned. When Hugh Miller had watched the sunsets of forty other summers, he "put in the sky" of his picture thus: "The sun had sunk behind the precipices, and all was gloom along their bases, and double gloom in their caves; but their rugged brows still caught the red glare of evening. The flush rose higher and higher, chased by the shadows; and then, after lingering for a moment on their crests of honeysuckle and juniper, passed away, and the whole became sombre and gray. The sea-gull sprang upward from where he had floated on the ripple, and hied him slowly away to his lodge in his deep-sea stack; the dusky cormorant flitted past, with heavier and more frequent stroke, to his whitened shelf high on the precipice; the pigeons came whizzing downwards from the uplands and the opposite land, and disappeared amid the gloom of their caves; every creature that had wings made use of them in speeding homewards; but neither my companion nor myself had any, and there was no possibility of getting home without them. . . . For the last few hours mountainous piles of clouds had been rising dark and stormy in the sea-mouth; they had flared portentously in the setting sun, and had worn, with the decline of evening, almost every meteoric tint of anger, from fiery red to a sombre, thunderous brown, and from sombre brown to doleful black."

All these things were seen by Hugh Miller, as he stood on the threshold of the cave, or looked out from within through its rock-hewn telescope; but it was not the Hugh Miller of twelve years who saw them; it was the Hugh

Miller of fifty who was transported by imagination to stand again in the entrance of the cave, or gaze again from its interior, and to see " what the eye brought with it the means of seeing." It was as if Turner at fifty had taken it into his head to paint the first sunset on which he had looked with boyish delight, and in so doing had thrown upon the canvas the science and subtlety of a life spent in the observation of nature.

CHAPTER IV.

SOON after the occurrence which has detained us so long, the boy proceeded on a visit to certain relatives in the Highlands of Sutherland; a visit which was repeated in two successive autumns. His faculties were thus exercised by new scenes and new acquaintances; he listened to discussions on the poems of Ossian, and began secretly to think it probable that the famed Celtic bard belonged to the ancient clan MacPherson; he added to the picture-gallery of his imagination a few fresh subjects, — long, low valleys in tender blue, enlivened by green-wooded knolls and delicately draped with wreaths of morning mist; reaches of quiet lake with gray ruins nodding on slim promontories; waterfalls glancing by the silvery boles of birch-trees, and sending up a steamy spray to fall gemlike on their drooping foliage; and he laid the foundation of that thorough comprehension of the character of the Highlanders, and of the condition of the Highlands, which made him in after life one of the best authorities on all Highland questions.

Whether in Sutherland or at home, his mind was constantly active, constantly growing. His school-fellows wondered and derided as they beheld him launching on the horse-pond a succession of mysterious vessels constructed

51

from the descriptions of Anson, Cook, and other voyagers. In the "Schools and Schoolmasters" we hear of one of these, a proa, similar to those used by the Ladrone islanders, but this was no more than a single specimen of his ship-carpentering. "I used," he wrote to Baird, "to keep in exercise the risible faculties of all the mimic navigators of the pond, with slim, fish-like boats of bark, like those of the North American Indians, awkward high-pooped galleys, like those I had seen in an old edition of Dryden's "Virgil," two-keeled vessels, like the double canoes of Otaheite, and wall-sided half vessels, like the proas of the Ladrone islands. Nor could I," he proceeds, "derive, like my companions, any pleasure from the merely mechanical operation of plain sailing. I had a story connected with every voyage, and every day had its history of expeditions of discovery, and cases of mutiny and shipwreck." Navigation gave place to chemistry, but his experiments were "wofully unfortunate." Then he tried painting; but, as the art seems to have required boiling of oil, and as he boiled it so effectually that the flame found its way out at the chimney-top, and a "sublime fire-scene," threatening to become more sublime than agreeable, was the result, the brush was thrown aside. The founding of leaden images was next attempted, but one of the busts being waggishly like a neighbor, and troubles arising in consequence, this, also, was abandoned. "My ingenuity gained me such a reprimand that I flung my casts into the fire." He now took a turn at "mosaic work," and this was followed by attempts to fashion watch-seals. "When I had worn the points of my fingers with cutting and polishing until the blood appeared, I forsook the grindstone." He fell in with a book on natural magic, palmistry, and astrology, and for a time went wool-gathering upon that particular range of the mountains of vanity. He became a sufficient adept in palmistry to make out, from a perusal of the mystic characters inscribed on the palm of his left hand, that his life was to be strange and eventful, that he was to become a revolutionary leader, and that he was to die, like Wallace, on the scaffold. Verse-writing, prose-writing, and "a third sort of composition which imitated the style of Macpherson's 'Ossian,'" were engaged in, probably with fitfulness, but with passionate enjoyment.

His principal amusement at this period, however, was one of which he has singularly enough omitted mention in the "Schools and Schoolmasters." He drew the map of a country in the sand, and, having collected quantities of variously colored shells from the beach, arranged them so as to represent its inhabitants. Appointing himself king of the miniature community, he designed its towns, roads, canals, harbors, and other public works. He ruled his dominions by every different form of government with which he was acquainted, and attacked or defended them by every stratagem of war with which books or his uncles had made him familiar.

In his fourteenth year all other amusements yielded to that of heading a band of his school-fellows, with whom, in the harvest vacation, he spent every day, from dawn to sunset, in or about a deep cavern, penetrating one of the steepest precipices which skirt the southern base of the hill of Cromarty. One of the brotherhood brought a pot, another a pitcher; the shore supplied shell-fish, the wood fuel, the fields potatoes, peas, and beans; and so they went a-gypsying the long summer day.

"The time not employed in cooking," says Miller in his letter to Principal Baird, "or in procuring victuals, we spent in acting little dramatic pieces, of which I sketched out the several plans, leaving the dialogue to be supplied by the actors. Robbers, buccaneers, outlaws of every description, were the heroes of these dramas. They frequently, despite of my arrangements to the contrary, terminated in skirmishes of a rather tragic cast, in which, with our spears of elder and swords of hazel, we exchanged pretty severe blows. We were sometimes engaged, too, in conflicts with other boys, in which, as became a leader, I distinguished myself by a cool yet desperate courage. Nor was I entitled to the rank I held from only the abilities which I displayed in framing plays and in fighting. I swam, climbed, leaped, and wrestled better than any other lad of my years and inches in the place."

With schooling, in the mean time, it fared as ill as possible. Hugh had made up his mind not to learn, and he could neither be coaxed nor beaten out of his determination. Sooth to say, he had become a self-willed, turbulent lad, and the haziness of conception on the subject of *meum* and *tuum*, indicated by potato-pilfering and orchard-robbing, was not the darkest shade which we have to bring into harmony at this period, as we best may, with the idyllic brightness of his boyhood. In the letter to Principal Baird and elsewhere, he mentions a fact or two which he omits from the " Schools and Schoolmasters," but which cannot be withheld consistently with biographic veracity.

Setting his schoolmaster, his uncles, and his mother at defiance, he played truant three weeks out of four, and cast off every trammel of authority. Distressed and alarmed, his relatives tried force. The stubborn will and intrepid spirit which he had inherited from his father were roused to fiercer opposition. He carried about with him a long clasp-knife, with which to repel any attack that might be made upon him by his uncles. They next had recourse to expostulation. They represented to him, with affectionate earnestness, that he was losing his sole chance of escaping a life of manual labor, and urged that the possession of faculties whose right use would enable him to rise in life, made it the more disgraceful in him to sink actually below his father's station. The arguments were unanswerable, and Hugh seems to have made no attempt to answer them, but he held his own course. His mother, profoundly afflicted by the seeming disappointment of her hopes, gave him up altogether, and bestowed her affection on his two sisters. In the winter of 1816, both the little girls died. Hugh loved them, and was deeply affected when the music of their voices, which had cheered the cottage so long, passed suddenly away forever. But keener far was the pang which struck to his heart when he overheard his mother remarking how different would her condition have been, had it pleased Heaven to take her son and leave one of her daughters. "It was bitter for me," he says, "to think, and yet I could not think otherwise, that she had cause of sorrow. both for those whom she had lost, and for him who survived; and I would willingly have laid down my life, could the sacrifice have restored to her one of my sisters." A noble impulse and sincere, but an impulse merely; in a few weeks he was again at the head of his band. "A particular way of thinking," he remarks, " a peculiar course of reading, a singular train of oral narration, had concurred from the period at which I first thought, read, or listened. in giving my character the impress it then bore, and it was not in the power of detached accident or effort to effect a change." He had, at this time, cast all religion to the winds. We have it explicitly in his own words that he became an atheist. "A boy-atheist." he writes to Mr. John Swanson. in 1828. "is surely an uncommon character. I was one in reality; for. possessed of a strong memory, which my uncles, and an early taste for reading, had stored with religious sentiments and stories of religious men. I was compelled, for the sake of peace, either to do that

which was right; or by denying the truth of the Bible to
set every action, good and bad, on the same level." His
atheism, however, was a mere affectation, — a drossy scum
on the surface of his nature, with no real basis either in
head or in heart. It was one form of his rebelliousness at
the time. He was obstinately wilful and irreligious, and
he thought it bold and fine and also logically consistent to
call himself an atheist.

Three schoolmasters in succession had an opportunity of
exercising their talents upon Hugh, and in each case the
failure was signal. His schooling ended when he was fifteen in a pitched battle with the dominie. His gains from
ten years of nominal education were small. Penmanship,
clear and strong, a smattering of arithmetic, spelling of
which a boy of ten might be ashamed, syntax which joined
substantives in the singular to verbs in the plural and *vice
versâ*, were his scholastic acquirements. His miscellaneous
reading, however, had been extensive; he had stored up a
vast amount of information in a capacious and retentive
memory; he composed freely in prose and verse, though
there is hardly any sign of vitality in his writings of this
period except the delight they evince in the work of composition. Before the close of the day on which his conflict
with the schoolmaster took place, he had avenged himself
in a copy of satirical verses, which, to say the least, show a
great advance, in flexibility and in command of language,
on those in which he first recorded the adventure in the
Doocot cave. As given in " Schools and Schoolmasters,"
they are much improved, the epithets freshened and burnished, and the best line in the whole,

" Nature's born fop, a saint by art,"

added. I find the lines in the " Village Observer," a

manuscript magazine in Miller's boyish handwriting, dated Feb., 1820.

Such was Hugh Miller at the time he left school. A rugged, proud, and stiff-necked lad, impossible to drive and difficult to lead, his character already marked with strong lines, and developing from within or through self-chosen influences. " I saw," said Baxter of Cromwell, " that what he learned must be from himself; " and the observation might already have been made of Hugh Miller. To his friends he was a perplexity and offence ; to his uncles, in particular, who knew him too well and were too sagacious to accept the off-hand theory of his schoolmasters that he was merely a stupid and bad boy, he must have seemed a mass of contradictions. Intellectual in his wildest play, fond of books, and capable of discerning excellence from its counterfeits in thought and style, passionately addicted to the observation of nature, and forgetting no fact he once ascertained, how could he be dull in the ordinary sense? If, again, capacity to influence one's fellows was a test of power, could it be said that he, who was undisputed sovereign of the boys of the place, was the stupidest of them all? A dunce who from childhood had entertained his companions with tales of his own invention, who fitted his play-fellows with dramatic parts by way of pastime, who was never weary when his pen was in his hand, who possessed more literary information than any one twice his age in Cromarty, was a phenomenon new to the experience of Uncle James and Uncle Sandy. It was a puzzle for them, and it is something of a puzzle for us.

Not a few — among them men of the highest eminence as thinkers and writers — will decide with impatient emphasis that Hugh's rebellion against the tyranny of grammar was the genial assertion of his native force, the bursting of the flower-pot by the oak sapling, the most propi-

tious thing which could have befallen him.   There is much
to be said on this side of the question.   The boy who was
dux of the school in Cromarty when Hugh Miller was
dunce, — the model boy, who was the delight of the schoolmaster, and who carried off the highest prizes when he
went to college, — the boy whom the story-books designate
for a Lord Mayor's coach and a handsome fortune, — became a respectable and useful minister of the Church of
Scotland, and would probably never have been heard of
beyond the circle of his parishioners, but for the circumstance of his having been mentioned in the works of his
friend, the dunce.   The name of the dux has been touched
by the pen of the dunce, and is likely to live as long as the
English language.   By taking the bit into his teeth, leaping the fences, and scouring the plain at his own wild will,
Hugh Miller obtained that freedom for his faculties which
is necessary to all vigorous growth, to all beauty and capricious grace of movement.   Had he received the technical training of a college professor, would college professors
have said that they would give their hand from their wrist for
the *curiosa felicitas* of his style? Take young creatures, colts,
or lambs, mew them up, feed and fodder them on the most
approved scientific principles; you will have them sleek
and fat, but will there be buoyancy or elastic strength in
their limbs; will there be the light of health and joy in their
eyes; will not the "poor things," like Tennyson's hot-
house flowers, "look unhappy"?   The law of freedom applies to all life, human as well as animal, and the finer and
fresher the mental qualities, the greater is the risk that
constraint will benumb or pervert them.   The grand thing
to be secured is mental force, and it is possible that laborious effort to attain skill in the expression of force may
draw fatally on the original force itself.   The faculties,
like over-drilled soldiers, may have no strength left to play

their part in life's battle. It is a Shakespearian opinion that

> "Universal plodding prisons up
> The nimble spirits in the arteries;
> As motion and long-during action tires
> The sinewy vigor of the traveller."

The worst possible result of school discipline is to take the edge from that exultant ardor with which a strong youth thinks of work, for mind or for body, as the supreme of pleasures. Hugh Miller's freedom was not unredeemed trifling; it was his native force developing in its own way and seeking its own nourishment. If he turned from the Latin Rudiments, he found a literature in which he never tired to expatiate, — a literature whose teaching he accepted with enthusiasm; a literature which acquainted him with foreign lands, and caused him to thrill at the deeds of brave men; a literature whose inmost spirit he vitally assimilated and made his own. If attention to his grammatical task in the dingy school-room pained him, his powers were concentrated in highest action when he accompanied Uncle Sandy in his researches on the shore at ebb-tide, or when, in solitary rambles, he looked carefully, constantly, lovingly, into the face of nature. Even in those doings with his brethren of the cave which seem to have occasioned his relatives most alarm, he was acquiring habits of self-possession, courage, fidelity, reticence, which are not always imparted by artificial training.

And let us not forget that stubbornness of purpose, inflexibility of will, the unpardonable sin in the eyes of most pedagogues, is after all the indispensable basis of character for any man who will do much. Acquire it as he may, the ability to go forward in the path he has chosen, to face the pelting shower and the scorching sun, to do wholly, heartily, inflexibly, what he deliberately wills to do, is of sovereign importance for a man. *Quicquid vult valde vult,* — this is the diploma of masterhood in nature's university; " unstable as water, thou shalt not excel," — this is the hopeless doom. " I sowed flower-seed," wrote John Sterling respecting his management of his garden in boyhood, " and then turned up the ground again and planted potatoes, and then rooted out the potatoes to insert acorns, and apple-pips, and at last, as may be supposed, reaped neither roses, nor potatoes, nor oak-trees, nor apples." The words are an epitome of Sterling's biography. Hugh Miller, even in boy-hood, had a purpose, and held to it, firmly resolved that he would not have his limbs straightened on the Procrustean bed prepared for him, conscious that he was neither dunce nor reprobate, but growing in his own way.

It must be carefully noted that the character always remained sound in the vital parts. Of meanness, untruthful-ness, cruelty, avarice, he showed no trace. Had his sensual passions been vehement as those of Burns or Mirabeau, the probability is that he would have fallen into debauch-ery ; but his wildest passion was a passion for freedom ; his dissipation was to wander in the wood or by the wave. Neither morally nor intellectually was he, at any time, dissolute.

And yet it is impossible to hide from ourselves that there is another side to all this. It is difficult to believe that insubordination, turbulence, habitual neglect of tasks with which a sentiment of duty is more or less associated, can be other than disadvantageous to the mind. To check the lawlessness natural to man ; to break self-will to the yoke ; to change the faculties from a confused barbarian herd or horde (*heer* of the old German tribes) into a disciplined or exercised company (*exercitus* of the Romans) must ever be an essential part of the training of youth. Educated human nature is more natural than uneducated. Shakespeare says, again : —

> "Nature is made better by no mean
> But nature makes that mean ; so, o'er that art,
> Which, you say, adds to nature, is an art
> That nature makes."

Does not this throw us back on the reflection that education of the highest kind, based on nature, guided by nature, yet raising nature to heights otherwise unattainable, is not to be easily attained? In every case where an original mind is concerned, education is too subtle a process, requiring too intimate and individual a communion of soul with soul, to be managed by the rough, common methods. A boy of genius would require a teacher of genius, one whose perceptions were so keen, whose sympathies were so fine and true, that he could understand the exceptional mind, obey its monitions as he led it on, apply to it a constraint which would be felt as gentleness, and a gentleness which would tell as constraint. Had Hugh Miller found such a teacher, the advantage to himself and the world might doubtless have been great. He had capacities in him for consummate scholarship, an exact and tenacious memory, great attention, great application, true taste, and clear judgment. Learning could never with him have been pedantry ; and it is indisputable that the man who can converse with the ancients in their own tongues commands a wider intellectual horizon than the man who knows only his native language. One cannot help wishing that Hugh Miller had seen Homer himself lead out Achilles to poise a javelin, or had perceived how different a person is the brawny, broad-shouldered, highly unrhetorical Ulysses of the "Odyssey," from the Ulysses whom Pope taught to look and speak " in a manner worthy of the times of civilization." Had Hugh

Miller's father survived, his shrewd sense and peremptory authority might have given a new color to the schooling of the boy; and, without sacrificing his freedom, Hugh might have taken enough along with him to go to college. Once at a university, the ambition of scholarship would have laid hold on him, and with genius unimpaired and materials extended, he might, in the first bloom of his manhood, have taken his place among the foremost intellectual workers of his time.

There is another consideration which lends a melancholy emphasis to these regrets. Hugh Miller came of a long-lived, strong-boned race, and we have learned from himself that he was the most athletic boy of his years in Cromarty. Had he proceeded to a University, he would have avoided those fifteen years in the quarry and the hewing-shed, during which his robust constitution was shaken, and the seeds of ineradicable disease were sown in his frame. In that case, the tear and wear of the severest of the intellectual professions, journalism, though combined with unremitting attention to science, might have failed to prevent his attaining a green old age. In his letter to Baird, he refers to the obscurity and hardship of his life as a mason, as " punishment for his early carelessness." But why follow these speculations further, or launch into the vainest and vaguest of all philosophies. the philosophy of what might have been? By natural endowment and the action of circumstances, — in one word, by the will of God, — Miller was fitted for the work appointed him, and this is all we require to know or can know.

BOOK II.

THE APPRENTICE.

———————•◆•———————

" Consider how, even in the meanest sorts of labor, the whole soul of a man is composed into a kind of real harmony the instant he sets himself to work."

" Befreit der Mensch sich der sich überwindet."

CHAPTER I.

BOYISH MAGAZINES — A LAD OF HIS OWN WILL — BECOMES
APPRENTICE — HARDSHIPS — ALLEVIATIONS.

BOY-LIFE, with its freshness of faculty, its exuberance of delights, its opulence of wayward force, lies behind Hugh Miller. In the autumn of 1819 his mother, after a widowhood of fourteen years, accepts a second husband, and he removes with her to the house of his step-father. " I had no particular objections to the match," he writes to a friend a few years later, " but you may be certain that it gave me much disgust at the time." It compels him to realize the fact that the world has changed for him, and that duty now demands that play shall cease and work begin. Half a year, however, glides away pleasantly enough, — his own expression is " very agreeably," — in the house of his step-father. He still continues those sportings with literature which have from infancy been among his choicest enjoyments. I have before me Nos. I., II., and III. of a tiny Magazine, written in Miller's hand, and entitled, " The Village Observer, or Monthly MSS." They are dated January, February, March, 1820. Hugh is the editor and principal contributor. It is in February of this year that he enters on his apprenticeship, and the March number closes the series. The pen gives place to the hammer — for a time.

These " Village Observers " are absolutely authentic documents of Miller's history at this time, and enable us to realize the circumstances of his life before any tint of fancy, or association from the pursuits of a subsequent period, had softened their harsher features. In the three numbers there is not the remotest allusion to his apprenticeship. This may be imputed to the disagreeableness of the subject; but it is somewhat remarkable that place is not found for a brief description of those rare and beautiful birds discovered by him in the quarry on the evening of his first day of labor, and delineated with enthusiastic minuteness in the "Old Red Sandstone." The one was a goldfinch, — very uncommon in the highlands of Scotland, — with " hood of vermilion and wings inlaid with gold; " the other a bird of the woodpecker tribe, " variegated with light blue and a grayish-yellow." Neither does Hugh, in capacity of village observer, give us, in his March number for 1820, any hint of that " exquisite pleasure " which, as we are told in the " Old Red Sandstone," he derived from contemplating the adjacent landscape when resting, on the second day, from his toil at the hour of noon. " All the workmen," he says in that book, " rested at mid-day, and I went to enjoy my half-hour alone on a mossy knoll in the neighboring wood, which commands through the trees a wide prospect of the bay and the opposite shore. There was not a wrinkle on the water, nor a cloud in the sky, and the branches were as moveless in the calm as if they had been traced on canvas. From a wooded promontory, that stretched half-way across the frith, there ascended a thin column of smoke. It rose straight as the line of a plummet for more than a thousand yards, and then, on reaching a thinner stratum of air, spread out equally on every side, like the foliage of a stately tree. Ben Wyvis rose to the west, white with the yet unwasted snows of winter, and as sharply defined in the clear atmosphere as if all its sunny slopes and blue retiring hollows had been chiselled in marble. They reminded me of the pretty French story, in which an old artist is described as tasking the ingenuity of his future son-in-law, by giving him, as a subject for his pencil, a flower-piece composed of only white flowers, of which the one half were to bear their proper color, the other half a deep purple hue, and yet all be perfectly natural; and how the young man resolved the riddle and gained his mistress by introducing a transparent purple vase into the picture, and making the light pass through it on the flowers that were drooping over the edge. I returned to the quarry, convinced that a very exquisite pleasure may be a very cheap one, and that the busiest employments may afford leisure enough to enjoy it." This is beautiful writing and excellent philosophy; but there is not a word in any degree resembling it, whether descriptive or philosophical, in the "Monthly MSS.," edited by Hugh Miller at the time. Nor is mention made of the ripple-marked sandstone, on beholding which, on the same day, he "felt as completely at fault as Robinson Crusoe did on his discovering the print of the man's foot on the sand."

What is, perhaps, still more surprising, there is a similar absence of reference to ornithological, geological, or æsthetic alleviations of his early toil in the account of this period, written by him ten years subsequently for Principal Baird. "My first six months of labor," he writes to Baird in 1829, " presented only a series of disasters. I was at the time of a slender make and weak constitution; and I soon found I was ill-fitted for such employments as the trundling of loaded wheelbarrows over a plank, or the raising of huge blocks of stone out of a quarry. My hands were soon fretted into large blisters, my breast became the seat of a dull, oppressive pain, and I was much distressed, after exertion more than usually violent, by an irregular motion of my heart. My spirits were almost always miserably low; and

I was so wrapped up in a wretched, apathetic absence of mind, that I have wrought for whole hours together with scarcely a thought of what I was doing myself, and scarcely conscious of what others were doing around me."

Both these narratives may be strictly consistent with fact. In that case they afford a striking illustration of Miller's own remark, that two varying descriptions may be given by the same person of the same events, and yet both be veracious. He said nothing, in the earlier documents, of the rare birds, the beautiful landscape, the rippled-marked stone, because it was not until afterwards that he regarded them as of importance. He mentally associated with his first years of labor feelings which belonged to a later time. He was an observer from infancy, and his observations gave him joy; his memory became stored with facts; but not until he studied geology did he apprehend that these facts had any scientific value. When geology took possession of Miller, the possession was complete. He thought, talked, wrote of geology; his leading articles, his discussions of political and religious questions, were full of it. From the boyish magazines he edited, it is absent; from the poems which he composed in boyhood and youth, it is absent; in the letters which he wrote to his favorite associates, of which we have an uninterrupted series, beginning a year or two later than the time at which we have arrived, we look for it in vain; and in the narrative composed at the request of Baird, there is not one throb of scientific enthusiasm. It was, I believe, at a time much later than that of his apprenticeship that Hugh Miller, though his eye had always beamed with delight when it rested on an object of beauty, learned to take a geological interest in the ammonite, "graceful in its curves as those of the Ionic volute, and greatly more delicate in its sculpturing," or to read, hour after hour, with scientific curiosity, in the "marvellous library of the Scotch Lias."

Boys and girls are moralists and politicians before they care about science. Charlotte Brontë and her brother and sisters also played at Magazines, and wrote solemn essays lauding the Duke and execrating the Whigs. Hugh Miller and his boy friends in 1820 were ardent politicians, censuring the conduct of government, bewailing the horrors of Peterloo, sternly criticising the motives and proceedings of the Reformers. One of the most important articles in their Magazine is a " Retrospective Essay," in which the events of the time are reviewed in an ethico-historical spirit. There is no name attached to the piece, but I take it to be Miller's, and it is at all events a specimen at first hand of the kind of speculation and of talk which went on in the circle of his acquaintance. The retrospective essayist thinks that the cruelties committed at Manchester in the Peterloo affair " will be held in as much detestation by future ages as the firing upon the inhabitants of Toulon, or the massacre of Glencoe." A clever simile, however, catches his eye, and he follows the bright game even at the risk of inconsistency. " Smollett," he says, " has somewhere observed that an English mob, like a dancing bear, may be irritated to a very dangerous degree of rage, yet pacified by firing a pistol over his nose. Such was it with our British Radicals ; those whose vivid harangues were inspired with all the spirit of heroism, and whom we would have supposed lions in the field, slunk frightened at the hostile preparations against them, and were heard of no more." Severities comparable *both* to the massacre of Glencoe and to the firing of a pistol over a bear's nose are not easily imagined, but it would be hard to debar boy *litterateurs* from saying *all* the fine things which turn up, in discussing a subject, merely because they occur on opposite sides of the question. Very young and very old politicians are generally Conservative, and the former invariably express the highest moral and religious sentiments. Our retrospective essayist has little or no sympathy with the patriots. "Reform," he writes, "was but the name which a few designing men had affixed to a daring rebellion; and whose aims were that, after having pulled down with the teeth of a deluded multitude those men whose tyranny was most obnoxious, to set themselves up as rulers, and in their turn be tyrants. Happily their conduct and principles were of such a nature as to exclude from their meetings men of piety or true independence. The religious opinions of Cobbett held back all true Christians from his standard, and the enthusiasm with which Carlyle was defended disgusted all men of sense or feeling. At their meetings it was impossible to be an oppositionist; and though they termed themselves men of liberty and forbearance, the man who dared openly to oppose their schemes ran the risk of having his brains beat out. Indeed, the liberty they would have secured for themselves was of no universal kind; it was a liberty which only bad men would have profited by, and from which the virtuous would have turned with disgust; those laws which bind the victorious would no longer have existed, and instead of a few there would have been a multiplicity of tyrants."

The last number of the "Village Observer" contains a few verses on criticism, headed "extempore," which seem to be by Miller. The two opening lines are not without spirit: —

> " Critics, like lions, make not carrion game;
>   The work has merit, or they'll ne'er condemn."

Perhaps the most significant trait which the number presents of Hugh is this from a "Journal of the Week:"

"Wrote a moral essay upon the advantages of industry, but tore it in pieces on considering that its author was one of the most indolent personages on earth, — did nothing, but still determined on reform."

Farewell, then, to the busy idleness of verse-making and magazine-editing. In the last days of February, Miller still has leisure to put together the number for March, but no other number follows. He binds himself verbally, but by no legal instrument, apprentice for three years to " old David Wright," stone-mason, brother-in-law of his mother. Old David was something of a character. The man who, standing on the thwarts of his boat, which had just sunk, the sea-water being at the moment up to his throat, could so accurately appreciate the points of his situation, and retain so clear a perception of the thing to be done, as to say, on seeing his snuff-box floating off, " Od, Andro man, just rax out your han' and tak' in my snuff-box," must have had an enviable firmness of nerve and quietness of self-possession.

Miller's uncles, who had taken the right measure of his capacity, and who had loved and watched over him as a son, have done their utmost to oppose this decision. Their sure instinct tells them that the place of this recruit is not in the ranks; they have earnestly wished to see him enrolled among the brain-workers of the community; and, like all Scottish peasants of the old historic type, they regard the ministers of the Church of Christ as taking precedence of all others in the intellectual aristocracy. They have told him that if he will only return to his books, and prepare for college, their home and their savings will be at his command. They have tried to appeal to his pride and desire for advancement. Uncle James has gone the length of hinting with some bitterness that if he has found books too hard for him, he may find labor harder still, and may turn from the latter with the same inconstancy with which he turned from the former. But Hugh, as James Wright knows and has said, is "a lad of his own will," and his mind is made up. As for his declinature of the clerical profession, he satisfies both himself and Uncle James on that head, by the consideration that he has no call to the sacred office. The feeling of independence, strong in Hugh Miller as in Robert Burns, rebels against the idea of his going to college, dependent on the bounty of relatives. Strangely enough, too, that passion for literature, whether in the form of reading or of writing, which had marked him from his childhood as the predestined author, drove him to the quarry. The conception of a literary career founded upon a complete University education, and commencing with the instruments and furtherances which ages have accumulated, had not dawned upon his mind. Literature had been to him a coy maiden, radiant, fascinating, but free and light-winged as a forest bird, and he shrank from formal irreversible espousals. He has observed that "Cousin George," a mason, though hard-worked during several months in the year, has the months of winter to himself. This decides him in favor of the trade of mason. In winter and early spring he will return to his beloved Muse, to dally with her in a life-long courtship; or, if it is to end in marriage, — for the thought of rising by literature does lurk, deep hidden, in his heart, — she will take his hand as a beneficent princess takes that of a knightly though low-born suitor, and lift him at once to fame and fortune. Uncle James' remark on the probability of his failing at labor as he has failed at study, he takes note of; it may be pleasant to teach Uncle James that he can will to work as well as will to play, and that, though others have lost the mastership of him, he has not lost mastership of himself. Enough; he declares unalterably for stone and lime, and becomes apprentice to his uncle, old David Wright. The engagement is understood to be for three years. In the chill February morning of 1820, he takes his way to the quarry.

Relieved or not relieved by touches of romance, Hugh Miller's first season of labor proves to be one of sternest hardship, putting to the strain his whole faculty of endurance. The dark side is given in all his contemporary or nearly contemporary renderings of the subject; the lights in the picture come out only when it is seen through the vista of years. Still quite a boy, slender and loose-jointed, unintermitted toil presses hard on him both in mind and in body. His spirits fail. He is constantly in pain, often prostrated by sickness. He shows at first no quickness or dexterity in acquiring his trade, and is the most awkward of the apprentices. Uncle David begins to be of opinion that this incomprehensible compound of genius and dunce is incapable of attaining the skill of an ordinary mechanic. The lad is sorely tempted to become a dram-drinker. We have two accounts of his triumph over this temptation, the one harshly realistic, of date 1829, the other more picturesque, dated 1853.

" It is probable," he writes to Baird, " that the want of money alone prevented me from indulging, at this period, in the low vice of dram-drinking." He thus describes the affair in " My Schools and Schoolmasters : "—" In laying down the foundation-stone of one of the larger houses built this year by Uncle David and his partner, the workmen had a royal ' founding-pint,' and two whole glasses of the whiskey came to my share. A full-grown man would not have deemed a gill of usquebaugh an overdose, but it was considerably too much for me ; and when the party broke up, and I got home to my books, I found, as I opened the pages of a favorite author, the letters dancing before my eyes, and that I could no longer master the sense. I have the volume at present before me, — a small edition of the Essays of Bacon, a good deal worn at the corners by the friction of the pocket; for of Bacon I never tired. The condition into which I had brought myself was, I felt, one of degradation. I had sunk, by my own act, for the time, to a lower level of intelligence than that on which it was my privilege to be placed; and though the state could have been no very favorable one for forming a resolution, I in that hour determined that I should never again sacrifice my capacity of intellectual enjoyment to a drinking usage; and, with God's help, I was enabled to hold by the determination." It was, therefore, not "the want of money *alone*" which prevented him from becoming a tippler; but we may be permitted to think that this little circumstance was a valuable auxiliary to Bacon.

Soon, also, there come alleviations of his hardship more practical than those derived from geological discovery and admiration of Highland scenery. As he does not sink under exertion, his physical stamina gradually asserts itself, and makes labor a source of strength. It was a characteristic of Miller during life that he progressed in any pursuit not by little and little, but by leaps. His master and fellow-workmen, who, during the first months of his apprenticeship, have regarded him as too awkward to learn his trade, are suddenly astonished to find him one of the most expert hewers in the squad. "So flattered was my vanity," he writes to Baird, "by the respect which they paid me on this account, and such satisfaction did I derive from emulating them in what they confessed the better department of their profession, that the coming winter, to which, a few weeks before, I had looked forward as good men do to the pleasures of another state of existence, was no longer an object of desire."

To throw down the tools, however, could not but be a relief, and the leisure of winter is hailed with satisfaction. After a pedestrian journey to Strath-Carron, in company with his cousin, George Munro, in the course of which he makes some observations, not of an important character, on an old Scotch forest of native pine, he returns to Cromarty. The education of toil has already done more for him than any previous education, and the unruly boy has become a thoughtful, docile young man.

CHAPTER II.

*F*ROM his early boyhood Miller had given proof of the blended faithfulness and tenderness of his nature by the affection with which he clung to one or two chosen friends. His friendship with John Swanson, him of the Doocot cave, already warm and confidential when Hugh was twelve and John ten, continued in freshness and intensity until the hour of Miller's death. Finlay, whom he describes as a gentle-spirited boy, who loved to share with him the solitude of the caves by moonlight, seems to have held the first place in his regard in the period immediately preceding his apprenticeship. In the " Village Observer" for January, 1820, I find " The Farewell," a copy of verses in which, on departing for the south, Finlay bids adieu to Cromarty, and which is alluded to and partly quoted in the " Schools and Schoolmasters." The five stanzas of which it consists, though boyish, are not without a certain pensive sincerity and sweetness : —

> " Ye pleasures of childhood, farewell,
>   In which I have oft had a part;
> Where mirth and where gladness prevail,
>   Without affectation or art.
>
> " How oft when the school set me free,
>   I've wandered amongst these green woods,
> When nothing was heard but the bee,
>   Or the cataract pouring its floods.

76

" Ye shepherds who merrily sing,
    And laugh out the long summer's day,
Expert at the ball or the ring,
    Whose lives are one routine of play ;

" To you my dear crook I resign,
    My colly, my pipe, and my horn ;
To leave you indeed I repine,
    But I must away with the morn.

" New scenes may arise on my sight,
    The world and its follies be new,
But never such scenes of delight
    Shall I witness secluded from you."

By far the most remarkable, however, of these early
friends of Miller was William Ross. There are many
memorials of Ross in Miller's papers, and I can perceive
that the account given of him in the " Schools and Schoolmasters " is not too highly colored. The child of parents
crushed into the dust by poverty, his father half imbecile, his
mother feeble in health and broken-spirited, his own energies depressed by perpetual sickness, he had received from
capricious nature a mental organization of exquisite delicacy,
enriched with fine and tender elements. Modest, gentle,
affectionate ; tremulously alive to the feelings and claims
of others ; depreciating everything in himself, exalting every
capacity and accomplishment of one he loved ; unaffectedly
religious, and unmoved by utmost calamity from simple
faith in a divine care and a heavenly love, — William Ross
was the very ideal of a bosom-friend. There is a letter
dated Nigg, 10th July, 1821, from Ross to Miller, which,
unimportant as it is otherwise, will serve to introduce him
to the reader. He had just lost by death one of the very
few who had been kind to him in his boyhood.

" Where think you have I sitten down to write you? In my grandmother's room, and before the very table at which I once used to read (in happier days) a chapter in the big old Bible and sing a psalm every night and .morning. I cannot tell you how I feel. The remembrance of the innocence and happiness of the days that are gone has softened my heart, indifferent as it has become to the pure feelings of devotion. I have done reading just now the three last chapters of the Gospel of St. John, and with the history of the sufferings of our Saviour I was never more affected. I feel my soul raised above the things of this world in the contemplation of the truly godlike patience with which, in his human nature, he bore the terrible evils which were inflicted on him, and his resignation to the will of his heavenly Father.

" Oh that I could fix the present mood, and render it permanent! What a world of happiness dwells in the bosom of the devout man; amid all the storms of adversity he has a fortress and a God. His hopes repose on that Providence who has the disposal of all events; not knowing himself what is good or evil of the things of this life, he does his duty, and trusts to his Father for the rest. How far different is God from man! If we ask his favor he will not withhold it. ' To the poor he is a friend, and he will not hide his face from the needy.' I find we must love him before we can truly love one another. I see this love as the master principle — as the purifier of the heart; it warms our affections to our friends, makes us grateful to our benefactors and forgiving to our enemies. Oh, my dear Miller, bear with me now as you have often done before! I am weak as a child.

" My mind is filled with recollections of the joys that are gone, and the dear sainted friend that has left me. I went to her house, but I did not see her waiting my approach, her feet did not sound in the passage as I entered the door; 'my dear Willie,' was not heard on my unexpected appearance. The good hand that once nursed me was not stretched out with an air of tender affection towards me. I looked to the place where she used to sit, but she was not there; in her bodily shape I did not behold her, yet her image was before me, and all the good she did me was present in my view. What a vacancy is here! what a change has death made to me! But I must have done; the last light of evening is taking its leave. Good-by."

The difference between the character of Miller, who met every check and insult with pugnacity, and that of Ross, whose gentleness was feminine, and who could not bear to be thought ill of even by those who acted to him meanly and unkindly, tended probably to cement their friendship. The proceedings of Ross on completing his apprenticeship, and commencing practice as a house-painter on his own account, illustrate in a touching manner his simplicity and kindliness. The master who had enjoyed his services for five years — and valuable services they were, for William's talent in his vocation was eminent — seems to have quite cast him off when his term expired. He writes to Miller : —

"Want stared me in the face; and, having determined not to be a burden to any, I meant to leave, if I possibly could, the place; for, though I had no prospect of employment, I deemed it better to starve among strangers (if nothing else awaited me) than in this country. . . . . On the Tuesday after you had left me I waited on Mr. ——, and told him what I meant to do if he would trust me. He would not; and after so downright a refusal you cannot imagine the perturbed state of my mind. What hurt me most was that he should have doubted my probity. I then went straight to Mr. ——, to see what he thought of me ; for after the first shock was over I was indifferent to what I might meet with. He was not quite so direct with me, but what he said amounted to a refusal too. Before evening I had paid them both, which so reduced my slender finances that I could go nowhere, and here, without money or employment, I could not well stay. The friend who would have sympathized with me was gone ; and perhaps, 'twas better that he was. The way in which I have been treated could not but have hurt you.

"Now that you have my worst news, I will tell you better. Colonel G—— sent for me to *refresh* the walls of his dining-room, and gave me 5s. when I had done. Soon after I saw Mr. ——, who asked me whether I was employed, and told me, on my replying in the negative, that his brother-in-law, Mr. ——, had bought paint at London, and was looking out for some one to paint his house for him by the day. I would do the work most readily, I said, but as my old master had thought of getting it for himself, I could not think of interfering. He assured me, however, that that was out of the question, as it was owing to the exorbitancy of my master's estimate that Mr. —— had procured the materials for himself. I accordingly went and settled with Mr. —— for the work at 3s. per day. This will make a sad change, I am afraid, in all I enjoyed of the favorable opinion of my master; but I can't help it."

Was there not a delicacy of honor in the reluctance of the lad, whom starvation actually stared in the face, to accept work which his old master had " thought of getting," such as is rarely met with in any rank of life? In a letter written shortly afterwards, we have this note of that master's conduct : " I came here to furnish brushes for the work, but my master would sell me none." Brushes, however, were obtained, and he proceeds : " I am happier in my mind than usual. There are glimpses of sunshine breaking out upon me, and a less troubled sky overhead. Oh. how grateful ought I to be to that bounteous Benefactor who knows our wants, and can and will supply them! I hardly know, my dear Miller, how to conclude. I trust I am grateful to *him* for you too." It must have been a sweetly toned nature which unkindness so bitter did not provoke to one angry word, and which was so easily stimulated to childlike gladness and to pious gratitude. In the deep forest one beam penetrates to the wounded bird, and it breaks on the instant into song.

We shall take another extract from these letters of William Ross. It is interesting not only from its references to himself, but on account of the few bold and vigorous strokes with which it sketches Miller's uncles, James and Alexander Wright, and still more because of its vivid glimpse of the boy Miller : " I trust I am no misanthrope ; but, with one exception, — and on that one I need not be very explicit in writing to you, — it is dead and inanimate nature that I derive all my pleasures from, not the world of men. I have but one friend. . . . . Really, my dear Miller, I am one of the weakest young fellows I ever knew. All that is worth anything in me lies on the surface of my character, — a little taste, perhaps, a little fancy, and more than a little warmth of heart ; but I have no energy of *will*, no strength of judgment ; I feel I cannot come in contact with superior men without sinking into a mere nonentity, and losing all command of even the few powers I have. I always felt thus when in company with your uncles : they are both strong-minded men. — strong in sentiment and intellect, — and there is a depth and massiveness in their character which common circumstances fail to render apparent to the unobservant, but which I have felt as if by instinct. Hence, perhaps, my profound

esteem for them; but hence, also, my want of sympathy
with them.   Had you yourself been other than a boy when
our intimacy was first formed, I would not now, it is probable, be on my present terms with you.   We met in an
hour propitious to friendship.   I could not feel myself inferior to the wayward, warm-hearted boy, who besought me
so anxiously to become attached to him, who admired my
bad drawings, and saw very superior sense in my simple
disjointed remarks.   Your force of character at the same
time was shown in but mere boyish rebellion which one
could laugh at; your firmness was but obstinacy.   You
were a mere cub, though a lion-cub, — a mere sapling,
though sprung from the acorn."

Such was the young man with whom Miller spent the
greater part of his time on being relieved from the labors
of his first year of apprenticeship.   He read his poems to
Ross, and showed him his drawings.   Hugh had formed a
high estimate of both, and the undercurrent of critical
severity which invariably accompanied his friend's applause,
though not strong enough to damp his ardor, was useful
in giving precision to his ideas of himself.   Ross had penetration enough to discern that a certain imaginative glow,
which threw out objects, as it were, in aerial perspective,
and cast over them a pleasing light of fancy or association,
belonged to Miller.   In their walks in the wood or by the
shore, he encouraged Hugh to cultivate literature, applaud-
ing " the wild vigor of his imagination," and hinting that
his word-pictures of the moment revealed more of poetical
genius than the formal productions either of his pencil or
his pen.   "There is in the vicinity of the town of Cromarty," writes Miller to Baird, giving him an illustration
of the kind of imaginative fantasia with which he used to
entertain his friend, " a beautiful, thickly-wooded dell,
through the bottom of which there runs a small streamlet.

This dell was one of our favorite night haunts. In winter, when the trees are bare of foliage, the moonbeams, when the moon is at full, find their way to the water, though the steep banks on either side are lost in the shade. The appearance when viewed from some of the overhanging thickets is exceedingly beautiful, and when contemplating it in the company of my friend, I have in the wild extravagance of fancy compared the little moonlight brook to, — I know not how many different objects, — to a pictured flash of pale lightning, — to a stream of lava, — to a rippling strip of the Aurora Borealis. I have termed the little dell a dark oblong mirror, and the bright streamlet in its centre the reflection of the milky way. I have described the trunks of the trees and the stones which were relieved by the light from the shade behind, as fays and spectres by which the place was tenanted. I have even given a minute detail of the particular expression of their features and the peculiarities of their attire."

Ross' advice to Miller on the whole was as follows: " Your drawings have but little merit, nor can I regard them even as works of promise; neither by any means do you write good verses. And why, do you think, do I tell you so? Only to direct your studies to their proper object. You draw ill, because nature never intended that you should do otherwise; whereas you write ill only because you write seldom. You are possessed of talents which, with due culture, will enable you to attain no common command of the pen; for you are an original thinker, your mind is richly imbued with poetry, and, though devoid of a musical ear, you have, from nature, something much better, — that perception of the harmonies of language which is essential to the formation of a good and elegant style." So far as I can judge, no critic in Europe could have more correctly estimated Miller's capacity at the time, or given him better advice.

A spectator, observing these lads, the one apprenticed to a mason, the other to a house-painter, would hardly have guessed the nature of their conversation. Had they been youths of aristocratic birth or university distinction, could their intercourse have been more completely that of *gentlemen?* We may note how steadily Hugh pushes forward what, without much conscious resolving on the subject, has become the purpose of his life, — self-culture. With quiet persistence, undistracted by the commencement of lifelong toil as a mason, he cherishes the ambition of maturing his powers of thought and expression. Attesting, also, the radical nobleness of his character, and the high tone of the society in which he had lived, this circumstance is to be noted, — that the ambition of making money never seized him. The big bells of Babylon dinning into all young ears, never more loudly than in our age, their invitation to make fortunes, had no persuasion for him. To extend the empire of his mind, to enrich and beautify the garden of his soul, this was what presented itself as a supreme object of ambition to our Scottish boy of eighteen, with a mallet in his hand.

CHAPTER III.

IN the spring of 1821 Miller resumed his labors. In the latter end of May, his master had finished the work contracted for in the district of Cromarty, and, as no more contracts were to be had, was compelled to descend from the position of master and seek employment as journeyman. The apprentice he had taken at the same time with Miller seized the opportunity of regaining his freedom, and setting up as journeyman on his own account; and one might have thought that the wilful, headstrong lad, who had set his uncles and his schoolmasters at defiance, would have followed this example. But Hugh was no longer the turbulent school-boy of sixteen, and among the qualities which had ripened in the wholesome atmosphere of labor was a profound sense of justice. He continued to serve old David Wright, and proceeded with him to the banks of the Conon, a river which falls into the Cromarty Frith at its western extremity. On reaching Conon-side, they found that the scene of their occupation lay a few miles farther to the west, and for four weeks they were employed in building a jointure-house for the widow of a Highland proprietor. Miller describes the country around as " somewhat bare and dreary, — a scene of bogs and moors, overlooked by a range of tame, heathy hills."

It was while here that he became acquainted with that remarkable maniac of whom he has left an account in the "Schools and Schoolmasters." Looking at midnight from the window in the loft in which he slept, he beheld a light moving among the ruins of an old chapel and the graves of the surrounding burial-ground. It was carried in the hand of the escaped maniac. He attracted her attention and secured her regard by interfering on her behalf when she was being chained down on the damp floor of her hut. Of a naturally powerful though completely disordered intellect, she had sagacity enough to discover that Miller was of a different strain from his fellow-masons, and entertained him with stories of the Highlands and anecdotes of her deceased brother, a preacher of reputation. She loved to discuss the most abstruse questions of metaphysical theology. That every human soul is immediately created by God, not transmitted from a human ancestor, she declared herself to be fully convinced; but, then, how to account for the influence exerted on all souls by the fall? It would take a powerful theologian, sane or insane, to answer this question. Miller informed her that a great authority thought it might be " by way of natural concomitancy, as Estius will have it; or, to speak as Dr. Reynolds doth, by way of ineffable resultancy and emanation." "As this," he adds, " was perfectly unintelligible, it seemed to satisfy my new friend." A singular pair on the black Ross-shire moor! It is only, I suppose, in Scotland that masons' apprentices and female maniacs engage in abstruse metaphysical discussions.

The jointure-house finished, Miller bids adieu to his mad friend, and returns to Conon-side. He is now, for the first time, introduced to the barrack or bothy life of a squad of masons. A description of the barrack and the scene it presented on his first becoming one of its inmates occurs in his letter to Baird. "I followed," he writes, "the horde into their barrack. It consisted of one large apartment. Along the wall, and across one of the gables, there was a range of beds rudely constructed of outside slab deals, and filled with straw, which bristled from beneath the blankets and from between the crevices of the frames in a manner much less neat than picturesque. At each bedside there were two chests, which served not only the purpose originally intended, but also for chairs and tables. Suspended by ropes from the rafters above, there hung, at the height of a man's head from the ground, several bags filled with oat-meal, which by this contrivance was secured from the rats; with which the place was infested. Along the gable furthest removed from the door there was a huge wood fire ; above it there were hung several small pots, enveloped in smoke, which, for lack of proper vent, after filling the whole barrack, escaped by the door. Before the fire there was a row of stones, each of which supported an oaten cake. The inmates, who exceeded twenty, had disposed of themselves in every possible manner. Some were lounging in the beds, others were seated on the chests. Two of them were dancing on the floor to the whistling of a third. There was one employed in baking, another in making ready the bread. The chaos of sounds which reigned among them was much more complete than that which appalled their prototypes, the builders of Babel. There was the gabbling of Saxon, the sputtering of Gaelic, the humming of church music, the whistling of the musician, and the stamping of the dancers. Three of the pots on the fire began to boil together, and there was a cry for the cook. He came rushing forward, pushed the man engaged in baking from out his way with one hand, and, drawing the seat from under the one employed in making ready the bread with the other, he began to shout out, so as to drown their united voices, for meal and salt. Both were brought him, and in a few minutes he had completed his task."

Wild companions, a wild lodging, and wild mode of life; nor can much bodily comfort be associated with the idea of a diet whose sole variation is from oatmeal in porridge to oatmeal in cakes; but Miller is not unhappy. He is now recognized as a good workman, and his frame is more capable of labor than in the previous season. His spirit is buoyant, and full of gay, hopeful humor; and his readiness to take and return a jest, together with his sprightliness and his obliging disposition, secure him the good-will of his companions. On the long summer evenings, when work is over, he can wander about the district, climbing its ridges of hill, exploring its ruins and natural curiosities, diving into the recesses of its woods, and following the course of its streams. He is still boy enough to enjoy the raspberries which grow in the woods, and the poetry of his nature finds aliment in the new and picturesque aspects of hill and plain which every eminence reveals to him.

The district of Miller's sojourn at this time, dreary and bare though he calls it, is not without its pleasing and impressive features. Gaunt hills rise everywhere, warming at autumn, when the heather blooms, into solemn glow of purple, but for the greater part of the year presenting a surface of black-brown, fringed here and there with fir or plumed with birch. The gray crag pierces the moor, the gray mist trails wearily along the hill-summits. A marked feature of the scenery is the gracefully drooping, delicately waving birch foliage, which stoops to the frequent watercourse, or hangs tremulous over the surface of the lake, the white stems relieved against the russet heath, or vying with the whiter foam of the cascade. Over all towers the bald forehead of Ben Wyvis, a thousand feet above the highest of the encircling hills, and with a few white snow-gleams lingering among its crags and corries even in the height of summer. Between the ridges and in the basins of the hills, the lakes are numerous, and from the higher elevations, as the eye looks through curtains of mist, opening and closing in majestic change, the broad flash of their golden mirrors, girdled by the ebon hills, is seen striking upwards with a resplendence never to be forgotten.

The gentler aspects of the scenery appear, however, to have chiefly attracted Miller. "Strathpeffer," he wrote to Baird, "one of the finest valleys in this part of the country, lies within five miles of Conon-side. My walks occasionally extended to it; and I still retain a vividly-pleasing recollection of its enchanting scenery, with the more pleasing features of the scenes through which I passed on my way to it. There is in its vicinity a beautiful little lake, which contains a wooded island. Along the banks of this lake I have sauntered for whole hours; and from the green top of Knockferrol, one of the hills by which the valley is bounded, I have seen the sun sink behind Ben Wyvis, without once thinking that I was five miles from my place of residence."

But he was not exclusively engaged on these occasions in view-hunting. "I have not even yet," he adds, "summed up the whole of my evening amusements. They were not all equally poetical. The country round Conon-side abounds with wild fruit, and I have feasted among the woods, during my long rambles, on gueens, rowans, raspberries, and blae-berries, with all the keenness of boyish appetite. The fruit furnished me with an ostensible object for my wanderings; and when complimented by a romantic young girl, who had derived her notions of character from the reading of romances, on that disposition which led me to seek my pleasures in solitude, I could remark in reply that I was not more fond of solitude than of raspberries."

Thirty years afterwards, in the "Schools and School-masters," he refers to his walks by Conon-side in these terms: "I greatly enjoyed those evening walks. From Conon-side as a centre, a radius of six miles commands many objects of interest, — Strathpeffer, with its mineral springs; Castle Leod, with its ancient trees, among the rest one of the largest Spanish chestnuts in Scotland; Knock-ferrol, with its vitrified fort; the old tower of Fairburn; the old, though somewhat modernized, tower of Kinkell; the Brahan policies, with the old castle of the Seaforths; the old castle of Kilcoy; and the Druidic circles of the moor of Redcastle. . . . . My recollections of this rich tract of country, with its woods and towers, and noble river, seem as if bathed in the red light of gorgeous sunsets."

In a letter, otherwise unimportant, to William Ross, written, as I conclude, after he had returned to Cromarty for the winter, there occurs this reference to the same period: "When the task of the day was over, and I walked out amid the fields and woods to enjoy the cool of the evening, it was then that I was truly happy. Before me the Conon rolled her broad stream to the sea; behind, I seemed shut up from all intercourse with mankind by a thick and gloomy wood, while the tower of Fairburn * and the blue hills behind it formed the distant landscape. Not a cloud rose upon the sky, not a salmon glided beneath me in the river, nor a leaf shook upon the alders that o'erhung the stream, but raised some poetic emotion in my breast."

It was late in the year when he returned to Cromarty. Nearly a month of winter had passed. Ross was now re-siding in the cottage of his parents, on the northern side of

* The accompanying drawing was executed by Miller a few years subsequently to the time when he worked in the vicinity of the old tower of Fairburn.

Cromarty Frith, and Miller lacked the stimulus of his literary sympathy. " What remained of the season," he wrote to Baird, " together with the greater part of the ensuing spring, was spent in profitless indolence. I neither wrote verses nor drew pictures, but wandered during the day through the fields and woods, and among the rocks of the hill of Cromarty ; and my evenings were commonly spent either in the workshop of my Uncle James, where a few of the more intelligent mechanics of the place generally met, or in the company of a new acquaintance." This was the helpless cripple, described in the " Schools and Schoolmasters " as " poor lame Danie," who, with his old mother, occupied " a damp, underground room." Miller formed a friendship with the suffering boy, and took delight in alleviating the tedium of his lingering illness.

CHAPTER IV.

THE working season of 1822 finds him again on Conon-side. He is now in the third year of his apprenticeship, and he feels that he has a position in the barrack. " I had determined," — the words are from the letter to Baird, — " early this season, to conform to every practice of the barrack, and, as I was an apt pupil, I had in a short time become one of the freest, and not the least rude, of its inmates. I became an excellent baker, and one of the most skilful of cooks. I made wonderful advances in the art of practical joking, and my *bon-mots* were laughed at and repeated. There were none of my companions who could foil me in wrestling, or who could leap within a foot of me ; and after having taken the slight liberty of knocking down a young fellow who insulted me, they all began to esteem me as a lad of spirit and promise."

The foreman of the squad with which he worked appears to have exerted some influence upon his mind. " When a young man," writes Miller, " he had bent his excellent natural parts to the study of his profession, and he became so

92

skilful in it as to be intrusted with the superintendence of a party of workmen while yet an apprentice. His early proficiency was a subject of wonder to his less gifted companions; he was much gratified by their admiration, and acquired that appetite for praise which is of so general experience, and which in many instances becomes more keen the more it is supplied with food. He had too much sense to be open to the direct flatteries of other people, but he was not skilful in detecting his own; and having attained, in the limited circle to which circumstances confined him, the fame of being talented, he set himself to acquire the reputation of being generous and warm-hearted; and this, perhaps, for he was naturally of a cold temperament, from that singular weakness incident to human nature, which has so frequently the effect of making even men of reflection derive more pleasure from the praise of the qualities or talents of which they are destitute, than of those which they really possess. When treating his companions, he was rendered happy by believing they entertained an opinion of him similar to that with which he regarded himself; and that they would describe him to others as one whose head and heart were the warmest and clearest they had ever met with. A few years' experience of the world convinced him that his expectations were miserably unfounded. He saw, or at least thought he did, that every man he came in contact with had himself for his centre; and, though unacquainted with the maxims of Rochefoucault, he concluded with that philosopher that the selfish principle is the spring of all human action. The consequence of this conclusion was a misanthropy of the most sincere and unaffected kind. So sincere was it that he made no profession of it; unlike those silly, would-be misanthropes who, while they affect a hatred of their kind, take care to inform them of that hatred, lest they should fail of attracting their notice."

" I was advised by this man," proceeds Miller, " to study geometry and architecture. With the latter I had previously been acquainted; of the former I was entirely ignorant. I had not even a single correct idea of it. The study of a few detached hours, though passed amid the distraction of a barrack, made me master of the language peculiar to the science; and I was then surprised to find how wide a province it opens to the mental powers, and to discover that what is termed mathematical skill means only an ability of reasoning on the forms and properties of lines and figures, acquired by good sense being patiently directed to their consideration. I perceived, however, that from prosecuting this study I could derive only amusement, and that, too, not of a kind the most congenial to my particular cast of mind. I had no ambition to rise by any of the professions in which it is necessary; and I chose rather to exercise the faculties proper to be employed in it in the wide field of nature and of human affairs, — in tracing causes to their effects, and effects to their causes; in classing together things similar, and in marking the differences of things unlike. The study of architecture I found more amusing; partly, I believe, because it tasked me less; partly because it gratified my taste, and exercised my powers of invention. In geometry I saw that I could only follow the footsteps of others, and that I would be necessitated to pursue the beaten track for whole years before I could reach that latest discovered extremity of it, beyond which there lies undiscovered, untrodden regions, in which it would be a delight to expatiate. Architecture, on the contrary, appeared to me a field of narrow boundaries. I could see at one glance both over it and beyond it. I have found that the grotesque cottage of a Highland peasant, the hut of a herd-boy, a cavern half veiled over with trailing plants, an opening in a wood, in short, a countless variety of objects of art and nature, supplied me with ideas which, though connected with it, had not become part of it."

From mathematics, therefore, as previously from classics, Hugh Miller turned aside. The circumstance is perhaps to be regretted, and yet with the former reservation, that any severe and systematic course of study would have interfered with that natural and spontaneous development which made him what he was.

His apprenticeship had begun with trying experiences, and its termination was marked also by extremity of hardship. In the September of this year, 1822, his master obtained work as a contractor on a farm a few miles from Cromarty, and he and Miller bade adieu to Conon-side. A wall was to be built and a farmsteading to be repaired, and, as the season was advanced, and David Wright could afford to employ no labor in addition to his own and that of his apprentice, Miller and he worked from dawn until nightfall. Their work was of the most painful kind: "day after day, with wet feet, in a water-logged ditch," laying stone upon stone, until the cuticle was worn away, and the fingers oozed blood. In the "Schools and Schoolmasters," Miller describes the labor of this time as "torture." "How these poor hands of mine," he says, "burnt and beat at night at this time, as if an unhappy heart had been stationed in every finger! and what cold chills used to run, sudden as electric shocks, through the feverish frame!" His health was affected: a dull, depressing pain weighed upon his chest, and there were symptoms of pectoral blood-spitting. He lost his spirits, and thought he was going to die.

Of his state of mind at this time we have two illustrations, the one given in the "Schools and Schoolmasters," the other in the letter to Baird. " Superstition," we quote from the published volume, " takes a strong hold of the mind in circumstances such as those in which I was at this time placed. One day, when on the top of a tall building, part of which we were throwing down to supply us with materials for our work, I raised up a broad slab of red micaceous sandstone, thin as a roofing slate, and exceedingly fragile. and, holding it out at arm's length, dropped it over the wall. I had been worse than usual all that morning, and much depressed; and, ere the slab parted from my hand, I said, — looking forward to but a few months of life, — I shall break up like that sandstone slab, and perish as little known. But the sandstone slab did not break up; a sudden breeze blew it aslant as it fell; it cleared the rough heap of stones below, where I had anticipated it would have been shivered to fragments, and, lighting on its edge, stuck upright, like a miniature obelisk, in the soft, green sward beyond. None of the philosophies or the logics would have sanctioned the inference which I immediately drew; but that curious chapter in the history of human belief which treats of signs and omens abounds in such postulates and such conclusions. I at once inferred that recovery awaited me; I was 'to live and not die,' and felt lighter, during the few weeks I afterwards toiled at this place, under the cheering influence of the conviction."

In the letter to Baird there is no mention of this waking experiment, but he records the following dream: " I dreamed that I was walking alone, in an evening of singular beauty, over a low piece of marshy ground, which lies about half a mile to the north of the place where I wrought. On a bank which rises above the marsh there is a small burying-ground and the ruins of an old chapel. I dreamed that I arrived at the burying-ground, and that it was laid out in a manner the most exquisitely elegant. The tombs were of beautiful and varied workmanship. They were of a style either chastely Grecian or gorgeously Gothic, and enwreathed and half hid by the flowers and foliage of beautiful shrubs which sprung up and clustered around them. There was a profusion of roses, mingled with delicate blue flowers of a species I never saw except in this dream. The old Gothic chapel seemed roofed with stone, and appeared as entire as the day it had been completed ; but, from the lichens and mosses with which it was covered, it looked more antique than almost any building I remember to have seen. The whole scene was relieved against a clear sky, which seemed bright and mellow as if the sun had set only a minute before. Suddenly, however, it became dark and lowering, a low breeze moaned through the tombs and bushes, and I began to feel the influence of a superstitious terror. I looked towards the chapel, and on its western gable I saw an antique-looking, singularly formed beam of bronze, which seemed to unite in itself the shapes of the hour-hand of a clock and the gnomon of a dial. As I gazed on it, it turned slowly on its axis until it pointed at a spot on the sward below. It then remained stationary as before. My terror increased, the images of my dream became less distinct, and my last recollection before I awoke is of a wild night-scene, and of my floundering on in the darkness through the marsh below the burying-ground. A few weeks after the night of this dream, one of my paternal cousins, in the second degree, was seized by a fever of which he died. I attended his funeral, and found that the grave had been opened to receive his corpse on exactly the patch of sward to which the beam had turned."

This dream he calls " a prophecy of contingency, — one of those few dreams which, according to Bacon, men remember and believe because they happen to hit, not one of the many which they deem idle and forget, because they chance to miss." To us it is interesting as showing, especially when taken in connection with the small experiment in necromancy previously related, how strongly, even at this early period, Hugh Miller's mental state was influenced by his physical condition. Brooding on early death by day, wandering among tombs in night-visions, his brain was rapidly approaching that degree of agitation at which will and intellect fall under the dominion of mania.

Both in the "Schools and Schoolmasters," and in the letter to Baird, he dwells upon the wretched and dissolute life of the two or three (we have two in the earlier account and three in the later) farm-servants who occupied the same bothy with himself and his master. In his twenty-seventh year Hugh Miller pronounced emphatic condemnation on the bothy system; he returned to the subject when fifty, and it was to enforce his opinion by the experience of his life. "There were," he writes to Baird, "two unmarried farm-servants who lodged with us in the barrack. They were both young men, and the life they were almost necessitated to lead was one of the most unfriendly possible to the formation of moral character. All day they were employed in the monotonous labors of the farm. Their evenings, as they had no home, were spent either in neighboring houses, where young people similarly situated with themselves were accustomed to meet, or in a small village, about a mile distant, where there was an ale-house. Their ordinary pleasures consisted in drinking, and amusements of a low and gross character; their principal enjoyment they derived from what they termed a ball, and scarce a fortnight passed at this season without one being held at the village. It was commonly midnight before they returned to the barrack. The effects of this heartless course of life were apparent in their dispositions and conduct. They were bound by no ties of domestic affection; and, though they were never apart, they seemed to have no other idea of friendship than that it was a matter of convenience which substituted the pleasures of society for the horrors of solitude. To a person of a degraded, selfish cast of mind it is misery to be alone; and hence it will almost invariably be found that the more careless a common man becomes of his fellows, the less can he live without them. The lads were besides extremely ignorant; they were of a gay, reckless disposition, and, as they entertained no affection for their employer, and had their moral feelings much blunted, the services they rendered him were profitless and inefficient, as those services generally are which are extorted by necessity, and regulated by only a dread of censure. I could not think without regret that they were yet to become husbands and the fathers of families; and at this time I was first led to perceive that the large farm system has been as productive, at least, of moral evil as of physical good. By the discoveries in the art of agriculture to which it has led, the soil has been meliorated and rendered more productive; but what have been its effects upon men? So far as it has extended, it has substituted two classes of character which may be regarded as opposite extremes equally removed from the intermediate line of excellence, for a class which occupied the proper medium. It has given us, for a wise, moral, and religious peasantry, gentlemen-farmers and farm-servants, — the latter, in too many instances, a class of debased *helots* of the character described; the former a body of men too often marked (though certainly with many exceptions) by a union of the worst traits peculiar to the opposing classes of country gentlemen and merchants, — the supercilious, overbearing manners of the one class; the unfeeling, speculative spirit of the other."

To the same effect is the latter statement of his views on the subject: "The deteriorating effect of the large farm system," he wrote, " is inevitable. . . . Farm-servants, as a class, *must* be lower in the scale than the old tenant-farmers, who wrought their little farms with their own hands ; but it is possible to elevate them far above the degraded level of the bothy ; and unless means be taken to check the spread of the ruinous process of brute-making which the system involves, the Scottish people will sink, to a certainty, in the agricultural districts, from being one of the most provident, intelligent, and moral in Europe, to be one of the most licentious, reckless, and ignorant."

If two men ever lived who knew the Scottish people, and were able to give an intelligent opinion concerning them, these two men were Robert Burns and Hugh Miller ; and their joint authority in favor of the old system and against the new, viewed in relation to the capacity of each to produce upright, independent, self-respecting men, will hardly be outweighed by the consideration that large farms, worked by men in bothies, send most meat to the London market.

It may be hoped that such bothies as that in which Hugh Miller lived at this time are no longer to be found in Scotland. The roof leaked ; the sides were "riddled with gaps and breaches ; " along the ridge, " it was open to the sky from gable to gable," " so that," he writes, " when I awakened in the night, I could tell what o'clock it was, without rising out of bed, by the stars which appeared through the opening." Even in this dismal place, however, he contrived to supply himself with the consolations of literature. From a wandering pedler he obtained the old Scottish poems of Gawin Douglas and William Dunbar, besides a collection of " Ancient Scottish Poems " from the MS. of George Bannatyne. These books he " perused with great interest, lying on the barrack floor, with the page spread out within a few inches of the fire." At last, even this resource failed him. The fuel used for warming the barrack became soaked with rain, and could not produce a blaze by which it was possible to read. There was nothing for it but to stick doggedly to work, passing as many hours of the twenty-four in sleep as was practicable. He found that, by a little judicious management, a great deal of sleep could be got into the twenty-four hours, and that sleep was not a bad makeshift in the absence of livelier entertainments. "I restricted myself," he writes to Baird, "to two meals per day, that immediately after taking dinner I might go to bed; and in a short time this new arrangement became such a matter of habit that I commonly fell asleep every evening about six o'clock, and did not rise, sometimes not even awaken, until near eight next morning. Since this time I have been accustomed to decide whether I am happy, or the contrary (a query of difficulty when one measures one's circumstances by the standards of either hope or fear), by a test extremely simple. I deem the balance to incline to the side of happiness when I prefer consciousness to unconsciousness, — when I consider sleep merely a thing of necessity, instead of regarding it as a refuge from the *tedium* of waking inanity, or unpleasant occupation. The converse leads me to a contrary conclusion." In the letter from which this is quoted he pronounces the spring and summer of the first year of his apprenticeship "the gloomiest seasons of his life;" in the "Schools and Schoolmasters," the closing period is declared to have been "by far the gloomiest he ever spent." At both periods he suffered about as much as man can suffer; but in the intermediate stages there were glimpses, nay, abiding gleams, of enjoyment. On the 11th of November, 1822, his apprenticeship came to an end.

He was now an accomplished workman, and perhaps in all his books there is no passage more weighty or valuable than that in which he gives his estimate of the importance of this fact, and impresses upon artisans the supreme necessity of being masters of their trade. "It is not uninstructive," he writes, "to observe how strangely the public are led at times to attach paramount importance to what is in reality only subordinately important, and to pass over the really paramount without thought or notice. The destiny in life of the skilled mechanic is much more influenced, for instance, by his second education — that of his apprenticeship — than by his first, — that of the school; and yet it is to the education of the school that the importance is generally regarded as attaching, and we never hear of the other.

The careless, incompetent scholar has many opportunities of recovering himself; the careless, incompetent apprentice, who either fails to serve out his regular time, or who, though he fulfils his term, is discharged an inferior workman, has very few; and, further, nothing can be more certain than that inferiority as a workman bears much more disastrously on the condition of the mechanic than inferiority as a scholar. Unable to maintain his place among brother journeymen, or to render himself worthy of the average wages of his craft, the ill-taught mechanic falls out of regular employment, subsists precariously for a time on occasional jobs, and either, forming idle habits, becomes a vagabond *tramper*, or, getting into the toils of some rapacious taskmaster, becomes an enslaved *sweater*. For one workman injured by neglect of his school education, there are scores ruined by neglect of their apprenticeship education. Three-fourths of the distress of the country's mechanics (of course not that of the unhappy class who have to compete with machinery), and nine-tenths of their vagabondism, will be found restricted to inferior workmen, who, like Hogarth's "careless apprentice," neglected the opportunities of their second term of education. The sagacious painter had a truer insight into this matter than most of our modern educationists."

During his apprenticeship the character of Miller began to reveal the essential traits which we afterwards find in it. "Gloomy" many of its seasons were; the "gloomiest" of his life, — at least until he became a literary celebrity and editor of a religious newspaper; but both its gloom and its gladness went to the making and maturing of his character. The aching joint, the fevered pulse, the breast oppressed with pain, the eye swimming in bewildered trance of agony and exhaustion; the meditative midnight hour, when his eye marked the stars as they crossed the rent in the roof; the evening wanderings in woodland and by stream when sunset clothed in ruddy light the old tower on the crag, — these constituted the true education of Hugh Miller. Henceforth we recognize him as the man he was, and are able to trace in his countenance those lines of fortitude and resolution which so strongly marked that of his father. He had won the first decisive victory of life, earnest of all other victories, — the victory of reason and conscience over momentary inclination, of intelligent will over laggard indolence and lawless impulse. He had disciplined the wayward activity of boyhood into manly force. He had chastened rude strength into ordered energy. Blustering self-assertion, juvenile conceit, had given place to deliberate self-respect; and that rebellious disposition which had perplexed his uncles and been the despair of his mother was calmed and concentrated into modesty, into self-command, into the gentleness of conscious power. The flawed and brittle iron had become steel. "Noble, upright, self-relying Toil," he exclaims, with grand enthusiasm, "who that knows thy solid worth and value would be ashamed of thy hard hands, and thy soiled vestments, and thy obscure tasks, — thy humble cottage, and hard couch, and homely fare !"

Not, however, to all men is toil an education and hardship a blessing. Hugh Miller came to his apprenticeship fortified against evil and prepared for good by that training in courage and truthfulness, in just thought and manly feeling, which he had unconsciously received in companionship with his uncles. Those gentlemen of nature's finest modelling were, though he knew it not, the examples by which he shaped himself. He acted on all occasions as he felt that Uncle James or Uncle Sandy would have acted in the circumstances. Nor can we err in affirming that the incidents and results of Miller's apprenticeship prove that there was a remarkable soundness in his original constitution, a fund of natural health, moral and intellectual, of genial humor and of homely wisdom. How bravely he makes the most of adverse circumstances! How cheerfully he accommodates himself to his situation! How kindly are the relations he establishes between himself and his coarse and riotous associates! There is nothing which he cannot assimilate and apply to his mental nutriment, and he is animated by a quiet, half-conscious, but steadfast ambition for self-culture. He has a deep-lying conviction of his ability to rise above the sphere in which he finds himself placed; but he has already got firm hold of a very ancient philosophy of life, a philosophy which has been of use to wise men in every age; and it has made him comparatively indifferent to what is called success. According to this philosophy, happiness is too subtle an essence to be purchased with gold, or to be dealt out wholesale to one class of men as distinguished from another; the rude fare of the peasant is as sweet to him as his dainties to the peer; the honest pride which warms the heart of the capable artisan is as instinct with joy as the aristocrat's pride of rank or birth; nature's face has a smile for all who will lovingly look into it; and rising in the world may mean falling in all that makes life precious, character illustrious, man happy.

BOOK III.

THE JOURNEYMAN.

———•◆•———

"Here also is a man who can handle both pen and hammer like a man."

CHAPTER I.

ON returning to Cromarty, Miller soon regains his health, and things wear for him on the whole a pleasant aspect. Old David Wright, who had occasionally been morose to his apprentice (his own distresses imperatively demanding that relief), now declares that, though unsecured to him by any written agreement, Hugh had been, "beyond comparison, more tractable and obedient than any indentured pupil he ever had." Uncle James, whose predictions of failure at work, as a natural sequel to failure at school, had contributed not a little to the support of Miller at the worst time, — for it would be exquisitely gratifying to punish and to please Uncle James by one and the same course of action, — does ample justice to the faithfulness, with which, from a mere sense of honor, he has completed his engagement, and owns that there is in him, after all, the making of a man.

His first employment as a journeyman is characteristic. To seek remunerative employment — to start in life for himself — would be his natural impulse. But the better and homelier part of his nature has now ripened, and kindness of heart, one of his deepest qualities, proves stronger than the prompting of ambition. "Aunt Jenny," a sister of his mother, who had long wished to have some dwelling which she could call her own, and in which her spinning-wheel and knitting-needles might supply her modest wants, had never surmounted the alarm occasioned by the prospect of paying rent. Hugh inherited a little piece of garden ground from his father. Part of this he now devotes to the purpose of building a cottage for Aunt Jenny. Money he has none, but the few pounds which his aunt has saved are enough to buy wood for the roof and to pay for carting the necessary stones and mortar, and he builds the cottage. The worthy aunt is saved from fear of rent for the remainder of her days, and Hugh has his reward. The cottage is still to be seen in the village of Cromarty, bearing witness, while stone and lime endure, to the competence of Hugh Miller as a stone-mason, and to the simplicity, solidity, and kindliness of his character. It is in little circumstances like this that one learns infallibly what is in a man. When the scenes are arranged, the audience assembled, the attitude given, it is easy to act the generous part; but the quiet heart-heroism, unseen by the world, unsurmised even by itself, which makes Hugh Miller pause, on the threshold of life, to build a cottage for Aunt Jenny, cannot deceive us.

This undertaking is completed in the spring of 1823, and the day has now come when employment must be sought in earnest. Some little time elapses — two or three weeks at most — during which he looks in vain. " I was a good deal depressed." he writes to Baird. " I was somewhat diffident of my skill as a workman ; and I felt too, very strongly, the force of that sentiment of Burns to which we are indebted for his excellent elegiac poem, 'Man is made to mourn.' 'There is nothing,' said the poet, 'that gives me a more mortifying picture of human life than a man seeking work.' "

During the brief interval between the building of Aunt

Jenny's cottage and his first engagement as a journeyman, he writes to William Ross, now in Edinburgh, and copies out for him a selection of his poems. The letter is not without interest from the enthusiasm of its affection for the friend to whom it is addressed.

"I have long since promised you copies of all my little poetical pieces which you were so good-natured as to approve of, and I now send you them. I am too vain to forget how much you used to praise them; but was it not as the productions of a half-taught boy that you did so? and if you loved them, was it not merely because they were written by your friend? I now see that many of them are extremely juvenile, and this could not have escaped *you;* but I dare say you did best in not telling me so. I would have been disheartened, and have, perhaps, stood still. And yet even now when I see many of their faults, like a true parent I love them notwithstanding; but it is more for the sake of the association connected with them than for their own sakes. Some of them were composed among the rocks of my favorite hill when I played truant; some of them in Marcus cave, when the boys who had chosen me for their leader were engaged in picking shell-fish from the skerries for our dinner; some of them in the workshed, some in the barrack. And thus, like the purse of Fortunatus, which was made of leather but produced gold, though not rich in themselves they are full of riches to me. They are redolent of the past and of you: remember how I used to run to your closet with every piece the moment I had finished it. that you might say something in its favor. You were the whole *public* for whom I wrote. You will not deem me paradoxical when I say that the pieces I send you are full of scenery and character, though poor in description and manner, and rich in thought and sentiment, though meagre, perhaps, and commonplace. Your affection for me will, I dare say, make them poetry to you too. Do you think I shall ever write what will be deemed poetry by anybody else? I deem my intimacy with you the most important affair of my life. I have enjoyed more from it than from anything else, and have been more improved by it than by all my books. Since you left me I have not advanced an inch; have you no means of impelling me onward when at a distance? or is it necessary, as in Physics, that before communicating motion to me, we must come in contact?"

The poems are fluent and vivacious, but display little original power or depth of melody. The following lines, probably written among the woods of Conon during his apprenticeship, are not without a certain pensive sweetness and sincerity.

THE DAYS THAT ARE GONE.

" On the friends of my youth and the days that are gone,
 In the depth of the wild wood I ponder alone,
 And my heart by a sad gloomy spirit is moved
 When I view the fair scenes that in childhood I loved.
 Harsh roars the rough ocean, o'ercast is the sky,
 The voice of the wind passeth mournfully by ;
 For winter reigns wide ; — ' sure 'tis winter with me,'
 But a spring to my winter I never shall see ;
 For aught of earth's joys 'tis unmanly to moan,
 Yet bursts the sad sigh for the days that are gone.
  The fair flowers of summer have vanished away,
 The green shrub is withered, and leafless the spray ;
 Yet memory, half-sad and half-sportive, still shows
 How bloomed the blue violet, how blossomed the rose.
 Say, shall not that memory as fondly retain
 Hold of joys I have proved as of charms I have seen?
 Yes — Nature's fair scenes are more dear to this heart
 Than the trophies of love or the pageants of art,

Yet more to this bosom those friends are endeared,
By whom in life's dawn the gay moments were cheered;
More cherished, though darker their memory shall be,
Than that of the rose or the violet by me.

    Ye rocks, whose rough summits seem lost in the clouds,
Ye fountains, ye caves, and ye dark waving woods,
In the still voice of memory ye bid me to mourn
For the joys and the years that must never return,
The years ere the gay hopes of youth were laid low,
Or hope half-despondent had wept o'er the blow,
The joys, ere my knowledge of mankind began
By proving the toils and the sorrows of man.

    Yet why should I sorrow? — poor child of decay,
Myself, like my pleasures, must vanish away,
And life in the view of my spirit may seem
The tossing confused of a feverish dream.
Yes, life is a dream, a wild dream, where the will
Striveth vainly the precepts of right to fulfil;
A dream where the dreamer to sorrow is tied;
A dream where proud reason but weakly can guide;
It controls not my spirit, despite of my will,
The joys of the by-past are haunting me still.

    And oft when all bright on my night slumbers break
The spirits of pleasures I prize when awake,
When I seize them with gladness and revel in joy,
Comes the beam of the morning my bliss to destroy;
Away on the light wings of slumber they fly,
While their memory remains, and I languish and sigh.
O days of bright pleasure! O days of delight!
From me ye forever have wingéd your flight.
But the calm, pensive Muse still remains to beguile
The day of dark thought, of affliction and toil;
By the gloom of the present the past to endear,
By the joys of the by-past the present to cheer."

In a poetical epistle to a friend, whom I take to be Ross
himself, we have a significant glimpse of Miller's feelings
with respect to the lawlessness of his school-days:

> "Oh! well to thee are all those foibles known,
>   Which to a stranger I would blush to own:
>   For well you knew me when in youth I strayed;
>
>   .   .   .   .
>
>   When of untutored genius weakly vain,
>   I spurned instruction with a vile disdain;
>   Yet dared to expect, unskilled in classic lore,
>   To song's proud heights the untutored Muse would soar.
>   Vain hope! These rude, unpolished lines must show
>   How weak my thoughts, how harsh my numbers flow."

It is a deeply characteristic trait that Hugh Miller should, as a school-boy, have been so conscious of his genius as to feel himself empowered to spurn instruction, and that, as an apprentice, a year or two after leaving school, he should have already convinced himself of the feeble vanity of the idea.

Occasionally there is a vividness of conception in these pieces, which presents the individual figure or picture in outline so distinct, and colors so brilliant, that it flashes in clear visibility upon the eye of the mind. The raven in the following sketch is as palpably bodied forth as Tennyson's wild hawk staring with his foot on the prey:—

> "Foulest of the birds of heaven,
>   O'er thee flaps the hungry raven;
>   Hark! his loud and piercing cry,
>   Pilgrim, hark! that faint reply;
>   Soon, on yonder rocky shore,
>   Shall he bathe his wing in gore,
>   Bathe each wing, while dives his beak
>   In a cold, wave-beaten cheek;
>   Cold,—the fierce tides o'er it flowing;
>   Cold, though now with life 'tis glowing."

A copy of verses, "written at the close of the year," is dated for us in two lines which occur in its most mournful passage:—

" Shall ill indeed no more annoy?
   Is life in truth a flowery plain? —
Ah, wherefore look for coming joy
   When all the past is black with pain?
That strong-winged Spoiler oft I've seen
   Around that checkered circlet flee;
(For, lo! this weary world has been
   These eighteen years a home to me.)
Yes, I have seen him pass away
Slow o'er misfortune's gloomy day,
Stern joy seemed his when sorrow laid
Her cold hand on the sufferer's head;
But ah! when aught resembling peace
For one short hour bade mourning cease,
Like light's fleet ray he sped him on,
And soon the tearless hour was gone.
   Still shall he fly, and joy and pain
Shall mark this checkered life again,
Till sorrow's soothing plaint be made
All lonely o'er the nameless dead;
And all that Fate or Fortune gave,
Be summed up o'er my tombless grave."

Not altogether tombless! The melancholy vein soon gives place to one of sprightlier flow, and perhaps more genuine feeling. Here is a rhymed contribution to that sad yet smiling philosophy of life to which allusion was lately made: —

" Let calm content, let placid rest,
   For the wild joys of fame suffice;
Nor grandeur, clothed in gorgeous vest,
   And tempting form, allure mine eyes;
But let the lowly Muse descend,
   With fancied bliss to glad my view,
And I shall hail her as a friend,
   And deem her dear delusions true,
For life's a long, dark, feverish dream,
   And he does best who dreams it well;
Whose paths with fancied pleasures beam,
   Whose griefs no sign of woe can tell.

.   .   .   .   .

'Tis madness to anticipate
The dark-browed, angry storms of fate,
Life of itself is hard to bear;
But wherefore drop the doubtful tear?
When gentle zephyrs fan the trees,
And daisies bloom and roses blow;
Why sad because the wintry breeze
Shall bring the bitter frost and snow?"

We may here take in the following somewhat high-flown account of himself, which served as preface to a second copy of his juvenile poems, with which he seems to have favored Ross: —

"CROMARTY, March 15, 1823.

"DEAR WILLIE: — 1823 would have sounded oddly seven years ago, about which time we first got acquainted; yet, by the natural course of things, it has become the present time, and the by-past years live only in the memory of the evil or good committed in them. In 1815 I was a thoughtless, careless school-boy, who proved his spirit by playing truant three weeks in the four, and his genius by writing rhymes which pleased nobody but himself. In 1823, that same school-boy finds himself a journeyman mason, not quite so free from care, but as much addicted to rhyming as ever. But is this all? Can he boast of no good effect produced by the experience of a space of time which brings him from his thirteenth to his twentieth year? Has that time passed away in a manner useless to himself and uninteresting to others? Not entirely so; for, in that time, he got acquainted with William Ross; in that time he changed the thoughtless hilarity of nature for the placid, tideless composure of sentiment; and in that time the gay hopes of fortune and of fame which engaged him even in the simplest days of his childhood have changed into a less noble, though not a less pleasing form. His happiness no longer depends upon the hope of the applause of others; not even upon the approbation of his friends; he acts and he writes for himself. His own judgment is his critic, — his own soul is the world to which he addresses himself; but do not imagine that his own tongue sounds his own praise, which I am afraid, if I went on any longer in this strain, you might justly say."

CHAPTER II.

ABOUT midsummer work turns up, and Hugh starts
again for Conon-side, whence he is ordered to
Gairloch, on the western coast of Ross-shire. A
month after his arrival he is confined to his barrack with a crushed foot, and takes his pen to write to a
friend in Cromarty. There is one letter complete, and part
of another. Readers will, perhaps, like to have these compositions as they came from the pen of Miller in his
twenty-first year : —

"GAIRLOCH, July, 1823.

"You may expect a very long letter. I was so unlucky,
two days ago, as to get my left foot crushed in a quarry by
a huge stone, and I am now completely chained to my seat.
My comrades are all out at work; I have no books, and
the hours pass away heavily enough; but I have just set
myself to try whether I cannot beguile them by conversing
with you. You are sitting before me on a large, smooth
stone, the only spare seat in the barrack (my own — for I
love to sit soft — I have cushioned with a sod), and I
have to tell you a long, gossiping story — which, after all,
is no story — of my journey thither, and of what I have

116

been seeing and doing since I came. Draw your seat a little nearer me, that I may begin.

" I came here about a month ago, after a delightful journey of two days from Conon-side, from whence I have been dispatched by my employer, with another mason lad, and a comical fellow, a carter, to procure materials for the building. Though the youngest of the party, I am intrusted with the charge of the others, in consideration of my great gravity and wonderful command of the pen ; but, as far as the carter is concerned, the charge is a truly woful one. He bullies, and swears, and steals, and tells lies, and cares for nobody. I am stronger, however, and more active than he, and must give him a beating when I have recovered my lameness, to make my commission good. My comrade, the mason, and I have been living in a state of warfare with him ever since we came here. On the morning we set out from Conon-side he left us to drive his cart and went to Dingwall, where he loitered and got drunk ; we, in turn, after waiting for him for two long hours at the village of Contin, drove away, leaving him to follow us on foot as he best might, — for at least thirty miles ; and he has not yet forgiven us the trick.

" You have never seen Contin, and so I must show it you. It is a beautiful Highland village, pleasantly situated on the sweep of a gentle declivity, which terminates behind the houses, on the banks of a river, and is covered a-top by the mansion-house and pleasure-grounds of Sir George McKenzie, of Coul, a gentleman not quite unknown in the literary world. Towards the north the gigantic Ben Wyvis lifts up his huge, burly head, like leviathan among the lesser inhabitants of the deep. There is a much smaller, but more beautiful, hill on the north-west, which rises out of the middle of a low valley, and is washed on two of its sides by the rivers Conon and Contin. It is of a pyramidical shape, and so regularly formed that one might almost deem it a work of art, and regard it not as a little hill, but as an immense pyramid. Farther away, and on the opposite side of the valley, there is a range of steep, precipitous mountains, barred with rock and speckled with birch, and varying in color, according to their distance, from brown to purple, and from purple to light-blue. In a corner of the landscape, and at the base of one of these hills, though considerably elevated above the river, we see the old time-shattered tower of Fairburn, — tall, gray, ghastly, and like a giant eremite musing in solitude. It is five stories in height, with only a single room on each floor, turreted at every angle, and irregularly perforated by narrow oblong windows and shot-holes. For the first century after its erection it is said to have been unfurnished with a door, and to have been climbed into by means of a ladder; but when the times became quieter, and the proprietors more honest, they struck out for themselves the present entrance, a door scarcely five feet in height. The earlier McKenzies of Fairburn (a family now extinct) are famed in tradition as daring freebooters, and men of immense personal strength. I have heard my uncle say that the two strongest men in the allied army of Marlborough and Eugene were Munro, of Newmore, and McKenzie, of Fairburn. The one could raise a piece of ordnance to his breast, and the other to his knee, which no third man of eighty thousand could lift from the ground. But I forget my picture. See, there are the hills. — steep, abrupt, jagged at their summit, and here and there streaked with snow. Two beautiful Highland streams wind through the plain below, which is partially covered with woods of birch and hazel, and dotted with little black cottages, while a line of large beeches and a snug little village occupy the foreground.

" A little beyond Contin, the road enters a birch wood, and forms the only object in view which reminds one of man. It is but a few years since it has been made : I even saw in a little recess in the wood the ruins of two of the unwheeled carts, (sledges rather) which were in use among the Highlanders here prior to its formation. We were met at the place by a company of men from Lochbroom, with their gray plaids, as the day was extremely warm, rolled up in a knapsack form on their shoulders, — three of the party had folded up their breeches in the same bundle. They were all travelling towards Ferintosh to the sacrament. A little farther on the appearance of the country is extremely pleasant. On our right there rose a ridge of abrupt rocky hills, from the hanging cliffs of which the hazel and mountain ash shot out their gnarled and twisted trunks almost horizontally over the road ; on our left, a small but beautiful loch filled the bottom of the glen. After driving a few miles further we were presented with quite a different scene, — a bleak, extended moor, through which a few sluggish streams rather oozed than flowed, with here and there a dwarf oak or birch, — the upper branches decayed and bleached white with the storms of winter. We saw at one place some very large and very old oak trees, — one of them standing, the others fallen. The one which stands is about six feet in diameter, and is so entirely divested of its upper branches that it resembles a green spire, and so hollow at bottom that it reminded me of a large tar-barrel. A still bulkier tree lies doddered and leafless beside it, and not many yards away there is an immense heap of sawn timber, originally of an inferior quality, rotting on the ground, — the property of some unfortunate speculatist. I thought at the time that I might have met with many things less characteristic of the past and present ages than the oak and the sawn wood. The one spoke of an age of barba-

rism, in which whole forests were either suffered to moulder
in the soil which had produced them or removed by fire as
positive incumbrances; the other, of the days of projectors
and bankruptcy.

"The sun disappeared behind one of the hills on our
right when we were yet several miles from our stage, and
the evening gave promise of a storm. The clouds thick-
ened as the night advanced, and there came on a chill,
drizzling rain. I had untied the bundle in which we had
packed up our bed-clothes, and with a thick coverlet, which
I raised on four pike handles, I was forming a tilt over the
cart, when a sudden turn in the road brought us full in view
of the solitary inn of Achnicion, and ere I had replaced the
coverlet we had driven up to it. We found in it a cheerful fire and an obliging landlord, — excellent things in themselves, and particularly so in the midst of a desert; and it
did not detract from our pleasure to hear the rain pattering
on the windows and the blast howling wildly over the roof.
From the door of the inn I saw a dreary prospect of a barren and mountainous country stretching away for several
miles, and clothed in the black-gray tints of a stormy summer evening. The hills were covered with wreaths of mist,
which, ever and anon rolling into the valleys, brought with
them a fresh deluge. And the sounds which predominated
were well-nigh as dreary as the scene. There was the sullen roar of a distant river, the louder and more rattling
dash of a large stream which rushes over a rocky declivity
beside the western gable of the inn, the howl of the wind,
the pattering of the rain, and, heard at intervals, the distant bark of a sheep-dog. The landlord of Achnicion is a
kind, active old man of about seventy, his wife an indolent
slattern of nineteen. The match was a love one, on at
least one side, — will you believe it? — on the side of the

lady, who would have broken her heart, it is said, had not the old man married her.

" We were awakened next morning by the carter storming, in an adjoining room, at both us and the landlord, who strove to defend us ; and so terrible was the noise he made that every person in the inn gathered round the door to see what was the matter. He actually *howled* out the story of his wrongs and of his sufferings. He had been galled during his journey with a pair of bad shoes and a large bundle, and knocked up about seven miles short of the stage, where he had to beg lodgings for the night, having drunk all his money before leaving Dingwall. Furious as he was, however, we succeeded in pacifying him, partly by dint of threats, partly through the mediation of a few gills of whiskey ; and then set out with him on our journey. The morning somewhat resembled the preceding night. Large volumes of mist seemed sleeping on the distant hills, and the long, low moors that lie around Achnicion appeared more dismally bleak beneath the shadow of the thick, heavy clouds which brooded over them.

" The weather cleared up as we proceeded. We had quitted the highway immediately on leaving the inn, and our path, which seemed to have been formed rather by the feet of animals than the hands of men, went winding for about seven miles through a brown, moory valley, whose tedious length was enlivened by a blue, oblong lake, — beautiful in itself, but reflecting, like the mirror of a homely female, the tame and unlovely features that hung over it. At its upper end we found the ruins of a solitary cottage, the only vestige of man in the valley. We then began to descend into a deep, narrow glen or ravine, through which there runs a little prattling streamlet, the first we saw falling towards the Atlantic. The hills rise to a great height on either hand, bare, rocky, striped into long furrows, mottled over with *débris* and huge fragments of stone, and nearly destitute of even heather. The day had become clear and pleasant, but the voice of a bird was not to be heard in this dismal place, nor sheep nor goat to be seen among the cliffs. I wish my favorite John Bunyan had passed a night in it at the season when the heath-fires of the shepherds are flaming on the heights above, — were it but to enable him to impart more tangibility to the hills which border the dark valley of the shadow of death. Through the gloomy vista of the ravine a little paradise seemed opening before us, — a paradise like that which Mirza contemplated from the heights of Bagdad, — of smooth water and green islands. 'There,' said my comrade, 'is Loch Marie; — we have to sail over it for about fourteen miles, as there is no path on which we could bring the cart with the baggage; but the horse and his master must push onward on foot.' The carter growled like an angry bear, but said nothing we could understand. Emerging from the ravine our road ran through a little moory plain, bordered with hills which seem to have at one time formed the shores of the lake. A few patches of corn and potatoes that, surrounded by the brown heath, reminded me of openings in a dark sky, together with half-a-dozen miserable-looking cottages, a little larger than ant-hills, though not quite so regularly formed, showed us that this part of the country had its inhabitants.

"We found out and bargained with the boatmen, left the carter and his horse to make the best of their way by land, and were soon sweeping over the surface of the lake. I have already fatigued you with description, but I must attempt one picture more. Imagine a smooth expanse of water stretching out before us for at least eighteen miles, and bordered on both sides by lofty mountains, — abrupt, precipitous, and pressing on one another, like men in a crowd. On the eastern shore they rise so suddenly from the water that the eye passes over them mile after mile without resting on a single spot where a boat might land; on the west their bases are fringed by a broken, irregular plain, partially covered with a fir wood. At the higher end of the lake two mountains, loftier and more inaccessible than any of the others, shoot up on either hand as if to the middle sky, and we see large patches of snow still resting on their summits, — gleaming like the banners of a fortress to tell us that they are strongholds held by the spirits of winter, — and from whence they are to descend, a few months hence, to ravage the country below. From one of these mountains there descended two small streams, which, falling from rock to rock, leaped into the lake over the lower precipice, and, whitened into foam by the steepness of their course, reminded me, as they hurried through the long heath then in blossom, of strips of ermine on a cloak of purple. Towards the north the islands seem crowded together like a flock of water-fowl. They vary in character, some barren and heathy, others fertile and tufted with wood. On the largest, which is of the better and more pleasing description, and bears, by way of distinction, the name of the lake, there is an ancient burying-ground, and, as I have heard said, a Druid or Runic monument. I would fain have landed on it, but night was fast coming on, and, besides, my time was my employer's, not my own.

"At the lower end of the lake we encountered a large boat full of people. A piper stood in the bows, and the wild notes of his bagpipe, softened by distance and multiplied by the echoes of the mountains, formed a music that suited well with the character of the scene. 'It is a wedding party,' said my comrade; 'they are going to that white house which you see at the foot of the hill. I wish you understood Gaelic; the boatmen are telling me strange stories of the loch that I know would delight you. Do you see that little green island, that lies off about half a mile to the right? The boldest Highlander in the country would hesitate to land there an hour after sunset. It is said to be haunted by wraiths and fairies, and every variety of land and water spirit. Directly in the middle of it there is a little lake, in the lake an island, and on the island a tree beneath which the Queen of the Fairies holds her court. What would you not give to see her?' Night came on before we got landed; and we lost sight of the lake while yet sailing over it. Is it not strange that with all its beauty it should be so little known? I never heard nor met with so much as its name, until it opened upon me with all its islands, except once, in a copy of verses written by a gentleman of the parish of Cromarty, — a Mr. Williamson. The voyage terminated about an hour after nightfall, our journey an hour after midnight.

"Good-by. My companions are just coming in to dinner. Shall we not have another *tête-à-tête* to-morrow?"

"GAIRLOCH, July, 1823.

"'Twas *as* well you didn't wait dinner with us yesterday! We have quarrelled with the minister's wife, who, to avenge herself, magnanimously refuses to sell us any milk, and so our only food, in the *material*, at least, is oatmeal, prepare it as we may. The carter steals fish and potatoes, and contrives to fare pretty well, but we who are honest come on badly enough. For my own part, however, I am not far from being happy, notwithstanding. Do look round, just for one minute, and see the sort of place in which a man can be happy. The sun is looking in at us through the holes in the roof, — speckling the floor with bright patches, till it resembles a piece of calico. There are two windows in the apartment; one of them filled up with turf and stone, the other occupied by an old, unglazed frame. The fire is placed against the rough, unplastered gable, into which we have stuck a pin, for suspending our pot over it; the smoke finds its way out through the holes of the roof and the window. Our meal-sack hangs by a rope from one of the rafters, at the height of a man's head from the floor, — our only means of preserving it from our thievish cohabitants, the rats. As for our furniture, 'tis altogether admirable. The two large stones are the steadiest seats I ever sat on, though, perhaps, a little ponderous when we have occasion to shift them; and the bed, which pray observe, is perfectly unique. It is formed of a pair of the minister's harrows, with the spikes turned down, and covered with an old door and a bunch of straw; and as for culinary utensils, yonder is a wooden cog, and here a pot. We are a little extravagant, to be sure, in our household expenses, for times are somewhat hard; but meal and salt, and every other item included, none of us have yet exceeded half a crown per week. You may now boast, like a true scholar, who looks only at the past, of Diogenes and his tub, and the comforts of philosophy.

"The Gairloch, as you will find by consulting your map, is an arm of the sea on the western coast of Ross-shire. Its length is perhaps somewhat more than eight miles, its breadth varies from three to five. Where it opens towards the sea the water is deep, and clear of sunken rocks; nearer its bottom there are several small islands. The shores, with the exception of two or three little sandy banks, are steep and rocky; the surrounding country is Highland in the extreme. The manse, beside which I reside, and at which I am employed, is situated on the northern shore, and about two hundred yards from the sea. There rises behind it a flat, moory hill, speckled with large, gray stones, and patches of corn, somewhat larger than beds of onions, only not quite so regularly laid out. Farther away there is a little scattered village, composed of such hovels as one commonly finds in the remote Highlands, and containing from eighty to a hundred inhabitants, who are *crofters* and fishermen. It is a fact that the Highlander of the present day, and the Highlander of four hundred years ago, live in huts of exactly the same construction; and their mode of agriculture here has been quite as stationary.

"I must enable you to form an estimate of it. The arable land is equally divided among all the families of the village; a long, brown moor which lies behind it affords pasture to their cattle, of which every one has an equal number, namely, two. The rents they pay the proprietor, and which they derive from the herring fishery, are of course also equal. There is neither horse nor plough in the village, — a long, crook-handled kind of spade, termed a *cass chrom*, and the hoe, supplying the place of the latter, the Highlander himself, and more particularly his wife, that of the former; for here (shall I venture the expression?), as in all semi-barbarous countries, the woman seems to be regarded rather as the drudge than the companion of the man. It is the part of the husband to turn up the land and sow it; the wife conveys the manure to it in a square creel with a slip bottom, tends the corn, reaps it, hoes the potatoes, digs them up, and carries the whole home on her back. When bearing the creel she is also engaged in spinning with the distaff and spindle. I wish you but saw with what patience these poor females continue working thus, doubly employed, for the greater part of a long summer's day. I frequently let the mallet rest on the stone before me, as some one of them passes by, bent nearly double with the load she is carrying, yet busily engaged in stretching out and turning the yarn with her right hand, and winding it up with her left. Can you imagine a more primitive system of agriculture, or wonder that I should be half inclined to imagine that, instead of having taken a journey of a few score miles to witness it, I had retraced for that purpose the flight of time for the last six centuries?

"I am now going to turn gossip, and to give you some stories of myself. I am a great egotist; but how can I help it? I have no second-hand narratives to relate, and of what I myself see I must tell you what I myself think. With all the different members of the minister's family I have become acquainted in some degree or other. The minister himself occasionally honors me with a nod; his wife, who has no particular quarrel with *me*, for 'twas not I who remarked that her milk 'smelt of the last week,' has once or twice had some little gossip with me. I am busily courting her three maids, who, though they have not a syllable of English amongst them, are very kindly teaching me Gaelic; and from a young lady, the governess of her children, I have borrowed a few books. One of these, though published in Inverness about twelve years ago, I have not had the chance of seeing before. It is a small volume of poems by a Miss Campbell, then a young lady of seventeen. At even that early age she was a poetess, and rich in those sentiments and feelings which we deem so fascinating in the amiable and accomplished woman. Even though occasionally the *girl* peeps out in most of her pieces, I like them none the worse; her puerilities, joined to no equivocal indications of a fine genius, leading one to entertain hopes of her future eminence; and certainly, if her riper years have but fulfilled the promise which her earlier ones have given, she must be now a very superior person indeed. I feel much interested in her, and wish much to know what has become of her." . . .

Thus abruptly ends the narrative. Miller's jesting allusion to the three maids whom he was "courting," suggests the remark that his insensibility to female attractions in his youth contrasts strongly not only with the impassioned admiration of Burns for every beautiful face he ever saw, but with the susceptibility to woman's charms common to vivid and poetical natures. "Miss A——," one of his acquaintances at Gairloch, asked him to write a poem upon love. He set about it with as much composure of mind as if she had asked him to carve an inscription on a gravestone. Here are the four opening stanzas: —

> "Though meanly favored by the Muse,
>   Though scant of wit and time,
> On theme by Celtic maid supplied,
>   I sit me down to rhyme.
>
> "But why should love demand my song;
>   It breathed from Hammond's lyre,
> On Cowley's page its meteors flashed,
>   On Moore's its wilder fire;
>
> "While I, who never proved its bliss,
>   Ne'er proved its restless smart;
> Who have, though much the fair I prize,
>   A free, unbleeding heart,
>
> "Can paint, alas! with little skill,
>   The joy which love inspires,
> Or tell of pangs I never proved,
>   Of hopes or fond desires."

On reading this, one begins to have misgivings as to the intensity of Miller's poetic fire.

> "All thoughts, all passions, all delights,
>   Whatever stirs this mortal frame,
> All are but ministers of Love,
>   And feed his sacred flame."

thus Coleridge struck the key-note when his theme was love. " The greatest bliss that the tongue o' man can name," sang Hogg, with lilting, lark-like melody, giving *his* experience on the subject. " I sit me down to rhyme," observes Miller, and, " though much the fair I prize, I am not disposed to exaggerate their good qualities." Miller does not, like Teufelsdröckh, find that his " feeling towards the queens of this earth " is " altogether unspeakable." Perhaps, however, his heart, though cold to the many, may prove responsive to one, and for him also there may bloom a paradise, " cheered by some fairest Eve." We shall see.

Rhyming or reasoning, courting or cogitating, Hugh Miller, during this season at Gairloch, is worth looking at. Not yet twenty-one, living in a hovel from which water, a foot deep, has been drained off to render it habitable, his food oatmeal without milk, his companions stone-masons, his employment manual labor, he bates no jot of hope or heart, but takes the whole with a frank effulgence of mirth, a rugged humor of character, which bears him victoriously through. It never strikes him that there is hardship in his own lot, but he has ready sympathy for the distresses of others. Might not some Scotch artist try to realize for us that picture, drawn by Miller of himself with so little thought of picturesque effect, when the pensive lad drops his mallet and looks at the Highland woman, bent nearly double with her burden, yet, as she wearily trudges past, working with both hands? One can see the kind, grave, deep-thoughted face. the steadfast blue eyes moistening with compassion, the lip touched, perhaps, with a faint, mournful smile of stoical, not cynical, acceptance of the sternness of fate.

Miller's poetical faculty, though not powerfully stirred by the nymphs of Gairloch, and though more felicitous, now and subsequently, in prose than in verse, did not at this time slumber. That picture of the old, gray tower of Fairburn, " like a giant cremite musing in solitude," is genuinely imaginative. His relations with the other inmates of the bothy are full of a strong, hearty, buoyant humor, which floods the rugged paths of life with sport. The doings of the carter, who " bullies, and swears, and steals, and tells lies, and cares for nobody," are manifestly productive of diversion more than distress. Miller, in fact, rather likes the man, though he feels that he will be improved by a beating. The carter is clearly one of those favorites of nature who obey her promptings and receive her rewards. He " steals fish and potatoes," and makes himself comfortable, while his virtuous brethren do penance on oatmeal. Such a man appeals irresistibly to that instinct of fallen humanity which makes us admire successful personages like Drawcansir and Reynard the Fox.

One of Miller's Gairloch fellow-workmen, who exerted a more important influence upon him, is described with some detail in the " Schools and Schoolmasters," but I have not found mention of him elsewhere. I refer to John Fraser, one of three brothers, who, if Mr. Darwin's theory is sound, were a variation of the human species adapted to found a race of superlative masons and stone-cutters, and to outlive and extirpate, by natural selection, all other masons and stone-cutters. Miller states, on the authority of " Mr. Kenneth Matheson, a gentleman well-known as a master-builder in the west of Scotland," that David Fraser, the most remarkable of the brothers, could do three times as much as an ordinary workman. John, even when advanced in life, could build against "two stout young fellows" and " keep a little ahead of them both." " I recognize old John," says Hugh Miller, " as one of not the least useful nor able of my many teachers ; " and the justice of the remark is attested by the admirably philosophic account which he gives of the lesson old John taught him. The secret of Fraser's power was that he saw "the finished piece of work," as it lay within the stone, and cut down upon the true figure at once, without repeating, like an ordinary workman, his lines and draughts. And is not this faculty of seeing with the mind's eye what the hand has to execute, — of conceiving the work as a whole, so that there shall be neither hurry nor delay in carrying it out, — essentially the faculty by which a Hannibal or a Napoleon wins battles, a Dante or a Shakespeare writes poems, a Titian or a Turner paints masterpieces?

Writing to Baird six years after this time, Miller relates the following dream, which belongs to the Gairloch season, and is omitted from "Schools and Schoolmasters." It is remarkable as containing a very definite prediction which proved incorrect. "About the middle of September, this year, I had a singular dream, the particulars of which retain even to this day as firm a hold of my memory as if they had been those of a real incident. I dreamed that my friend William Ross had died, and that I was watching the corpse in a large, darkened apartment. I felt sad and unhappy. Suddenly there appeared near the couch where the body lay an upright wreath of thin vapor, which gradually assumed the figure of my deceased friend. The face of the spectre was turned towards the body, and the robes of white in which it was dressed appeared, compared with the winding-sheet beside it, as a piece of cambric exposed to the rays of the sun would to another piece hung up in the shade. The figure turned round and I spoke to it ; but though, from the splendor of the dress it wore, and the placid expression of the face, which was of feminine beauty, I inferred it to be a spirit of heaven, by one of those inconsistencies common in dreams, my question to it regarded the state of the damned. ' I know nothing,' it said, ' of the damned.' 'Then describe to me,' I rejoined, 'the happiness of the blest.' The reply was strong and pointed: Live a good life, and in seven days, seven weeks, and seven years you shall know.' I must add that I have since thought much oftener of the prediction than of the advice." No particular incident of any kind appears to have taken place in the history of Miller at the time specified.

The work at the manse completed, Miller removed, with two of his brother workmen, to a village in the neighborhood, to build a house for an innkeeper. Their lodging here was as bad as at the place they left. One half of a large cellar used for storing salt, of which half had been pulled down to furnish materials for the proposed building, was their barrack. They hung mats across the open end, through which the wind blew cold at night, awakening them sometimes by dashing the rain in their faces. Their fare was improved by a supply of excellent milk, and the innkeeper made a point of inviting them to dine with him on Sunday. "He was a loquacious little man, full of himself, and desirous of being reckoned a wit," but without capacity to play the part. Miller, less talkative than his fellow-workmen, was supposed by mine host to be available as a butt, and was made the object of sundry small witticisms. He took this in good part for a while, but one day he retorted upon his entertainer and reduced him to silence. The consequence was, that he was excluded from the invitation next Sunday, and left to regale himself on oatmeal and milk in the solitude of the barrack. He took his revenge in a way gratifying at once to his pride and his kindliness. One of the favored workmen had bargained with the innkeeper to give the latter a hammer and trowel, but, after receiving the money for the articles, had played him false. "I was informed of the circumstance," says Miller to Baird, "when on the eve of setting out for the low country; and taking my hammer and trowel from my bundle. I presented them to the innkeeper's wife, — alleging, when she urged me to set a price on them, that they were a very inadequate return for her husband's kindness to me during the two first weeks of our acquaintance." It was a mode of revenge to which neither Uncle James nor Uncle Sandy could have taken exception.

Before quitting the Gairloch scene we may take this final picture of one of its landscapes: "There is a steep, high hill, rather more than a mile from the manse of Gairloch, to the summit of which I frequently extended my walks. The view which the eye commands from thence is of a character wilder and more sublime than can be either rightly imagined or described. Towards the east and south there spreads a wide savage prospect of rugged mountains, towering the one over the other from the foreground to the horizon, and varying in color, in proportion to the distance, from the darkest russet to the faintest purple. They are divided by deep, gloomy ravines that seem the clefts and fissures of a shattered and ruined planet; and their summits are either indented into rough naked crags, or whitened over with unwasting snows, — forming fit thrones upon which the spirits of winter might repose, each in a separate insulated territory, and from whence they might defy the milder seasons as they passed below. To the north and west the scene is of a different description; it presents a rocky indented shore, and a wide sea speckled over with islands. On both sides, however, though the features are dissimilar, the expression is the same. Scarcely more of the works of man appear visible in the whole wide circumference than appeared to the gaze of Noah, when he first stood on the summit of Mount Ararat, and contemplated the wreck of the deluge.

"It was on a beautiful evening in the month of June

that I first climbed the steep side of this hill and rested on its summit. I was much impressed by the wide extent and sublime grandeur of the scene. Part of the eastern skirt of the Atlantic was spread out beneath me, mottled with the Hebrides. In one glance I had a view of Longa, Skye, Lewis, Harris, Rona, Raza, and several other islands with whose names I was unacquainted. The sky and sea were both colored with the same warm hue of sunset, and appeared as if blended together; while the islands which lay on the verge of the horizon seemed dense purple clouds, which, though motionless in the calm, the first sea-breeze might sweep away. Towards the south my eye was caught by two gigantic mountains, which, as if emulous of each other, towered above the rest, like the contending chiefs of a divided people; while towards the east I beheld a scene of terrible ruin and sublime disorder, — mountain piled upon mountain, and ravine intersecting ravine. All my faculties of reason and imagination seemed at first as if frustrated and held down by some superior power; the magnitude of the scene oppressed me; I felt as if in the presence of the Spirit of the Universe; and the apology of the Jewish spies recurred to me, ' We were as grasshoppers before them.' "

This was written when Miller was twenty-seven. It is remarkable for the absence of all geological allusion, and for the strong human element in the imagery. When he had lived for another quarter of a century he again described the scene, and the pencil is now in the firm hand of a master. But so completely has the geological interest taken possession of him that he throws it back into a period prior to that at which it exerted any powerful influence upon his mind, and makes the imaginative boy of twenty look through the eyes of the scientific man of fifty. Here is the scene as he rendered it for the last time : —

"How exquisitely the sun sets in a clear, calm, summer evening over the blue Hebrides! Within less than a mile of our barrack there rose a tall hill, whose bold summit commanded all the Western Isles, from Sleat in Skye, to the Butt of the Lewis. To the south lay the trap islands; to the north and west the gneiss ones. They formed, however, seen from this hill, one great group, which, just as the sun had sunk, and sea and sky were so equally bathed in gold as to exhibit on the horizon no dividing line, seemed in their transparent purple, — darker or lighter according to the distance, — a group of lovely clouds, that, though moveless in the calm, the first light breeze might sweep away. Even the flat promontories of sandstone, which, like outstretched arms, enclosed the outer reaches of the foreground, — promontories edged with low red cliffs, and covered with brown heath, — used to borrow at these times, from the soft yellow beam, a beauty not their own. Amid the inequalities of the gneiss region within, — a region more broken and precipitous, but of humbler altitude, than the great gneiss tract of the midland Highlands, — the chequered light and shade lay, as the sun declined, in strongly contrasted patches, that betrayed the abrupt inequalities of the ground, and bore, when all around was warm-tinted and bright, a hue of cold neutral gray; while immediately over and beyond this rough, sombre base, there rose two noble pyramids of red sandstone, about two thousand feet in height, that used to flare to the setting-sun in bright crimson, and whose nearly horizontal strata, deeply scored along the lines, like courses of ashlar in an ancient wall, added to the mural effect communicated by their bare fronts and steep, rectilinear outlines. These tall pyramids form the terminal members, towards the south, of an extraordinary group of sandstone hills, of denudation unique in the British Islands, which extends from the northern boundary of Assynt to near Applecross. But though I formed at this time my first acquaintance with the group, it was not until many years after that I had an opportunity of determining the relations of their component beds to each other, and to the fundamental rocks of the country."

The winter of 1823 was spent, as usual, in Cromarty. William Ross was in Edinburgh, and Miller had no friend of his own age with whom he cared much to associate. He seems to have been in a trivial mood, and to have made business of amusement. "There was," he says, "a little mischievous boy of about ten years of age whom I chose as a companion for lack of a better. He was spirited and sensible for his years, and deemed me a very superior kind of playfellow. I taught him how to climb and leap and wrestle, how to build bridges and rig ships, and how to make baskets and rush caps. I told him stories, and lent him books, and showed him how to act plays, and lighted fires with him in the caves of the hill of Cromarty, and, in short, went on in such a manner that my acquaintance began to shake their own heads and to question the soundness of mine. My Uncle James, who used sturdily to assert, in the face of all opposing evidence, that my powers of mind averaged rather above than below the common standard, seriously told me about this time that if I would not act more in the manner of other people, he would defend me no longer." ʹ

CHAPTER III.

MILLER is now to enter upon a scene in all respects new, — new in temptation, new in instruction, new in companionship. He exchanges the rustic murmur of Cromarty and the solitudes of Gairloch for the sights and agitations of the metropolis of Scotland. He has acquired an accurate knowledge of the character and circumstances of the Scottish Highlander; he is to bring his faculty of observation to bear upon the inhabitants of the Lowlands. In both instances his observation is as yet almost entirely confined to the working-class.

In the autumn of 1823 he comes of age, and is therefore competent to exercise rights of proprietorship over a wretched tenement on the Coal-hill of Leith, which has been a constant source of loss and annoyance to his mother from the time of his father's death. His own wish, and that of his friends, now is, that he may be able to dispose of it, and, with a view to investigating the affair on the spot, he sails from Cromarty for Leith in the spring of 1824. I have before me a manuscript containing "Descriptive Letters," written by him to his uncles in the course of the summer. It enables us to trace his course from the moment of his stepping aboard ship until the series abruptly terminates with part of a letter written in the last days of the year. As might have been surmised from the affection and gentleness of his disposition, he thinks more at first of the home he is leaving than of the new world into which he is to enter.

"LEITH, 4th June, 1824.

"The ship in which I was a passenger left Cromarty upon Sunday forenoon; and, as the day was warm and pleasant, I remained upon deck till evening, with my eyes steadfastly fixed upon the land I had so lately left. Every moment it was lessening and growing more indistinct; but fancy strengthened my powers of vision, and in a half-sad, half-sportive mood, I was marking out every spot which in the by-past had been the scene of my juvenile sports or pleasures. There, thought I, looking toward the hill of Cromarty, will some of my friends be stationed with their eyes fixed upon the departing vessel, and though she appear but a small, an almost imperceptible speck, yet will they deem her an object of greater interest than any of the scenes the eye commands from that eminence. The thought was tender and pleasing. There was something in it that told me of the affection of the friends I was leaving, and of the coldness of those with whom I was soon to mingle. But perhaps 'twill be for the better; that coldness may rouse the sleeping energies of my character, and when I find myself as if alone in the world, instead of resting upon the exertions of others, I shall learn to depend on my own. Such were the thoughts with which I beguiled the time, —

Till the gray mists of eve arose, and wrapt
My native hills in dark and formless gloom.

" Scarcely had the sun risen when, curious to know in what part of the Moray Frith we now were, I rose and went upon deck. . . The sun hung on the verge of the horizon, and illuminated that part of the water which seemed to lie beneath with a splendor not less dazzling than its own. A solitary porpoise was tumbling around our vessel in unwieldy sport. A " killing " of sea-gulls at a little distance were screaming over their morning banquet; while, at intervals, an overgrown seal raised his round black head above the waves and gazed upon us with a long and very curious stare. Upon the north I perceived the land stretching from Tarbat-ness to John-o'-Groats, while upon the south and east, at about three miles' distance, rose the bold, rocky, and romantic shores of Moray and Banff. Tower and town, hill and promontory, in their turns engaged my attention, and after having. in the course of the day, passed Portsoy, Banff, Macduff, and Fraserburgh, I again sought my bed, and spent this night. as I had done the preceding, in calm and refreshing sleep.

" Two days of our voyage had passed pleasantly, but upon the morning of the third I was surprised and somewhat disheartened when, upon getting on deck, I perceived nothing but a dark rolling sea. and a dense cloud of mist closing upon the vessel upon every side. . . Often as I paced the narrow space the deck afforded me did I behold in fancy the scenes I was soon to visit, and as often was that fancy carried back to picture the regrets and joys of home. But that you may better know what my thoughts were, I insert the copy of a short, I should rather say unfinished, poem I composed that morning. It will show you what ideas I had formed of Edinburgh, and how little the hope of its pleasures appeared when compared with the well-proved joys of the home I had left : —

"Thou mayst boast, O Edina, thou home of delight,
  For thy gallants are gay, and thy ladies are bright,
  August is thy palace, thy castle, sublime,
  Has braved the rude dints of fire, battle, and time.

"Thou mayst boast, O Edina, thou faméd abode
  Of the wise and the learned, of the great and the good,
  Thou mayst boast of thy worthies, mayst boast of thy towers,
  Thy halls and thy temples, thy grots and thy bowers.

"Yet lovelier by far and more dear to this heart
  Than all your gay trophies of labor and art,
  Is the home of my fathers, the much-lovéd land,
  Of the dauntless of heart and the mighty of hand.

"'Tis there the gray bones of my fathers are laid,
  'Twas there that my life's sunny friendships were made,
  And till death chills my bosom and closes my e'e,
  These friends and that land shall be dear unto me."

"The weather was still extremely thick, and, though my eyes were earnestly fixed in that direction, I could see but little of Edinburgh. Once indeed I saw the chimneys of the new town appearing through the mist, like the shocks of a field newly reaped, and several times the rugged summit of Arthur's Seat came full in sight, as if passing through the dark cloud which obscured its base. These were but transient glimpses, but of the town of Leith I had a full and distinct view. A young lad, one of the passengers, was pointing out to me the harbor, docks, and public buildings, and between the amusement his remarks afforded me and the pleasure I took in looking at the vessels we passed and repassed in the roadstead, an hour or two flew away very agreeably.

"By a signal from the shore we were made to understand that the water in the channel had risen to a requisite height. The vessel's head was immediately turned that way, and in a few minutes I found myself in the town of Leith, my head dizzied with the confused cries of watermen and carters, and my thoughts scattered by a multiplicity of objects, any of which I might have thought curious, but all of which only tended to confuse."

This, it must be admitted, is a rather commonplace epistle, and the verses are so poor that an apology may seem necessary for presenting them to the reader. But here we have at least the lad Miller in his habit as he lived, with no gleam from the after-time to disturb the artless unconsciousness of modest, simple-hearted youth. Both in his letter to Baird and in the "Schools and Schoolmasters" there are elaborate pictures of his first sight of Edinburgh ; but what first impressed him in the scene — the emergence of the chimneys of the new town and the summit of Arthur's Seat, from the mist — always reappears. It is well, also, to remember that the bareness in the record of his impressions which meets us in these contemporary letters on Edinburgh, may arise partly from his inexperience in composition, and partly from the restraints imposed upon epistolary correspondence in days long antecedent to the introduction of the penny post. We may believe that it was not merely in the autobiographic retrospect that he "felt as if he were approaching a great magical city — like some of those in the 'Arabian Nights' — that was even more intensely poetical than nature itself;" and that reminiscences of Ramsay and Ferguson, Smollett's "Humphrey Clinker" and Scott's "Marmion," heightened the interest with which he looked through the canopy of mist upon the spires and roofs of Edinburgh.

The great city — to one who had never seen a larger town than Inverness it was very great — threw him at first out of all his habitudes. He frankly confesses, "though conscious that by so doing he will lay himself open to mer-

ited censure," that on the first four Sundays after his arrival
he absented himself from church and "strolled through the
streets of Leith and Edinburgh;" that the fifth was occupied in scaling Arthur's Seat and viewing the city and adjacent country from its summit; and that "a few more"
were passed in the company of some townsmen of his own,
who, "Cameronian-like, preferred the open air to a church."
The impressions formed in this leisurely survey of Edinburgh are described at some length to his uncles, and they
set before us the Hugh Miller of twenty-one, with a distinctness so vivid and a simplicity so naïve, that we feel
still more strongly than before how completely the profound
reflective vein of the autobiography prevents us from realizing what the writer was at the various stages of his career.

The fervor of his nationality is one of the first things
which attracts our notice. "Holyrood House," he says, "I
viewed with the same emotion which a pilgrim feels when
prostrating himself before the shrine of a favorite saint.
With this building, long before I saw it, I had connected
associations of a high and venerable character, but I was
not prepared for the sudden, the spontaneous burst of enthusiasm, which rose from my very soul when I stood fronting the gateway and saw the arms of Scotland, as if it was
still an independent kingdom, frowning in the gray stone,
and directly above them the crown of her ancient kings.
It was no time to sum up the advantages which we derive
from the union, — the very thought of it was revolting, —
and I looked upon the sentinel who paced before the door
as one who had no business there. I have often heard of
classic and of holy ground; to me the space upon which
this pile stands is both. But why need I say so? To you,
or to any other Scotsman acquainted with the history of his
country, and proud (as most of us are) of the fame of her
ancient grandeur, it must appear the same. Under the

piazza which runs round the inner court I walked for a considerable time, and was not a little struck with the death-like stillness, — a stillness interrupted by nothing except the measured footfall of the sentry."

He is much disappointed with the High Street, having been led by something he had read in the works of Smollett to fancy that it was "one of the finest in Europe." He looks with great contempt upon the equestrian statue of Charles II. in Parliament House Square. "This lascivious and dissipated monarch," he says, "is attired in the garb of an ancient Roman; and, by his appearance, a person un-acquainted with the history of his reign might suppose him to have been a sapient and warlike prince, dauntless in the field and wise in the council. . . . . . When I first saw the statue, I could not help quoting a few lines from Thomson's ' Liberty,' which will appear to you as it did to me, the character of Charles the Second faithfully drawn, maugre the inscription and the Roman dress : —

> " ' By dangerous softness long he mined his way.
> By subtle arts, dissimulation deep,
> By sharing what corruption showered profuse,
> By breathing wide the gay lascivious plague,
> And pleasing manners suited to deceive,
>   A pensioned king,
> Against his country bribed by Gallic gold.' "

The natural and unaffected manner in which Miller alludes to Smollett and Thomson is not without significance. How completely this young mason is already a literary character !

After describing his impressions on the effigy of Charles II., he proceeds in a very different spirit to refer to another and less pretentious effigy then visible in Edinburgh. "At the lower end of High Street" — these are his words — " is a house, from a window of which, in the earlier days of the Reformation, John Knox frequently used to preach. To preserve the memory of this, in a small niche, a bust of the illustrious Reformer appears, as if still holding forth to the people. At his right hand, in low relief, a circle representing the sun, upon which the name of God is inscribed in Greek, Latin, and English, appears as if emerging from a thick cloud. The sculpture of the whole was rude when at its best, and the wasting hand of Time has rendered it still more uncouth; nevertheless, some person, doubtless of more zeal than judgment, has got the bust painted, and surrounded it with a tawdry pulpit. I need hardly tell you that these ill-judged alterations have given it a caricatured appearance; and yet I felt more impressed when looking at it from the very spot upon which some of the original's auditors stood, than I did when standing before the horse and man of Parliament Square: for, with a feeling which perhaps the venerable Reformer would have censured, as savoring too much of the idolatry he abolished. I uncovered my head and bowed very low to his effigy."

His estimate of Edinburgh College is high, and the terms in which it is couched prove that he had already acquired some technical knowledge of architecture. "The College in my opinion is the finest building in Edinburgh, either taken in its parts or as a whole. It forms a square, the exterior of which displays all the chaste simplicity of the Doric order, and the interior the lighter graces of the Ionic and Corinthian."

He visits the burying-grounds of the city: here is an interesting note. "I have seen the grave of poor Ferguson, and the plain stone placed at its head by his brother in misfortune and genius, Robert Burns. I felt much affected when standing above the sod which covers the mortal remains of the young poet, and could have dropped a tear to his memory and to the memory of his still greater successor, but I was not Shandean enough to command one. You know I never could weep except when insulted and stung to the heart by those whose unkindness I could not or would not resent, and then the tears I dropped were those of grief, rage, hatred, in short, the offspring of any passion except tenderness." This is a touch of self-portraiture worth whole chapters of retrospective delineation.

In another of these letters, dated 10th October, 1824, and addressed to his Uncle James, we meet with the following careful sketch of Dr. McCrie. " I had long wished to hear a discourse from Dr. McCrie, the elegant historian of Knox and Melville, but it was some time before I found out his meeting-house. At length I discovered it, and, being obligingly shown to a seat by one of his elders, I sat with some little portion of impatience till the doctor made his appearance. The laudable end to which he has dedicated his great talents in rescuing from unmerited contumely the memory of our venerable Reformer had long prepossessed me in his favor, and this prepossession his appearance was well calculated to confirm. In age and figure I know not where to point out any one who more resembles him than yourself. His countenance is pale and expressive, and his forehead deeply marked with the lines of thought; the spareness of his habit reminded me of long study and deep research, and his demeanor, at once humble and dignified, finished the portrait. You may doubt — when I tell you that the discourse he that day delivered was one of the best I ever heard — that my partiality blinded me to its defects. This was not the case; for, though partial to the doctor. it was his superior talents that made me so, and had his discourse been of that dull, commonplace kind which I have often heard in a church that shall be nameless, my disappointment would have been great in proportion to my expectation. I need not tell you that, as an historian, Dr. McCrie ranks very high. At a time when every witling thought himself licensed to ridicule the firmness or denounce the boldness of the Reformers of our religion, the doctor stood forth in their defence, and, endowed with powers equal to the task, dispersed the dark cloud of obloquy in which partial or designing men had enveloped their names. If we consider him as a preacher, he will appear in a light as favorable. His manner is calm yet impressive, and his sentiments (always beautiful, and ofttimes highly original) are conveyed in language strong and nervous, yet at the same time plain and simple. In short, Dean Swift's definition of a good style, 'proper words in their proper places,' can be very well exemplified in his. I have now heard him several times. One Sunday his voice, which is not naturally strong, was nearly drowned by loud and continued coughing, which arose from every corner of the church. For some time he went on without any seeming embarrassment, but just when in the middle of an important argument made a full stop. In a moment every eye was fixed upon the doctor, and such was the silence caused by this attention that for the space of a minute you might have heard a pin fall. 'I see, my brethren, you can all be quiet enough when I am quiet,' was his mild and somewhat humorous reproof, and such was its effect that, for the remainder of the day, he received very little interruption. There was something in this little incident that gave me much pleasure. I thought it told more truly of the discernment and good temper of the doctor than even his discourse did, beautiful and instructive as that was."

Very little is added to this in the "Schools and Schoolmasters." There is indeed a quiet accuracy in the portrait, which shows that Miller was beginning to find his hand as a master of English prose. The pale complexion and expressive features, the deep thought-written lines of the forehead, the spare habit, the humble yet dignified demeanor, which appear in the sketch of the mason lad from Cromarty, bring Dr. McCrie visibly before us. The doctor was indeed a notable figure in the Edinburgh of that time. He exercised a profound influence upon the intellectual society of Scotland, and left behind him at least one work, the biography of Knox, which has an imperishable place in the literature of Europe. Connected ecclesiastically with a very small religious denomination, he rose by a natural and effortless ascent, through the force of his solitary genius, until he found his level among the most eminent men of his time. Miller, long afterwards, finely compared him, in relation to the co-religionists which clustered round him, to a village church rearing its tower amid a group of cottages.

But it was not only to burying-grounds and churches that Miller betook himself during his residence in the neighborhood of Edinburgh. In our last extracts he has appeared somewhat in the light of a philosopher and critic, but we are reminded, as we accompany him to the panorama, that he has not yet thrown off the boy. It was rather hard in the autobiographer of fifty to omit all notice of the event chronicled in the following animated sentences : —

"Upon the earthen mound where the good people of Edinburgh see shows and sights of all descriptions, from the smoking baboon to the giant of seven feet and a half, stands a circular wooden building, which in size and appearance reminds the reader of Gulliver's travels of the washing tubs of Brobdignag. In this building all the panoramic scenery which is painted in or brought to Edinburgh is exhibited. The battle of Trafalgar, together with a series of scenes representing the Emperor of France, from the skirmish of Genappe till his death in the solitary island of St. Helena, was, when I came here, the subject of exhibition. Of this species of entertainment I had formed no idea, and willing to fill up the blank which a name unaccompanied with an idea leaves in the mind, and perhaps not a little urged by a natural fondness for sights of the amusing description, I left my work one evening about an hour sooner than usual, called upon my friend, Will Ross, as I passed his way, and accompanied by him made directly for the panorama. We were ushered into a darkened gallery, the sides and ceiling of which were covered with green cloth. Our eyes were immediately turned towards an opening about thirty feet in width, through which, by a striking illusion, we perceived the ocean stretching out for many leagues before us, and upon it the British fleet, commanded by Nelson and Collingwood, bearing down, a double line, upon the enemy, who at a little distance, in the form of a crescent, seemed to await their coming. Not even in a camera obscura have I seen anything so natural. The sun seemed beaming upon the water; the British pendant was unfolding to the wind; the vessels appeared as if gently heaving to the swell, while upon their decks all was bustle and activity. The marines were loading their muskets; the seamen were employed about the great guns; some of the officers were busied in giving orders, and others with great anxiety were looking through their glasses as if to catch every movement of the enemy. In truth, the deception was so complete that, forgetting the ground upon which I stood, I fancied myself just on the eve of a great battle, and felt my mind impressed with that indescribable emotion which, in the reality of such a circumstance, the young soldier always feels. This scene was soon changed, and in its place another represented which displayed all the terrible confusion of the engagement. The first only showed us the cloud that concealed the storm; here it was represented as if bursting in its full fury. It was the deck of the 'Victory,' as it appeared at the moment Nelson received his death wound. You will have some idea of the size of the picture when I tell you that there were above two hundred figures, all as large as life, at once under my eye. In the middle of these was Nelson; the sword was falling from his hand; his features were distorted as if by sudden and acute pain; and the pale, cadaverous hue of his countenance betokened speedy dissolution. The attention of the figures nearest him seemed to be entirely engrossed by his fall; an anxious expression of the countenance or a sudden turn of the head showed that those at a greater distance had some faint perception of what had happened, while others in the outskirts of the picture were busied in working the guns, or in supplying those who wrought them with ammunition. A few paces from Nelson, a young officer was eagerly pointing out to a marine the main-top of one of the vessels with which the 'Victory' was engaged, from which the fatal bullet was supposed to have come, and he, with great deliberation, was levelling his musket in that direction. The third scene was of a terrific description. It represented the battle as if drawing near its close. In the foreground was the 'Redoubtable,' a French ship of the line, on fire. The flames were bursting out furiously from window and gun-port, tinging the waves below with a red and fiery glare. Some of the crew were seen throwing themselves overboard; while others, with despair depicted on their countenances, were clinging to the vessel's sides as if uncertain which death to choose. The fourth and last scene was of a calm, but, though it represented the hour of victory, of a gloomy character. In the distance a few of the fugitive vessels were seen giving their broadside and crowding on every sail to expedite their flight. In the foreground all was desolation. Dismasted and shattered vessels, huge fragments of rigging to which a few shivering wretches still clung, and a sun again shining through a clearing atmosphere on the madness and the misery of man, made this scene, like the last of a tragedy, by far the saddest."

From the panorama he turns to the theatre. Much of his reading, he says, had been of a description approved by Uncle James, but he had read more plays and novels than would have been sanctioned by that stern moralist. He cannot see that they have done him much harm, and, sure enough, "no small portion of the pleasure he had experienced in this world had been derived from them." He will not, however, undertake to defend this species of reading; he means only to introduce the remark that, being largely acquainted with plays and novels, and possessing a fancy naturally strong, he had formed too high an idea of theatrical representation, and, when he saw the theatre, was disappointed. "When reading," he says, "the plays of Shakespeare or of Otway, of Rowe or of Addison, I saw with the mind's eye their heroes not as actors, but as men; and the scenes they described brought to my view not the painted scenes of the stage, but the real face of nature, in the same manner that a beautiful portrait gives us the idea of a real person, not of a mask. But when I saw men who neither in appearance nor reality came up to the idea I had formed of the characters they represented, I rated them in the bitterness of my soul as mere pretenders who could not act their part upon the stage so well as common men do the parts assigned them in the great drama of life."

He appears to have grown ashamed in a few years of the boyish delight with which he gazed upon the panorama. In the letter to Baird, he passes over his visit with the single remark, " I was more pleased with the panorama

than with the theatre." His account of his theatrical experiences contains indications of the extent of his dramatic
reading. " I several times attended the theatre, but I did
not derive from theatrical representation half the pleasure
I had anticipated. I had read a great many plays of the
different English authors from the days of Shakespeare
down to those of Cumberland and Sheridan. I had perused,
too, translations of Terence and Molière. My acquaintance with this department of literature was perhaps prema-
ture ; for I perused most of these works at too early an age
to appreciate their merits as compositions, or to draw comparisons between their *dramatis personæ* and the people of
the world. The impression, however, which the more striking scenes and characters had left on my imagination was
ineffaceably vivid. Most of the scenes were identified in
my mind with the beautiful scenes of the hill of Cromarty.
The cliff of Dover, even in Shakespeare, could not surpass
in grandeur of feature the rock of the *Apple-yardie*, a
rugged, hoary, perpendicular precipice, nearly three hundred feet in height, — crested by a dark wood, — skirted by
a foaming sea, — partially mantled with ivy, — caverned
at its base, and continually lifting up its voice in hollow
echoes as if holding converse with the waves that toil beneath it, or the innumerable flocks of sea-birds that scream
around it. The Jacques of my imagination moralized in a
solitary opening in the thicket above, from which a long
vista that pentrates into the recesses of the wood, and
becomes narrower and darker in the distance, is seen to
terminate in a small circular opening which, when the
evening sun rests on the hill behind, may remind one of
the beacon of a lighthouse. I found it the easiest thing
imaginable to convert the cavern in which I had been once
imprisoned into the cave of Belarius ; and an old vault in a
ruinous chapel dedicated to St. Regulus, and nearly buried

among the woods of the hill, furnished me with a proper tomb for the Capulets. The other scenes were of as suitable a character; and the figures with which I peopled them were as strongly, though in some instances more whimsically, defined. I conceived of Caliban as a monster that scarcely less resembled a huge beetle than a human creature, and that walked erect and on all fours by turns. The witches of Macbeth appeared to me in the forms of some of the most disagreeable-looking old women in the country, — not, however, in their living aspects, but in those which I fancied their corpses would have assumed, should they, after being committed to the grave, be possessed by evil spirits. The ideas of female grace and elegance which I connected with the heroines of Shakespeare, and the lady of the Mask of Comus, were mostly derived from a beautiful painting in Cromarty House, — a copy of Guido's famous Aurora, which, when a boy, I have contemplated for hours together. It was in consequence of my having acquired such ideas as these of the characters and scenes of dramatic poetry that I was *now* displeased with both actors and the stage. The stage I regarded as merely a little area floored with fir deal and surrounded by painted sheets; — the actors as a company of indifferent-looking people who could bear no comparison with either the ideal *dramatis personæ* of my imagination, or the real characters whom I had seen acting their parts in the great drama of life. On the evening I first sat in the Theatre Royal of Edinburgh, I felt as if, after having admired an exquisite portrait, which the art of the painter had almost awakened into life, I should be asked whether I could not recognize the original of it in an inanimate image of wax."

CHAPTER IV.

MILLER soon found employment in his trade.
The scene of his labor during his residence
near Edinburgh was the village of Niddrie,
where he was one of a company of workmen
engaged in building an addition to Niddrie House. To
give ourselves a vivid idea of the locality, exactly as it
impressed itself upon him at the time, we cannot do better
than avail ourselves of his own description, which we find
in a letter to Uncle Alexander, dated 15th December,
1824 : —

"We shall, if you please, ascend the highest pinnacle of
Niddrie House, and from thence survey the country. As
far as the eye can reach in an east or southerly direction, a
low, unvaried flat presents itself, gradually rising, as it re-
cedes from the sight, into low, swelling hills, and falling
with a sweep as gradual towards the Frith of Forth, which
from this elevation appears in all its extent, glittering with
many sails. Upon the north and west the face of the country is of a bolder character. Arthur's Seat and Salisbury
Crags upon the one hand, and the blue, heathy Pentland
hills upon the other, will remind us of the beautiful and
picturesque scenery which surrounds our native town. . .

153

To the grounds about Niddrie my work gives me access. Often, in the fine summer evenings, have I sauntered through its fields and woods, alone, but not solitary, watching the last beam of the sun as it tinged with a purple hue the Pentland hills, or as it streamed on the roofless walls and dismantled turrets of Craigmillar Castle. . . . Niddrie House is a large, irregular building, bearing date in one part 1636, and in another not yet finished. The modern addition will, when the winter storms of a few years have soiled the natural hue of the stone and rounded the angular mouldings, appear by far the most antique, as it is executed in the heaviest style of the Saxon Gothic. The large, mullioned windows are crowned with rich labels, and the walls deeply indented with moulded embrasures. Octagon turrets rising above the roof project from every corner, and instead of those large stacks of chimneys which disfigure many modern houses, here every one has its own airy column, connected at top to the rest by a star-like cope. When finished, you might suppose this building, from its antique appearance and secluded situation, to have been some nunnery founded by that church-endowing monarch, David I. Adjoining the house is a large garden, which, from its irregular and partial cultivation, differs very little in appearance from the surrounding pleasure-grounds. In that corner of it which lies nearest the north-west gable of the house is a vault in which the Wauchopes of Niddrie, time immemorial, have been interred. Its front is screened by a huge bush of ivy, which, overshading the door and twining about a sepulchral urn that rests directly above, gives the whole a gloomy yet picturesque appearance. Death does not move the bodies of the proprietors of Niddrie far from the house which sheltered them when living; the dead Laird in his vault is not thirty feet distant from the living one in his bedchamber. Bounding the other extremity of the garden is a burying-ground, in which the humbler inhabitants of the country and village adjacent find their last resting-place. It is a solitary spot, embosomed in wood, and at a considerable distance from any house. These circumstances, which in the north country would make a burying-ground after nightfall the supposed haunt of restless spirits, here affords the violator of sepulchres opportunity to tear from its grave the newly deposited body, and to convey it to some of the dissecting-rooms about Edinburgh. Such is the barbarous audacity of these wretches, that they frequently break and overturn monuments which lie in their way ; and, without any desire of concealing their depredations, leave the violated graves half open, and scatter around them, as if in derision, the cerements that wrapped the body. I hope I am not bloodthirsty, yet I think I could level a musket at the villain who robbed the tomb of the body of one of my relatives, with as much composure, and with as little compunction, as I would feel in taking aim at a wooden target.

" The house, or rather cottage, in which I at present lodge stands upon the side of the Dalkeith road. It is sheltered on the north and west by the Niddrie woods, and on the east fronts a wide though not diversified prospect of corn-fields and farm-steadings. From the door at night, through a long, wooded avenue, I see the Inchkeith light twinkling in the distance, like a star rising out of the sea."

Thus does he nourish a youth hardly sublime, yet not without its genially fostering elements and influences; sauntering among the leafy woods, watching the sunset as it streams along the broad valley from the west, and deepens into purple the green-blue of the Pentlands, looking through the wooded avenue until the Inchkeith light flashes out above the darkening sea. " *Nunquam minus solus quam cum solus,* — " alone," as he puts it, " but not solitary," — he communes with his own heart, ponders on men and things, and lays up fact after fact, conclusion after conclusion, in a memory which, from his sixth year, appears to have lost not one gleaning of his experience. With the peace and beauty of nature around him, and Edinburgh at hand, his circumstances might at first sight be pronounced favorable.

There was, however, a very important drawback. It was a serious misfortune for Miller, and one which left deep traces of its injurious influence upon his mind, that the men in company with whom he worked at Niddrie were, for the most part, dissolute and worthless. Nor were the exceptions of a kind likely to inspire him with any enthusiasm for the order to which he provisionally belonged. They were men of strong religious sentiments, but narrow intellects, unable, save by the silent eloquence of their moral superiority to the rest of the squad, to make any impression either upon him or upon their comrades. The others were as bad specimens of their class as it is possible to conceive. Selfish and wilful as spoiled children, brutishly sensual, flippantly, because ignorantly, infidel, habitually profane, they showed Miller how base a thing a working-man can be, and to his dying day his opinion of working-men retained the stamp which it received in the society of these reprobates. Owing to the building mania, which was at its height at this time, they had abundance of work and high wages; but they were mean enough to be jealous of the workmen from the North, and Miller found himself exposed to the thousand nameless vexations which spiteful cunning can suggest to mechanics wishing to subject a comrade to humiliation. It is often necessary for a stone-cutter, in order to have the block which he hews placed conveniently for the chisel and mallet, to be assisted by his fellow-workmen. This customary civility was refused to Miller, whose pride prevented him from begging a favor, or complaining of its being tacitly refused. The ablest, and, except himself and the religious workmen, the best in the squad, was a young man whom he calls " Cha." He was the " recognized hero " of the band, and his heart seems to have smote him on account of the base combination against a stranger. He put an end to it by stepping out one day to assist Miller, when he was being left to roll up to his block-bench a stone of the size which two or three commonly united to place.

Even Cha, however, was not merely a blackguard, but, in all that relates to moral sanity and self-respecting manhood, a fool. Like the majority of his fellows, he celebrated the fortnightly payment of wages by two or three days of drunkenness and debauchery. He was leader in the following feat, the account of which I extract from the letter to Baird, as one or two of its traits are omitted from the autobiography : " On a Saturday evening three of the Niddrie workmen, after having received a fortnight's wages, which in all amounted to more than six pounds, went to Edinburgh, and there spent the night in a house of bad fame. Next morning they hired a coach, and. accompanied by three women of the town, set out for Roslin on a jaunt of pleasure. They came back to Edinburgh in the evening, passed the night as they had done the preceding one, and returned to Niddrie on Monday without a single shilling." Such was Cha, and to his taking the lead in expeditions of this kind he appears to have in large measure owed his reputation for cleverness and spirit. The revolting exploit just mentioned was spoken of with enthusiasm in the shed, and the workmen regaled each other for days after with accounts of similar feats which they had executed, or of which they had heard. " I was told," proceeds Miller, " of an Edinburgh mechanic, a mason, who on the death of a relative received a legacy of about eighty pounds. He was no sooner paid the money than he carried home his tool-chest, and shoved it under his bed. He then commenced a new course of life. He bought an elegant suit of clothes, hired a hackney-coach by the week, attended all the fashionable amusements of the place, and regularly, once in the day, called in his carriage on his brother-workmen. In six weeks the whole of his money was expended. He then took out his tool-chest from under his bed, and returned to his former employment." This fellow seems to have had a trace of humor in him.

At first hated as an intruder, and ridiculed as a Highlander, Miller, being found to be not only capable of holding on his own path, but superior in the valued accomplishments of swimming, leaping, running, and wrestling, rose into something like popularity among his fellow-workmen. It was impossible, however, that between him and them there could be any communion; and, tacitly accepting these sixteen masons of Niddrie as representatives of their class, he acquired a profound distrust, sharpened and embittered by contempt, for workmen in general. It cannot be denied that, so far as these unfortunates were concerned, he gave working-men a fair trial, and looked candidly and boldly into their ways and habits. He permitted himself to be carried along in the stream when the masons of the district turned out on strike, and he forced himself to endure one or two dreary hours in accompanying them to the foul subterranean haunt where they enjoyed the sport of badger-baiting. Everything he beheld in the character and conduct of these workmen offended his higher nature. They were too far below him to exert any such influence as might have tempted him to a fellowship with them. In an atmosphere of profanity, sensuality, and the most coarse and sordid selfishness, he continued an Apollo among neat-herds, pure, proud, and lofty-minded.

As was to have been expected, the strike in which these masons engaged seemed to him unreasonable, and we need not doubt that his view of the matter was correct. In point of fact, there was no redeeming feature in his experience of working-men during his residence at Niddrie to modify the sternly unfavorable opinion which he formed of the class. He concluded that they were incurably disqualified for promoting their true interests by combination. He declared against trades' unions, and from this decision he never swerved. Finding that William Ross was not only member of a house-painters' union, but one of the officials of the society, he told his friend that his union would never benefit the house-painters as a class, and advised him to resign his clerkship. He gives us in the autobiography the argument which he addressed to Ross, and as it was substantially the argument he continued to urge against trades' unions to the end of his life, it is as well to quote it here : " There is a want," he said, " of true leadership among our operatives in these combinations. It is the wilder spirits that dictate the conditions ; *and, pitching their demands high, they begin usually by enforcing acquiescence among their companions. They are tyrants to their fellows ere they come into collision with their masters, and have thus an enemy in the camp, not unwilling to take advantage of their seasons of weakness, and prepared to rejoice, though secretly, mayhap, in their defeats and reverses. And further, their discomfiture will be always quite certain enough when seasons of depression come, from the circumstance that, fixing their terms in prosperous times, they will fix them with reference rather to their present power of enforcing them, than to that medium line of fair and equal adjustment on which a conscientious man could plant his foot and make a firm stand. Men such as you, able and ready to work in behalf of these combinations, will of course get the work to do ;

but you will have little or no power given you in their direction ; the direction will be apparently in the hands of a few fluent *gabbers;* and yet even they will not be the actual directors ; they will be but the exponents and voices of the general mediocre sentiment and inferior sense of the mass as a whole, and acceptable only so long as they give utterance to that ; and so, ultimately, exceedingly little will be won in this way for working-men. It is well that they should be allowed to combine, seeing that combination is permitted to those who employ them ; but until the majority of our working-men of the south become very different from what they now are, — greatly wiser and greatly better, — there will be more lost than gained by their combinations. According to the circumstances of the time and season, the current will be at one period running in their favor against the masters, and at another in favor of the masters against them ; there will be a continual ebb and flow, like that of the sea, but no general advance ; and the sooner that the like of you and I get out of the rough conflict and jostle of the tideway, and set ourselves to labor apart on our own internal resources, it will be all the better for us."

Of the reasoning by which his correspondent attempted to rebut these arguments we have no sample, but Ross, though modest and diffident to excess, was not convinced, and retained his place in the union. Of the force of Miller's statements, so far as they go, there can be no doubt ; the question is whether his inference is not based on too narrow an induction of facts. That cacklers were generally the leaders of the unions at the time he wrote, and that they are too often the leaders now, may be admitted. But he seems to assume that there is a natural necessity in this state of things, and to conclude that no schooling by experience will suffice to teach working-men that the leadership of the wise man is better than the leadership of the fool. Stump-oratorical leadership has been proved long ere now to be no necessity in the organizations of working-men. The charge of tyrannically repressing individual energy may still be brought against unions; but it is an established fact that these associations have been the means of keeping tens of thousands of families out of the workhouse, and have dispensed to tens of thousands of workmen comforts and necessities in time of illness. Nearly twenty years have elapsed since Miller wrote his autobiography, and perhaps none of our institutions have partaken more largely in the general improvement which has characterized that period than trades' unions. It is not impossible that, with the comprehensive information before him which has been furnished by the Committee appointed to inquire into the subject by the Social Science Association, and by the Royal Commission which investigated the question in the summer of 1867, he would have divested himself more fully than he ever did of the evil impression made upon his mind by the abject squad in which he had the lamentable misfortune to work at Niddrie.

Be this as it may, his nature, purified and elevated by the influences of his training, remained uncontaminated by the baseness of his companions. Retaining his erect human attitude, he breathed freely and without hurt in this Grotto of Dogs, while the canine creatures perished. He had, besides, the society not only of William Ross, whose friendship and converse were a perpetual solace to him, but of a cousin and a few other rational persons. And the trees were leafy, the skies were blue, the white clouds over the Pentlands radiant in their stainlessness, and, when the wind raged in the wood behind the cottage at midnight, he could dream that it was the roll of the surge among the crags beside his beloved Cromarty. While his fellow-workmen in the shed indulged in clumsy jest or obscene tattle, he could " croon " to himself the " Boatman's Tale," getting into shape during these weeks. The poem will not rank high as a work of art, but there were a few at that time in Edinburgh, — Scott, Jeffrey, and Wilson in that number, — who would have heard with interest that it had been composed by a mason lad of twenty-one, who, in the very moments of composition, held mallet and chisel in a shed at Niddrie. The first two parts were written here, the remaining three at Cromarty. We shall glance at the poem.

The " Boatman's Tale " is varied in scene and incident, but the gist of the story is that Walter Hogg, a seafaring man, beheld a vision of fiendish creatures who predicted his death : that this death took place as announced, with appropriate circumstances of horror and terror, and that the ghost of Walter appeared to his friend and informed him that the demons, spite of their happy guess, were beings of no great potency, and that he was in a state of blessedness. The following stanzas are evidently a version of the episode of the apparition in " Jack Grant's Tale " : —

" Oh ! all was dark as dungeon gloom :
 Still louder swelled the roar
That rushed above, and howled behind,
 And dashed and raged before,
When gleamed a light, shadeless and bright,
 On cordage, mast, and oar.

" Now mock me not; our stern upon
 I saw a lady stand;
A waxen taper, straight and tall,
 She held in either hand;
Her lightly-flowing garb appeared
 Of shining silvery green,
Her face was calmly pale, her eyes
 Were stars of dazzling sheen.

> " High rose our bows; when passed the wave,
>   Again as low they fell;
>   Yet all unmoved that lady stood;
>   No sailor man, of flesh and blood,
>   Had kept her berth so well."

The scene of the apparition of Walter was also on ship-board, but the vessel had evidently never been on the stocks at Cromarty or elsewhere : —

> " Her sails were white as summer cloud,
>   Her mast a boreal ray,
>   A fiery star bedecked her prow,
>   Begemmed with light her stern below
>   The circling eddies play.
>   .   .   .   .   .   .
>
> " Now mark me : on her silver deck
>   Unharmed did Walter stand;
>   And on each side, and round behind,
>   There watched a seraph band.
>
> " The rainbow of the shower ye've seen,
>   The dazzling sun ye see :
>   Oh ! orbs and hues of heaven alone
>   To the good may likened be,
>   When they doff their garb of fragile clay
>   To bathe in eternity.
>
> " And lovely was the smile that dwelt
>   On Walter's placid face;
>   'Twas — but 'twere vain to strive to tell,
>   For words can ne'er express
>   The beauty of that sinless smile
>   Of perfect happiness."

On the subject of the demons which had appeared to him when on earth, the ghost becomes homiletic : —

> " Thou sure hast read in Heaven's own book
>   (Oh, search that volume well!)

How that of old the seraph tribes
   Grew proud and did rebel;
And how that from the height of heaven
   To deepest woe they fell.

" Of these the band whose dark presage
   Did sore my heart dismay;
Yet harmless in the lonely wood
   And in the storm are they.
But ah ! right fearful, though scarce feared,
   When in man's heart they stay.

" Oh, dread them when the wanton smiles,
   And when the bowl is set;
Oh, dread them when thy heart is glad,
   And when thy cheeks are wet.

   .   .   .   .   .   .

" But if on Heaven thy trust be laid,
   To fear thou dost not well,
For stronger is one Christian man
   Than all the fiends of hell."

The two last lines really do credit to the mason lad.
One can imagine him giving a vigorous stroke or two with
his mallet as he " crooned " them out.

The influence of Coleridge's " Ancient Mariner " and of
Hogg's " Queen's Wake " are traceable in the " Boatman's
Tale."

After working two seasons at Niddrie, Miller returned to
Cromarty. The voyage was long, and in its course he composed the verses which are quoted in the autobiography as
" Written at Sea." His uncles, his cousin George, and
other friends and relatives, welcomed him on the beach.

CHAPTER V.

THE STONE-CUTTER'S DISEASE — LINES TO SISTER JEANIE — RENEWS HIS FRIENDSHIP WITH SWANSON AND CORRESPONDS WITH ROSS — WRITES AN ODE ON GREECE AND OFFERS IT TO THE "SCOTSMAN."

MILLER returned from Edinburgh in unbroken spirits. Whatever the drawbacks of his Edinburgh sojourn, he had never ceased to be happy. and his mood, as we learn from an expression used in a letter to William Ross, had commonly been that of exuberant gayety. But one circumstance connected with his work while at Edinburgh now comes into view, to which it is impossible to refer without mournfulness. While the young journeyman, so brave of spirit. so modestly content with his exile from the society he was fitted to adorn, was cutting blocks into pillars in the shed at Niddrie, the seeds of painful and ineradicable disease were being sown in his constitution. The hardships of his apprenticeship had brought him to the gates of death, and although he seemed to have recovered his strength, it is probable that his lungs were of less than average vigor when he entered as a journeyman upon the occupation of stone-hewing. In two seasons he became so deeply affected with "the stone-cutter's malady," that he had to choose between throwing himself loose for a season from his employment and certain death. "So general," he says, "is the affection, that few of our Edinburgh stone-cutters pass

165

their fortieth year unscathed, and not one out of every fifty of their number ever reaches his forty-fifth."

For the first month or two after his return to Cromarty, he deemed it probable that his illness had gone too far for recovery. " I still remember " — these are his words — " the rather pensive than sad feeling with which I used to contemplate, at this time, an early death, and the intense love of nature that drew me, day after day, to the beautiful scenery which surrounds my native town, and which I loved all the more from the consciousness that my eyes might so soon close upon it forever." It was at this time that he composed the lines " To Jeanie." The little girl of five, to whom he addressed them, was his mother's eldest daughter by her second marriage. With that gentleness which ever characterized him, he made friends with Jeanie, and led her by the hand in his quiet walks. The lines are in the Scottish dialect, of which Miller was never such a master as Burns. They are not distinguished by power or originality, but are interesting as a reflex of his mood at the time, and breathe — the closing stanzas especially — an unaffected and artless pathos : —

"Though to thee a spring shall rise,
    An' scenes as fair salute thine eyes ;
    An' though, through many a cludless day,
    My winsome Jean shall be heartsome and gay ;

" He wha grasps thy little hand
    Nae langer at thy side shall stand,
    Nor o'er the flower-besprinkled brae
    Lead thee the lownest an' the bonniest way.

" Dost thou see yon yard sae green,
    Spreckled wi' many a mossy stane ?
    A few short weeks o' pain shall fly,
    An' asleep in that bed shall thy puir brither lie.

" Then thy mither's tears awhile
   May chide thy joy an' damp thy smile;
   But sune ilk grief shall wear awa',
   And I'll be forgotten by ane an' by a'.

" Dinna think the thought is sad;
   Life vexed me aft, but this mak's glad;
   When cauld my heart and closed my e'e,
   Bonny shall the dreams o' my slumbers be."

But he is young, and though his lungs have been permanently and incurably injured, the energy of his constitution, aided by repose and by peace of mind, is sufficient for the present to conquer the disease. With returning health return his interest in life and his intellectual ambition. He renews his friendship with John Swanson, who had recently abandoned a growing business in Cromarty with a view to devoting himself to the work of the Christian ministry in connection with the Church of Scotland, and opens a correspondence with William Ross. Swanson who, six years previously, had been one of his most intimate friends, he finds improved in all respects. John had thrown off a habit of sarcasm which formerly disguised his kindness of heart, and "his judgment," says Miller to Baird, "had attained a strength and niceness of edge which I had not before found equalled." In a few hours after they met, the friends were more closely knit in the bonds of amity than they had ever been. "After parting with him for the evening," says Miller again, "my spirits were so exhilarated that I felt as if intoxicated."

While he worked as a stone-cutter, Swanson had been preparing himself by a regular education for the duties of a learned profession. "I found my friend," writes Miller, "to be one of the few persons who become wise in proportion as they grow learned." He adds the following characteristic estimate of the effect of formal culture upon a certain order of minds: "My acquaintance with men of education, though not very extensive, is yet sufficiently so to convince me that the people whose capacities average between mediocrity and the lower extreme of intellect are rather injured than benefited by being made scholars. Men of this kind, when bred up to a common mechanical profession, are generally quiet and unpretending, useful to society and possessed of an almost instinctive knowledge of those rules of conduct, an attention to which makes easy the passage through life. As scholars, however, they frequently bear a character much the reverse of this. I have met with such newly set loose from college, and have taken an inventory of their intellectual stock: A smattering of Greek and Latin; an affected admiration of writings whose merits they have neither taste nor judgment to appreciate; a few confused philosophical notions; a few broken ideas, the imperfect transcripts, not of things, but of other ideas; an ability of conveying trite thoughts in common language; a pride that gloats enraptured over these attainments; and a sincere contempt for the class of people whom they deem the ignorant. Parnell's beautiful description of a lake when perfectly calm and when ruffled by a pebble illustrates happily the minds of men of true and of fictitious learning. The sensoriums of the former are mirrors of the universe; those of the latter present only scenes of broken fragments."

Swanson, like most young men of ability who study in the Scottish colleges, was an eager metaphysician, immersed in the study of Locke, Hume, Berkeley, and Reid. On the lighter departments of literature he looked with indifference, tempered by disdain. Miller's pursuits and preferences were of precisely the opposite character. He was addicted to poetry, and thought metaphysics dry and displeasing. "In a few months, however, he (Swanson) had become an admirer of the elegances of composition, and I (Miller) of metaphysical acuteness. He perused the 'Paradise Lost' of Milton with astonishment, I the Essays of Hume with admiration."

Strongly contrasted with the vigorous, practical Swanson, is Miller's other friend, of whom we have already heard so much, William Ross. If in any one of his early associates there was a ray of genius, it was in this hapless youth. What he wanted was at bottom nothing else but health. He blamed himself, and his friends blamed him, for indolence ; but it was not indolence, it was the lassitude of failing life, the weariness of approaching death, that palsied his energies. Keen and clear in his intellectual perceptions, he had a half-consciousness of this, but he did not know it well enough to silence his self-upbraidings. He told Miller that he, Ross, lacked the stamina which would one day raise his friend above the crowd, and regarded his own efforts with melancholy contempt. But for the sympathetic tenderness of Hugh's nature, there could have been no friendship between him and Ross ; the men were very different. "I need not remind you," writes Hugh, from Cromarty. in May, 1825, "that, though ever desirous of each other's company, we were not always very happy together. There was so much whim on the one side, and so little philosophy on the other, — the one was so low-spirited, the other so madly-spirited, — that not husband and wife (and that is saying a good deal) could agree worse together."

Miller felt the genuine worth of Ross, appreciated his fine qualities. and with a beautiful assiduity of friendship strove to woo him from his listlessness and his depression. The poor fellow struggled fitfully, but in vain. " O Indolence !" Ross exclaims in one of his letters, " thou demon who hast ever had such power over me (never more than now). accept the heartiest, bitterest curses of thy victim.

Unnerved by thy baneful influences, I have loitered in the dark valley of obscurity until the day of life is far spent; until clouds have arisen and obscured the bright vistas through which I once hoped my path would lie. I am even losing the little ground I have gained. I am sliding backwards. The want of natural abilities, the want of a proper education, the want of a rational confidence, — each of these throw rough, steep obstacles in the path of many a poor sojourner; but when thou, O fiend! seizest the will and makest it thine own, we struggle no longer against these obstacles. No! we sit down at thy feet and merely think of them. But why address the fiend?" In a more pensive mood, he contrasts his own situation with that of Miller: " I can scarce say I desire anything. Here I live as an exile, without a friend or a scene near me that I love, without anything to wish or enjoy. How grateful ought you to be to the great Benefactor who has placed you in a situation so truly delightful! I can in imagination picture you at work on the chapel brae, where everything around you is so still, so fresh, so beautiful. I can see green woods and yellow fields; a little, quiet town at a convenient distance, with the blue waves half encircling it, and the blue hills peeping over it. Did I say I had sunk into such an apathy as to be too indifferent to desire anything? If so, I have spoken amiss, for there are things which I can still desire. Did I say you ought to be grateful to the Giver of all good? Alas! discontented, restless thing that I am, I have much cause for being grateful also." He has a deep affection for Miller, and a pride in his friend. " You complain, my friend, of melancholy. Had I such a heart as yours, I think I could be happy even in grief. It is of a gentler and more delicate cast than I had imagined, and I am glad of it."

Occasionally Ross introduces a similitude so apt and so

beautiful that we feel keenly how real, how fine, if slender, was his vein of genius. Remarking that all who knew him think well of him, he proceeds, with his usual self-depreciation, to account for the fact: " All these men only see me in part, and (for such is the nature of all earthly things, when viewed from a distance) what they do see of me appears other than what it is. The clouds which so gloriously encircle the setting sun, and whose beauty in description no comparison can heighten. are but wreaths of watery vapor ; and the distant hill, though its azure hue vies in depth and beauty with that of the cloudless firmament. is a mass of rock and earth, half covered with a stunted vegetation. What am I in reality? What is my heart? A cold, vicious thing, devoid of energy, affection, and peace." This is a far deeper thought than Thomson's about the enchantment of distance. Mr. Ruskin expands what is essentially the same idea as the poor consumptive house-painter's into one of the most eloquent passages in his works ; * but the ap-

* " Are not all natural things, it may be asked, as lovely near as far away? Nay, not so. Look at the clouds, and watch the delicate sculpture of their alabaster sides, and the rounded lustre of their magnificent rolling. They were meant to be beheld far away ; they were shaped for their place, high above your head ; approach them, and they fuse into vague mists, or whirl away in fierce fragments of thunderous vapor. Look at the crest of the Alp, from the far-away plains over which its light is cast. whence human souls have communion with it by their myriads. The child looks up to it in the dawn, and the husbandman in the burden and heat of the day, and the old man in the going down of the sun, and it is to them all as the celestial city on the world's horizon ; dyed with the depth of heaven, and clothed with the calm of eternity. There was it set, for holy dominion, by Him who marked for the sun his journey, and bade the moon know her going down. It was built for its place in the far-off sky ; approach it, and, as the sound of the voice of man dies away about its foundation, and the tide of human life, shattered upon the vast aerial shore, is at last met by the Eternal ' Here shall thy waves

propriate and beautiful application of it to the judgment of human character belongs to Ross alone.

Still finer, perhaps, is the following : " The virtuous man has not only the approbation of others, but his own. It is said by philosophers that the air we breathe would be a most oppressive burden to us did it not penetrate the pores of our bodies, and, by filling every cavity within, render us unconscious to the weight which presses from without. Thus the self-approbation of the virtuous man renders the approbation of others an invigorating, refreshing thing ; but without it (I speak from experience) the voice of praise appears a cruel irony, — a weight which bends the consciously unworthy soul to the very dust." Poor fellow ! He was so good and so gifted that all who knew him loved and admired him ; and so gentle-hearted, so modest, and self-accusing, that even their admiration gave him pain. In the same letter we have a glimpse of the country about Perth : " The scenery about Perth is exquisitely beautiful. The day upon which I first came within sight of it was calm and pleasant, and, then in its decline, was clothing the woods, hills, and fields with a yellow light. The Tay, speckled with boats and small vessels, like a vein of silver winded through the landscape. The distant town, half mixing with an azure cloud which rested above it, seemed (to use the words of my favorite poet)

" A town of fairy-land, a thing of earth and sky,"

while the aerial hue of the distant hills spake of the skill of nature's painting, — a hue evidently intended to sort with,

be stayed,' the glory of its aspect fades into blanched fearfulness; its purple walls are rent into grisly rocks, its silver fretwork saddened into wasting snow ; the storm-brands of ages are on its breast, the ashes of its own ruin lie solemnly on its white raiment." — *Stones of Venice.*

to melt into the hues of the firmament. The sun lingered a while on the top of his hill. as if admiring the scene, and then sunk beneath it. For a time the golden clouds, like the ministers of a good king deceased, strove to be what he had been; but the attempt was above their power; they languished, and the scene became duller and blacker, until at length the gray mantle of evening was spread over it." Are there not tones and touches here of what Mr. Carlyle calls nature's " masterpiece and darling, the poetic soul"? That such a soul should have been placed amid the desolate circumstances of William Ross — hopelessly poor, hopelessly ill — suggests some of the deepest questionings in the stern mystery of human life.

It was in September of 1826 that Hugh Miller made his first attempt to address his countrymen in the columns of a newspaper. He wrote an " Ode on Greece," and commissioned William Ross to hand it into the office of the " Scotsman." A note was at the same time addressed to the editor. " The enclosed Ode," writes Hugh. with the anxious dignity of the young author, " was written at a time when the cause of the Greeks appeared desperate, by one who has looked upon their glorious struggle for independence with a wish and a sigh. Had his powers of mind equalled his feelings in strength or vivacity, his poem would rouse like the blast of a trumpet; but, alas! you will soon perceive that it displays little of the art — perhaps little of the spirit — of the poet. He who can only court the Muses in the few intervals of rest which a laborious occupation affords, must be indeed fortunate if he prove a favored suitor." The " Ode " is hardly above the average standard of juvenile compositions, though here and there a vigorous note breaks through. echoed from Byron. The poet has no mercy on the doctrine of non-intervention, and addresses his own country in tones of haughty rebuke.

" Alas for Greece! but not alone
    For wretched Greece the tears shall flow;
Adorned by glory's brightest zone,
    Her fame shall soothe her woe.
But thou, proud home of wealth, for thee
Heavy the patriot's heart must be.
Say, dark of spirit, hast thou sold
The souls of men for sordid gold,
And plied each art of niggard trade
When hapless patriots toiled and bled,
And filled thy coffers o'er the dead?"

He exhorts Greece to bestir herself, and is very angry with
the Turks.

" Rouse thee, O Greece! a fearful sign
    Is pictured on the awful sky;
Ruin awaits the Moslem line,
    Mahomet's faith shall die!
The falchion cleaves the turbaned head,
    The Koran's darkened page is torn,
And Turkey's streams are rolling red
    With blood of the unborn.

.   .   .   .   .   .

Alas for hapless Greece! again
    The dark clouds gather round her head;
Her Byron's lyre was swept in vain,
    In vain her children bled.
But vengeance loads the coming gale,
    And ere the tyrant grasps the rod,
His soul shall shrink, his strength shall fail,
    Beneath the brand of God!"

How this trumpet-blast might have influenced the Greeks
we cannot tell. The editor of the "Scotsman" proved a
Trojan on the occasion, and Miller's Ode was returned upon
his hands.

Not long after. Hugh refers to the subject in a letter to
Ross, and bravely decides that the piece might not have

been worth publishing after all. " Perhaps "— he thus expresses his philosophical resignation — " my Ode was ill-timed ; perhaps its merits are of so doubtful a kind that no one except myself can discover them ; perhaps — but I have said enough. Why should I be a seeker after fame? Fame is not happiness ; it is not virtue. Bad men enjoy it ; wretched men attain it. It rewarded the deeds of Erostratus as largely as those of Leonidas." With equal judiciousness and self-severity, he touches upon his efforts in the way of mental improvement. " It is the remark of a celebrated writer that without long and serious application no man, however great his natural abilities, can attain the art of writing correctly. At one time I flattered myself with the hope of becoming a correct writer ; and, with the intention of applying myself sedulously to the study of the English language, I collected several works that treated of grammar and composition. Besides these helps I also calculated upon the assistance of my friend, John Swanson. But though repeatedly warned by experience, I did not calculate upon that volatility of mind which I have ever found as difficult to fix upon any single object, whatever may be its importance, as to fix quicksilver on an inclined plane ; and now I can look back upon my half attempt at becoming an English scholar, just as I can upon every other speculation in which I have been engaged. I see a fine foundation laid, but no superstructure. I still propose, however, to become a correct writer, but it must be in the manner in which Cowley became a grammarian. That ingenious poet, speaking of himself, says : ' I was so much an enemy to all constraint, that my masters could never prevail on me, by any persuasion or encouragement, to learn without book the common rules of grammar, in which they dispensed with me alone, because they found I made a shift to do the usual exercise out of my own reading and observation.'"

In a letter written about the same time, we have sundry remarks on literary subjects. " You ask me whether I now read Byron or Ovid. I reply in the affirmative. I do read every work of ability that falls in my way, whatever the opinions or intentions of their authors were ; but in reading these works I always strive to keep in view certain leading truths, which serve as tests to discover and separate sophistry from argument, and as lights to dissipate those shades of obliquity which are cast over virtue, both by its artful enemies and injudicious friends. At the birth of our Saviour, the shrine of Apollo and Delphi spake no longer with its mysterious organs of what was, or of what was to come. He who was the truth had come into the world, and every oracle of lies had become dumb. At His death, the veil of the temple was rent in twain, and truth was no longer a mystery. Thus, by His power, that which was false, and that which was true, became alike evident. The Gospels are still in our hands, and they, like Him of whom they speak, silence falsehood and discover truth. He who takes up the writings of Byron, Ovid, or Moore, or any of the many writings of those men who have so fearfully misapplied the talents which God gave them, will, if impressed with a deep sense of the true religion, run no risk of being allured and led astray by the blandishments of vice. But what can induce, it may be asked, a man of religious principle to peruse a volume in which he must, of necessity, come in contact with the allurements of vice : in which all that he loves will be made to appear in its least lovely form, all that he hates or has to fear in its most engaging and dangerous? To this I would reply that it is no very honorable safety which is procured by flight. Why should a man who stands upon the advantage ground of truth and

virtue yield to the emissaries of vice and error? May he
not, as did Gideon the son of Joash, descend into the camp
of these Midianites, and listen to the ominous visions which
perplex them, or examine the unsocial sophistries upon
which they have founded their systems, or expose the futility of the vain beliefs upon which they have founded their
hopes? But, to speak in plainer language, there are many
advantages which may be derived from a real philosophical
perusal of the writings of these men. Many of them were
endowed with extraordinary talents, were the friends of
civil liberty, and excelled in the art of reasoning and of
writing well. I cannot read the Essays of Hume, without
seeing the necessity of entrenching myself behind the bulwarks of Christianity. All those outworks which are raised
in every direction around these bulwarks, some of them by
mistaken good, and others by designing bad men, must be
forsaken; for I find I have to do with a foe who can lay
bare the designs and demolish the sophistries of the designing priest, who can crush at one blow the boasted illu-
minations of the enthusiast and fanatic. But when I retire
within the citadel of Christianity, I see from it the ingenious
philosopher becoming a sophist, the powerful warrior as-
sailing a rock of adamant with a battering ram of straw .
. . The 'Don Juan' of Byron is an extraordinary poem,
in my opinion ten times more so than the 'Hudibras' of
Butler. It displays a thorough knowledge of human character, — of the crimes and frailties of mankind."

"*Feb.* 20. — Since I conversed with you I have toiled
and played, I have ate and drank, walked and slept; I
have been happy and indifferent, and — no, not sad. And
now I am again with my friend; draw then your chair a
little nearer, and I shall tell you of my toils and amusements. I have been quarrying at Navity shore stones for
a house, which my cousin Robert Ross is going to build,

and with my uncles and cousins have brought home several
boat-loads of them. You remember Navity, with its rough,
bold shore, steep precipices and sloping braes, so I need
not tell you that there are few places where he who labors
is so ready to forget that labor is a curse. Nor need I tell
you how pleasant I found it to sweep on the calm wave in
a fine frosty morning, past the rude bays and steep promontories of the Gallow Hill, or how grand and awful the
wide caverns, rugged precipices, and wooded brow of that
hill appeared when our boat crept round its shores, heavy
laden in a clear moonshine night." His amusements are
principally verse-making and solitary walks. He proceeds
to describe one of the latter. " I left the house about four
o'clock in the evening, passed along the shore, climbed the
rock at the dropping cave, descended again, and in half an
hour from my setting out found myself at the Doocot Cave.
I have attempted a description of this cave and the surrounding scenery in my ' Tale of Youth.' I next struck
a light, kindled my torch, and proceeded to explore the
cavern. Its depth is a hundred and fifty feet, its height
varies from eighteen to twenty. Its sides are incrusted by
a beautiful white stone, resembling marble, and formed by
springs of a petrifying quality which ooze through its roof,
while its floor is composed of a damp, mouldy earth, strewn
over with fragments of rock. In a clear day, from the
height and straightness of the cavern, the light penetrates
to its inmost recess, but as yester evening was dull and
cloudy, fifty feet from its entrance was dark as midnight;
even the rays of my torch seemed lost in the gloom. As I
proceeded, however, and as the sides of the cavern approached each other, and its roof lowered, the light appeared to gather strength. When I had gained the extreme
end. I tied my torch to a pillar of stone which depended
like an icicle from the roof, and then groped my way back

to its entrance, from whence I contemplated the scene. Have you not observed in a stormy night, when the sky is covered with clouds, how bright and clear the stars which look down through a small opening appear? Only imagine these clouds darker. and one solitary star looking through them brighter than you have ever seen cloud or star, and you will have some idea of the appearance which the Doocot Cave presented when my torch twinkled in its deepest recess."

CHAPTER VI.

POEMS ADDRESSED TO ROSS — SERIOUS THOUGHTS — CORRE-
SPONDENCE WITH SWANSON — FREAKISH HUMOR — DE-
SCENDS INTO THE TOMB OF THE URQUHARTS — IS CATE-
CHIZED BY MR. STEWART — WRITING IN THE OPEN AIR —
A PROSELYTIZING BORE — CORRESPONDENCE ON RELIGION.

TWO of Miller's early poems are addressed to William Ross, the one entitled an Ode, the other an
Epistle. Neither is of importance, but in the Epistle, written in the Scottish dialect, occur the following lines, part of an enumeration of the joys of wealth : —

> " The power o' aiding honest men
> Should be itsel' a heaven o' pleasure."

These, I think, are worthy of Burns.

The Epistle is sad throughout. It is Miller's design, as
he informs Ross in prose, to give him a " faithful picture "
of his mind " when overcast by those clouds of constitutional melancholy that obscure it so often."

> " The lover's joy, the star o' fame,
>   The Muse, the bliss that waits upon her,
> The ray that gilds the warrior's name,
>   The tags and toys o' boastful honor,
> Are shades that on the calm, smooth wave
>   Shine bonny as the northern streamer;
> But they fade and die when the wild blasts rave,
>   And leave to woe the wakened dreamer.

" There reigned a king in ancient time,
    The wisest ever swayed a sceptre;
His deep, sly saws, and songs sublime,
    Shine bright on the fair page o' Scripture.
And he, the wyliest sure o' men,
    For bliss tried ilka scheme o' living,
But he found at length his labors vain,
    And life a scene o' crime and grieving."

Light, however, breaks through. In a tone of earnestness which contrasts strongly with his references to religion in his earlier productions, prose or verse, he exclaims : —

" Hark! wherefore bursts that rapturous swell?
    Why are the night's dark shadows riven?
'A Saviour sought the depths o' hell,
    That such as thee might rise to heaven.'

" My cares, my hopes, my wishes climb
    To reach that Friend who reigns above me;
Truth's best perfection dwells in him,
    And he has sworn to aid and love me."

The composition of these stanzas is connected with a revolution which has been silently transacting itself in the mind and character of Hugh Miller, and which will come under our notice as we review his correspondence of this period with John Swanson.

We have seen that from his childhood he had displayed a fine natural disposition; that he was fearless, unselfish, affectionate. Of the baser passions, avarice and cruelty, he never exhibited a trace; and of that less ignoble passion which has frequently coexisted with high and generous attributes of character, but which has frequently also, as in Mirabeau, Burns, and Byron, made wreck of the palaces of the soul, he was singularly destitute. The extravagances of his boyhood, — the pranks of a wild, free, gipsying life, — reaching their climax of wickedness in robbery of an orchard and rebellion against an uncle, would not be regarded even by a morose school of moralists as portending a vicious manhood. The lessons which he received from Uncle James and Uncle Sandy had sunk deep into his heart, even when he chafed under their inculcation; and while he passed through the severely salutary discipline of his apprenticeship, his feelings towards those admirable men had gradually settled into a profound and filial regard. As we mark him, therefore, among his comrades of the bothy and the shed, we are struck by the moral nobleness, the virgin purity, which constantly attend him, and which render him undefilable by the foulness amid which he moves. But religion had not become the supreme influence in his mind; he was still — he knew it himself, and his friends knew it — " in the camp of the unconverted."

We saw that, on returning from Edinburgh, he renewed his acquaintance with John Swanson, and that the closest friendship was soon established between them. Swanson, as we said, had recently thrown up a growing business in Cromarty, had resolved to become a preacher of the gospel, and had proceeded, shortly after the renewal of his intimacy with Miller, to Aberdeen, in order to pursue his studies. His robust and healthful nature was aglow with the impassioned ardor of first faith and first love. " Oh!" he exclaims to Miller, in a letter dated Aberdeen, July, 1825, " I pant after that time when I may be fully assured that you are travelling towards Zion! Oh, there is much encouragement held out to us in the Scriptures to come to Christ! His love, how amazing! The subject has an effect on my feelings; but if I would speak of it, I feel my tongue tied. Angels cannot do justice to his love; how infinitely short, then, must we come! How forcible does that expression appear to those who have considered it aright: ' It passeth knowledge'! I cannot bid him God-speed who would deny His willingness to save us. No! the more I consider the subject, the more am I persuaded that he delighteth in mercy!'"

There was doubtless an answer to this from Miller, but I have not found it. In Sept., 1825, Swanson again writes, and still, apparently in response to hesitation exhibited, or objections started, by his correspondent, insists upon the plenitude of the divine mercy. "He is described as holding out His hands all day long to a rebellious and gainsaying people, and shall we impiously dare to say that He is unwilling to receive any? 'Tis true there are mysterious doctrines in the Bible; 'tis true, election, etc., are spoken of; but, if I know aught of the spirit of the Scriptures, these were never meant to keep a returning sinner back from God. Indeed, I presume we often mistake this very doctrine. It appears to me not as intended for our use before conversion, but after it. It seems to me given for the support and consolation of the saints, and not as a question for the returning penitent. We never hear of the apostles making use of such expressions as these to an inquirer: 'It may be you are not elected. It may be, though you tell us you believe, you are deceived.' But we find them asking this question, 'Dost thou believe?' Believe what? That Jesus is the Christ. And I ask you, my dear Hugh, dost thou believe? Do you believe that he lived? that he was the Sent of God? that he died to save sinners? I know that thou believest. Well, is your life and conversation corresponding to this belief? Do you pray? read the Scriptures? obey the injunctions of Christ?"

Miller, however, is shy of coming to close quarters. In a letter of 18th November he takes a sportive tone, and chats lightly on miscellaneous matters. Here is a jotting which may be read with interest. Rummaging, one evening, among his papers, he comes upon the uncompleted manuscript of the "Boatman's Tale." He seizes it. "Off we went," he proceeds, "and in the twinkle of an eye arrived at Marquis shore. Daily did my fires smoke in the cave there until I had completed my tale. By the way, I found your fire-box extremely useful. Marquis cave has ever since my childhood been a favorite haunt of mine. If the romantic scenery of the great world has an effect of moulding the fancies of the little one, I know no place where with better success that species of poetry which I have attempted in my tale may be studied. I would send your favorite Pope to write verses in some august palace, where his eye might rove over the chaste ornaments of architecture, or rest upon gay statues and gorgeous thrones. I would place Milton on the blue summit of Etna. When the sun laughed upon the world which stretched beneath his feet, I would fancy him enjoying its beauties. When an earthquake made hills tremble and destroyed cities, or when some furious storm dashed upon the base of his throne, I could imagine him elate in the midst of horror and death, mingling his song with the music of the tempest. To my master, Coleridge, I will dispose of Marquis cave. There, on the rude mass of granite, which I have rolled from the beach, let him sit and enjoy the fire I have kindled. There let him listen to the roar of the ocean as it beats against the rocks, or to the blast roaring above his head through shattered crags and ragged furze; and when his mind is filled with the wild images which on every hand present themselves, let him sing of bewildered mariners and wretched spirits. Are you not tired? I am sure I am. My spirits are wretchedly low at present, and I write bombast because unable to write anything better."

But Swanson is in a mood far too earnest to be pleased with Miller's light humor, and he gently rebukes the levity of this letter. It "yielded" him, he frankly says, "some degree of disappointment." He returns at once to his point, and puts the direct question, "Have you made your peace with God?" Hugh can now fence no longer. He confesses that he had been prevented from responding to his friend's appeals by a "backward, mistrustful pride and bashfulness." In simple-hearted reliance on the friendliness of a correspondent who justified the confidence reposed in him, he gives an account of himself. "At times I have tried to pray. At times I have even thought that these prayers were not in vain. I have striven to humble my proud spirit by reflecting on my foolishness, my misery and guilt. I have thought to be reconciled to that God who, in his awful justice, has doomed the sinner to destruction, yet who, in his infinite mercy, has found out a way of redemption; but I am an unsteady and a wavering creature, nursing in my foolishness vain hopes, blinded by vain affections; in short, one who, though he may have his minutes of conviction and contrition, is altogether enamored of the things of this world, and a contemner of the cross."

The letter in which this passage occurs is dated December, 1825. About this time Swanson becomes so absorbed in his studies that he finds it impossible to devote time to correspondence, and he writes Miller briefly, on the 14th of January, 1826, to that effect. "Go on, my dear Hugh,"—he says, in reference to the chief subject on which they had exchanged thoughts,—"go on, and the Lord himself will bless you. If you are not under the teaching of the Spirit of God, I am deceived, and if I do not find you soon established in the way of happiness, peace, and life, I shall be miserably disappointed."

One cannot help remarking, by the way, that this correspondence is creditable to these young friends. "How," exclaims Miller in one of his letters, "can I repay you for that deep, that generous interest which you take in my spiritual concerns! How can I make a suitable return for a friendship which, unlike the cold, selfish attachments of earth, approaches, in its nature and affectionate disinterestedness, to the love of heaven? Perhaps I say too much, — I am certain you will think so, — but with a heart so full a wiser man could hardly say less." Modest, noble, kind-hearted Hugh! How many would have resented Swanson's interference in affairs which jealous pride and sensitive independence might so plausibly allege to lie solely between a man and his Maker! From the meanness of such pride and the bitterness of such independence, Miller's true heart guards him well. He is deeply grateful. Swanson, for his part, thrilling with joy in the possession of the pearl of price, yearns to share the treasure with his friend, and to seal their friendship with the seal of immortality.

Pleased, perhaps, for the moment, that his correspondence with Swanson should take a less earnest turn, Miller recurs, in his next letter, to his vein of light, miscellaneous writing. On the 26th of February he gives his friend an account of a solitary excursion undertaken by him, some weeks previously, to the Dropping Cave. The day was tempestuous. "Availing myself," he writes, "of the moment when a huge wave in retiring left the beach uncovered, I sprung forward and gained the cave. There I seated myself on the very rock where, as tradition informs us, the naked, gray-bearded man, a few nights before a shipwreck, seats himself and looks mournfully on the sea. Shakespeare says something very severe of the man who does not love music; my ear is wretchedly dull, but as there are three kinds of music which have the power of raising my passions. I hope I am not obnoxious to his anathema. The first of these is the rolling of artillery, especially when the sound, prolonged by echo, returns upon the ear three or four times, each time fainter and more hollow. The second is the pealing of thunder. This is the most sublime of all sounds. I never hear it without feeling that, though a little and weak creature, I am not meaner nor more inconsiderable, when laid in the balance with Him whose voice is then lifted up, than are the mighty ones of the earth, who, in their rage, their sport, or to make themselves a name, desolate kingdoms or raise pyramids. The third is that combination of wild sounds which, in a tempest. pleases yet stuns the ear. In the Dropping Cave, like a solitary Triton divested of his shell, I was listening to such a concert, — a concert of the elements ; and my mind, as if sympathizing with the winds and waves, was overcast by a mist of wild thoughts. which arose and passed away even as did the gray clouds which at that time hurried over the face of the heavens. I sung verses of war-songs. I repeated, or rather shouted out, pieces of poetry descriptive of battles or tempests, or, turning to the recesses of the cavern. I challenged the spectre by which it is haunted to come forward that we might hold converse together. You see how well your friend can act the madman when under the guidance of imagination, yet, volatile as my mind is, I do not envy the gravity of the men over whose judgments fancy never triumphs."

This wild and buoyant humor was not, however, constant with him. "You seem," he writes, "to have been in low spirits. Are you also subject to those strange rises and falls of spirit which, without any assignable cause, make your humble servant happy, miserable, and mad by turns? I wish the college session over, and you fairly settled at your mother's fireside. I am really vexed on seeing you determined on killing yourself. Is he not as much a suicide who swallows death in the form of a mathematical problem, as he who takes an ounce of opium? The latter is certainly the easiest way of getting out of the world, — there is no pedantry in it." Affecting words, when read in connection with the history of Miller's closing years! How little did he think, while rejoicing in the freedom of the hill-side and the sea-shore, and warning his friend with gentle earnestness not to overtask his brain, that he should himself yield to the terrible temptation, and pay the penalty with his life! "Happy and miserable and mad by turns:" the expression is striking and strange.

The strutting and declamation of this visit to the Dropping Cave are not the sole illustration we have of an extravagant and freakish humor indulged by Miller in this period of his life, — *tolerabiles ineptiæ*, the trifling of a powerful mind which has not yet found its work. Some years later, in February, 1830, he details to a correspondent the particulars of an attempt made by him to " create incident " by descending into the vaulted tomb of the Urquharts, in the ancient burying-ground adjoining the ruinous chapel of St. Regulus or St. Rule in the neighborhood of Cromarty. " A few weeks ago," he writes, " upon a dark and stormy night, I procured a tinder-box, three torches, and a small quantity of fuel, and went to the old chapel of St. Rule. I descended to the ruinous vault, struck a light, lighted the torches, and placed them at equal distances against the gable wall. The light rendered visible a scene, which, heightened by association, was of no tame or common character. The floor below was strewn over with fragments of hewn stone, gray with lichens, or green with moss, and in the interstices there were brown, discolored fragments of human bones. From the crevices in the wall there sprung a few weeds which had pined throughout the summer for the fresh air and the sunshine, but now, as they were beyond the reach of the frost and the cold, they were green and rank, and spread their tiny branches over the rough. damp stones, like silk foliage on a ground of gray worsted. The arched roof above is covered over with a whitish stalactitical matter, and stained with the damps which have oozed from the soil over it. From the light of the torches it assumed a pale, shroud-like, death-like appearance. The square opening above seemed a chasm of darkness; and the recesses of the vault furthest from the light were enveloped in so dismal a twilight that I could almost have fancied that the whiter masses of stone or building, which stood out like rude columns from the darker wall, were some of the old tenants of the place, who had risen to inquire after the cause of my intrusion. The sounds which were conveyed to me in this place formed a music worthy of such a hall. The night, I have said, was stormy. The rain was heard to patter on the flat stones above, the wind roared terribly through the trees with which the burying-ground is enclosed; and the stream which runs through the neighboring ravine, the bottom of which is many yards lower than that of the vault. joined its hoarse dash with the roar of the wind and the pattering of the rain. In order that I might vary the scene, I piled up a little rude altar on the floor, and kindled a fire on it. The wind above prevented the smoke from rising; the atmosphere of the vault became dense and cloudy; the three torches on the wall appeared from the halo with which each of them was encircled three mock suns; and the features of the scene, which were before characteristic of the wild and the ghastly, were now shrouded ‧ in the dun hues of earthquake and eclipse,' and assumed the terrible. From above, the mouth of the vault appeared, through the darkness, like the crater of a volcano."

Such were the " pleasures of the imagination " in which young Miller could at all times find more enjoyment than in any society, except that of his most esteemed friends. It may be interesting to view him for a moment in a more subdued aspect. It is, or was, the custom in the parishes of Scotland for the pastor at stated intervals to publicly examine the members of the congregation in the Westminster Assembly's Catechism. It appears to have become the practice to catechise working-men and their children, but not to offend the sensibilities of the richer heads of families by putting them through the ordeal in presence of the congregation. Miller at least thought that Mr. Stewart, his pastor, of whom he subsequently learned to entertain a different opinion from his present, displayed " something very like cowardice " in his choice of persons to be examined. " Our *betters*," he says " (forgive me the use of this meanest of all Scotticisms), can, by attending the diets of catechism, which are held in church, be either instructed or made merry at our expense." Neither in the way of merriment, however, nor in the way of instruction, could much be derived from the appearance of Miller, which he thus chronicles : " I was catechised to-day (Feb. 30, 1826), by Mr. Stewart. It is an unpleasant thing to stand exposed point-blank to the gaze of two or three hundred people, each man more provokingly keen-eyed than the other. Had you seen me standing before the minister this day, as conspicuous as Saul among the people, — my face changing from crimson to pale and from pale to crimson by turns, — you must either have pitied my confusion or laughed at it. I will strive to recollect the questions which were asked me and the words with which I answered them. 'Who is the Spirit?' — 'The Third Person of the Trinity.' — 'Is he a person?' — 'He is termed so.' — 'Yes, he is. Do you recollect any particular passages of Scripture which show him as a distinct person?' Here I was silent. 'I thought, from your readiness in answering me my two first questions, that you would answer me this one too. In what form did the

Spirit appear at the baptism of our Saviour?'—'In the form of a dove.'—'Yes. The Spirit, then, is a person, not a mere influence proceeding from the Father and Son, as some believe. In what manner were we baptized?'—'With water, in the name of the Father, Son, and Spirit.'—'Yes. The Holy Ghost is a person. What is the work or province of the Father?'—'He created all things, and from him all things proceed.'—'You speak of him as the Creator. I desire to know what share he has in the redemption of sinners?'—'He sent the Son.'—'Yes. What did the Son do?'—'He died for us.'—'And what was the work of the Spirit?'—'He applies Christ.' Here he spoke a good deal which I forget, and concluded by desiring me to sit down. I did so most willingly, for my legs were trembling beneath me."

He gives a more satisfactory account of himself to his cousin, William Munro, in a letter dated 1st of May. "I am writing at this moment in the open air, under the shade of a honeysuckle. The sun is peeping through its leaves, and casting upon my paper spangles of a bright hue and strangely fantastic form. As I look upon them I cannot avoid recognizing a picture of my own mind. It is thus its lights and shadows blend together. A little cloud has passed over the sun, and my page has become dark and sombre; and is it not thus that my fair hopes and gay imaginings ofttimes pass away, and leave behind them a cloud of darkness?" This picture may be somewhat high-wrought, as Miller had announced to William Ross his intention to send his cousin "a fine sentimental letter, resembling that of a boarding-school miss."

On the 19th of August he writes to Swanson, and his correspondence touches again upon matters of importance. The town of Cromarty was at this time the residence of a Baptist gentleman of decided views and proselytizing tendencies. He appears to have considered the poetical mason a desirable acquisition for his church. " A few days ago," writes Miller, " when at work in the old chapel burying-ground, I was favored by a visit from Mr. M——, the Baptist. He and I had a long conversation together. Our subject was the peculiar tenets of his sect, and (if you allow me the expression) the opposing ones of mine. It was he who attacked, and I who did not defend; but I leaned most manfully upon my arms and looked on. And what did I see, do you ask? Why, I saw much of the strength and of the weakness of his cause, and much of his strength and weakness as an individual. I am pretty certain he saw none of mine. In his opinion concerning Church government I agree entirely with him. But this is no change of mine; for long since, when angered by the unjust encroachments on civil liberty of proud Churchmen, — men to whom, in describing, Hume and Voltaire have done justice, — I was led to examine the ground upon which they had founded their pretensions, and saw it to be a forced mass, uncemented except with the blood of persecution or by the unsolid sophistry of the schools. But though, by an inference seemingly reasonable, I see a connection subsisting between the baptism of Mr. M—— and the apostolic form of Church government, I can also see that upon this connection, discovered by this seemingly reasonable inference from Scripture, not by Scripture itself, can Baptists alone build. This, when I consider the fallacy of several Scripture inferences which appear as reasonable, I think an unsolid foundation. I could prove by an inference deduced from Scripture data that the mental and bodily sufferings of one man could not in justice be accepted as an atonement for the crimes of another. Where would inferences seemingly reasonable, deduced from the doctrine of predestination, lead us? To impiety the most horrible. I need not remind you of Carlyle's inferences, or of some others which you will find in the writings of Kaimes and Hume. This may not be argument; but where, suffer me to ask, is a doctrine upon the knowledge of which man's salvation depends, which is not fairly stated in Scripture, repeated oftener than once, and viewed in a variety of lights? Then let me be shown where He who spake as man never spake, or any of his servants, the apostles, has, or have said, ' Baptize not your children, but suffer themselves to come forward, when awakened by the Spirit, to be baptized,'— show me this, or a passage of like meaning, and I will become a Baptist.* During the course of our conversation I perceived in some of Mr. M——'s remarks traces of that foul spirit which can, like the harpies who settled upon the viands of Æneas, perch upon the soundest creeds. Will you believe that he dared tell me that a good Christian pastor of the Church of Scotland did more harm to the true Church than a mere hireling? How, think you, did he prove this? ' The good man,' said he, ' through a mistaken zeal, supports the impure Church of which he is a member, and thus unwittingly does evil; the hireling, on the other hand, by disgusting the sensible and well-inclined, hastens its downfall, and thus unwittingly does good.' What think you of this? For my own part, I will just remark that it

* It is interesting to see how another eminent Pedobaptist put the *onus probandi* of this question entirely on the other side: " If I should inform any one," says Coleridge, " that I had called at a friend's house, but had found nobody at home, the family having all gone to the play; and if he, on the strength of this information, should take occasion to asperse my friend's wife for unmotherly conduct, in taking an infant six months old to a crowded theatre, would you allow him to press on the words ' nobody ' and ' all the family ' in justification of the slander? Would you not tell him, that the words were to be interpreted by the nature of the subject, the purpose of the speaker, and their ordinary acceptation, and that he must, or might, have known that infants of that age would not be admitted into the theatre? Exactly so, with regard to the words, *he and all his household*. Had baptism of infants at that early period of the Gospel been a known practice, or had this been previously demonstrated, then indeed the argument, that in all probability there were infants or young children in so large a family, would be no otherwise objectionable than as being superfluous, and as sort of anti-climax in logic. But if the words are cited as the proof, it would be a clear *petitio principii*, though there had been nothing else against it. But when we turn back to the Scriptures preceding the narrative, and find repentance and belief demanded as the terms and indispensable conditions of Baptism, then the case above imagined applies in its full force." — *Vol. I., p. 335, Saml. Taylor Coleridge's "Complete Works." — Am. Pub.*

strengthens by experience an opinion I have long held. It is, that in the field of religious controversy the rankest and most poisonous weeds do spring. What a wretched thing is it that a man, in his zeal for truth, should run himself headlong into error; that in his haste to establish a few doubtful notions belonging to the head, he should starve the good, and indulge the evil, feelings of the heart!"

So Hugh Miller, the lay champion of the Free Church, was in his twenty-fourth year of the same opinion "concerning Church government" with the Baptists! Does this imply that he was at that time a Voluntary? I know not. His sentiments on the subject of religious controversy are also noteworthy. Were they modified by his subsequent experience of ecclesiastical discussion? I think not.

To Miller's letter of the 19th of August, Swanson replies on the 29th of the same month. Passing hastily over matters of minor importance, he comes to what lies nearest his heart. "I have experienced here great kindness among my Christian friends. Oh that I could with confidence rank you among the number! I cannot think that you are aware how near you are to my heart. Blessed be God that Christ is still nearer! I pray and hope that you will one day be one with me in him. I wait but for your confession to recognize you as a brother. . . . My dear Hugh, my metaphysical speculations are entirely exploded (oh, let me never cease to pray that I may be preserved from again setting up blind reason as a God to worship; thousands have perished at his shrine; why was I not left?), and, since exploded, I have learnt to take the word of God simply as I find it, and the consequence is peace and joy. I long much to see you. Oh, will you not accept of Christ? You believe the truth of God. See, then, the freeness and fulness of the gospel offer made to you. Believe the record, that God hath given to us eternal life, and this life in his Son; believe this, and all shall be well."

On the 2d of September, — almost as soon, therefore, as he can have received Swanson's letter, — Miller replies to it. He declares himself " exhausted, dull, lazy, sick, melancholy." and quite unable to write an interesting letter. For his reluctance to write there is, he confesses, another cause. " I feel that, after your earnest and affectionate exhortation, it would be something worse than unfriendly of me not to unbosom myself before you ; yet what have I to confess? Were I an unbeliever, though I would assur edly lose my friend by confessing myself one, still that con fession would be made. I would scorn to hold the affec tions of any one by appearing what I am not. Or if, on the other hand, I were a Christian in the true sense of the word, I hope I would have courage enough to avow my pro fession, not only to you or to those from whom I could expect nothing except kindness, but even to the proudest and boldest scorner. But what profession can the luke warm Laodicean make? — the man who, one moment, is as assured of the truth of the gospel of Christ as he is of his own existence, and who, in another, regards the whole scheme of redemption as a cunningly devised fable. It will not do! I am not at present collected enough to give you a faithful account of what is my religious belief; I will just say that, as far as the head is concerned, my creed is a sound one, but alas for the heart ! "

The remainder of the letter accords well with this profes sion of indifference, or at least of vacillation and vicissi tude, in spiritual affairs. He speaks of other matters, and bewails his bashfulness in society. " In that proper assur ance which is opposed to bashfulness," he says, " there is scarce a young girl in the country who is not my superior." He knows that this is a weakness, but declares that he can not help it. " In one of Shenstone's larger poems," he pro ceeds, " there is an exquisite description of a bashful man when in company ; and were it not that he is represented as possessed of talent and virtue, I would lay my hand on the page, and say, this is a portrait of H—— M——.

> " ' But ill-starred sense, nor gay nor loud,
> Steals soft on tiptoe through the crowd,
> Conveys his meagre form between,
> And slides like pervious air unseen,
> Contracts his known tenuity
> As though 'twere ev'n a crime to be,
> Nor ev'n permits his eyes to stray
> To win acquaintance in their way.
>
> In company, so mean his air,
> You scarce are conscious he is there,
> Till from some nook, like sharpened steel,
> Occurs his face's thin profile,
> Still seeming from the gazer's eye
> Like Venus newly bathed to fly.
>
> Disused to speak, he tries his skill,
> Speaks coldly and succeeds but ill,
> His pensive manner dulness deemed,
> His modesty reserve esteemed,
> His wit unknown, his learning vain,
> He wins not one of all the train.' "

Swanson receives this letter on the 5th of September. He answers it the same day. He implores his friend to get rid of the melancholy which preys upon his mind by a "full, free, and simple acceptation of the gospel. Pardon me, my dear friend," he adds, " when I say that I fear you have religious opinions not derived from the Bible. Read it as if you never heard a word concerning it before." On the 30th of September Miller writes again: "I am still employed on the chapel brae in hewing a second tombstone for Colonel G——. That spot is now beginning to lose its charms; every breeze which passes over it carries a shower of withered leaves upon its wings; the herbage is assuming a sallow hue, and I stand alone in the midst of desolation, in all except sublimity of feeling the prototype of Campbell's last man. I do not know whether I am advancing in wisdom as in years (I rather suspect not), but somehow the thought of death often presses upon me in these days. I look upon the little hillocks which are laid above men and women and children, the traits of whose features are pictured in my memory, and when by its aid I conjure up their forms when, gay and restless, they followed the businesses or the pleasures of life, and then when, in the eye of the imagination, I behold them stretched in the dark coffin, cold, and black, and mouldy, without form or motion, I pause and ask, What is this Death, this mighty Death, that turns mirth to sadness, that unnerves the arm of the strong and pales the cheek of the beautiful?

" I remember to have seen, many years ago, old Eben, the sexton, digging a grave. He raised a coffin, which, though much decayed, was still entire, and placed it on the earth he had thrown out. I was a mere boy at the time, and out of a foolish curiosity, when his back was turned, I raised with the edge of his spade the lid of the coffin. The appearance of the mouldering remains which it contained, nothing can erase from my memory. I see them even now before me, in all their sad and disgusting deformity, and still when I hear or read of the empire of death, — of the wrecks of death, or of the change which death works on the human frame, — imagination immediately reverts to a long, black skeleton, clothed over with a mouldy earth to which, in some places, the rotten grave-clothes are attached. This is a disgusting image, but it is not a useless one, for when, thinking of death, I bare my arm and look at the blue veins shining through the transparent skin, — when I look and think that the day may not, cannot, be far distant when it shall become as black and as mouldy as that of the skeleton, — I start, for there is something in the contrast which removes all the accumulation of commonplace which the habit of hearing and speaking at second hand of death hath cast upon that awful thing.

"But what is the fruit, you will ask, of these cogitations? Follow me a little farther and you shall see. If the soul be a mere quality affixed to matter, which shall die when that matter is changed from animate into inanimate, then, though the thought of the havoc which death works on the human frame tends to lower the pride of the haughty, it is not a harassing one to the philosopher. Life is full of evil and unhappiness; death is a state of rest. When the tyrant Edward invaded this country; when Wallace, its bravest defender, was betrayed and slain; when the carnage of Flodden filled Scotland with mourning, or the defeat of Pinkie with fear, — I was neither sad, nor angry, nor afraid, for I was not called into existence until twenty-four years ago. And in a few years after this, if the soul be not immortal, I shall again have passed (if I may use the expression) into a state of non-existence, and though my mouldering remains may raise horror in the breasts of the living, the vacuum which once existed shall not sympathize with them. But that the soul is immortal, if it be the same wise God that created the heavens and earth who formed man, I must believe; and if that soul, after it has departed from its fleshly nook, is to be punished or rewarded according to the deeds done in the body, — this I also must and shall believe; then death becomes not the herald of rest, but the messenger of judgment. Thus far unassisted reason can go. Socrates went still further, for, when other philosophers were raving of an absurd, because unattainable, virtue, by the possession of which men were to be made happy both in this world and the next, he taught of the evil that dwelleth in the human heart, and of the help which cometh from God. But it is to the pages of Revelation we must turn, if it be our desire to learn with certainty how to prepare for death by making the Judge our friend.

"You have often urged me with a friendly zeal, both in speech and by writing, to forsake sin and turn to God.

Your letters and conversations have had an effect, — I wish I could add the desired one. I give some of my time to the study of the Scriptures, and have become perhaps nearly as well acquainted as the mere theorist can be with the scheme of redemption. Nay, more, I pray. But the day-beam has not yet, I am afraid, dawned upon me, — the light vouchsafed is not a clear and steady one like the beam of the morning; it is rather like the reflection of lightning in a dark night, — a momentary glimpse succeeded by an hour of gloom. My prevailing disposition is evil, and though I have oftener than once experienced a feeling strange indeed to the human heart, — a feeling of love to God, — the cares of the world and the allurements of pleasure draw away my affections, and the old man is again put on.

"The town clock has struck the hour of twelve, — so, for the present, adieu!"

Swanson replies on the 9th of October. The speculative part of Miller's letter he passes by, and fixes on the statement that he had begun to pray. "Have you indeed, then," he exclaims, "set your face towards Zion? Have you indeed begun to call upon the name of the Lord? Feeble as your beginnings may be, can you doubt that he will hear you? Can you dare? Would you wish to draw back? . . . . You have now closed with Christ, and, closing with him, I trust closed more fully (if that were possible; and it was) with me. Oh, it is sweet to join heart and hand and to put them thus joined into the hand of Christ! . . . . O Hugh, I have not a single complaint to make; my cup is running over! With regard to the manner in which God will dispose of me, I am, at present, quite ignorant. I have no prospect, and no earthly friend who, while he would wish to do anything for me, has it in his power. Before the end of this session I believe I shall be without a shilling, and I have no hand to look to. No hand, did I say? Nay, I have the hand of Omnipotence to look to, and he will aid me. Oh, it is sweet to depend on him for everything coming directly from him!"

A month elapses before Hugh replies, and his answer has none of the warmth of feeling for which we might have looked. "After perusing your last letter," he writes, " I sat down to tell you that I was not a little alarmed by your recognizing me as a Christian brother; I then stated my grounds of alarm; and, willing to furnish you with a kind of data by which you would be enabled to judge of the spiritual state of your friend, I recommenced a historical detail of the fluctuating opinions of my mind for the last seven years. But I now see that a narrative so long, and in which I will require to be so careful of error, will engross more of my time than I can conveniently devote to it at present."

The " historical detail," here referred to, in so far as it appears to have ever been written down, is contained in an unfinished letter, dated October, 1826. It is a somewhat rough, though not a careless, sketch, and, from the expressions just quoted, a doubt may be reasonably entertained whether Miller considered it, even in the part which he completed, perfectly accurate. What is more to be regretted, it was never finished. The dark side of his spiritual history is portrayed in what he wrote, but the bright side and the transition between the dark and the bright continue unrevealed. The want, it is true, can, in all essential respects, be supplied from other letters, or from passages in his works. There is no ground for doubt as to the conclusion, theoretic or practical, at which he arrived. But a delineation by himself of his spiritual experience at this crisis of his religious history would have had a nice verisimilitude which no description by another hand can attain. It is important to observe that he takes the tone of one describing a process which has reached its issue; he believes himself to have "a changed heart," and he aims at explaining to his friend how the change took place. Every subsequent year of Miller's life bore testimony that, on this point, he was not mistaken. Here is what remains of the "historical detail:"—

"I know not in what words to confess that your last letter, friendly and affection-breathing as it was, alarmed and in some degree rendered me unhappy. You recognize, you address me as a Christian brother; and, when I look within and see how doubtful the signs of a radical change of heart are, when I see how little there is to justify even the limited profession I made when I last addressed you by writing, I tremble lest you are throwing away your affections on a deceiver who is now even less worthy of your friendship than when he confessed himself a stranger to Christ. But why tremble on this account? If I am a deceiver, I am not a wilful one; for the hypocrite only trembles when detected or on the verge of detection, and if, by mistaking an excited imagination for a changed heart, I deceive both my friend and myself, I am surely rather unfortunate than guilty.

"I have for some time had the intention of writing for your perusal a history of my mind, with its various and varying opinions for the last seven years. For this I have more than one reason. I would wish, by showing you what I am and what I have been, to furnish you with data from whence you might draw whatever conclusion your judgment or experience warranted. I would wish to give you a faithful picture of my mind, and thus add to your knowledge of human nature by casting light on the only point with which you are not already acquainted as well or better than myself. I would also wish, by calling to recollection, and then examining, the vague and foolish opinions that once formed my belief, to prevent the Tempter from reigning over me a second time by laws whose injustice I have discovered, or shaking me by quibbles of whose insolidity I have had experience.

" I believe I may term my education a religious one. I was examined in the Catechism by my uncles every Sabbath night, and forced to attend regularly at church. This, you will say, is a poor definition of the words religious education, but in nine cases out of ten it is all that is meant by them. As I advanced into the latter years of boyhood I became impatient of this restraint, and, after many struggles, in which I showed a fierceness and desperation of character worthy of the liberty for which I strove, I became, as some of my friends satirically termed me, a lad of my own will. As a lad of my own will, I was a Sabbath-breaker, and a robber of orchards; and, as strange, foolish thoughts, passages of Scripture, and questions on the subject of religion would at times either flash upon my recollection or rise in my mind, just for the sake of peace, I also became an atheist. A boy atheist is surely a strange and uncommon character. I was one in reality, for, possessed of a strong memory, which my uncles and an early taste for reading had stored with religious sentiments and stories of religious men, I was compelled, as I have already said, for peace' sake, either to do that which was right, or, by denying the truth of the Bible, to set every action, good or bad, on the same level, and I had chosen the latter as the more free and pleasing way. My mind, as you will see in the sequel of my story, long retained the bent which it at this time acquired; but my actions, restrained by a rising pride, by notions of honor, perhaps by a conscience which, though fast asleep, had its dreams, became less reprehensible. I became what the world calls honest; and, from a dislike of drink and noisy company, had all along preserved a habit of sobriety, but to every other vice to which a young man of sixteen is exposed, I was addicted. You are aware that, much earlier than this, I composed pieces in rhyme, which I called poems. One of the drawers of my desk is filled with copies of these youthful effusions, which I preserve both for the sake of the recollections attached to them, and for the history I can trace in them of the growth of my mind and its varying opinions. The short piece I here insert, with a few subsequent alterations, was written in my sixteenth year. You will see in it, confused with a good deal of mythologic nonsense, a confession of the school of morals to which I then belonged. What is said of wine and Bacchus, you are to recollect, is mere imitation : —

"HOW TO LIVE.

"Oh, free as air, light as the wind,
　　Let us spend Life's years away,
To coming evil wisely blind,
　　Still be glad when glad we may.
For what is philosophic lore,
　　What the schoolmen's boasted rules?
Go, sound it loud as ocean's roar, —
　　The cloak of knaves, the boast of fools.

"Bright wine and love shall banish care,
　　Pleasure all our thoughts employ;
Let Bacchus be our god of prayer,
　　Bacchus and the Paphian boy.
Let mirthful Momus, laughing, still
　　O'er our harmless feasts preside,
And lovely nymphs be there to fill
　　The cup to dry, grave lips denied.

"Thus years shall pass when age steals on,
　　Ere the last joys of life are gone;
Jocund, let us rise and say
　　Sweet has passed life's stormy day.
And when Time strides gravely in,
　　To warn us that our sands have run,

"Gay, ere fails our latest breath,
     Let our song be, ' Welcome Death.'
     When life, save pain, can nothing give,
     When wine disgusts, and cold is love,
     Rather than live in pain and fear,
     Welcome the shroud, the grave, the bier!"

" About a year after I had written this piece, I had several argumentative conversations with my cousin G. on the subject of religion. I boldly and impiously declared to him that I considered it as a cheat, and when he began to support his opinions, which were directly the reverse of mine, by Scripture quotations, I told him that I considered the Bible and Alcoran as of equal authority. I made use of some other imprudent and impious expressions at that time, which I still remember, and now heartily regret. G. was so much scandalized at what he then heard, that he threatened to inform my uncles and other friends, nay, more, every one who was in the least acquainted with me, of my scepticism. This alarmed me, for I had wisdom enough to see that, though the ' religious' be no numerous or formidable body, the prejudiced are ; and that men who were no better Christians than myself would look upon the professed atheist with horror and detestation. Notwithstanding his threat, he was silent on the subject of our conversations, but the recollection of it, and the anticipation of its consequences, had the effect of making me so prudent, that is, so hypocritical, that whenever religion became a subject of conversation in any company of which I formed one, I gave a passive assent to whatever was said in its favor.

" About the end of the year 1820 I had a fearful dream, which, for the time, had the effect of converting me into a kind of believer, — a believer of I knew not what. I dreamed I was wandering through a solitary and desert country ; that I was alone, restless, and unhappy. All at once the skies became dark and overcast, and a gloom like that of a stormy winter's evening seemed to settle over the face of nature. By one of those changes so common in dreams, the country appeared no longer unpeopled; but the figures I saw were so dark, so indistinct, so silent, that in my terror I regarded them not as men, but spirits who were wandering about in unhappiness until the time came in which they were to reanimate the bodies in which they once dwelt. A fearful presentiment arose in my mind that the day of judgment was at hand; I felt the petrifying influence of despair pervade every faculty, yet, though my agony was extreme, I could neither weep nor pray. In a little time the clouds began to disperse, and through a clear, blue opening I perceived a large, cloudy scroll spread on the face of the heavens, which, with a flickering, undulating motion, at one moment resembled a dark, sulphureous flame, and at another reminded me of a banner waving in the wind. I fixed my eyes upon it in fear and astonishment, and perceived that in its centre a few dark characters were inscribed. I strove to decipher them, but could not. In a few seconds, however, the coloring of the scroll deepened gradually, as the hues of the rainbow increase from dimness to brilliancy. I read its startling motto, 'Take warning!' and awoke. My mind was dreadfully agitated. The sweat, which, during my dream, had flowed from every pore, was cooled upon my brow, but my heart was still burning. In my terror I vowed that, for the future, I would be no longer a sinner, and I began to pray; but my prayers were addressed, not to the God of the Christian, but to the God of the heathen philosopher. I was awakened to a painful consciousness of sin. I had heard that God was merciful, and on the strength of that attribute I addressed myself to him; but alas! I did not know that his justice is as infinite as his mercy, and that no sinner can be accepted by him unless he appeal to the sufferings and righteousness of that Saviour whom his sins have pierced.

" The recollection of my dream haunted me for about ten days, during which time I prayed. A natural bashfulness withheld me from making any show of sanctity, but my heart was very proud of its newly acquired purity, and I regarded myself as a much better man than many of my acquaintances. But the foundation on which my hopes were raised was not one of sand, — a sandy foundation would have served me until the day of the tempest, whereas the thin vapor upon which I had built sunk of itself without being once assailed. Suffice it to say that, as my fears subsided and my pride increased, my prayers became more and more a matter of form, until at length they ceased altogether, and except that I believed in the being of a God, and continued to see a beauty in moral virtue, I became, in thought and feeling and action, the same man I had formerly been.

" In the working season of the two following years I wrought and resided at Conon-side, — a gentleman's seat and farmsteadings, situated on a bank of the River Conon, near where it falls into the Cromarty Frith. When there, there was no one for whose good opinion I cared a pin within twenty miles of me, so I felt myself at liberty to do or say whatever I thought proper. In a short time I became a favorite with my brother workmen. " He is a good-natured, honest, knowing fellow," they would say, " but desperately careless of Church." This was just the character I wished to bear ; as for Church attendance, I thought it rather a dubious virtue. Indeed, I had seen too much of the prejudices of mankind, and knew too little of true Christianity, to think otherwise.

" When at Conon-side, I had an opportunity of studying several characters of the grave, serious cast, but the knowledge of them which I acquired there did me no good. One, a Mr. M——, was a man of a grave, taciturn humor, whose definition of the word ' Christian' would be, as I apprehended, ' a hearer of the gospel for Mr. McDonald's sake.' He was exceeding reserved and unsocial in his manners, and little loved by his fellow-workmen. Once or twice I have seen him grow very angry when some parts of the conduct of his favorite preacher were censured, — censured, too, as I thought, with reason. There was another of the workmen with whom I wrought, who was of the grave, serious cast. He contributed quarterly to the support of the Bible Society, was regular in his attendance at church, and reproved swearing or indecent language every time he chanced to hear it among his companions. But it did not escape my observation that this man was so censorious that not even his brother saint, Mr. M——, was exempted from the severity of his animadversions, and so proud of his purity of life that the errors and misconduct of others afforded him pleasure. Perhaps he regarded them as foils to the virtues he possessed.

" Besides these two there were some others who made a profession of religion with whom I became partially acquainted ; but the tenor of their lives was ill qualified to impress my mind with a high opinion of the sanctifying influences of Christianity. One was a hard, austere man, of obtuse feelings, who seemed determined, whatever he thought of the world to come, to make the most he could of the present ; a second was silly and weak ; and a third was what I termed a Sabbath Christian, — that is, one who attends church, calls the preacher precious man, can tell a great many of the strange legends of the Scottish Church, and reprobates the poor wretches who prefer common sense to fanaticism. And are these men Christians? thought I. I have often heard divines bid that part of their congregations which they termed men of the world look at the life of the Christian, and grow convinced of the power and truth of Christianity by that example which is superior to precept. I have obeyed them. I have observed his actions, and through these actions have striven to discover his motives, and what have I found? In good truth, the philosopher who sees clearly that he who believes and he who does not believe, only differ in that the one practises the grave and the other the gay vices of humanity, may well laugh at the pretensions of these divines, and tell them that they either speak of they know not what, or wilfully deceive because it is their interest to do so.

" I remember one Sunday, after my companions had gone to church, and I remained behind, as was my custom, that, to pass away the time, I took a solitary walk in the woods of Conon-side. The day was pleasant, but, from a kind of nervous melancholy which hangs pretty often on my spirits, and is, as I believe, constitutional, I could not enjoy it. I felt quite unhappy, and after having had recourse to every species of wonted amusement, sat down on a green knoll, in despair of enjoying solitude for that day. A train of the darkest thoughts began to rise and pass through my mind. I looked upon what I had done in the past, I thought of the unhappiness of the present, I formed surmises of the future. There was a voice from within which incessantly whispered in my ear, ' You are doing wrong! you are doing wrong! and how then can you expect pleasure?' and so miserable did I feel from these cogitations and these questionings, that I started from my seat, and strove to dissipate them by strong bodily exertion. In a few hours after, my spirits had regained their usual tone, and I could look back upon what I had felt, and say. ' Have I experienced what men call an awakened conscience? What, then, is conscience? The breast of the murderer and the dishonorable, mean man may well be the haunts of remorse; but surely, with one who neither does nor wishes any man ill, conscience is but the ashes of early prejudices raked together by a disordered imagination.'

"In the latter end of the autumn of this year (1822) I wrought and resided at Pointzfield for several weeks. My constitution is naturally delicate, and by building in stormy weather on a wet, marshy spot of ground, I caught a severe cold, which hung about me for several weeks; I felt my strength wasting away; my breast became the seat of a dull, oppressive pain, and, imagining I was becoming consumptive, I began seriously to think of death. So assured was I at this time of approaching dissolution that even through the perspective of hope I could only look forward on a few short months of life. and, as I could not bring myself to doubt of a separate existence of soul or of a judgment according to deeds done in the body, I began seriously to think of a preparation for death. But how was this preparation to be made? I knew prayer to be the only language by which the sinner could intercede with the Deity for pardon; but then experience had shown me how unable I was of myself to bring my mind into the frame of devotion, or to preserve that frame unchanged when it was produced by fear, disgust, and the mingling dictates of reason. At length I bethought me of an expedient which I hoped would preserve me from that falling off or apostatizing, of which I had experience two years before: for, awakening the sincere fervency of feeling which my expedient was to render lasting, I had before me the fear of death. For the three previous years, when I had freely and seriously pledged my word in a matter of importance, to any of my brother men. I had a pride of rigidly adhering to it. From this I concluded that, were I to pledge myself to God by oath, I would have a restraining bond upon me strong enough to preserve me for the future from known sin. I would thus be shut up by every principle of honor to serve God, — of loving him I had no idea. I made and took my vow to be I knew not what, called God to witness it, and for a few following days persisted in praying twice a day. But prayer soon became an irksome duty; proud thoughts over which I had no control, and strong desires that would not be repressed by a few light words, came rushing on my mind in a mingled torrent, and swept before them every vain resolve. To add to their strength my health began to amend, and it not only appeared an impracticable, but even a foolish, thing to strive any longer to be religious.

" I passed the winter of this year and the spring of the following one at home, and there became acquainted with an old companion of my uncles. He had resided at Edinburgh for many years, and, though a clever, was neither a steady nor respectable man, but for the sake of becoming acquainted with his character, which was eccentric in the extreme, I courted his company and conversation. At Edinburgh he had been a member of one of those deistical clubs so common in large towns; and, by a natural quickness, and from the habit of speaking at their meetings, had acquired the faculty of arguing extempore with a good deal of skill. My uncles, whose principles and opinions were in almost every particular the reverse of his, impressed by early recollections, still continued attached to him, but, as might be expected, frequently attacked opinions which he was by no means slow to defend. The doctrine of predestination, that hobby-horse of disputants, was brought frequently on the carpet, as was also the doctrine of universal, as opposed to partial, redemption. At first I merely listened to these verbal controversies, but seeing that my uncles, though well-grounded in the doctrines of Christianity, were ill-qualified to answer every objection raised against it by a veteran quibbler, out of a desire of assisting them, I set myself to examine the different bearings of the doctrines they defended. Predestination first engaged me. I read all that is said of it in Scripture, drew conclusions from the prescience of God, and from Plato's Dialogues of Socrates, and some other philosophic writers, and endeavored to produce data from whence to show that predestination is not a doctrine peculiar to revealed religion. I had long looked upon controversial divinity as the worst kind of nonsense; and since my argumentative conversation with my cousin G. had entertained an antipathy against verbal controversy of every kind; this, added to a hesitating manner of speech, and a consciousness of an inability to preserve my ideas from becoming confused when I waxed warm on any subject, after all my preparation, withheld me from attacking my brother deist.

"Had any one told me at that time that I was in reality brother in belief to a deist, I would have complained of injustice. In fact, my opinions were so wavering that, with a due regard to truth, I could not tell what I did or did not believe. I saw there were two schools of deism.— the high and the low. Epicurus of the ancient philosophers and Hume of the modern, men who, while they remained sceptical on the subject of future rewards and punishments, and of the Providence of God, cherished virtue for its own sake, both by example and precept, I regarded as members of the first; while I looked upon the brood of half-bred wits, who, with Paine at their head, battled with religion because it gave a deeper and stronger sanction to the laws of morality, as the masters of the second. The leaders of the former I considered to be good, wise men (indeed, I am still readier to regret their defects than censure them), while the whole body which composed the latter I regarded as a band of conspirators against all that is good or noble in human nature. I looked upon the Edinburgh deist as a pupil of the school last described; indeed, the irregularity of the life he led lent this opinion a strong sanction.

"The more I thought and read, the more wavering and unsettled my opinions became. I began to see that the precepts inculcated by the Christian faith are equal if not superior in purity to those taught in the school of philosophy; but then the strange, mysterious doctrines which mingled with these precepts had in them something repulsive. I could believe in many things which I did not understand; but how could I believe in things evidently not beyond the reach of reason, but directly opposed to it? I could believe that man is either a free agent, or chained down by the decrees of God to a predestined line of conduct; but how could I believe that he was at once free and the child of necessity? And yet the contradiction (as it appeared) seemed to me to be the doctrine of the Bible.

"I regarded the main doctrine of Christianity as one of those which lie not beyond the reach of reason, but, as I have said, are directly opposed to it. How, thought I, can one man who is a criminal be pardoned and rewarded because another who is none has, after meriting reward, been punished? How can it be said that he who thus pardons the guilty and punishes the innocent is not only just, but that he even does this that he may become just and merciful? It appeared still more strange than even this that the only way of becoming virtuous was, not by doing good and virtuous deeds, but by believing that Christ's death was an atonement for sin, and his merits a fund of righteousness for which they who thus believed were to be rewarded. Certainly, thought I, if the Christian religion be not a true one, it is not a cunningly devised fable; for its mysteries are either not far enough removed from the examination of the rational faculties, or too directly opposed to the conclusions which they must necessarily form. The mystery of the Trinity I regarded as an exception to this; the nature of God is so little known to man that I could neither believe nor doubt it."

In this abrupt and unsatisfactory manner the document ends. It will appear in the sequel that evidence exists in other quarters, enabling us to trace the essential facts of Miller's spiritual history.

CHAPTER VII.

POVERTY, HONORABLE AND DISHONORABLE — FIRST IMPRES-
SIONS OF THE REV. MR. STEWART — LOOKS INTO HIS
FATHER'S BIBLE — THE SELFISH THEORY OF MORALS —
NEW-YEAR'S-DAY MUSINGS — IMPORTANT COMMENT UPON
AND ADDITION TO THESE TEN DAYS AFTERWARDS — THE
CHANGE EFFECTED IN HIS SPIRITUAL STATE.

ONE or two threads of our biographical narrative have slipped through our hands, and it will be necessary to gather them up before proceeding with the delineation of Miller's religious experience. Swanson, as we saw, alluded to his prospects of pecuniary support, and exulted in his trust in God. This was in October. In November Miller replied. " You tell me that you are becoming (like myself) very poor, but you also inform me that you are very happy. I know by experience that simple, unambitious poverty and happiness are not such enemies as is generally imagined ; but, oh, how I detest the mean, cringing poverty that prompts a man of God's forming to cast himself in the dust before his brother man ; that compels him to smile at the stupid, cruel jibe that wounds him ; that teaches his knee to bend and ties his tongue. This is poverty of spirit. I merely detest it ; but I cannot think of those mean insults which, coming from the little great, make poverty truly bitter, without wishing for the return of the earliest days of barbarism. My master in the rudest stage of society would have, at least, two of nature's advantages, he would be brave and strong; but, in its present state, he may be at once an idiot, coward, and knave."

Swanson had asked for information about the Rev. Mr. Stewart. The account of his relations with his parishioners, and the estimate of his character, which Miller gives in reply, are very different from what he would subsequently have written. " When, after leaving Edinburgh, I returned to this place, I scarce met one of my old acquaintances who did not tell me of the extraordinary parts and merits of their new minister. He was so humble, said his admirers, that he did not, like many foolish parsons, speak of the priesthood as a body of good, perfect men, who were sorely toiling to convert vile lay sinners, — no, when he spoke of sinners, he said You and I. His sermons, too, with all the solidity of orthodoxy itself, were so interesting and eloquent that no one could sleep in his church. The very reserve of his character was praised; it was bashfulness; it was modesty. This general opinion has now given place to another as general. His humility, it is said, was affected, for his reserve is not that of bashfulness, but of pride. No one gives less to the poor, or is fonder of money. His very sermons are now different from what they were once, — they still display talent, but they are cold and unanimated, and ill-calculated to rouse or comfort his hearers. These two contrary opinions were and are those entertained by the middle class of Mr. Stewart's parishioners; do not imagine, however, that either of them in every particular was or is mine. I know too little of his character as a man to say whether he be generous or niggardly, proud or humble; but, as a minister, I believe I may dare decide of his merits. His sermons are the offspring of natural talent polished by learning. Few men understand better what subjects are susceptible of that eloquence which at once engages the understandings, imaginations, and hearts of men. His views of a subject are generally clear, and his style, though apparently unstudied, is pure and express- ive. But, on the other hand, he is an unequal, ofttimes a careless, preacher. His sermons were such as I have de- scribed only for the first ten or twelve months after he received the presentation to this parish. At particular seasons, such as the time of a sacrament, he still exerts himself, and I am cheered by flashes of that spirit the blaze of which once delighted me ; but his common, every- day discourses are dry and doctrinal. They address them- selves to the understanding, but not to the heart. The knowledge they display of human nature is often vague and general, and such as is to be taught by books. Of that partic- ular and striking kind which is to be acquired by the study of our own hearts, or of the characters of others, there is to be found in them but few instances. That cold reserve of character, which has now become so disgusting to Mr. Stewart's parishioners, is surely an unfortunate thing in a minister of the gospel. In a private individual, though often feared and reviled, it has its apology ; but it has none in the man who is bound down both by the command of God, and every principle of honesty recognized among men, to devote his whole life to the gaining of souls from Satan. What is merely a singularity in the parishioner is a crime in the minister."

Of the seriousness of Miller's mood at this time we have traces in his correspondence with his other friend. He has, he tells William Ross, but two friends, and can as ill afford to lose one of them as he could to lose " an eye or an arm."—" Alas ! Willie," he says in a letter of December 8th, " whether wise or foolish, we are no longer boys ; last October a note of my father's handwriting in the first page of the big Bible, which was once his and is now mine, informed me that I had then completed my twenty-fourth year. Since the first page of that Bible furnishes me with a fact of so serious a nature, do you think it would be lost time should I spend a few minutes every day in considering the facts which are laid down in its other pages? My friend, J. Swanson, assures me it would not."

In a letter to Swanson of December 15th, we meet with the following decided repudiation of what is called the selfish theory of morals : "Are you still," he asks, " a member of that school of philosophy which resolves every feeling expressive of affection into mere selfishness? I hope not. I have, ever since I heard of it, hated it as heartily as ever I did any of the schools which perplexed me in the days of my boyhood, and the more I examine myself by patiently tracing the connection which subsists between my feelings and the circumstances which excite them, the more am I convinced that selfishness does not supply all the ties of that connection. . . . I hate the selfish school of philosophy. I wish I could hate it as practically as St. Paul did."

On the 1st of January, 1827, he writes to Ross. His reflections are not of a jocund character : " The first sun of the year has not yet risen, but I have trimmed and lighted my lamp, and set myself down to write by the assistance of its little red flame. . . . Many are the reflections which a closing and an opening year suggest. You have often seen that Egyptian symbol, an adder holding its tail in its mouth ; and I am sure that you have observed that the slender circular body of that adder is but a dull-looking thing, varied as it only is by a slight difference in bulk, or a still slighter difference in the loops of its scaly coat ; while, upon that part of it where its head and tail meet, the eye can rest with pleasure. It is said that this adder is a symbol of the year ; and certainly as the eye is attracted more by its head and tail than by any part of its body, so the attention of the moralist is excited more by the beginning and close of the year than by any of its intermediate parts. The moralist, do I say? Alas! true moralists are by no means common characters, yet serious reflection at such a season as this is not confined to a class of men so extremely rare. I remember that at a stage of life little removed from childhood, on a New-Year's day, not all the halfpence my friends gave me could make me happy. A certain vague regret for the days of sport that had passed away, and a fearful anticipation of the days of care and toil which I knew were coming on, conspired to cast a gloom over my mind. But in this the boy indulged in a folly not always avoided by the man. When I looked at the head and tail of the snake, I thought of the sting which in reality both of them bear, but not of the antidote growing near. I now perceive that it was unwise thus to suffer the clouds of unavailing regret and dismal antici- pation to cast their shade over my enjoyments. He who taught that there is but one thing truly needful taught also that 'sufficient unto the day is the evil thereof.' It is an opinion of mine, that all the drinking and feasting so com- mon at this season were at first resorted to for the sake of dissipating gloomy thoughts like those with which I was once perplexed. The more I think of this, the more I am confirmed of its truth. Judging from experience, it appears reasonable enough that the man who is unprepared to die should strive to forget that he is mortal ; but it is monstrous to suppose that, deeming, as most do, death the greatest evil, he should yet joy at its approach. If an opening year warned a boy of the toils which awaited him, it may surely whisper to men of death. And it does! Get one of the most stupid of those who are revellers at this season to make a single moral remark, and that one will be, that he is now by a year nearer his grave than he was twelve months ago. From reflections like these, though custom, by giving its sanction to the festivities of the season, has, after its usual manner, obscured every circumstance of its own beginning and growth, I can regard that loud huzza which has penetrated even to this recess, as that of madness raised to drown the deep, low murmurings of thought. Many are the reflections which a closing and opening year suggest, and yet the writer who would set himself to collect and arrange these would find that there is little to be said of the years which commenced and concluded seven hours ago, which has not been already said (perhaps well said) of some preceding ones. . . . But in morals, regarded as the rules of life, there is nothing commonplace. Filled with a desire of making new acquirements and a love of novelty, man is generally moving onward in knowledge, — there is a law in his very nature which urges him on ; but for that which is morally good he has no natural inclination. Before he quit his vicious habits he must be threatened with the horrors of eternal punishment, — nay, perhaps made to feel in conviction a foretaste of these horrors. Before he commence a course of virtuous actions, he must be presented with the strongest motives, assurance of eternal peace and joy, and, what is necessarily superior to any motive, he must be powerfully assisted by the Spirit of God. Ah, my dear friend, there can surely be no commonplace in morals, whether by the word we mean virtuous actions, or the precepts which enjoin or the considerations which enforce them. The uncertainty of time and the certainty of death, the guilt and madness of misspending time, and the sure coming of judgment, all of these are topics extremely commonplace for an author, but truths which to every human creature are important in the highest degree. I cannot look back upon the past year with a feeling of pleasure, and yet

I should look upon it with one of thankfulness. I am certain I have not marked it by a single meritorious deed, and yet, by the good mercy of God, I have been preserved from actions notoriously vicious. I have at times, I trust, by his help, cleared my heart of its viler affections, and repressed its evil desires. I have besought his assistance, and experienced within me the workings of gratitude. But, alas! at other times I have wilfully opened the floodgates of passion; I have courted rather than resisted temptation; I have apologized for known sin in my heart; and in thought many times oftener than once indeed have I committed evil."

Thus by the "little red flame," in the chill hour before the dawn, on the first day of 1827, does Hugh Miller jot down for his friend his stern and sad communings with himself. The drear glimmer of the lamp-light is traceable on the page, and the remarks on the festivities of Christmas and New Year's day are too harshly puritanic for his sunnier and wiser hour; but the severity of his self-judgment, and the deep and humble piety which pervades the letter, makes it valuable as a revelation of his state of mind at the time. Let us therefore proceed: —

"In that awful day when things shall appear as they really are, how shall I apologize for the evil I have committed in that portion of time which was measured out by the past year? The more I consider the more clearly do I see that the evil I have committed in it was of a positive, the good merely of a negative, kind. All that I can urge in my defence is, that I might have entered still deeper into evil than I have done. But will this defence serve? Were it to serve in an earthly court, the vilest criminal could with justice allege it; and will God, in whom dwelleth, and from whom cometh, all wisdom, accept it from his creatures? Alas! hope itself cannot build on a foundation

like this. If mankind have no better plea they are surely
lost; yet self-love, in the very face of reason, whispereth
the contrary. Ah, William, there can be no greater deceiver than self-love, — no flatterer more dangerous, — for
there is none we suspect less. Often, when we think of a
future state of being, of an Almighty Judge, and of our
own appearance before him, in our imaginations we not
only picture that Judge as merciful, but we even conceive
of him as possessed of feelings and .partialities, and consequently of weaknesses, like ourselves. We deem him to be
One who will look upon our faults with the same favorable
eye with which we ourselves regard them, — as One who will
give us credit for the merits which we think we possess.
Alas! we do not consider that one half of these imagined
merits are fictitious, the children of our fancy; and that
the other half of them consist of natural talents and pro-
pensities which have, for wise ends, been given us, but
which we have misapplied. And what, then, remains?
As I have said already, I must say again, that man's best
plea, if he ground his defence on works, is, that he has not
committed all the evil which he might have committed;
and I must say again that, if mankind have no better plea
than this, they are surely lost. But, dear William, Christianity is not the cunningly devised fable I once thought it.
There is a Saviour, and he who believes upon him with
that true, earnest belief which conquereth evil, shall, for
the sake of the sufferings of that Saviour, have his sins forgiven him, and for the sake of his righteousness be rewarded. I once thought this an absurd doctrine; now,
though I have more experience of men and things than I
ever had before, and though my reason has strengthened,
and is, as I hope, still strengthening, I can regard it as a
wonderful display of the wisdom of God.

"Many are the reflections which an opening and a closing year suggest! How impenetrably dark is that cloud which hangs over the future! How dubious and uncertain do the half-remembered incidents of the past appear! And what, since we have so little left us to bear witness of the past, — since we have nothing to assure us that in this body the future shall be ours, — what is that present time which we dare challenge as our own? Is it a day, an hour, a minute, a moment? No, it is simply a line of division, a thing which has neither solidity nor extension, breadth nor thickness. And is this nonentity all we can call our own? Cowley, in his essay on the danger of procrastination, gives a translation of an epigram of Martial, which, as it falls in with my present train of thought, and is, of itself, very ingenious, I shall here insert. By-the-by, I recommend Cowley to you as an excellent and shrewd fellow, who, if you court his company and conversation, will, I am sure, give you much pleasure, and, perhaps, some instruction. He is a true poet, though of a rare school. But the epigram : —

> " ' To-morrow you will live, you always cry;
> In what far country does this morrow lie?
> That 'tis so mighty long ere it arrive,
> Beyond the Indies does this morrow live?
> 'Tis so far-fetched, this morrow, that I fear
> 'Twill be both very old and very dear.
> To-morrow I will live, the fool does say.
> To-day itself's too late; the wise lived yesterday.'

" What is, or where is, to-morrow? is the question of the Roman epigrammatist. I would in like manner ask what is, or rather what was, yesterday? It has left a few marks upon the face of the earth. Yesterday, a field was ploughed, a house built, and a grave dug; and these marks and scarce anything else make yesterday different from the dream of yesternight; but the grave must very soon be closed, the ploughed field will soon become a piece of green sward, and to Him with whom a thousand years are as a day it will appear but a short space when the foundations of the house will become a piece of green sward also. Yet things like these are the monuments of yesterday. But what is yesterday itself? what was it, rather? It was a space of time, measured by the sun, which was given to men that in it they might prepare for death; and instead of preparing for death, the whole power of their bodies and every energy of their souls have been employed in building and ploughing and in other such occupations, even though they saw graves opening and closing before them. What though those wasting monuments of yesterday which men have raised or inscribed on the face of the earth were eternal,—what has the soul of man to do with these external things? If his soul be immaterial, as many judicious philosophers affirm, then, though mysteriously connected with a material body, it can surely have no proper and natural connection with the earth in which vegetables grow or the stones with which houses are built. But I am quaintly deducing a moral from an uncertainty, which I can simply and with ease deduce from a known truth. I am also speaking rather loosely of the particular provision to be made for the soul, and making no allowance for that which must of necessity be made for the body. Be it sufficient that I mention the last, since the proportion which the interests of the body bear to those of the soul must be that which finite bears to infinite.

"The particular provision which must be made for the soul is, as I firmly believe, specified in those revealed books which compose the Old and New Testaments. The uncertainty to which I refer is the immateriality of the soul. The truth—the truths, I should rather say—which concern the separate existence of the soul and the resurrection of the body, are those of God.

"And now I will just conclude, for I become, though very serious, very tiresome, by remarking that, since time past is little more than a shadow, since time coming is something less, it is man's true wisdom to entrench himself within himself, — not in selfishness; it is selfishness which prompts him to wander, and in his wanderings to form connections with unfit objects such as earth and stones, — not in selfishness, but with a love to God greater, and a love to his neighbor equal to that which he bears to himself, entrenching himself in a good conscience and a rational (that is, a scriptural) hope of salvation, perceiving that to himself his own soul is everything. And, dear William, is it not truly everything? All that to us remains of the past lies in the storehouses of our memories or the books of our consciences; all the surmisings which we form of the future are drawn from the experiences of the past, which we have laid up in these storehouses; while our imaginations sit retired, each in its own recess, drawing pictures of these experiences, and of the images which are preserved along with them, joining or disjoining them at pleasure. Oh, how strange and varied are the powers of that soul which is destined to immortality! It can be made of itself, just as we deal with it, either a heaven or a hell. And now I have done. No, not yet. I must, by quoting Shakespeare, forestall some of your remarks.

"'When I did hear
The motley fool thus moral on the time,
My lungs began to crow like chanticleer,
That fools should be so deep contemplative;
And I did laugh sans intermission
An hour by his dial.'"

This remarkable letter was not sent away at once. On the 10th of the month Hugh took it up, and added a few words. The "thoughts and modes of expression" seem, he says, as new to him "as if they had been found by some other person." From this he infers that, if he and his two friends made copies of their letters, the volume containing them, if of no great interest to third parties, would be not only interesting but extremely useful to the correspondents. "You may see," he proceeds, "that I am bent on making this experiment." Miller carried out his intention to a very considerable extent, and seems never, while he resided in Cromarty, to have grudged the labor of copying for preservation what he wrote.

Reverting to his letter, he remarks justly that it is "too much in the style which a preceptor would assume," while some of the observations "are commonplace and ill connected, and others of them unpardonably quaint." He assures Ross that the preceptorial tone is "only in seeming, not in reality, and that he does not suppose his correspondent to be ignorant of anything he has written. "The blockhead who sets himself up as an adviser of others is always one who is very far indeed beyond the power of advice to reclaim." By way of practical conclusion to the whole matter we have the following: "But why, you may ask, why then write me that which I already know? The question, though a simple, is truly a hard one, and I can answer it in no other way than by saying that I wrote from my feelings; that, from seeing the connection which the passing time and my wasting life have together, I was insensibly led to think of time and eternity, life and death, and, as I was, when my mind was thus occupied, writing my friend, to commit these thoughts to paper for his perusal. But besides general there are in these pages particular facts. I have told you that what I now believe I did not once believe, and I have told you how I have determined, relying on the help of God, to make the doctrines of Christianity the rule of my belief, its precepts that of my conduct. Ah, William, how easy it is to write of virtuous deeds! how difficult to perform them! How easy is it to make a good resolve! how difficult to abide by one! But the power, truth, and goodness of God are infinite, and he has promised to give his Holy Spirit to them that ask it."

From this point Hugh Miller never receded. A profound change had passed over his spiritual nature, a change none the less penetrating or pervasive that its operation had taken place in the silent chambers of his soul and had manifested itself in few external signs. Through no paroxysms of self-accusing agony did he make his way into the temple of his spiritual rest. By no raptures of religious enthusiasm did he announce his arrival at his Father's house. With the deliberate assent of reason, conscience, and feeling he embraced the Gospel of Christ, and solemnly cast in his lot with those who confessed Christ before men. On this point there was to be no further debate. By one supreme act of resolution he defined the future of his soul's life. Aided, as he reverently believed, by the Divine Spirit, he placed his trust in the power, truth, and goodness of the Infinite One, as revealed in Jesus of Nazareth. But the religion of Miller, though from this time it lay entwined with the deepest roots of his being and was the supreme and determining element in his character, came little to the surface. It was an unseen force, a hidden fire, influencing him at all moments, but never obtruded on the public eye. It would have been offensive to all the instincts of his modest and manly nature to unveil the secret places of his soul to the general observer.

The reader may have remarked that, in his letters to Ross, Miller assumes that part of Mentor, which, in the other correspondence, is taken so decisively by Swanson. The influence emanates from Swanson, and Hugh passes it on to Ross. His relations with the latter appear to have been of a more tenderly confidential character than his relations with the former.

CHAPTER VIII.

HUGH MILLER, then, as we meet him on the threshold of his twenty-sixth summer, has passed through the stages of boyhood and youth, with their changes of mood and development of faculty, and acquired that fundamental type of character which he subsequently retained. Steadily prosecuting the enterprise of self-culture, he is animated by the purest spiritual ambition, and experiences, in faculties invigorated and knowledge increased, that deep joy which is the student's reward. He has derived, it is scarce necessary to say, inestimable advantage from the completion of that religious process which had long been going on in his mind. The event which he would have called his conversion, and pronounced of transcendent importance in relation to all other occurrences in his life, has taken place. He knows what he believes. The atmosphere of his soul is clear and calm, and the unfathomable azure of heaven touches with softening radiance all its clouds. Placid resolution, energy peacefully fronting the tasks of life, a thoughtful gayety and smiling fortitude, attest the genial

228

firmness with which he now wields the sceptre of his mental realm.

A letter to Ross, dated May, 1828, bears some reflection of the peace and clearness to which he had attained. This letter, indeed, does much to compensate for the loss of which we had to complain in last chapter.

"I was employed in the church-yard in hewing a tomb-stone, at which, as I wrought late and hard, I fatigued myself considerably, when my cousin George Munro brought me your letter. There was scarce light enough to read it, the evening had so far advanced; the little I did decipher of it, however, acted upon me as a spell. I forgot the labors of the past day, and, in short, everything except that I was happy in my friend, and had much cause of gratitude to my God. Surely the best of his gifts, if we except the great gift of the Son and the Spirit, is a true friend! Everything temporal must decay and perish. The soul, if it dwells long in the body, must see many of the things of the material world, upon which it puts a value, because it deems them conducive or essential to its happiness, dropping away, or so changing as to be no longer matters of comfort or use. Even supposing them of a less transient or changeable nature, it is certain they are completely lost to the soul when it separates from the body, that piece of earth being the only medium through which it can enjoy them. It is not thus with friendship. The soul cannot decay, and we have assurance from Scripture that that which we term death is not to those who love God a death to affection. I trust that in the friend to whom I now write, I have one whom I will love and by whom I shall be beloved forever. Is not this a noble hope, and does it not deserve to be cherished?

"I have read somewhere (in Byron's 'Don Juan,' if I mistake not) that virtue is but another name for romance.

Unbelief alone could have made a remark like this, but I think it so shrewd that, were there no such thing as Revelation, and consequently nothing like assurance of a future state of rewards and punishments, I would at once assent to its truth, so far as what I may term active virtue is concerned. I make a distinction when I say active, the passive being essential to the happiness which Epicurus sought after. Believing, as I assuredly hope I do, in Revelation, I shall dare imitate this remark so far as to say that romance is the shadow of religion, and religion the truth of romance; and, if you have patience enough to follow me, I shall endeavor to explain what I mean when I say so. We both know from experience the character of the romantic man. He is one who casts the reins to his imagination, and believes in all the promises that are given him by hope. He is a day-dreamer that lives in an ideal world of his own creation. If of a kind, unsuspicious temperament, his dreams are of a peaceful description. Love and friendship are his guiding stars.

> " ' He hopes a Sylph in every dame,
> A Pylades in every friend; '

and the world of his dreams, the world which these noble beings inhabit, is so far from resembling that one of which other people have experience, that neither pain, sorrow, accident, nor the evils which folly and villany produce, have any part in it. If the visionary be of a venturous, restless spirit, and imbued with love of fame, the world presented in his dreams is of a less quiet and guiltless disposition, but, to balance its disadvantages, he beholds himself as a god in that world. He sees himself a conqueror over all those whom he hates or fears, and an object of admiration to all those whom he loves. Such are the dreams of romance, and him who indulges in such we term romantic.

The people of the world, who in general do not abound in good nature, make his folly the butt of their ridicule, and the realities of life, which to a man of this cast are misfortunes, are sure to make sport of it. But religion is the truth of romance. It promises more than hope does, and it performs all that it promises. We are given to know with assurance that our eyes have never seen, neither have our hearts conceived, a blessedness equal to that which God has prepared for those that love him. The glories of heaven are too bright for our conceptions, but this we know, that in the future world we shall associate with none except the good, and that we shall love them, and be beloved by them. This is just a fulfilment of the highest promise which hope gives the visionary. In heaven we shall also hold close communion with God. There is nothing like this in all the provinces of romance. We know, too, that in heaven misfortune shall have no place, and that we shall be there triumphant over all that we now fear and all that is evil, over death and hell and temptation. As for fame, we are assured that there is joy in heaven over one sinner that repenteth. 'Well done, good and faithful servant,' is the address of the Omnipotent to the man who by his works has glorified His name. I need not follow this subject further; I have said enough to show what I mean by saying that romance is the shadow of religion, and religion the truth of romance.

"Religion, my dear friend, is a very different thing from what the people of the world think it. Four years ago I deemed the love of God a passion altogether chimerical. When I looked towards the sky, I saw that the sun was a glorious and sublime object, and a very apt image of the God who had created it and all things; but I thought I could as rationally love that sun as I could the invisible Being of whom I deemed it the best type. I found what I reckoned admirable things in the writings of Plato. Socrates I regarded as a very excellent, talented man; his reasonings on the immortality of the soul, on the love of God, on prayer, and on the nature of holiness and of man, delighted me. But though I never once thought of bringing forward arguments to weigh against his, I could not consider what he taught in the light of serious truths. I felt the same pleasure in perusing his dialogues, or in reading fine moral poems and discourses, as I felt when looking at an elegant statue or picture; but I thought as little of taking the precepts I found in these pieces as rules to live by as I did of paring my limbs or features to the exact proportions of those of the Apollo Belvidere or the Hercules Farnese. As for the religion of the New Testament, I could not at all admire it. Some of the morals it inculcated I thought good, though in the main rather calculated to make a patient than an active man, and better adapted for the slave and the vanquished than for the freeman and the conqueror. The scheme of Redemption and its consequent doctrines I regarded as peculiarly absurd. I held it impossible that a man of taste and judgment could in reality be a Christian. As for those men who were evidently possessed of both these faculties in a high degree and yet professors of religion, I interpreted their seeming assent to its dogmas as the effect of a prudence similar to that which made Plato, Seneca, and some of the other ancient philosophers, profess a belief in the mythologic fables of Greece and Rome. I was myself an imitator of these men, and I looked upon the professed atheist or deist, not perhaps with as much abhorrence as the serious believer would regard him with, but with a much higher contempt; for it seemed to me a thing childishly imprudent for any one to assume the character of a free-thinker, when all to be acquired by opposing the current of what I regarded as popular prejudice was the unqualified hatred and detestation of nineteen-twentieths of one's countrymen and relations. I therefore professed, as you will perhaps remember, a great respect for religion, though always ready to confess to any one who was seriously a Christian that I had no experimental knowledge of its truth. I found the doctrine of predestination very serviceable as a kind of shield to protect me against the advices (you may smile at the term) of such. You may see from what I have written what it was made me think it possible that your profession of respect for religion was insincere; but you will pardon me, as you know how natural it is for a man to judge his neighbor by himself.

"But though misled for once by this method of judging, I shall yet avail myself of it in forming an opinion of that formidable body, the men of the world, so far as their regards for religion are concerned. My present self takes my former self as a specimen of these men; ay, and conceit goes so far as to say that former self may be regarded as no unfavorable specimen either. 'Tis true I was not one of the most acute though one of the most prudent of freethinkers. I will not arrogate to myself the powers of a Paine or a Hobbes, yet, setting conceit apart, I think I may say that my natural acuteness and acquired knowledge at the time I deemed the historical part of the Bible a collection of fables, and its doctrinal a mass of absurdities, were far superior to the acuteness or knowledge of the generality of such men as harbor similar opinions. I mean such of them as think for themselves; and it is proper to make this distinction: for I can assure you, however much the men who arrogate a faculty of detecting impostures the rest of the world are deceived by, may boast of the superior power of mind lavished on their sect, that there are blockheads who are sceptics as well as weak men who are Christians, nay, more. that there are men who profess themselves free-thinkers who were not born to be thinkers at all.

"The few intelligent sceptics I have been acquainted with, I have invariably found as ignorant of religion as I myself was four years ago, and from my present knowledge of it I conclude (and it would be difficult to prove my conclusion false) that all its enemies, even the most acute, are thus ignorant. I have perused the Essays of Hume, one of the best reasoners, perhaps, the world ever produced, and on rising from that perusal this estimate appeared to me juster than ever. Holding this opinion, I can pity these men, but I feel little disposed to fear their arguments, having experience of their futility; nor yet do I feel uneasy at the thought of being the object of the contempt of such; for my memory must altogether fail me before I forget that with a contempt similar to theirs I once regarded men well skilled in that wisdom the beginning of which is the fear of God.

"With the second class, the non-thinkers, it is not so easy to deal. They are so numerous as to compose nearly two-thirds of the inhabitants of our large towns, and even in our villages and in the country, whose inhabitants, forty years ago, were a superstitious, it may be, but certainly a moral and decent people, they are springing up like mushrooms. Consummately ignorant of religion, and deficient in all general knowledge, they ridicule and defame all those who, professing a belief in the doctrines of the Bible, make its morality the rule of their lives. They are searchers after truth on the plan laid down by my Lord Shaftesbury. Men of the firmest minds find it a hard task to keep themselves cool and undisturbed when made the butts of ridicule. The ridicule of the fool, too. is peculiarly bitter. I have had occasion to feel it at times, having oftener than once come in contact with persons of the stamp described;

and I have felt hurt at finding myself made their butt; but as there is no character I regard with so much contempt as a coward, I have been solaced at finding, from repeated experience, that none except arrant cowards set upon me in this manner. These pusillanimous mockers never venture singly to attack a man. They fight in companies, have no chance if the person they single out be strong in judgment or in humor, unless they can drown his arguments or wit in their laughter. For any two of the fraternity, unless they be more ignorant and stupid than common, I find myself an overmatch. Argument or the sallies of wit confound them. They can do nothing except laugh, and not even that when alone.

"But as I have detailed the opinions which I formerly held of religion at some length, it may not be improper to state, as a *per contra*, a few of those I at present hold respecting it. I have now so far changed my opinion of religion as to think, with a celebrated poet, that Christian is the highest style of man, and that, by the New Testament, men of the greatest powers of mind and the deepest learning may be taught wisdom. Nor can I deem. as I did once, the scheme of morals which this book contains mean and contemptible. I am convinced that, were that scheme universally acted upon, earth would become a heaven; and further, that no one can act upon it unless possessed of the highest and noblest fortitude, — a fortitude, indeed, too noble to have any place in the natural human heart, but which God has promised to infuse into the hearts of all such as believe Jesus to be the Christ. As for taste, I cannot help wondering how I could at any time be so very absurd as to think the doctrines of Christianity opposed to this principle, especially when I understood and relished the larger poems of Cowper and Milton. Through the Revelation by which I am taught of all that Christ has done and suffered for sinners, the God whom I would formerly regard with a cold feeling of admiration I can now love as my God and Father. I feel him brought near unto me, and that, too, in a way against which my pride of heart had formerly revolted, and which my reason deemed as unworthy of divine wisdom to devise as of human to trust to.

"This is not merely an avowal of a change of opinion. There is implied in it a change of heart. Though still sinful and foolish in a degree I would be ashamed to confess even to my friends, I trust I am now less selfish and possessed of a more affectionate heart than I was before I believed. My friends are dearer to me than they were formerly, and yet I do not now, as I did once, make their approbation the rule of my actions. I am, perhaps, still too fond of praise from such of my fellow-men as I respect and love, but I find that my desire of avoiding that which is bad and dishonorable follows me into solitude, and that my belief in God's omnipresence (may I not hope the assistance of his Spirit also?) gives me strength to accomplish this desire. But you will not be satisfied if I run on in this strain to the end of my letter. Let me close this part of it, then, in the words of one of the many texts which point out the principle upon which the change I have been describing hinged: 'Whosoever believeth that Jesus is the Christ, is born of God.' Mark what follows: 'Whosoever is born of God overcometh the world.' . . . .

. . . . Rousseau was certainly in the right when he said that the art of writing well was of all others the most difficult to acquire. I have been wishing, ay, and striving, too, as hard as my indolent, volatile nature suffered, for these three years past to acquire this art; and all I have yet attained is an ability of detecting my mistakes and of seeing how incorrect my modes of expression are. . .

"There is a general stagnation in this part of the country

in all kinds of trade. The season favorable to my department is fast advancing, but except two tombstones (and one
of these is not yet finished) I have done nothing this year.
I have some thoughts of putting into execution a plan which
has been revolving in my mind these several months back.
I engrave inscriptions on stone (conceit apart) in a neater
and more correct manner than any other mason in this part
of the country. The masons of Inverness, as I have been
informed, are very deficient in this art. My plan is to go
to that town, take lodgings in some cheap part of it, and
make myself known by advertisement as a stone engraver.
What think you of this? The want of friends and of a due
confidence in one's self are, it is true, disqualifying circumstances, but time and chance happeneth to all."

Of the pursuits, projects, and aspirings of this period we
have further record in a document drawn up by Miller in
the spring of 1828, headed "Things which I intend doing,
but many of which, experience says, shall never be done."
It is too characteristic to be omitted : —

"PART FIRST. GEOMETRY, ARCHITECTURE, SCULPTURE, DRAW-
ING, ETC.

"1. To fill a book containing from thirty to forty pages
with such problems of practical Geometry as are of use to
the architect and builder.

"2. To execute in the best style a complete set of archi-
tectural drawings, beginning with Egyptian, and ending
with Gothic architecture.

"3. To study the proportions of the human figure as
exemplified in the works of the Grecian school of sculpture.

"4. To practise cutting in stone, foliage, shells, heral-
dic figures, the Ionic, Corinthian, and composite capitals, etc.

" 5. To fill about a dozen pages with the varieties of the Roman, Italian, old English, and Saxon alphabets ; the letters of each to be formed in my best and neatest manner, and the whole to be shown to strangers as a specimen of my skill in inscription engraving.

" 6. To make a set of drawings of such of the old buildings of Ross-shire as I have taken sketches of in the course of my casual peregrinations through that country, such as the Tower of Fairburn, Castle Leod, Craighouse, Lochslin, Balconie, Balnagown, etc.

" 7. To make a set of drawings of the scenery of the parish of Cromarty, including two views of the town, one from the west, the other from the east ; two views of Cromarty House, one from the old chapel, the other from the green in front. One from the hill above the Laigh Craig of the Bay of Cromarty, another of the same from the Sutor Road. One view of the Laigh Craig from the wood adjoining. One of the Sinkan Hillock from the Sach Craig. One of the Apple-Garden from the Red Nose. One of the Murray Frith from the Gallow Hill. One of the Gallow Hill from the Murray Frith. One of Mac-Arthur's Bed. One from Hespy Home, and three to be taken from different points in the Burn of Craighouse.

" 8. To try how I will succeed in portrait and landscape in oil colors.

" 9. To practise the old hand until the best judges would be unable to distinguish between a piece of my writing in the ancient style and a manuscript two hundred years old.

" 10. To make a set of drawings of all the fine wild flowers and pretty colored butterflies to be found in this part of the country.

" 11. To make a piece of mosaic work of fine stones

found on the shores of Cromarty, or in the caves of the Gallow Hill.

"PART SECOND. LITERATURE : PROSE COMPOSITION.

"1. I intend writing a work, humorous and descriptive, to be entitled, 'Four Years in the Life of a Journeyman Mason.'

"2. I intend writing a history of my varying thoughts of men and manners, right and wrong, philosophy and religion, from my twelfth to my twenty-sixth year.

"3. I intend writing a description of the town and parish of Cromarty, its traditional history and a character of its inhabitants.

"4. I intend writing a memoir of my father's life.

"5. I intend writing the life of my uncle, Alexander Wright.

"6. I intend making a collection of all the letters I have written my friends, and all I have received from them.

"7. I intend writing an essay on the Book of Psalms.

"8. I intend writing a memoir of my friend, Will Ross.

"9. I intend writing a memoir of my townsman, David Henderson.

"10. I intend writing an essay on the doctrine of predestination as connected with that of faith, for the perusal of my friend, Will Ross.

"11. I intend writing letters to George Corbett on sermon writing and sermon writers, and also a sermon for him on a given text.

"12. I intend completing my letter to Clericus, and writing out a fair copy of it for my friend, J. Swanson. I intend writing a collection of miscellaneous essays in the manner of the 'Spectator,' to be entitled 'The Egotist.'

"13. I intend writing two letters descriptive of the Herring Fishery, and containing its traditional history.

"PART THIRD.   LITERATURE : POETRY.

"1. I intend collecting all my Juvenile Poems into one volume, correcting and altering them as I see proper.

"2. I intend writing 'The Widow of Dunskaith,' a legendary poem.

"3. I intend writing 'The Lady of Balconie,' a legendary poem.

"4. I intend writing 'The Chapel,' a descriptive poem.

"5. I intend writing 'The Leper,' a sacred poem.

"6. I intend new modelling and completing 'An Hour at Eve,' a moral poem.

"7. I intend writing an Ode to the Ness.

"8. I intend writing an Address to the Northern Institution."

There are several things worth noting here. Observe, in the first place, the practical nature of the scheme. Our stone-mason has high aspirings, but he is no day-dreamer. Sketching, in the heyday of early manhood, the tasks of the ensuing years, he begins with a series of undertakings bearing directly upon the calling by which he is to live. The basis of all his activity is the attainment of a comfortable livelihood, and a creditable position as a hewer of stone. In the next place, his literary activity centres in himself and his local connections and interests. The two largest works which he intends to produce in prose are to be about himself, and it seems probable that in the series of essays to be entitled "The Egotist," he would be the central figure. It is remarkable, in the third place, that we find, in this summary of Hugh Miller's intentions at the age of twenty-six, no trace of scientific enthusiasm, no vestige of scientific ambition. Literature, and those aspects of nature which delight the poet and the painter, possess his heart. He is to execute many drawings, but not one geological diagram. Lastly, we may observe that, though the contrite anticipation of partial failure in achievement was of necessity verified, yet the correspondence between this chart of his voyage and the course he actually pursued was more than usually close. Proof exists that Miller accomplished a large proportion of what he at this period intended to attempt. His autobiographical plans ultimately took shape in the "Schools and Schoolmasters." His letters on the Herring Fishery will claim our attention in the immediate sequel. The drawing of the old tower of Fairburn, which we have been able to lay before the reader, was probably one of several which he executed about this time, but which having, as I surmise, been given to friends, are lost. This drawing not only proves him to have possessed considerable skill as a self-taught draughtsman, but exhibits, in the opinion of Mr. Ruskin, some power of composition. The problems in practical geometry were worked out and entered in a manuscript book, as proposed. His description of the town and parish of Cromarty was published in the Statistical Account of Scotland, and is a most accurate, lucid, and comprehensive performance. From all this we may conclude that Hugh Miller, instead of being, as he calls himself, volatile and indolent, has become a man of singularly calm and resolute mind. He looks habitually before and after; calculates the force at his command; and disposes it with strategic method for the conduct of life's campaign.

CHAPTER IX.

THE plan of seeking work in Inverness, which he carried into effect in the course of the summer, had important consequences, but they proved to be by no means of the kind he anticipated. Thinking, with somewhat less, it must be admitted, than his usual shrewdness, that, by demonstrating his power to write grammatically in the poetical corner of a newspaper, he might obtain employment as an engraver of epitaphs, he wrote an Ode to the River Ness, and offered it for insertion in the " Inverness Courier." No one trusts a versifying mechanic in his *own* art; and the inhabitants of the capital of the Highlands, dowered with quite sufficient conceit, would have been more likely to resent the implication that they could not compose inscriptions for themselves, than to employ a stone-cutter who proposed, however melodiously, to compose inscriptions for them. But we need not speculate on the effect which the appearance of the Ode to the Ness in the columns of the " Courier " might have produced

242

in the way of orders for gravestones. The editor did not insert the verses; they are, in truth, uncommonly poor. Miller. however, piqued by their non-appearance, and confident in his poetical powers, resolved to print on his own account, and with this view made application afresh at the office of the newspaper.

He thus formed the acquaintance of Mr. Robert Carruthers, then, as now, editor of the " Inverness Courier," and the acquaintance ripened rapidly into a friendship which continued during the life of Hugh Miller. With that critical acumen which all the world has learned to acknowledge in the biographer of Pope. Mr. Carruthers discerned the originality and worth of Miller, and though he came in the guise of a stone-mason. shy, taciturn, ungainly, with a quire of rugged verses in his pocket, admitted him at once to the enjoyment of that equality and that fraternity which have from of old prevailed in the republic of letters. Miller had indeed made a notable acquisition. and he did not fail to appreciate it. The perfect judgment, the perfect temper, the literary sympathy. not less intelligent than warm. the indestructible cordiality, unchilled by forty years' editorial experience, which have endeared Mr. Carruthers to thousands from London to Inverness, won his confidence and his heart. To his dying day there was no newspaper which he read with half the interest with which he hung over the " Inverness Courier."

An address to the Northern Institution, — an antiquarian and scientific society which had its head-quarters in Inverness. — though couched in the pompous rhetoric proper to such addresses, and written out in that old English hand which was one of Miller's valued accomplishments, was as unsuccessful. in the light of a business speculation. as the Ode to the Ness. The task of soliciting employment, directly or indirectly, thus discovered to be intolerably irksome and utterly unprofitable, was relinquished. He would ask no more favors of any one, and "strode along the streets, half an inch taller on the strength of the resolution." Whether it was the defiant glance expressive of this resolution, or a lingering forlornness in his appearance which still betrayed the mechanic out of work, that attracted the attention of a recruiting sergeant, we are left to guess. Certain it is that he was offered the king's shilling on the streets of Inverness, and civilly declined the same.

Meanwhile, his poems began to be put into his hands in a form which, though he probably had them by heart, made them nevertheless new to him, to wit, in print. The effect was memorable. His critical faculty realized with startling and painful, but quite convincing, vividness, that they fell far below the mark of good English poetry. Hugh Miller was hardly one of those who "can hear their detractions and put them to mending," for his pugnacity always awoke when he was attacked ; but he was one of a class, perhaps still smaller, who can estimate their own performances with austere justice, and abide by that estimate in face of contemptuous disparagement, on the one hand, and the most ingenious and plausible encomiums on the other. The "Poems written in the Leisure Hours of a Journeyman Mason" met with a success which, had Miller been a rhyming artisan of the ordinary calibre, would have turned his head. Issued from a newspaper office in the north of Scotland, they were recognized as imbued with true excellence in periodicals of the first order, and by critics of culture and authority. The "Lines to a Sun-dial placed in a Church-yard" were quoted in magazine and newspaper throughout the length and breadth of the United Kingdom, and the author was assured that they displayed " a refinement of thought, an elegance and propriety of language, that would do honor to the most accomplished poet of the day." Had Miller *not* had the making of a poet in him, the like of this would have led him at once to exalt his horn as a prodigy of genius, too fine to work at his craft, who had only to put his name to a copy of verses to make them immortal, and whom the human species were bound to supply with the necessaries of life gratis. The plaudits profoundly gratified Miller, but did not move him a hair's-breadth from the rhadamanthine sternness of his judgment on himself, or shake in his bosom " that serene and unconquerable pride which no applause, no reprobation, could blind to its shortcoming or beguile of its reward."

The question may be gravely put, whether he did not err in determining, as he did, to abandon poetical composition and devote himself, for a time at least. to prose. The pieces which he printed were no doubt defective, and his best verse is inferior, in poetical qualities, not only to his best, but to his second or third-rate prose. The essential point to determine, however, is whether there are grounds for believing that. if he had brought the whole energies of his soul to the task of perfecting his verse, — if he had invincibly striven to beat out those notes of music, delicate and strong, which lay deep in his nature and were never clearly articulated, — he would or would not have realized a higher beauty, and expressed a deeper truth, than he actually attained. It was within the capacity of Miller to produce reflective and descriptive poetry equal to any in the English language. On the other hand, he fell short both in lyrical passion and dramatic sympathy, and his imagination, though powerful, was cold. His ear, too, may have been naturally better fitted to the modulation of prose than of verse. It is bootless to speculate on the subject. The army of the Muses is like that of Gideon. All who are fearful or afraid, all who do not serve for life or for death, not only may but must quit it ; and Miller was critic enough to know the " intolerable severity" of Apollo. Some of our most eminent writers, Mr. Carlyle and Mr. Ruskin, for instance, impatient of the deluges of mediocre poetry which flood our literary thoroughfares, and angry that attention should be diverted by anything short of transcendent excellence from the wealth of choicest song with which the literature of England is already stored, would maintain that, in deliberately abandoning verse, amid the acclamations which greeted his earliest efforts, Hugh Miller presented an example which specially deserves to be followed, and gave one of the noblest proofs afforded by his career of sterling ability and massive sense. Mrs. Miller informs me that his relinquishment of the lyre was but provisional; and that it was his intention to resume verse in a poem to be entitled "The Leper." It will be recollected that among the projects which we saw him form was one for the composition of a poem thus named.

From the ideal woe of perceiving for the first time ·that he stood at an immeasurable distance below the great masters of English poetry, he was recalled to the hard reality of grief by the intelligence that his Uncle James had died; and, on proceeding to Cromarty, in consequence of this intelligence, he learned that William Ross also was no more. Uncle James, as we well know, had been as a father to him; or rather as one among ten thousand fathers; for, if the affection with which he regarded his nephew was as that of a tender parent, the counsel, the example, the sympathetic forbearance, the just appreciation, which Miller experienced at his hands, were such as the fewest parents can bestow. From Uncle James, as by a fine moral contagion, Hugh derived that proud integrity, that sensitive honor, in money matters, which was with him, as with Burns, a passion.

The death of Ross, though at the moment his preoccupation with grief for the loss of his uncle prevented him from feeling the full force of this second blow, must also have touched him keenly. Among his early friends Swanson had his deepest respect, but the tenderest of his friendships was with Ross. Of him alone among his boyish companions did Miller speak as possessed of genius, and we have seen enough to prove that his estimate was not extravagant. Ross could sympathize with much which elicited no response from the Puritan rigor of Swanson, and with his delicate feeling for beauty were combined a feminine gentleness and depth of affection which greatly endeared him to Miller. The circumstances of his death have a pathos deeper than the pathos of romance. He was living in Glasgow, occupying the same rooms with a brother mechanic, when this last was seized with consumption. For several months he was unfit for work. Ross, who had been consumptive in his most vigorous years, and in whom the vital flame was now waning fast, continued to toil for both; and as his fine talent, incomparably superior to that of the ordinary house-painter, enabled him to execute work which required delicate handling rather than exertion of physical energy, he found remunerative employment as long as his fingers could hold a brush. Having thus shielded against want the comrade who was dying only a little faster than himself, Ross beheld him sink into the grave, and, the last task which bound him to earth accomplished, speedily followed. "My hope of salvation is in the blood of Jesus. Farewell, my sincerest friend." These were the closing words of William Ross's last letter to Miller.

The Journeyman's Poems were dedicated to John Swanson, the name disguised in asterisks. In a dedicatory epistle to his friend, written in prose, Miller declares him to be " the best scholar and truest philosopher he ever knew," and avows his gratitude to him for " having convinced one who possibly might have done some mischief as an infidel, that the Religion of the Bible is not a cunningly devised fable." Of his own book he ventures to state the opinion, " that a spirit of poetry may be found in it, wrestling with those improprieties of language consequent on imperfect education, just as the half-formed animals of the Nile, that are warmed into life by the beams of the sun, struggle to free themselves from the mud and slime in which they are enveloped." He virtually takes upon himself the blame, however, of whatever defect of education the volume may display, confessing that, in the present age, " ignorance implies rather want of mind than want of opportunity for cultivating the mental faculties." True words; and specially brave and modest from the lips of a poetical mechanic.

CHAPTER X.

AVING committed the body of Uncle James to the grave, and piously recorded on his tombstone that he had " lived without reproach and died without fear," Miller did not return to Inverness, but resumed his employment in the church-yards of Cromarty and its neighborhood. The publication of his poems, whose authorship was well known in the locality, was sufficient to make him a person of some importance in his native town. He associated himself with the better portion of its inhabitants, those who combined a moderate liberalism of political opinion with literary or scientific tastes and strong religious principles. His acquaintance with the Rev. Mr. Stewart, which had formerly been slight, now deepened into intimacy, and no sooner had he an opportunity of knowing Mr. Stewart well, than he conceived for him the highest esteem, and dismissed forever from his mind, as the mere fruits of misunderstanding, what he had formerly fancied to the disadvantage of his minister. Miller's profession of religion, also, was more decided than formerly, and he began to teach in the Sunday school.

249

Hewing under sunny skies on the chapel brae, he often finds Mr. Stewart or some intelligent friend stealing to his side to give and take an hour's conversation, and sometimes his visitors are of the fair sex. The journeyman mason has become the literary lion of Cromarty.

But " nature's noblest gift " to Miller, his " gray goose-quill," has not been laid aside. Turning his attention to prose, and availing himself of the columns of the " Inverness Courier," which his friend Carruthers gladly throws open to him, he writes, in the summer of 1829, five letters on the Herring Fishery, which, " in consequence," said Mr. Carruthers, " of the interest they excited in the Northern Counties, and in justice to their modest and talented author," were issued in pamphlet form in September of the same year. They are written with much vivacity, and abound with pertinent remarks and fine descriptive passages. In addition to what he had personally witnessed in connection with the Herring Fishery, Miller puts on record not a little which he learned from his more aged townsmen. To the latter is due the following graphic picture of Cromarty Bay, when in possession of an extraordinary shoal of fish : —

" I have heard one season spoken of as very remarkable from the quantity of fish on the coast. One day in particular, in the beginning of autumn, the Bay of Cromarty presented a scene not easy to be forgotten. The appearance was as if its countless waves were embodied into fish and birds. No fewer than seven whales, some of them apparently sixty feet in length, were seen within the short space of half a mile. When they spouted, the jet seemed, in the rays of a noon-day sun, as if speckled with silver, an appearance given by shoals of *garves* (a smooth-coated, pretty little fish) which they drew in with the water, and thus ejected. Some of the birds that flocked round them to pick up the small fry which were stranded on their backs, were hurried aloft in the jet, like chaff or feathers in an eddy, to the height of thirty or forty feet. The water round them bubbled like a caldron. There were in the immense heterogeneous mass through which they swam, herrings, mackerel, sand-eels, garves, cod, porpoises, and seals."

The exact observation and firm grasp of detail, which contributed so much to make Miller a master of description, are already traceable in the following account of the Bank of Guilliam, a noted resort of herrings in the Moray Frith: " The Moray Frith Herring Fishery commences in the middle of July, and the fish commonly leave the coast in the end of August, or first of September. For the first few weeks the shoals are small and detached; and the fishings only average from two to five barrels per boat. Herrings are caught at this early stage of the fishing on the coast of Moray, nearly opposite the mouth of the Spey; but they swim in no determined track, — advancing, in some seasons, through the middle of the frith, and in others towards its eastern or western shores. As the season advances they come up higher, form into large bodies, and pursue a route tolerably certain. At this second stage, the quantity of barrels caught by each boat averages from eight to fourteen. The point at which the shoals unite is a long, narrow bank, which lies in the middle of the frith, nearly opposite the Bay of Cromarty, and which the fishermen term Guilliam, from three little conical hillocks, on the northern shore, so called. These hillocks are situated near a deep ravine, about half a mile south of the little fishing-town of Shandwick; and when boatmen bring them to appear as if rising out of the middle of the ravine, and see at the same time the Gaelic chapel of Cromarty in the line of the Inlaw, — another conical hillock near the southern base of Ben Wyvis, — they are on the fishing ground. The position of the bank is also ascertained by the depth of the water, and the nature of the bottom. The soundings on the north side vary from twelve to eighteen fathoms, on the south from twenty-five to thirty, while the depth of the bank does not average more than ten fathoms, and the bottom, which on the one side is sand, and on the other mud, is a hard gravel, and in some places a smooth, level rock covered with sea-weed. The breadth of the ridge does not exceed half a mile, but its length is nearly thrice as much. A greater quantity of herrings have been caught on this bank than upon any other of equal extent on the coast of Scotland. There have been repeated instances of fishings prosecuted on Guilliam, for the space of a whole week, at the average rate of eight hundred barrels per day; and it has become so famous among Moray Frith fishermen, that they are regarded as meaning the same thing when they express their wish for a prosperous season, or for a week's fishing on Guilliam. It is sufficiently strange, that several thousand barrels of herring should be caught in the course of a week, on a bank whose extent of surface does not exceed one-half of a square mile, and still more so, that near the close of such a week the fish appear in as great a body upon it as they do at the commencement. When the herrings make a lodgment on Guilliam, the fishings are invariably good; when, after making a short stay on it, they proceed farther up the frith, the quantity caught is immense, and salt and cask commonly fail the curers before the fish leave the coast; but when the shoal quits the frith before it settles on this bank, the fishing is so scanty as scarcely to cover the fishermen's expenses in fitting out their boats. This, though not generally known, is so well understood by those concerned, that an intelligent fisherman could mark a chart of the Moray Frith with cross lines, like the index of a thermometer, and affix a statement of what the average profit or loss of the respective seasons would prove, in which the fish turned and went off at the different places marked."

It was on this Bank of Guilliam that Hugh Miller passed a night in a herring boat ten years before the time at which he wrote. The letter in which his experiences on the occasion are recorded is the most carefully executed of the series, and derives additional interest from containing, in their original form, the extracts from the Herring-Fishery letters which he included, many years subsequently, in the "Schools and Schoolmasters." They thus enable us to compare his descriptive manner in 1829 with that which he ultimately preferred. Miller seems never to have been able to let a sample of his composition leave his hand without making it as good as, at the time of its quotation, he was capable of making it. Some may be disposed to think that in the easy and artless vigor, the youthful animation and freshness, of the earlier style, there is something to compensate for the studied compactness and elaborate polish of the later.

A NIGHT ON GUILLIAM.

"In the latter end of August, 1819, I went out to the fishing then prosecuted on Guilliam, in a Cromarty boat. The evening was remarkably pleasant. A low breeze from the west scarcely ruffled the surface of the frith, which was varied in every direction by unequal stripes and patches of a dead calmness. The Bay of Cromarty, burnished by the rays of the declining sun, until it glowed like a sheet of molten fire, lay behind, winding in all its beauty beneath purple hills and jutting headlands; while before stretched the wide extent of the Moray Frith, speckled with fleets of boats which had lately left their several ports, and were now all sailing in one direction. The point to which they were bound was the Bank of Guilliam, which, seen from betwixt the Sutors, seemed to verge on the faint blue line of the horizon ; and the fleets which had already arrived on it, had, to the naked eye, the appearance of a little rough-edged cloud resting on the water. As we advanced, this cloud of boats grew larger and darker ; and soon after sunset, when the bank was scarcely a mile distant, it assumed the appearance of a thick, leafless wood, covering a low, brown island.

" The tide, before we left the shore, had risen high on the beach, and was now beginning to recede. Aware of this, we lowered sail several hundred yards to the south of the fishing-ground, and, after determining the point from whence the course of the current would drift us direct over the bank, we took down the mast, cleared the hinder part of the boat, and began to cast out the nets. Before the ' Inlaw' appeared in the line of the Gaelic chapel (the landmark by which the southernmost extremity of Guilliam is ascertained) the whole drift was thrown overboard, and made fast to the swing. Night came on. The sky assumed a dead and leaden hue. A low, dull mist roughened the outline of the distant hills, and in some places blotted them out from the landscape. The faint breeze, that had hitherto scarcely been felt, now roughened the water, which was of a dark blue color approaching to black. The sounds which predominated were in unison with the scene. The almost measured dash of the waves against the sides of the boat and the faint rustle of the breeze were incessant ; while the low, dull moan of the surf breaking on the distant beach, and the short, sudden cry of an aquatic fowl of the diving species, occasionally mingled with the sweet, though rather monotonous, notes of a Gaelic song. ' It's ane o' the Gairloch fishermen,' said our skipper ; ' puir folk, they're aye singing an' thinking o' the Hielands.'

" Our boat, as the tides were not powerful, drifted slowly

over the bank. The buoys stretched out from the bows in an unbroken line. There was no sign of fish; and the boatmen, after spreading the sail over the beams, laid themselves down on it. The scene was at the time so new to me, and, though of a somewhat melancholy cast, so pleasing, that I stayed up. A singular appearance attracted my notice. 'How,' said I to one of the boatmen, who a moment before had made me an offer of his great-coat, 'how do you account for that calm, silvery spot on the water, which moves at such a rate in the line of our drift?' He started up. A moment after he called on the others to rise, and then replied: 'That moving speck of calm water covers a shoal of herrings. If it advances a hundred yards farther in that direction we shall have some employment for you.' This piece of information made me regard the little patch, which, from the light it caught, and the blackness of the surrounding water, seemed a bright opening in a dark sky, with considerable interest. It moved onwards with increased velocity. It came in contact with the line of the drift, and three of the buoys immediately sunk. A few minutes were suffered to elapse, and we then commenced hauling. The two strongest of the crew, as is usual, were stationed at the cork, the two others at the ground baulk. My assistance, which I readily tendered, was pronounced unnecessary; so I hung over the gunwale watching the nets as they approached the side of the boat. The three first, from the phosphoric light of the water, appeared as if bursting into flames of a pale-green color. The fourth was still brighter, and glittered through the waves while it was yet several fathoms away, reminding me of an intensely bright sheet of the aurora borealis. As it approached the side, the pale-green of the phosphoric matter appeared as if mingled with large flakes of snow. It contained a body of fish. 'A white horse! a white horse!' exclaimed one of the men at the cork baulk; 'lend us a haul.' I immediately sprang aft, laid hold on the rope, and commenced hauling. In somewhat less than half an hour we had all the nets on board, and rather more than twelve barrels of herrings.

"The night had now become so dark that we could scarcely discern the boats which lay within gunshot of our own; and we had no means of ascertaining the position of the bank except by sounding. The lead was cast, and soon after the nets shot a second time. The skipper's bottle was next produced, and a dram of whiskey sent round in a tin measure containing nearly a gill. We then folded down the sail, which had been rolled up to make way for the herrings, and were soon fast asleep.

"Ten years have elapsed since I laid myself down on this couch, and I was not then so accustomed to a rough bed as I am now, when I can look back on my wanderings as a journeyman mason over a considerable part of both the Lowlands and Highlands of Scotland. About midnight I awoke quite chill, and all over sore with the hard beams and sharp rivets of the boat. 'Well,' thought I, 'this is the tax I pay for my curiosity.' I rose and crept softly over the sails to the bows, where I stood, and where, in the singular beauty of the scene, which was of a character as different from that I had lately witnessed as is possible to conceive, I soon lost all sense of every feeling that was not pleasure. The breeze had died into a perfect calm. The heavens were glowing with stars, and the sea, from the smoothness of the surface, appeared a second sky, as bright and starry as the other, but with this difference, that all its stars appeared comets. There seemed no line of division at the horizon, which rendered the illusion more striking. The distant hills appeared a chain of dark, thundery clouds sleeping in the heavens. In short, the scene was one of the strangest I ever witnessed; and the thoughts and imaginations which it suggested were of a character as singular. I looked at the boat as it appeared in the dim light of midnight, a dark, irregularly shaped mass; I gazed on the sky of stars above, and the sky of comets below, and imagined myself in the centre of space, far removed from the earth, and every other world, — the solitary inhabitant of a planetary fragment. This illusion, too romantic to be lasting, was dissipated by an incident which convinced me that I had not yet left the world. A crew of south-shore fishermen, either by accident or design, had shot their nets right across those of another boat, and in disentangling them a quarrel ensued. Our boat lay more than half a mile from the scene of contention, but I could hear, without being particularly attentive, that on the one side there were terrible threats of violence immediate and bloody, and on the other threats of the still more terrible pains and penalties of the law. In a few minutes, however, the entangled nets were freed, and the roar of altercation gradually sunk into silence as dead as that which had preceded it.

"An hour before sunrise I was somewhat disheartened to find the view on every side bounded by a dense low bank of fog, which hung over the water, while the central firmament remained blue and cloudless. The neighboring boats appeared through the mist huge misshapen things, manned by giants. We commenced hauling, and found in one of the nets a small rock-cod and a half-starved whiting, which proved the whole of our draught. I was informed by the fishermen, that even when the shoal is thickest on the Guilliam, so close does it keep by the bank that not a solitary herring is to be caught a gunshot from the edge on either side.

"We rowed up to the other boats, few of whom had been more successful in their last haul than ourselves, and none equally so in their first. The mist prevented us from ascertaining by known landmarks the position of the bank, which we at length discovered in a manner that displayed much of the peculiar art of the fisherman. The depth of the water and the nature of the bottom showed us that it lay to the south. A faint, tremulous heave of the sea, which was still calm, was the only remaining vestige of the gale which had blown from the west in the early part of the night, and this heave, together with the current, which at this stage of the flood runs in a south-western direction, served as our compass. We next premised how far our boat had drifted down the frith with the ebb-tide, and how far she had been carried back again by the flood. We then turned her bows in the line of the current, and in rather less than half an hour were, as the lead informed us, on the eastern extremity of Guilliam, where we shot our nets for the third time.

" Soon after sunrise the mist began to dissipate, and the surface of the water to appear for miles around roughened as if by a smart breeze, though there was not the slightest breath of wind at the time. 'How do you account for that appearance?' said I to one of the fishermen. 'Ah, lad, that is by no means so favorable a token as the one you asked me to explain last night. I had as lief see the *Bhodry-more*.'—'Why, what does it betoken? and what is the *Bhodry-more?*'—'It betokens that the shoal have spawned, and will shortly leave the frith; for when the fish are sick and weighty they never rise to the surface in that way: but have you never heard of the *Bhodry-more?*' I replied in the negative. 'Well, but you shall.'—'Nay,' said another of the crew, 'leave that for our return; do you not see the herrings playing by thousands round our nets, and not one of the buoys sinking in the water? There is not a single fish swimming so low as the upper baulks of our drift; shall we not shorten the buoy ropes, and take off the sinkers?' This did not meet the approbation of the others, one of whom took up a stone, and flung it in the middle of the shoal. The fish immediately disappeared from the surface for several fathoms round. 'Ah, there they go,' he exclaimed, 'if they go but low enough; four years ago I startled thirty barrels of light fish into my drift just by throwing a stone among them.'

" The whole frith at this time, so far as the eye could reach, appeared crowded with herrings; and its surface was so broken by them as to remind one of the pool of a water-fall. They leaped by millions a few inches into the air, and sunk with a hollow, plumping noise somewhat resembling the dull, rippling sound of a sudden breeze; while to the eye there was a continual twinkling which, while it mocked every effort that attempted to examine in detail, showed to the less curious glance like a blue robe sprinkled with silver. But it is not by such comparisons that so singular a scene is to be described so as to be felt. It was one of those which through the living myriads of creation testify of the infinite Creator.

" About noon we hauled for the third and last time, and found nearly eight barrels of fish. I observed, when haul-ing, that the natural heat of the herring is scarcely less than that of quadrupeds or birds; that when alive its sides are shaded by a beautiful crimson color, which it loses when dead; and that, when newly brought out of the water, it utters a sharp faint cry somewhat resembling that of a mouse. We had now twenty barrels on board. The *east-erly har*, a sea-breeze, so called by fishermen, which in the Moray Frith, during the summer months and first month of autumn, commonly comes on after ten o'clock A. M., and fails at four o'clock P. M., had now set in. We hoisted our mast and sail, and were soon scudding right before it.

" 'The story of the *Bhodry-more*, which I demanded of

the skipper as soon as we had trimmed our sail, proved interesting in no common degree, and was linked with a great many others. The *Bhodry-more* * is an active, mischievous fish of the whale species, which has been known to attack and even founder boats. About eight years ago a very large one passed the town of Cromarty through the middle of the bay, and was seen by many of the townsfolks leaping out of the water in the manner of a salmon, fully to the height of a boat's mast. It appeared about thirty feet in length. This animal may almost be regarded as the mermaid of modern times; for the fishermen deem it to have fully as much of the demon as of the fish. There have been instances of its pursuing a boat under sail for many miles, and even of its leaping over it from side to side. It appears, however, that its habits and appetites are unlike those of the shark; and that the annoyance which it gives the fisherman is out of no desire of making him its prey, but from its predilection for amusement. It seldom meddles with a boat when at anchor, but pursues one under sail, as a kitten would a rolling ball of yarn. The large physalus whale is comparatively a dull, sluggish animal; occasionally, however, it evinces a partiality for the amusements of the *Bhodry-more.* Our skipper said that, when on the Caithness coast, a few years before, an enormous fish of the species kept direct in the wake of his boat for more than a mile, frequently rising so near the stern as to be within reach of the boat-hook. He described the expression of its large goggle eyes as at once frightful and amusing; and so graphic was his narrative that I could almost paint the animal stretching out for more than sixty feet behind the boat, with his black marble-looking skin and cliff-like fins. He at length grew tired of its gambols,

* Properly, perhaps, the musculus whale.

and with a sharp fragment of rock struck it between the eyes. It sunk with a sudden plunge, and did not rise for ten minutes after, when it appeared a full mile astern. This narrative was but the first of I know not how many of a similar cast, which presented to my imagination the *Bloedry-more* whale and hunfish in every possible point of view. The latter, a voracious, formidable animal of the shark species, frequently makes great havoc among the tackle with which cod and haddock are caught. Like the shark, it throws itself on its back when in the act of seizing its prey. The fishermen frequently see it lying motionless, its white belly glittering through the water, a few fathoms from the boat's side, employed in stripping off every fish from their hooks as the line is drawn over it. This formidable animal is from six to ten feet in length, and formed like the common shark."

The letters on the Herring Fishery were fitted to interest many to whom the poems of the journeyman mason would be a sealed book. Whatever might be his rhyming capabilities, the Cromarty mason was clearly a man of sense and talent. The circle of his friends and admirers continued, therefore, to widen. In character of occasional correspondent, he contributed items of news and occasional articles to the " Inverness Courier." These are admirably done, and in some of them we detect impressions and opinions cherished by Miller to the last. The following occurs in an article on the departure of two hundred emigrants from Cromarty for Canada : " A few years ago we were led by business into the central Highlands of the north. We passed on a half-obliterated path through a succession of those wild scenes of savage sterility and rude grandeur, which, if not peculiar to the Highlands of Scotland, only occur in countries whose high destiny it is not to be conquered by a foreign enemy. They suggested to us a series of pleasing reflections. Abrupt, craggy hills, separated from each other by deep, gloomy ravines, which seemed the rents and fissures of a shattered and ruined planet, and which varied in color, according to their distance, from the faintest azure to the darkest purple, filled our whole space of view from the foreground to the horizon. Such, we thought, are the barriers which, in defiance of the armies of Rome and of England, maintained the spirit of freedom in this country during the early ages of its history, and which, in the present times, oppose an insurmountable wall of defence to the advances of an enemy equally potent and more insidious. That luxury, whose waves are rolling over and obliterating every better trait of character which once distinguished the Lowland Scotch, shall find its boundary of shore on the skirts of these mountains. Nations, like individuals, become old, and they at length expire; but, though symptoms of age are apparent in the southern districts of the kingdom, those of the northern Highlands are still full of the vigor of youth; and, while the moralist may find reason to describe the inhabitants of the latter as a remnant of people happily preserved from the inundation which has devastated the plain below, the patriot may as rationally regard them as thews and sinews of the State, ready to be exerted in preserving to our otherwise enfeebled country her name and place among the nations.

"These agreeable reflections were dissipated by the contemplation of a scene the most melancholy we ever witnessed. Our path lay along the brow of a hill, overlooking a valley that, unlike the others which we had previously seen, was comparatively level and of considerable extent. A small stream winded through the centre, and on either side there were irregularly shaped patches of vivid green, which were encircled by the brown heath, like islands by the ocean. As we advanced, we saw the ruins of deserted cottages, and perceived that the patches adjoining had once been furrowed by the plough. All was solitary and desolate. Roof-trees were decaying within mouldering walls; a rank vegetation had covered the silent floors, and was wavering over hearths the fires of which had been forever extinguished. A solitary lapwing was screaming over the cottages, a melancholy raven was croaking on a neighboring eminence, there was the faint murmur of the stream, and the low moan of the breeze; but every sound of man had long passed from the air, — the tones of speech and the voice of singing. Alas! we exclaimed, the Highlander has at length been conquered, and the country which he would have died to defend is left desolate. The track of an eastern army can be traced many years after its march by ruined villages and a depopulated country. Prophets have described scenes of future desolation, — lands once populous grown 'places where no man dwelleth nor son of man passeth through,' — and here in our native country is a scene calculated to illustrate the terrible threatenings of prophecy, and the sad descriptions of Eastern historians."

Among the latest of these contributions to the "Inverness Courier" is one which, though otherwise unimportant, is useful in a biographical point of view as helping us to trace one of the most interesting stages in Miller's intellectual history, the transference, namely, of his enthusiasm and ambition from literature to science. A short newspaper article on crab-fishing marks the point at which the stream of scientific acquirement which had long, with gathering volume, been flowing underground, rose to the surface. Miller writes as one who has from infancy been familiar with the natural objects and appearances of the Cromarty beach, and who had not written about them sooner merely because it did not occur to him that they could afford occupation to his pen. He does not yet adopt a scientific nomenclature. But he describes natural objects with exquisite precision and lucidity, and dwells upon details of structure which the mere literary sketcher or anecdotic sportsman would have regarded with indifference. He has learned also to contemplate, not in vague wonder but with reverent and delicate appreciation, the mystery and miracle of God's work in nature. "I am confident," he says, in concluding a description of the sea-urchin, "that there is not half the ingenuity, or half the mathematical knowledge, displayed in the dome of St. Peter's, at Rome, or St. Paul's, at London, that we find exhibited in the construction of this simple shell." It is not without interest that we note a like impression made by an examination of the same animal upon the mind of Edward Forbes. "The skill of the Great Architect of Nature," observes that celebrated naturalist, "is not less displayed in the construction of a sea-urchin than in the building up of a world."

CHAPTER XI.

REFERENCE has been made to the additions to the previously limited number of Miller's friends and acquaintances, occasioned by the publication of his poems. It is in no ordinary degree pleasing to observe the friendliness which he experienced from persons greatly his superiors in social position, and the manner in which that friendliness was responded to by him. On the one hand, there was cordiality without the faintest trace of the " insolence of condescension ;" counsel and furtherance of every kind to the utmost limit permitted by genuine respect, and by sympathetic apprehension of what a sensitively proud and independent nature required ; unfeigned recognition of the intellectual rank of this artisan, and of the title it gave him to be treated as a gentleman. On the other hand, there was perfect appreciation of all this ; gratitude not for patronage to the mechanic, but for fellowship and sympathy with the man ; independence not petulantly insisted upon, not obtrusively displayed, but quietly, unaffectedly, almost unconsciously worn as habit of soul and principle of deportment.

Principal Baird, at this time one of the most eminent

ministers of the Church of Scotland, was among the first to stretch out a friendly hand to the Cromarty poet. Miller was introduced to him in Inverness by Mr. Carruthers, shortly after the appearance of the poems, and Baird suggested that he should draw up that account of his education and opinions which has been so frequently mentioned. The first part of the narrative was soon ready, and Miller despatched it, in the autumn of 1829, to Baird in Edinburgh. He took occasion, at the same time, to thank Baird for " the very favorable critique " on the poems which had appeared in the " Caledonian Mercury." The critique in question had been written by Dr. James Brown, working editor of the " Encyclopædia Britannica," and Baird hastens to declare that he " had no hand whatever, directly or indirectly," in its publication. " But you say nothing," adds Baird, " in your letter as to my suggestion, when at Inverness, of giving your busy hours to your profession here during the ensuing winter, and your leisure hours to reading books, and plying your pen, and extending your acquaintance with the living as well as the dead world of literature." These words occur in a letter dated November 24, 1829. We have Miller's reply, bearing date the 9th of the following December : " From my engagements here and at Inverness, I cannot avail myself of your kind invitation to spend the winter at Edinburgh, but I appreciate its value and feel grateful for your kindness. My acquaintance with the dead world of literature is very imperfect, and it is still more so with the living; instead, however, of regretting this, I think it best to congratulate myself on the much pleasure which from this circumstance there yet remains for me to enjoy. If I live eight or ten years longer, and if my taste for reading continues, I shall, I trust, pass through a great many paradises of genius. Half the creations of Scott are still before me, and more than half those of every other modern poet. But though I can appreciate the value of an opportunity of perusing the works of such authors, there are opportunities of a different kind to be enjoyed in Edinburgh, which, from a rather whimsical bent of mind, I would value more highly. My curiosity is never more active than when it has the person of a great man for its object; nor have I felt more delight in anything whatever than in associating in my mind, when that curiosity was gratified, my newly acquired idea of the personal appearance of such a man with the ideas I had previously entertained of his character and genius. When I resided in the vicinity of Edinburgh, I have sauntered for whole hours opposite the house of Sir Walter Scott, in the hope of catching a glimpse of his person; and several times, when some tall, robust man has passed me in the streets, I have inquired of my companions whether that was not Professor Wilson. But perhaps I am more ambitious now than I was five years ago. Perhaps I would not be satisfied with merely seeing such men. and I am aware that I have not yet done anything which entitles me to the notice of the eminent, though in one instance I have been so fortunate as to attain it. I must achieve, at least, a little of what I have hoped to achieve before I go to Edinburgh. But even this intention must not be followed up with too great eagerness. Ortogrul of Basra, after he had surveyed the palace of the vizir, despised the simple neatness of his own little habitation. I must be careful lest, by acquiring too exclusive a bent towards literary pursuits, I contract a distaste for those employments which, though not very pleasing in themselves, are in my case, at least, intimately connected with happiness. I do not think I could be happy without being independent. and I cannot be independent except as a mechanic."

It is evident, from the terms in which Dr. Baird refers to

the suggestion made by him to Miller, of coming to Edinburgh, that the latter slightly misunderstood its purport. The account of the interview given in the " Schools and Schoolmasters " forces us to conclude that Miller supposed Baird to have advised him to abandon the chisel on coming to Edinburgh. " The capital furnished," he said, — the quotation is from the " Schools and Schoolmasters," — " the proper field for a literary man in Scotland. What between the employment furnished by the newspapers and the magazines, he was sure I would effect a lodgment and work my way up." Baird's words are that the " busy hours " were to be given to the stone-cutter's profession, and the " leisure hours " to literature. Carruthers, too, was as prudential in his advice to the workman as he was ardent in his admiration of the poet. " We have learned," he said, in a commendatory notice of the poems, " with much satisfaction that he (Miller) has confined his devotion to the Muses strictly to his leisure hours ; thus his industry in pursuing a laborious occupation has been unremitting." The friendliness both of Dr. Baird and of Mr. Carruthers was too genuine to permit indulgence in the cheap flattery of bidding Miller abandon his trade and launch into the perils of a literary life ; and he had the manliness and sense to appreciate their discretion while valuing their applause. Miller, not unnaturally, in writing the " Schools and Schoolmasters," saw the advice of Baird through the coloring medium of many years of literary eminence.

Among those who interested themselves in the success of his first venture, none were more zealous than Mr. Isaac Forsyth, of Elgin. But the efforts of Mr. Forsyth to dispose of the copies sent him from Inverness were vain, and that although he had " never embarked in any such concern with so much enthusiasm, nor took so much pains to secure success." There is a chivalrous delicacy in Miller's reply ;

he contrives to extract from the failure of his friend an additional cause for gratitude : —

"When I look back to the fate of my literary speculations with a composure approaching to indifference, I trust my gratitude to the gentleman who has so generously exerted himself in striving to forward these is not at all in proportion to the success with which his exertions have been repaid. Nay, sir, I consider your claim on me to have gained in strength from the circumstance of your having encountered disappointment in my behalf. I trust I may affirm that nature has bestowed upon me a disposition which enables me to conceive of the sentiment conveyed in the remarkable text, 'It is more blessed to give than to receive :' and though fortune seems to have determined that I shall be no bestower of benefits, I yet know from experience what it is to confer an obligation, and what it is, after having striven to oblige, to be thwarted in the intention. In the one case I have derived a full compensation for what I had done from that lightness of heart which accompanies success, and from the consciousness that, by benefiting a fellow-creature, I had in some degree added to the sum of human happiness. But in the other I have felt differently. In that depression of spirit which is almost always a consequence of unsuccessful exertion, I have looked for solace to something external ; and have felt that I had a claim on the gratitude of the party in whose cause I had interested myself, not only for what I had attempted to do, but also for what I had suffered from the disappointment which attended the failure."

So much by way of acknowledgment and consolation to Mr. Forsyth ; now for the effect of his literary failure upon himself : —

"With respect to literary pursuits, I have every claim to be regarded as one of the *incurables* mentioned by Goldsmith. At this moment, when I can look back to the complete failure of my speculation, I am as determined upon improving to the utmost my ability as a writer as I could have been had the public, by buying my work, rendered the speculation a good one. With only my present ability to judge of my own powers, the event can alone determine whether, when I have attained the art of writing, I shall succeed or fail in making myself known. But could I decide whether I possess or be devoid of true genius, it would be an easy matter for me to anticipate the result. If destitute of this spirit, I shall certainly not rise to eminence; for my situation in life is not one of those in which fortune or the influence of friends can supply the want of ability, or in which mediocrity of talent can become admirable by clothing itself in the spoils of learning. My education is imperfect; I cannot even subsist except by devoting seven-eighths of my waking hours to the avocations of a laborious profession; and I have no claim from birth to either the notice of the eminent or the patronage of the influential. But if nature has bestowed upon me that spirit of genius which ultimately can neither be repressed nor hidden, then, though fortune should serve me as Jupiter did Briareus when he buried him under Etna, I shall assuredly overturn the mountain."

Thomas Pringle, editor at this time of an annual publication called "Friendship's Offering," had seen some of Miller's productions, and wrote to Mr. Smith, a friend of Mr. Forsyth's, pronouncing him "a person of no ordinary talent and character." Mr. Forsyth enclosed Pringle's letter in that to which Miller is now replying, and Hugh proceeds, in the paragraph which follows, to comment upon it. "I am acquainted with Mr. Pringle as a poet, — and an admirable poet he is, combining in his beautiful pieces the simplicity of the ancient ballad with that elegance of style and delicacy of sentiment, which are the characteristics of classical poetry. I shall not venture, however, on addressing him by letter. The friendship of such a man, however valuable, and however much an honor, would scarcely afford me the pleasure which ought to be derived from it unless I were conscious I had done something to deserve it; and at present I can have no such consciousness. I am as yet only a little fellow, and with all the jealousy of a little fellow I shall conceal my insignificance, — not by stalking on stilts into the company of the gigantic, but by immuring myself in my solitude, from the loopholes of which I shall peep at them as I best may; — solicitous both to see and to avoid being seen." He next touches on his correspondence with Principal Baird. "I have not of late heard from the Principal; and I think I have a shrewd guess of the cause of his silence. In accordance to his advice, I sent him two hundred copies of my Poems, which he was to use his influence in getting sold; but that influence, great as it necessarily is, has, I suspect, proved insufficient to bring into notice a work destined not to be known, — perhaps not very deserving of a higher destiny, — and, with his characteristic benevolence, he is unwilling to give me pain by telling me so. I trust, however, that I shall yet have an opportunity of convincing him that, though only an indifferent poet, I am more than a tolerable philosopher."

It was remotely and but for a moment that Hugh Miller and Thomas Pringle came into relation with each other, and yet it is impossible to pass on without saying a word of one whose poems justify Miller's fine and appropriate eulogy, and whose life merited eulogy more enthusiastic still. Scotland, among her many noble sons, has hardly sent into the world a nobler than the high-souled, brilliant Pringle. As a poet, he had much reputation in his day, and some of his pieces are not likely soon to drop into oblivion. Coleridge declared that his stanzas, entitled " Afar in the Desert," are to be classed " among the two or three most perfect lyric poems in our language." His " Lion and Giraffe" seems to be the original from which Freiligrath paraphrased his universally known " Lion's Ride." Nay, if one could trust his ear, and the general impression conveyed by the poems, it might be suggested that the ring of Pringle's " Lion Hunt" was in the head of a greater than Freiligrath when he wrote, " How they brought the Good News from Ghent to Aix." Browning's poem is far and away the greater of the two, but its picturesque vividness and manner of poetic touch recall to my mind at least the earlier strain : —

> " Mount — mount for the hunting — with musket and spear !
> Call our friends to the field, — for the Lion is near !
> Call Arend and Ekhard and Groepe to the spoor ;
> Call Müller and Coetzer and Lucas Van Vuur.

> " Side up Eildon-Cleugh, and blow loudly the bugle ;
> Call Slinger and Allie and Dikkop and Dugal ;
> And George with the elephant-gun on his shoulder, —
> In a perilous pinch none is better or bolder."

And if all else that Pringle sang were to pass away, surely that one verse of his Farewell to Scotland will be immortal : —

> " My native land, my native vale,
> A long, a last adieu,
> Farewell to bonny Teviotdale,
> And Cheviot's mountains blue."

But the poet Pringle yields precedence to Pringle the man. His very defects were those which characterize heroic minds. Calculating shrewdness, caution, mercantile prudence, — all those stunted virtues which, like the treasure-guarding dwarfs of mediæval legend, keep the portals of worldly success, — were indeed lacking in his mental constitution.   But what capacity of self-sacrifice, what chivalrous generosity, what unquenchable ardor of goodness, dwelt in his breast!   Of all the voices raised on behalf of the slave, not one was more purely, passionately earnest than Pringle's.   And not for the slave alone, for every human being to whom he could do good, was Pringle zealous.   From his youth he had experience of straitened circumstances, he knew the most malignant spite of foes, the bitterest apathy and listlessness of friend and patron ; but in the heavenly well of that heart the wormwood and the gall were turned to sweetness.

CHAPTER XII.

THOUGH an interested and intelligent observer of the political occurrences of his time, and a cordial supporter of Catholic Emancipation, the Reform Bill, and those other measures by which the genius of liberalism was then putting its mark on the institutions of the country, Miller was never what is commonly understood as an ardent politician. One of the ideas which he most firmly grasped, and which had throughout his whole career a powerful influence on his mind, was that the share which the inhabitants of any particular locality can take in shaping the legislation or directing the policy of the country at large is necessarily too small to deserve their close and constant attention. When a great constitutional battle was to be fought; when the fate of an important measure depended, as in the case of the Reform Bill, on the unanimity and vehemence of the popular support, — he would exert himself to the utmost. But he held that, in ordinary times, it was business of a more local and less political kind which came home to the bosoms of sensible men. He was keenly alive to everything which touched upon the relation in which he stood to his parish minister, and became naturally the spokesman and leader of those Cromarty citizens who were, in matters parochial, like-minded with himself. Questions which, seen from this distance, may seem to be mere illustrations of the infinitely little, became topics of agitating concern for him, and called him, pen in hand, into the field of controversy.

The " Cromarty Chapel Case " has vanished from the thoughts and recollections of almost every living man; but, in the summer of 1831, it was profoundly interesting to Hugh Miller. The minister of the Gaelic Chapel, in Cromarty, had petitioned the Presbytery of Chanonry. that he should be either assigned a parish within the bounds of the parish of Cromarty, or a collegiate charge with the Rev. Mr. Stewart. By granting the petition, the Presbytery would have done one of two things, — placed all Mr. Stewart's parishioners under the authority of the pastor to be associated with him, or disjoined one-half of the parishioners from Mr. Stewart altogether and handed them over to the petitioner. The latter had not been in any sense chosen as their minister by Mr. Stewart's congregation; they had chosen Mr. Stewart, and were exceedingly well pleased with him; they pronounced, therefore, almost unanimously against the proposed arrangement. As the petition, in the event of its being pushed forward by its promoters. would ultimately come before the General Assembly of the Church of Scotland, a legal gentleman of Edinburgh was employed to prepare the way for its favorable reception by writing it up in an Edinburgh newspaper. Hugh Miller replied, as " the representative of nearly eight hundred" of his fellow-parishioners. The style of his letter is certainly equal to the grandeur of the occasion. It is " the cause of civil and religious liberty" which he advocates, and he is willing " to dare the worst in defence of either." He concludes with a fine testimony to the merits of Mr. Stewart. " Permit me," Mr. Editor, " before taking leave of you and the public, to state once more, for myself and my townsfolks, one great cause of our hostility to the deprecated measure. It threatens to separate us from our minister. Mr. Stewart was the man of our choice. The high character and admirable talents of this gentleman were alone taken into account when we called upon him to preside over us in spiritual things; after an acquaintance with him of nearly seven years, we can now testify to the purity of that character, and to the strength and brilliancy of these talents; much of our knowledge of human life and of human nature, of the depravity of man and of the goodness of the Almighty, has been derived from him. By means of his powerful discourses a beneficial impulse has been given to our powers of thought; in these discourses no inapt images or absurd conclusions disturb the conviction that the doctrines of Christianity are indeed fraught with the wisdom of God, and address themselves not more to the hearts than to the understandings of men; but, on the contrary, they are marked and striking examples of the established law of criticism and logic, that nothing but what is just in argument, and apt and beautiful in illustration, should be associated with what is morally good and spiritually holy."

This letter, signed " One of the People," naturally elicits a reply from the man of law; and, in July, 1831, Miller's rejoinder appears in shape of a thirty-six page pamphlet. In it Miller plays to perfection the part of the village Junius. " To no man will I yield, at least without a struggle, those rights and privileges which have been bequeathed to me by my ancestors, and which I consider it my duty, so far as my modicum of power renders me accountable, to transmit uninjured to my countrymen of a future age." There is one passage in this pamphlet which has considerable biographical value, as proving that Miller had already conceived that intense aversion for Radicalism which he continued throughout life to cherish. Sincere and steady as he was in his Whiggism, he called himself a Whig of 1688, rather than a Whig of 1789. "There is a class of men," — such is his deliverance on Radicalism, in 1831, — "which, in the present day, infests almost every civilized country of Europe. Like the desolating locusts of the East, the members of this class are terrible when gathered into multitudes, though the individuals, singly considered, be tiny and contemptible as insects. Opposition, either implied or direct, is their peculiar vocation. Though sometimes apparently united in aim, neither in principle nor conduct have they anything in common with that better tribe who are the friends and advocates of rational liberty. There was a happy allusion made to the two classes by a philosophic and honest statesman in his late admirable defence of a popular measure. He described that measure to be as a firmament which would separate the pure waters above from the gross and turbid pollution of the waters below. To the one class we owe the Reformation, and every right and institution which is dear to us as people of Scotland. From the other have proceeded many of those terrible inflictions on mankind which the historian shudders to relate. We trace the slime of those reptiles on almost every dark page of the annals of modern Europe. They have catered for that demon of Radicalism which has prowled in the streets and lanes of our cities, and lighted the torch of that fiend of Incendiarism which so lately stalked out into our fields. They are fast defacing the glories of the second revolution of France; and their names are recorded in blood on the frightful atrocities of the first. I have seen much of the people of this class in their character as individuals, and regard them in this character, however much I may dread them in the aggregate, with, I trust, a proper contempt. I have ever found them to be as devoid of genuine talent as of sterling principle."

Miller takes leave of his antagonists in words which, when we think of his subsequent championship of the Free Church, may strike us as almost prophetic: "I care not, though it be recorded as my epitaph, that when the civil and religious rights of the people of this northern parish were assailed by a hired gladiator of the law, I, one of that people, encountered the hireling on his own field, and vanquished him at his own weapons. For the future you are safe. Should I again appear on the rough arena of controversy, it will be when the barriers are encircled by a deeper line of spectators, and to grapple with some more powerful opponent." Could the strut and stare of Junius have been more felicitously mimicked? The petitioners were utterly routed, and the rights and privileges which Miller and his followers had derived from their ancestors in the parish of Cromarty continued unimpaired. Though Whig in his view of national affairs, he commonly acted in local matters with the Conservatives of the district.

CHAPTER XIII.

MISS FRASER — HER PARENTAGE, RESIDENCE IN EDINBURGH, POSITION IN CROMARTY — SOCIETY OF THE PLACE — MILLER'S MANNER AND APPEARANCE — A FASCINATING COMPANION — HE AND MISS FRASER BECOME LOVERS — GLIMPSES OF ROMANCE — METAPHYSICAL LOVE-MAKING — A NEW AMBITION AWAKES IN MILLER — FABLE OF APOLLO AND DAPHNE REVERSED — LETTER TO MISS FRASER — AND TO MRS. FRASER.

BUT there were better things to entertain Hugh Miller at this time than what Mr. Carlyle might call the highly unmemorable polemics of the parish of Cromarty. In the summer of 1831 he first saw Miss Lydia Mackenzie Fraser. About a year before, when residing with relations in Surrey, this young lady had received a letter from her mother, in which, among other descriptive touches relating to Cromarty, occurred the following: "You may guess what are its literary pretensions, when I tell you that from my window at this moment I see a stone-mason engaged in building a wall. He has just published a volume of poems, and likewise letters on the herring fishery; both of which I now send you." Miss Fraser was quick, intelligent, interested in literature; this announcement naturally excited her curiosity. On coming to Cromarty she did not for some time see the poetic stone-mason, and, when she did, he was not aware that her eyes rested on him. She and her mother had stepped in to have

279

a look at a school recently opened on " the brae-head " of Cromarty, when a man, entered, looking like a working-man in his Sunday dress, who, as a whisper from her mother informed her, was Hugh Miller. She was struck by the deep thoughtfulness of his face and by the color of his eyes, " a deep blue, tinged with sapphire." The first occasion on which, for his part, he heard her name, and cast an attentive glance upon her features, was that which is described in the " Schools and Schoolmasters." He was talking with two ladies beside a sun-dial which he had set up in his uncle's garden, when she " came hurriedly tripping down the garden-walk " and joined the group. " She was," he adds, "very pretty ; and, though in her nineteenth year at the time, her light and somewhat *petite* figure, and the waxen clearness of her complexion, which resembled rather that of a fair child than of a grown woman, made her look from three to four years younger." Evidently, though he saw her but for a few minutes, and did not exchange a word with her, she made an unusual impression upon him.

The probability, in fact, was, that this young lady would form an important addition to the circle of his acquaintance, and to that of the intellectual " upper ten " in Cromarty. Both beauty and talent had been among the attributes of the stock from which she sprung. The " lovely Barbara Hossack," and several other women noted in the Highlands for their personal attractions, had been of her ancestry on the female side ; Provost Hossack of Inverness, trusted friend of President Forbes and honored intercessor with the Duke of Cumberland for the vanquished of Culloden ; Mr. Lachlan Mackenzie, famed Highland preacher, of whom tradition in the northern Scotch counties has much to report ; and the Mackenzies of Redcastle, " said to be the most ancient house in the north of Scotland," had been among her kindred in the line of male descent. Her father, notably handsome in youth, and famous in Strathnairn as a deer-stalker, entered, later in life, into business in Inverness, and was at first prosperous, but, being generous and unsuspecting to a fault, was robbed by a clerk and beguiled by a relative, and at last overborne by disappointments and difficulties.

After the death of Mr. Fraser, his widow, possessing some small property of her own, went to live in Cromarty. His daughter had been taken away by relatives in Surrey when his affairs were getting into confusion. She had received the best education obtainable at the time by young ladies. Having resided in Edinburgh in the house of Mr. George Thomson, the correspondent of Burns, she had had the benefit not only of being instructed by Edinburgh masters, but of being introduced to a singularly pleasant and rather distinguished circle of society. George Thomson attracted to his musical parties the most skilful and enthusiastic votaries of Scottish music in Edinburgh. Nor were literature and art unrepresented at those gatherings. Scott himself, never out of his element when kindness and intelligence ruled the hour, had appeared sometimes among Thomson's guests, though this was before Miss Fraser became an inmate of his dwelling. James Ballantyne and his brother Alexander were frequently of the number. James had the gift of singing "Tullochgorum" with rough heartiness. Alexander was an exquisite violinist. Pieces from Beethoven, Mozart, and their compeers, were performed at those parties, Thomson's preference for Scottish music by no means rendering him insensible to the claims of other schools. Thomson of Duddingston, who, when clear and unapproached pre-eminence has been allowed to Turner, must be placed high among the landscape painters not only of Scotland but of Great Britain, was sometimes present, attracted, perhaps, by the original portrait of Burns by

Nasmyth, or Wilkie's Auld Robin Gray, both of which adorned George Thomson's drawing-room. Mrs. Grant of Laggan and Tennant of "Anster Fair" figured among the literary celebrities.

A young lady, of great natural ability, accustomed to polite society in Surrey, and advantageously educated and introduced in Edinburgh, would be likely to shine in the intellectual circle of Cromarty. For a very small town, Cromarty was happy in the quality of its inhabitants. The Rev. Mr. Stewart was the central star in its social firmament, his supremacy beginning about this time to be disputed by Miller. Not that there was any thought of rivalry or of jealousy on either side; they were the closest and most faithful friends; but that the reputation of Miller even in its dawn shot its rays to a wider horizon than had as yet been reached by Mr. Stewart's, and that the culture of the minister was, in all save theological reading and grammatical knowledge of Greek and Latin, narrower than that of the parishioner. A colonel, a captain, both intelligent beyond the average of their class, with ladies to match, a banker who had been an officer in the navy, and retained professional enthusiasm enough to make him study naval history until he became a walking encyclopædia of information on sea-battles, — these, with a variety of studious and accomplished ladies, eminent, some for Calvinistic metaphysics, some for geological predilections, made up the cluster of notabilities which circled round Alexander Stewart and Hugh Miller, the Duke and the Goethe of this miniature Weimar. The women had their full share of the intellect of the place, or more. "By much the greater half of the collective mind of the town," says Miller in one of his letters, "is vested in the ladies." It speaks for the sterling worth as well as the intellectual penetration of the Cromarty notables, that they welcomed to a footing of perfect social equality the man who was to be seen any forenoon, bare-armed, dusty-visaged, with mallet in hand and apron in front, making his bread by cutting inscriptions in the church-yard. With Miller any intercourse but that of perfect equality would have been impossible. Diffident in company as he was, his pride was as inflexible as that of Burns, and, if possible, more sensitive. The slightest trace of condescending patronage would have driven him away, and forever. The colonels and captains who were to be found in country towns at this period were generally men of the French war, men who had seen enough of life and action to bring out the stronger lines in their character, men frank of bearing, direct of speech, and perfectly brave. In the Highland towns they were likely to be cadets of old Highland houses. Constitutional fondness for war, concurrently with shallowness of the paternal purse, had led many such into the army. Pride as well as courage was likely to be hereditary with these military gentlemen, and it is, I repeat, to the credit of those of Cromarty that they recognized Miller for what he was, a man qualified to adorn and delight any circle.

Once the singularity of admitting a stone-mason to social fellowship was got over, the charm of Miller's acquaintance would secure his footing. All who knew him with any degree of intimacy have testified to the fascination of his presence. For women in particular his manner and conversation had an exquisite charm. The leonine roughness of his exterior, the shaggy hair. the strong-boned, overhanging brows. the head carried far forward and shoulders bent as with brooding thought, the working-man's gait and gesture, lent the enchantment of a delicate surprise to the deep gentleness which they disguised. Never was the difference between the conventional gentleman and the true gentleman — the possibility that one may be every inch a true gentleman and yet every inch *not* a conventional gentleman — more signally illustrated than in the case of Miller. A fine and tender sympathy, the soul of politeness, enabled him, spontaneously, unconsciously, to feel with every feeling, to think with every thought, of the person with whom he conversed. The faculty of skilful and kindly listening is rarer even than that of fluent and brilliant talk, and Miller had it in fine perfection. He had, however, the gift of captivating speech, as well. His conversation, though never voluble, impulsive, precipitate, exhibited the action not only of a powerful but of an educated intellect, practised in logic and trained to the expert use of its linguistic instruments. He never was at a loss for an idea, never at a loss for a word, and the stores of his memory afforded him an exhaustless supply of illustration from what he had seen in nature or read in books. There was a pensiveness, also, in his tone, a profound sadness in his eye, a touch of egotistic melancholy about him, which is a spell of absolute enthralment for most women, and, indeed, for most men. "The bewitching smile," says Mr. Disraeli, "usually beams from the grave face. It is then irresistible."

Miss Fraser, as we should have expected, was not without admirers of the other sex at the time when she formed the acquaintance of Hugh Miller. They were "younger and dressed better" than the stone-mason, and had chosen "the liberal professions." But no man has so strong an attraction for a superior girl as a man of brains, and Miller's seniority of ten years was in his favor rather than the reverse, in the contest with more juvenile rivals. Miss Fraser, meeting him here and there in society, was interested by his conversation. On sunny forenoons, she might pause in her walk to have a chat with him in the churchyard. On which side the friendship first glowed into a warmer feeling need not be determined; probably they became lovers almost simultaneously; and it is certain that this his first and last love took entire possession of Miller's heart.

A number of materials, — letters of the period, memoranda, note-books, — illustrative of this part of his history, have come into my hands, and from these I have selected at my own discretion, and on my own responsibility. Here is a glimpse of him from an authentic source, when he seems to have been already pretty far gone : " One evening we (Miss Fraser and Hugh Miller) encountered each other by chance in a wooded path of the hill, above which slope a few cultivated fields skirted by forest. Hugh Miller prevailed on me to accompany him to a point which commands a fine view of the frith and surrounding country. We sat down to rest at the edge of a pine wood, in a little glade fragrant with fallen cones, and ankle-deep in the spiky leaves of the firs. I sat on the stump of a felled tree. He threw himself on the ground, two or three yards from my feet. The sun was just setting, and lighted up the pillared trunks around with a deep, copper-colored glow. Hugh took out a volume of Goldsmith. When did he ever want a companion of that description? He read in a low voice the story of Edwin and Angelina. It was then I first suspected that he had a secret which he had not revealed."

Things had reached this rather critical posture when Mrs. Fraser, alarmed at the notion that her daughter might bestow her heart and hand on a mechanic, commanded that the intimacy should be broken off. The young lady was disconsolate; wept much; felt " like a poor little parasite which had succeeded in laying hold of some strong and stately tree, and which a powerful blast had laid prostrate in the dust." Under these circumstances the following entry from the same hand will not seem surprising : —

" It was late on the evening of a very hot summer•Sabbath during the time of interdict, that, feeling listless and weary, I crept out a little to breathe the air. I had no intention of walking, — did not even put on bonnet or shawl. I stole down the grassy garden-path and listened to the murmur of the sea, whose waves beat on the shore at a stone's throw beyond. But the night was still sultry, and I imagined that, by getting to the top of some eminence, I might find the cooling breeze for which I longed. So I found myself, I scarcely knew how, at the ancient chapel of St. Regulus. There the trees which line the sides of the ravine by which it is surrounded waved the tops of their branches, the blue sea looked forth between, and as the twilight gave place to night the stars began to twinkle forth. I stood on the edge of the hill enjoying the slight breeze and the soft brightness of earth and sky, when suddenly I perceived that Hugh stood beside me. He spoke of the sweetness of the evening, the beauty of the landscape, and so on; but his speech was cold and reserved, and he made no allusion to our peculiar position. Possibly his pride was touched by it. At that very time, however, as he afterwards told me, he cut a notch in the wood of a beam which crossed the roof of his cottage for every day on which we had not met. He stayed but a short time there, leaving me standing just where he had found me; but there was no notch on that day. I on my part knelt at a cold gravestone, and registered over the dead a vow, rash and foolish perhaps; but it was kept."

From these suggestive glimpses, readers of imagination and sensibility will gather all the information that is necessary upon the subject. This love affair was clearly romantic, but not the less real on that account. A judicious mother, reflecting probably that young ladies of nineteen are not likely to cease to love for being told to do so, removed the interdict, and, though marriage was for the present to be considered as out of the question, the young people were permitted to enjoy each other's society.

It would be a mistake to suppose that the intellectual benefit of their intercourse was entirely on the side of the lady. Her mind, if not so well stored, so deliberate, so patiently thoughtful, as that of her lover, had the piercing clearness and acuteness of good female intellect, and would sometimes strike direct to the heart of a subject when circumspect and meditative Hugh was gyrating round and round it. On one occasion, for example, — one probably of many, — the pair had enjoyed a game of chop-logic *àpropos* of that venerable problem, the origin of evil. Miller's argument, as placed before Miss Fraser, I cannot state in his own words, but its substance is derivable from a letter of his to Miss Dunbar of Boath. "May not evil," suggests Hugh, who, however, pronounces the question, in the essence of it, unanswerable, "be the shade with which good is contrasted that it may be known as good, the sickness to which it is opposed as health, the deformity beside which it is shown forth as beauty? Nay, may it not be affirmed that the plan of the Deity would not have been a perfect one if it did not include imperfection, nor a wise one if it admitted not of folly, nor a good one if evil did not form a part of it? Is there not something like this implied in the remarkable text which informs us that the weakness of God is mightier than the strength of men, and his foolishness more admirable than their wisdom?" All which plausible balancing of advantage and disadvantage, Miss Fraser brings front to front with the sheer mystery of pain. "Allowing," she writes, "that the actual contrast between good and evil, ease and suffering, increased our value for the ease and the good, how reconcile with our ideas of justice the fact that there are thousands born to suffer continual pain and to be depraved forever? Two

thousand gladiators once lay expiring in the Roman Am-
phitheatre, but does it reconcile us to the fact that hundreds of thousands of spectators were delighted with the
scene?' This metaphysician, for all her *petite* figure,
waxen clearness of complexion, and childlike appearance,
has not, to my knowledge, received a satisfactory answer
to her question either from Hugh Miller or any one else.
Such a lady-love was capable of furnishing intellectual dia-
mond dust of very superior quality for the sharpening of a
man's wits.

Miss Fraser's intercourse with Miller — the relation in
which he was now placed with her — was beneficial to him
in another way. It broke up the theory of life which he
had formed for himself, and replaced it by one of a more
masculine character. Profoundly imbued as he was with
the ambition of self-culture, and loving praise with the ardor of a born literary man, he was nevertheless firmly persuaded that, in the rank of mason, in the town of Cromarty,
he could enjoy as much happiness as it was possible for
him to enjoy on earth. A wife, he thought, he could dis-
pense with; no passion, except the passions of the mind,
had ever seriously moved him; and though he took special
delight in conversation with clever women, he could have
that conversation without marriage. He would ply the
mallet in the summer days; he would owe no man a six-
pence; he would read his favorite books in the evenings of
June and the short days of December; he would train himself to ever-increasing vigor and grace of style, and would
write with the fresh enthusiasm of one for whom literature
was its own reward. Thus was he contented to live and to
die; the world, it was his inflexible conviction, had nothing better than this to offer him. If the question were simply of more or less happiness, it would be difficult to prove
that in all this he was wrong. The quality, however, of the

happiness would not have been the highest, and he might have awakened from his idyl of intellectual luxury to the consciousness that, in evading the pains of action, he had missed the sternest but the noblest joys of life. When Miss Fraser taught him to understand the love-poetry of Burns, as he expressly says she did, he bade adieu forever, though not without a sigh, to the tranquil hopes which had hitherto inspired him. He told Miss Fraser that she had spoiled a good philosopher, and it was with no exultation, though with calm and fixed resolution, that he felt the spirit of the philosophic recluse die within him and the spirit of the man arise. The classic fable was reversed. Daphne overtook and disenchanted her lover. Miller awoke from the dream which was stealing over him; the roots which had already struck deep into his native soil, and which promised to bind him down to a mild, tree-like existence on the hill of Cromarty, were snapped asunder; a stronger circulation swept in fierce thrills along his veins; and with new hope, new ambition, new aspiration, he girded up his loins for the race of life. Hitherto, " he professed just what he felt, to be content with a table, a chair, and a pot, with a little fire in his grate and a little meat to cook on it." He professed such contentment no longer; for himself he could have lived and died a working-man, but he could not endure the idea of his wife being in any rank save that of a lady.

Habitually self-conscious, observant of every event in his mental history, Miller did not fail to mark the change which had passed over him. In a letter written in the summer of 1834 he describes it with grace, naïveté, and lightness of touch, to her who was its cause. The first part of the letter is unimportant, but it may as well be inserted for the illustration it affords of his simple and pleasurable mode of life in Cromarty at this period : —

"Cromarty, Wednesday, 12 o'clock.

"I am afraid you are still unwell. Your window was shut till near ten this morning, and as I saw no light from it last evening I must conclude you went early to bed. How very inefficient, my L——, are the friendships of earth! My heart is bound up in you, and yet I can only wish and regret, and, — yes, pray. Well, that is something. I cannot regulate your pulses, nor dissipate your pains, nor give elasticity to your spirits; but I can implore on your behalf the great Being who can. Would that both for your sake and my own my prayers had the efficacy of those described by simple-hearted James! * They are sincere, my L——, when you form the burden of them, but they are not the prayers of the righteous. . . .

"My mother, as you are aware, has a very small garden behind her house. It has produced, this season, one of the most gigantic thistles of the kind which gardeners term the Scotch, that I ever yet saw. The height is fully nine feet, the average breadth nearly five. Some eight years ago I intended building a little house for myself in this garden. I was to cover it outside with ivy, and to line it inside with books; and here was I to read and write and think all my life long; not altogether so independent of the world as Diogenes in his tub, or the savage in the recesses of the forest, but quite as much as is possible for man in his social state. Here was I to attain to wealth, not by increasing my goods, but by moderating my desires. Of the thirst after wealth I had none, — I could live on half a crown per week and be content; nor yet was I desirous of power, — I sought not to be any man's master, and I had spirit enough to preserve me from being any man's slave. I had no

---

* "The effectual, fervent prayer of a righteous man availeth much." — James v. 16.

heart to oppress; why wish, then, for the seat or the power of the oppressor? I had no dread of being subjected to oppression; did the proudest or the loftiest dare infringe on my rights as a man, there might be disclosed to him, perchance,

> " 'Through peril and alarm
> The might that slumbered in a peasant's arm.'

Even for fame itself I had no very exciting desire. If I met with it in quest of amusement, well; if not, I could be happy enough without it. So much for the great disturbers of human life, — avarice and ambition, and the thirst of praise. My desires were not tall enough to penetrate into those upper regions which they haunt; I was too low for them. and for the inferior petty disturbers of men's happiness I was as certainly too high. Love, for instance, I could have nothing to fear from. I knew myself to be naturally of a cool temperament; and, then, were not my attachments to my friends so many safety-valves! Besides, no woman of taste could ever love me, for I was ugly and awkward; and as I could love only a woman of taste, and could never submit to woo one to whom I was indifferent, my being ugly and awkward was as an iron wall to me. No, no, I had nothing to fear from love. My own dear L——, only see how much good philosophy you have spoiled. I am not now indifferent to wealth or power or place in the world's eye. I would fain be rich, that I might render you comfortable; powerful, that I might raise you to those high places of society which you are so fitted to adorn; celebrated. that the world might justify your choice. I never think now of building the little house, or of being happiest in solitude; and if my life is to be one of celibacy, it must be one of sorrow also, — of heart-wasting sorrow for — but I must not think of that."

One other letter upon this subject we must not omit. It was addressed by Miller to Mrs. Fraser: —

"MY DEAR MADAM: — I trust ingratitude is not among the number of my faults. But how render apparent the sense I entertain of your kindness in so warmly interesting yourself in my welfare? Just by laying my whole mind open before you. Two years ago there was not a less ambitious or more contented sort of person than myself in the whole kingdom. I knew happiness to be altogether independent of external circumstances; I more than knew it, — I felt it. My days passed on in a quiet, even tenor; and though poor, and little known, and bound down to a life of labor, I could yet anticipate, without one sad feeling, that in all these respects my future life was to resemble the past. Why should I regret my poverty? I was independent, in debt to no one, and in possession of all I had been accustomed to regard as the necessaries of life. Why sigh over my obscurity? My lot was that of the thousands around me; and, besides, was I not born to an immortality too sublime to borrow any of its grandeur or importance from the mock immortality of fame? Why repine because my life was to be one of continual labor? I had acquired habits of industry, and had learned from experience that, if labor be indeed a curse, the curse of indolence is by far the weightier of the two. It will not surprise you, my dear madam, that, entertaining such sentiments, I should have used no exertions, and expressed no wish, to quit my obscure sphere of life for a higher. Why should I? I carried my happiness about with me, and was independent of every external circumstance.

"I shall not say that I still continue to think and feel after this manner, for, though quite the same sort of man at present that I was then, I have, perhaps, ascertained that my happiness does not now centre so exclusively in myself. To you, I dare say, I need not be more explicit. But though, in consequence of this discovery, I have become somewhat solicitous, perhaps, of rising a step or two higher in the scale of society, I find it is one thing to wish and quite another to attempt. I find, too, that habits long indulged in, and formed under the influence of sentiments such as I describe, must militate so powerfully against me, if that attempt be made, as to leave little chance of success. My lack of a classical education has barred against me all the liberal professions; I have no turn for business matters; and the experience of about twelve years has taught me that, as an architect or contractor (professions which, during at least that space of time, have been the least fortunate in this part of the kingdom of all others), I can indulge no rational hope of realizing what I desire. There is one little plan, however, which is rather more a favorite with me than any of the others. I think I have seen men not much more clever than myself, and possessed of not much greater command of the pen, occupying respectable places in the ephemeral literature of the day as editors of magazines and newspapers, and deriving from their labors incomes of from one to three hundred pounds per annum. A very little application, if I do not overrate my abilities, natural and acquired, might fit me for occupying a similar place, and, of course, deriving a corresponding remuneration. But how push myself forward? Simply in this manner. I have lately written, as I dare say you are aware, a small traditional work, which I have submitted to the consideration of some of the literati of Edinburgh, and of which they have signified their approval, in a style of commendation far surpassing my fondest anticipations. I shall try and get it published. If it

succeed in attracting any general notice, I shall consider
my literary abilities. such as they are, fairly in the market;
if (what is more probable) it fail, I shall just strive to forget the last two years of my life, and try whether I cannot
bring a very dear friend to forget them too. God has not
suffered me in the past to be either unhappy myself or a
cause of unhappiness to those whom I love, and I can
trust that he will deal with me after the same fashion in the
future. I need not say, my dear madam, that I write in
confidence, and for your own eye alone. If I fail in my
little scheme, I shall bear my disappointment all the better
if it be not known that I built much upon it, or looked
much beyond it. In such an event, the pity of people who,
in the main, are less happy than myself (and the great bulk
of mankind are certainly not happier) shall, I trust, never
be solicited by,

"My dear madam," etc.

CHAPTER XIV.

NEW OUTLOOK IN LIFE — DIFFICULTIES OF PUBLICATION — LETTERS TO MISS FRASER.

THE quiet of intellectual luxury and philosophical contentment broken up by the agitation of a more genially inspiring hope; the pride of the stonemason who has been accepted as lover by a lady forbidding him to place her in any position in which the world might fail to recognize her for what she was, — Miller now looked anxiously round him for some means of bettering his social status. He often thought of the backwoods of America; but, though the project of emigration may have had some charms for his fancy, it never laid hold on his heart. He may have seen himself, with the mind's eye, a brawny pioneer of civilization, making clear, with stalwart arm and glowing forehead, a space in the primeval forest, to be occupied with field and garden and homestead, and at moments there may have been fascination in the view; but his affections were anchored in Scotland. His favorite idea, therefore, as we saw in the preceding letter, was that he might undertake the editorship of a Scottish newspaper. Some offer of the kind reached him from Inverness, but he did not consider it eligible. He shrank from the risk of depending for a livelihood upon promiscuous contribution to periodicals, and had the shrewdness to be aware that, neither by his poems nor by his letters on the herring fishery, had he attained celebrity enough to command, for his productions, a ready sale and a high price in the market of current literature. His disposition was at all times the reverse of sanguine, and the largest and most radiant possibility had a less attraction for him than a very small certainty.

For the present, therefore, he determined to watch and wait, concentrating his efforts on the improvement of his prose style, and preparing a prose work which might conclusively scale for him the heights of literary distinction. Soon after the appearance of his poems, we find him at work on a traditional history of his native parish, and, at the time when his engagement with Miss Fraser commenced, he had composed enough to fill a goodly volume. To remove its blemishes, heighten its beauties, and procure its publication, were for several years his chief endeavors. Against publishing by subscription he had objections which were, for a long time, invincible. The stubborn independence of his nature, the profound contempt with which he looked upon those mendicant friars of literature who, incompetent to succeed as mechanics and failing to sell their manuscripts to booksellers, hawk subscription-lists about country districts, and make beggary more hideous by conceit and affectation, and the dainty exclusiveness of his appetite for fame, loathing the very idea of a reputation he did not owe to his unaided efforts, all combined to dissuade him from this mode of publication.

Ultimately he gave way on the point, influenced by satisfactory reasons of which we shall hear; but the difficulty was evidently unresolved at the time when Miss Fraser addressed to him the following note. Its precise date has not been preserved, but I take it to have been written in 1833. "You are in difficulty about the printing of your book, and I might render you some assistance. Can I help, at least, satisfying myself whether or not it be in my power? I have a little hoard of money (about forty pounds), which I may put in trinkets or in the fire, and no one know anything of the matter. Will you not let me put it to a nobler use? . . . Dear Hugh, do not refuse me; if it will pain you to fancy yourself indebted to me, make it a loan. I shall indeed receive my own with usury when it shall have been of service to you." To which the reply was decisive, and, I have no doubt, prompt. "Not all that industry ever accumulated could impart to me so exquisite a feeling as your kind and generous offer. My heart still throbs when I think of it, and yet during the greater part of last night, — for I have not slept for two hours together, — I could think of nothing else. Could I avail myself of it, however, I would but ill deserve the affection which has prompted it. . . . . God bless and reward you; every new trait I discover in your character, while it draws me closer to you, shows me how ill I deserve you."

Miss Fraser, with a view to assisting her mother and finding a channel for her own energies, taught a class of young ladies. In the eyes of these, Hugh Miller, whose relation with their mistress they knew, was naturally a person of importance, and when they had anything to coax out of her they thought it good policy to apply to him. Little children, sweet-tempered women, light-hearted, laughing girls, — all gentle and innocent creatures, — loved and trusted this man, and "found their comfort in his face." The old Scottish customs of Halloween, immortalized by Burns, had not yet become obsolete in Cromarty, and Miss Fraser's pupils were disposed to celebrate their Halloween in the room usually devoted to study. Miss Fraser's consent was required; and one day, when Hugh was at work in the church-yard, he was "waited upon by a deputation" of the girls with a request to write a petition for them. He complied.

" To Miss Fraser, the humble petition of her attached and grateful pupils,

" Sheweth,

" That your petitioners had great-grandmothers who were young, unmarried women about the beginning of the last century. Like most young women of our own day, they were all exceedingly anxious to know what sort of husbands they were to have, or whether they were to have any husbands at all. And, that they might satisfy themselves on this important matter, they burnt nuts and ate apples every Halloween, and with such singular success that they all lived to see themselves married, — married, too, to men who had the honor of being the great-grandfathers of your humble petitioners.

" That your petitioners have, therefore, acquired a profound respect for the ancient and laudable practice of burning nuts and eating apples. They are desirous, too, to have a peep into the future, not only for the sake of their grandmothers, but also for their own, being not a little solicitous, as every Halloween for the last five years has given them a new set of husbands, to ascertain the exact number which is to fall to the share of each.

" That your petitioners deem Happiness a very excellent sort of lady, and know many wiser women than themselves who are of the same opinion. There is that in her character which makes people regard even the places in which she has visited them with feelings similar to those which incited the old Greeks and Romans of our story-books to raise temples and altars on the hill-tops on which their gods had alighted. Now it so happens that your petitioners have sent her a card of invitation for next Halloween, to share with them in their nuts and apples, and she is to be with them without fail. And they would fain meet with her on this occasion in that apartment in which their dear mistress has done so much to render them wiser and better. For so sincerely do they love it that they are desirous of loving it more, and this by rendering it a scene of splendid hopes, rich promises, and good fun, — by associating with it recollections not of long lessons or false grammar, but of fine husbands, gilt coaches, nuts, gingerbread, and apples.

" May it therefore please you to grant to your humble petitioners full possession, during the coming night of fun and prediction, of that interesting apartment in which you have so often imparted to your petitioners more of good than they have been all fully able to carry away. As you have already so liberally given to them of the kernel, may it now please you to add the shell. And your attached and grateful petitioners shall in return sacrifice an entire egg to your happiness and prosperity."

The petition was successful.

One thing is clear : Hugh Miller's existence at this time was bright and cheerful. At peace with himself, and, if we except a fierce Cromarty Radical or two, with all the world; exempt from every care which gnaws the human heart; happy in friendship, happy in love; hope and ambition touching his horizon with bright auroral hues, but not inflaming him with any feverish heat, — he was indeed most fortunate. For events, there were occasional trips to Inverness, fishing excursions to the rocks, exploring rambles on the shore. picnics to the Burn of Eathie. All the time, he was pursuing his enterprise of self-culture with the steady enthusiasm of a Goethe. He never wrote a letter or penned a paragraph for the " Inverness Courier " without striving to make it a means of improving himself in composition. He grudged no toil in writing and re-writing his Traditions, resolutely bent upon bringing them, in style, thought, and interest, to his high standard.

It need not seriously qualify our estimate of his felicity

to know that the business of getting his volume into print proved for him, as it has proved for so many authors, a business of difficulty. Sir Thomas Dick Lauder — known to literature by his novel, "The Wolf of Badenoch," and to science by his account of the great Morayshire floods and dissertation on the parallel roads of Glen Roy — had formed a high opinion of the Cromarty poet's capacity, and exerted himself to procure the publication of his book. Sir Thomas submitted the manuscript to an Edinburgh critic, an expert, it appears, in the tasting department of the literary guild, whom he describes as "one of the first literary judges of the day." The response was more flattering than satisfactory. "I do not," wrote this minister of fate, "pretend to have read the whole with much care; but I have read quite enough to impress me with a decided opinion of his [Miller's] very extraordinary powers as a prose writer." There is, however, an objection to the history, to wit, "its great lengthiness;" and though the great man repeats his conviction that Mr. Miller is "a very extraordinary person," he does not say that he will recommend any of the purveyors of literary viands whom he professionally advises to place it on their bill of fare. Messrs. Oliver and Boyd and Mr. Andrew Shortrede, to whom respectively the volume is offered, are almost equally complimentary and equally tantalizing. Mr. Miller's manner of treating his subject "does him great credit." It is difficult to say what will succeed, but "as easy as ever to say what ought to succeed, and under this class no one can hesitate to rank the Traditional History of Cromarty." But "the work would require considerable pruning to suit the public taste," and, on the whole, "we regret that we cannot avail ourselves of your kind offer." Mr. Shortrede would "risk the printing," if any one would "venture the other expenses;" but farther than this not even Mr. Shortrede, though he evidently hankers after the thing, will go. He proposes to forward the MS. to his London correspondent, "to ascertain his opinion" before returning it. Sir Thomas, who felt that he " had no chance with Black, Cadell," or other publishers, apprised Miller of his want of success, trying to put the discouraging tale as tenderly as possible. "The difficulty," he said, " of getting out a *literary* work at present is immense. I have never been able to get my first volume of Legends launched, and I now begin to despair of doing so." In short, our aspiring Ixion cannot have the real Juno, but here is a cloud, as like her in form and color as a cloud can possibly be, and he is most civilly invited to derive what satisfaction he can from embracing it.

Sir Thomas' note is dated 14th October, 1833; Miller replies on the 18th of the same month. He is disposed to make as much of the cloud as is feasible, but sees well that it is a cloud after all.

" HONORED SIR : — I little thought, when writing you last spring, of the world of trouble to which my request and your own goodness were to subject you ; had I but dreamed of it I would not now, perhaps, be possessed of your truly valuable opinion of my MS., — an opinion which has given me more pleasure than I dare venture fully to express. I set myself down in my obscure solitudes to seek amusement in making rude pictures of my homely ancestors and the scenes of humble life by which I am surrounded, and find that my careless sketches have elicited the praise of a master.

" In a work composed as mine has been and on such a subject, by a person, too, so acquainted with the taste of the public and the present aspect of the literary world, what wonder that there should be a good deal which would be perhaps better away? The circumstances which have barred upon me those magazines of thought which constitute the learning of the age have prevented me from acquiring its manners or becoming familiar with its tastes. And yet, as it was probably these very circumstances which led me to think on most subjects for myself, I must just bear with the misfortune of being uncouth and tedious in some of my pages for the sake of being a little original in the rest. . . . Some of my dissertations, too, are, I suspect, sad, *leaden* things, though they amused me not a little in the *casting;* and some of my minor traditions, though recommended to me by my townsfolks, are, I am aware, like reptiles in a bottle of spirits, hardly worth the liquid which preserves them. . . . Some of my acquaintance here, who seem much more anxious to see my history in print than I am myself, are urging me to publish by subscription; and this they assure me I could accomplish through the medium of my friends without the meanness of personal solicitation, or, indeed, without meanness of any kind; but I am still averse to the method, and at any rate will not determine with regard to it until my MS. has been submitted to Mr. Shortrede's correspondent. Even should his opinion be an unfavorable one, and the dernier scheme prove unfavorable too, still my fate as a writer shall not, I trust, be decided by that of my Traditions. The same cast of mind which has enabled me to overcome not a few of the obstacles which my place in society and an imperfect education have conspired to cast in my way, and this, too, at a time when the approval of such men as the gentleman whom I have now the honor of addressing was a meed beyond the reach of even my fondest anticipations, shall, I trust, enable me to persist in improving to the utmost the powers which I naturally possess. And should I fail at last, it will assuredly be less my fault than my misfortune.

"I am wholly unable to express the sense I entertain of

your goodness, but believe, honored sir, that I can feel and appreciate it. My days are passing quietly and not unhappily among friends to whom I am sincerely attached, and by whom I know myself to be regarded with a similar feeling; and though that depression which affects the trade of the whole country bears so low that it has reached even me, I can live on the little which I earn, and am content. Still, however, I indulge in hopes and expectations which I would ill like to forego, — hopes perhaps of being somewhat less obscure, and somewhat abler to assist such of my relatives as are poorer than even myself; but the future belongs to God. Winter, my season of leisure, is fast approaching, and should I live to see its close I shall probably find myself ten or twelve chapters deep in the second volume of my Traditions, maugre the untoward destinies of the first."

The reference to Mr. Shortrede's London correspondent was unavailing. Nothing remained but to fall back upon the scheme of publication by subscription. "I stated," he writes to Sir Thomas Dick Lauder, in June, 1834, "when I had last the honor of addressing you, that some of my townspeople and acquaintance seemed to be more anxious to see my history in print than I was myself, and that they were urging me to publish it by subscription. It is not difficult to be persuaded to what one half-inclines; my chief objection to the scheme arose out of a dread of subjecting myself to a charge of meanness by teasing the public into an unfair bargain, — giving it a bad book, and pocketing money not counterfeit in return. But I am assured that the book is not bad, and that there would therefore be nothing mean or unfair in the transaction; and the partiality for one's own performances, so natural to the poor author, has rendered the argument a convincing one. I publish, therefore, by subscription, so soon as three hundred subscribers at eight shillings can be procured. Pecuniary advantage forms no part of my scheme; and, though not very sanguine, I trust I shall succeed. . . . If ever my Traditions get abroad I find they will be all the better for having stayed so long at home. Since sending you my MS. I have thought of alterations which will materially improve some of the chapters."

The subscription scheme was attended with complete success. Miller's townsmen and friends exerted themselves strenuously in his behalf, and in due time his book saw the light. But we must not anticipate.

His correspondence, while these negotiations on the subject of his volume were in progress, had been copious, and some portion of it must be laid before the reader. No further introduction is required to the following selection from his letters of the period addressed to Miss Fraser. Whenever Miller left Cromarty, whether for Inverness or elsewhere, he commenced writing to Miss Fraser, and seems to have carried a pen and ink-horn along with him, so that he might put his impressions into black and white for conveyance to his mistress at every resting-place on the way.

"Inverness, 10 o'clock at night.

"Your criticisms, my Lydia, came rather late; but when I receive my proof-sheets I shall bring them to you that we may talk over them. You are a skilful grammarian, but in some points we shall differ, — you know we can differ, and yet be very excellent friends. I might try long enough ere I could find a mistress so fitted to be useful to me, — so little of a blue-stocking, and yet so knowing in composition. I am glad you are better, and that you slept so well last night, even though your slumber abridged your letter. I saw you to-day as I passed your mother's. You were standing in the door with a lady, and looked, I thought, very pale. O my own Lydia, be careful of yourself! Take little thought and much exercise. Read for amusement only. Set yourself to make a collection of shells, or butterflies, or plants. Do anything that will have interest enough to amuse you without requiring so much attention as to fatigue. I was sadly annoyed in the steamboat to-night by a sort of preaching man, — one M——, a Baptist. He has little sense and no manners, and his religion seems to consist in finding fault. Of all nonsense, my Lydia, religious nonsense is the worst ; of all uncharitableness, that of the sectary is the bitterest. We too often speak of intolerance as peculiar to classes who chance to have the power of exercising it, — as inseparably connected with Church establishments and a beneficed clergy ; but it is not with circumstances or situations that it is connected ; it is with inferior natures, — it is with bad men. The proud, heart-swollen Churchman who condemns heretics to the flames of *this* world, and the rancorous heresiarch, his opponent, who can only threaten them with the flames of the *next*, possess it in an equal degree. Nay, it may rage in the breast of the Dissenter and find no place in that of the Churchman. I saw as much of it in M—— to-night (and yet no man could denounce it more earnestly) as might serve a Grand Inquisitor. I had no dispute with him, as I saw it would be an easier task to find him argument than comprehension ; besides, I wished to see the fellow, horns and all ; and had I touched him he might have drawn in the latter. Goodnight, my Lydia ; these are commonplace remarks, but they have an important bearing on the present time. A persecuting, intolerant spirit directed against our national Church animates the great body of our Dissenters, and there cannot be a fairer specimen of the more active of the class than M——. Good-night : fine thing to be able to write to one's friends."

"I have been walking about the streets for an hour, looking at people's heads and faces, and at the booksellers' windows. I wish I knew the house you were born in; I would pay my respects to it with a great deal more devotional sincerity than some pilgrims feel when kneeling before the Virgin's house at Loretto. I have been walking in the suburbs; it is still too early to call on any of my acquaintance. You little know, my lassie, how covetous I have become. I have hardly in the course of my walk seen a snug little house with woodbine on the walls and a garden in front, without half ejaculating, ' Here with my Lydia, and with a very little of that wealth which thousands know not how to employ, I could be happy.' Well, though not born to riches, I have been born to what riches cannot purchase, — to the possession of an expansive heart that can be sincerely attached, and happy in its attachment, and to the love, the pure, disinterested, unselfish love of a talented and lovely woman."

"DRYNIE FARM, Friday morning.

" After leaving Mr. Sutor, I called at the ' Courier ' office. Mr. Carruthers himself had not yet come in, and in the interim I took a stroll with the head printer of the establishment, to the building now erecting on the Castle Hill, where I saw more than twenty masons, but knew only two of the squad. Ten years, and so long is it since I wrought at any public work, have well-nigh worn out my acquaintance with my brethren of the mallet; but many of them in this part of the country who do not know me personally have a kind of favor for me as one who does them no discredit; and I saw some of them whom I had been pointed out to (do smile at my vanity!) looking at me with something like complacency. Masons are in general rough-looking fellows, and their occupation is dusty and toilsome, but I know not a manlier or a better suited to exemplify Bacon's remark on laborious as opposed to sedentary employments.

"On my return I saw Mr. Carruthers. He was very kind, and showed me his library, and kindly offered me the loan of any of his books. I saw with him a fine — shall I say affecting? — print of Cowper. It bore in the fixed lines of the face the marks of a vigorous intellect and a fine, playful wit, but, oh, the expression of withering blight and hopeless despondency that rested on the features! There was sadness in the beautiful eye and on the expansive forehead, — a sadness which the voice of friendship or of fame, or the bright rays of genius, vainly strove to dissipate; and the meek firmness of the lips was a firmness which seemed to contend with agony. I could almost cry as I contemplated it."

"Gray Cairn, half-past 3 o'clock.

"Here, my own Lydia, have I sitten down to write you after a rather smart walk of about eleven miles; and my first thought is of you. Have you ever visited the *gray cairn*, or surveyed the bleak barren moor that spreads around it? It towers high and shapeless around me, gray with the moss and lichens of forgotten ages, — a mound striding across the stream of centuries, to connect the past with the present, — a voucher to attest the truth of events long forgotten, — a memorial carved over by the fingers of fancy with a wild, imaginative poetry. How very poetical savage life appears when viewed through the dim vista of time! The savages of the present day we regard as a squalid, lazy, cruel race of animals, — disgusting mixtures of the wolf, the fox, and the hog, who live, and love, and fight, not with the wisdom, gallantry, courage of men, but with the craft, the brutality, the ferocity of wild beasts.

Not such the sentiment when we look through the clouded avenue of the past on the deeds and habits of our painted ancestors. The poetical haze of the atmosphere magnifies the size of the figures, smooths down their various hardnesses of outlines, and softens and improves their colors. On the wild moor before me have some of them fought and died in some nameless but hard-contested and bloody conflict, — nameless now, though long celebrated among their descendants, and often sung at their rude hunting-feasts and war banquets. See how we are surrounded by vestiges of the fray! Observe yonder rectangular, altar-like tumulus, — the scene, it is probable, of human sacrifice; — mark how thickly those grave-like mounds are scattered over the moor, and how regularly they run in lines. And then turn to the cairn behind, — the monument of some fallen chief. Give yourself up for a moment, my Lydia, to the sway of imagination. The moor is busy with life, the air rent with clamor. Do you not see waving arms and threatening faces, the glittering of spears, the flashing of swords, eyes flaring, wounds streaming, warriors falling? See, the combatants are now wedged into dense masses, now broken into detached bands; now they press onward, now they recede; now they open their ranks, now they close in a death-grapple. There are the yells of pain, the roarings of rage, and the shouts of exultation. Passion is busy, and so is death. But the figures recede and the sounds die away, till we see only a wide, solitary moor, with its mounds and its tumuli, and hear only the wind rustling through the heath."

"CROMARTY, half-past 6 o'clock.

"Here am I once more in my little room. Mother is preparing tea for me; and I have just given, as is my wont after returning from a journey, half pennies apiece to the children and to Angus, the idiot boy, who has been sadly annoyed at my absence. The degree of fatigue incurred by walking nearly eighteen miles in a warm day has in some slight degree blunted the edge of my mind, but it has spared my affections, — I can love as warmly as ever. Dear me, here is Bell, — I am to see you and to get tea from you to boot."

"Thank you, my own kind lassie, for your long and excellent letter. I wish you but knew how much I enjoyed it on the first perusal and admired it on the second. But, my own dearest Lydia, am I not tasking you overmuch? . . . . Do not be so careless of yourself. You are already much too pale and thin, my Lydia; do not become paler and thinner over the midnight oil. Your mind and body are not, I am afraid, very equally matched; the energies of the one wear out the powers of the other. Be generous, my lassie, and take part with the weaker side. Write me not continuously, but just a few lines now and then when you chance to be in the mood; — now at the grassy side of the *Leap* — now beside the beechen tree; and that I may be able to take your portrait at each sitting and to revert to the time of it, state over each paragraph the localities and the hour. But if I continue to lecture you in this way you will care little for either writing me or hearing from me.

" Tell me, my Lydia, why is it that I fear so much more for you than for myself? I hold life by quite as uncertain a tenure; and I do not know — for my constitution is by no means a strong one — if I be a great deal less subject to indisposition. But somehow sickness and death do not appear half so terrible to me when in looking forward I see them watching beside my own path, as when I see them lurking beside yours. Do I love you better than I do myself? or does the feeling arise out of one's confidence in one's own ability to resist or endure, which Young describes as making 'men deem all men mortal but themselves'? . . . I remember that when on my rock excursions with parties of my school-fellows I used to leap from crag to crag with the agility of the chamois, as cool and unconcerned when on the edge of a precipice as when on the level shore. If, however, I saw any of my companions in places of danger, I felt miserable. I had full confidence in myself, but so little in them, that at every step they took I expected to see them topple down headlong. It has been said, my own Lydia, that a philosopher in petticoats is a loveless thing; when I converse with you in this fashion, it is in the full conviction that few females' minds have been cast in a more philosophical mould than yours; but surely there is little truth in the remark, for never yet was there woman more warmly or more tenderly beloved."

"You and I, my Lydia, must converse some time or other on the unlucky subject of Friday night; — not for the sake of argument, — there are many subjects for us to exercise our wits upon without meddling with religion, — but that we may arrive at the truth. I was sorry to perceive that you were seriously displeased; and that in consequence of a rather unskilful statement of doctrine on your part, which was, I dare say, occasioned by the use of language rather bold than correct on mine, Mrs. —— was led to deem your opinion heretical. I am confident that in reality we are at one on this subject. Neither Mrs. —— nor I ever doubted for a moment that we ought to make Christ our pattern and example; for who can doubt that his whole life was just the entire *law* of his Father reduced to practice; and who does not know that the *law* is the rule which God has revealed for our obedience? On the other, neither Mrs. ——, nor you, nor I can doubt that the injunction 'Do this and live,' whether applied to the *law* as embodied in written commands or as exemplified in the life of Christ, is the now impossible condition of the old covenant, not the glorious watchword of the new; and that under this better covenant the ability of imitating Christ is a grace bestowed, not a condition exacted. All this, my Lydia, might have been said and agreed to without any angry feeling or personal remark; but we are so weak and foolish, my lassie, that we cannot so much as contend for the necessity of imitating Christ without showing by something more conclusive than argument how impossible it is for us to imitate him aright. Perhaps in some of our solitary interviews we may derive something better than amusement from talking over the subject, and something more than ordinary satisfaction in finding that in the more important of our beliefs we cordially agree. However diverse in our tastes, however different in our opinions, however dissimilar in our philosophy, let us at least *desire*, my own dearest Lydia, to be at one in our religion. Whatever befalls us in the future, — whether from the edge of some solitary forest of the West our prayers shall ascend for assistance and protection, or whether in some happy dwelling of our own land they shall rise in gratitude to Him the benefactor, would it not be well for us, my dearest, that they should rise together addressed to the same God through the same Mediator, and in quite the same way; that each should be employed in seconding the requests of the other, not in internally lodging a protest against them?

"Sir Thomas has sent me my manuscript, accompanied by a brief and exceedingly hurried note from Professor Wilson, in which he promises to write him a letter on the subject in a few days. I must say, I expect very little from the Professor. I question whether he has read my first chapter. Besides, our style and manner of thinking are so very unlike, that I do not well see how he can approve of my writings without passing a sort of tacit censure on his own. He is one of the most diffuse writers of the day; I am concise. His thoughts are detached; mine are consecutive. His descriptions, gorgeous with color and exquisite in form, delight only the sight; mine, though less splendid, appeal to the sentiments. His narratives are hung over with splendid draperies; mine are naked. He rarely reasons on the nature of man; I often. He is a Tory; I a Whig. What can I expect from such a critic?"

"SCHOOL-HOUSE OF NIGG, Monday Evening.

" Here am I set in Mr. Swanson's sleeping-room beside a not bad collection of books. I find I am not nearly so great a literary glutton now as I was fifteen years ago; there was a keenness in my appetite at that time which I have hardly ever seen equalled. The very heaven of my imagination was an immense library; and my fondest desires asked nothing more from the future than much time and many books. Have you marked the progress of your mind from the days in which you dressed your doll, to the days in which you are addressed by your lover? I remember that from my fourth to my sixth year I derived much pleasure from oral narrative, and that my imagination, even at this early period, had acquired strength enough to present me with vividly colored pictures of all the scenes described to me, and of all the incidents related. My mind then opened to the world of books. I began to understand the stories of the Bible, and to steal into some quiet corner, that I might peruse tales and novels unmolested by my companions. In my twelfth year I could relish a volume of the 'Spectator' and some of the better essays of Johnson; in my fifteenth I was delighted with the writings of the poets. About a year after I found that 'twas better to be solitary than in company; my mind had acquired strength enough, as nurses say of their children, to stand alone; and a first consequence of the improvement was that I exchanged my many companions for a few friends. I became a thorough admirer of nature for its own sake; before, I had only affected to love it from finding so much written in its praise. I was first delighted by the mild, the calm, the beautiful, next by the wild, the terrible, the sublime. Years passed on, and man became my study. I delighted in tracing the progress of the species, from the extreme of barbarism to that of refinement, and in marking the various shades of intellectual character. Studies of a more abstract class succeeded, and I became a metaphysician. I strove to penetrate into the first causes and to anticipate the remoter consequences of things; and reasoned on subjects such as those which employed the fiends in Milton when they 'found no end in wandering mazes lost;' but I soon perceived that the over-subtle thinker reaps only a harvest of doubt, and that, when truth is our object, it is quite as possible to miss the mark by overshooting as by falling short. In the progress related, and I cannot trace it further, habits have been successively formed and relinquished, and appetites acquired and satiated. But, though many of these have long since ceased, much of that which they accumulated for me still remains, — wrought up in some degree into one entire mass, but in some degree also bearing in their separate portions the color and stamp of the period at which they were acquired. I find, too, that as in the progress of my mind (to use your own happy language) 'what were at one time the subjects of thought and reason to me have become first principles,' so habits and modes of thinking which have been formed under the influence of our second nature —

custom — have become to me what seem primary tendencies of the mind; and that if there be much of originality
in my thoughts, I, perhaps, owe it in nearly as great a degree to the peculiarity of my education as to any innate
vigor of faculty. But you will deem me dull and an
egotist."

"ROADSIDE, Tuesday, 11 o'clock.

"I am on my way to Chapel-Hill; the day is so oppres-
sively hot that the grass and corn look as if half boiled,
and there is a dense cloud of flies buzzing about my head.
I saw, two minutes since, a large weasel quitting its hole to
drink. My eyes are so dazzled by the glare of the sun on
the white of your letter, which I have been again perusing,
that I hardly see the characters I am forming. You have
embodied very happily, in your description, the yawning
tedium of some of our Cromarty parties, and caught to the
life the tone of the sort of flippancy which has to pass in
them for wit. 'Tis a sad waste of time, my own Lydia, to
be engaged in such; how much better could we not contrive to spend an evening with only ourselves for our
guests! But I suppose *parties* everywhere are almost
equally profitless. They were profitless even in Athens, in
its best days. 'Why,' says Socrates, 'do the people call
in musicians when they entertain their friends? Is it not
because they have not learned to converse?'"

"BAYFIELD-WOOD, 2 o'clock.

"Where are you at present, my Lydia, or how are you
employed? Am I with you as you are with me, or has my
idea for a time entirely left you? Would that you were
now beside me. I always feel as if at home when in a
wood. One wood is so like another, and every wood so
like the one I am best acquainted with, — that which covers
the hill of Cromarty. Heigho! when shall we spend our

days together? and where? I breakfasted at Inverness with a very happy couple, a Mr. and Mrs. T——, and, more for our comfort, the husband is fully twice the age of the wife; I, you know, am only ten years older than you. The match was a love one on both sides, — in reality, whatever the world may think, the most prudent matches of any. I saw, in my journey, a second and still more striking proof of this. J. S—— has several aunts who prudently married men in rather easy circumstances, and one aunt (Aunt Barbara), who was so foolish as to marry a man who was poor, — merely because she loved him, — and who had little else to recommend him in the eyes of the unprejudiced than the possession of more sound sense and sterling worth than fell to the share of all the other husbands put together. The match, as you may think, was very rationally deemed a bad one; but, somehow, circumstances are less fixed than the characters of men, and it has so chanced that Aunt Barbara's husband holds, at this time, a rather higher place in society than the husband of any of the others; the match has, in consequence, become a good one. What if ours, you imprudent, foolish girl, should yet become a good one too!"

"MANSE OF KILMUIR, half-past 7 o'clock.

"I was on the way to the ferry this evening, but John impressed me to accompany him on a visit to Mr. M——. We crossed the sands of Nigg together, — a long, dreary flat, roughened by the cord-like hillocks of the sand-worm, and speckled with shells. Barren and dreary as it may seem, I know no part of the country busier with life. Myriads of sea-cockles have grown up and perished in it, age after age, till the shells have so accumulated, that in some places they form beds many feet in thickness; and, though thousands of cart-loads have of late ·years been carried away for lime, the supply seems as great as at first. As we passed through, immense shoals of shrimps and young flounders were striking against our naked feet, — reminding me, from their numbers and their extreme minuteness, of the cloud of flies that buzzed round my head at noon. I saw the sand-worms lie so thickly that their little pyramids fretted the entire surface nearly as far as the eye could reach, reminding one of the ripple raised by a light breeze on a sheet of water, while the remote horizon was darkened by endless beds of mussels and periwinkles. I am certain there is more of animal life in a few acres of this waste than is comprised in the human population of the entire world. In some comparatively recent era, — recent, at least, in the chronology of the geologist, — the sea seems to have stood several fathoms higher on our coasts than it does at present. Large beds of shells have been found in the interior of the valley, the opening of which is occupied by the sands of Nigg, more than two miles beyond the extreme rise of the tide; and John tells me that, not many years since, the bones of a fish of the whale species were found in the parish of Fearn, at a still higher level.

"I was shown, on quitting the sands, two fine chalybeate springs, which gush out of a rock of veined sandstone among the woods of Tarbat-house. They are thickly surrounded by pine and willow, in a solitary but not unpleasing recess, and their waters, after leaping to the base of the rock, with a half-gurgling, half-tinkling sound, unite in a small runnel, and form a little melancholy *lochan*, matted over with weeds, and edged with flags and rushes. The waters of both are strongly though not equally acidulous, and the course both along the rock and through the runnel is marked by a steep belt of ferruginous matter, which might be converted into a pigment, resembling burnt-sienna."

"FERRY DALE, Wednesday, half-past 11.

"How delightful the grounds about Cromarty look from this side the bay! Sir George Mackenzie, of Coul, has remarked, and I dare say he is quite in the right, that they are unequalled in at least all Ross-shire, but that the taste displayed in laying them out belongs to the obsolete school of a century ago. The hill-side, for instance, instead of being divided into square parks, should have been tufted with clumps of coppice, the edge of the wood ought to have been broken by the trees advancing in some places and retiring in others, and the enclosures should have run in waving rather than in straight lines. How innumerable, my Lydia, are the associations connected with the scene before me! Yonder is the burying-ground of my father, and yonder the house of my mother. There is hardly a spot my eye can rest on that is not wedded to the past by some interesting tradition; and then, how enriched is the whole scene by my recollections of you! Yonder is the beechen tree, and yonder the *Lover's Leap*, and yonder the little rocky recess in which I met with you last winter, with so little hope of ever meeting with you again. Yonder, too, is the old chapel of St. Regulus, yonder the *Ladies' Walk*, and yonder the house of Mrs. F——. What little, insect-looking things we are! Quick and sharp as my sight is, were you in the opening at the foot of the garden, I would see you merely as a little speck.

" 'Butler' I must return you unread; as between writing, working, and thinking of you, I have no time to devote to him. But here comes the ferry-boat."

CHAPTER XV.

EXCEPT Miss Fraser, Miller's most favored correspondent at this time was Miss Dunbar of Boath.
She read and admired his poems soon after their
appearance, and his correspondence with her began
some two years before he saw Miss Fraser. He refers to
her in terms of admiring affection in the "Schools and
Schoolmasters," and the letters which passed between them
prove that the feeling on both sides was one of ardent esteem and tender enthusiasm. She was about twenty years
his senior, and her tone in speaking of his plans and prospects is that of motherly solicitude, almost of motherly
pride. The tender strength of the affection with which,
unconsciously and without effort, he inspired her, is remarkable. The fascination of his gentleness and sincerity, and
of the gleams of beauty in which his genius revealed itself
when he spoke, is nowhere more strikingly evinced than in
the spell which he cast over this noble woman. He visited
her twice in Forres, and she spent three weeks in Cromarty,
principally in order to enjoy his society. These and other
circumstances of their intercourse are alluded to in the correspondence. Along with the letters of Miller to Miss Dunbar are given one or two passages from hers to him : —

318

"CROMARTY, November, 1829.

"I have perused two of the works you have so obligingly
sent me, — the volume of poems and the 'Wolf of Badenoch.' Both have afforded me much pleasure, and added, I
trust, to the stock of my ideas.

"It has been remarked, and I believe with justice, that,
while the historian immortalizes other men, the poet immortalizes only himself. A reason may be assigned for this.
We deem the historian merely a medium through which we
become acquainted with men and events, and are taught by
him without growing intimate with our teacher, — just as
we admire the figures in a painting without once thinking
of the canvas on which they are portrayed. It does not
fare so with the poet. From creation we infer a Creator,
and from the creations of the poet we rise by an unavoidable associative process to the poet himself. We consider
him not as our teacher, but as our friend. He is not like
the canvas of a picture, but like the groundwork of a piece
of embroidery, — a thing which blends with and relieves
every flower and figure raised on it. . . .

"From what I have read of Spenser, I find reason to
deem him both a true poet and a sound philosopher; but
from the suddenness of the transition from the 'Wolf of
Badenoch' to the 'Faëry Queen,' I am led (shall I make the
confession?) to institute a comparison between the two
works which does not very much exalt my opinion of the
latter. I am no critic. Spenser is, I doubt not, a finer
poet and a greater genius than Sir Thomas, but certain I
am that Spenser does not amuse me half so much. His
heroes and heroines are not real men and women like Sir
Thomas', nor do they come crowding round me in my solitary walks, like his. The one work is full of a stirring, day
reality, my recollections of the other blend with those of
my dreams. I shall, however, I doubt not, relish Spenser

better when my remembrance of the creations of Sir Thomas wax fainter."

"Forres, 15 January, 1830.

" I was very much pleased with your letter, and gratified to find I had been the means of procuring you so much pleasure as you have derived from the perusal of ' Wolf' and the poems.

" Sir Thomas Dick Lauder said, on seeing your letter to me : ' The author of the " Wolf of Badenoch," *whoever that might be,* had reason to be proud of the opinion you expressed of it.' I have no doubt you will read Spenser with all the enthusiasm proper to a young poet, when you go to it with a mind dispossessed of other subjects.

" Miss Smith tells me you are going to Inverness to work at your handicraft. I suppose you will occasionally work for Mr. Carruthers ; he seems to be a clever man, and I think the ' Courier' bespeaks him a man of independence. I hope he will continue to prove himself such in a place distracted by low politics and a narrow party spirit, too often vented in ungenerous, personal reflections. I conjure you to be on your guard, and preserve yourself from any share or feeling in these contests. Do not lend your fine talent to either or any side ; next to your integrity to Heaven, maintain your independence ; be courteous to every one, but render party service to none, and you will make yourself many friends and no enemies."

Miller's next letter is not dated, but it was evidently written at Cromarty soon after the preceding : —

" Ever since I knew myself I have hovered on the verge of two distinct worlds, — the one a gay creation of happy, animated dreams, the other a dull scene of cold, untoward realities. Into the former I have often been drawn by inclination; into the latter, dragged by necessity. I have enjoyed so much in the one, and suffered so much in the other, that I have sometimes been disposed to regard them as the opposing scales in which good and evil were to be doled out to me by Providence. Had I indulged, however, in so fanciful a theory, a few events of late occurrence would have overturned it; the real scene has begun to present an aspect not very unlike that of the imaginary; and that I should be held not unworthy of the notice of such as Miss Dunbar, is a circumstance which I deem characteristic of the change.

" Your kind intention of introducing me to the notice of Professor Wilson has, I believe, been anticipated by Principal Baird. . . . A Mr. Gordon, Secretary to the Highland Society, who himself writes for 'Blackwood,' made me a similar offer; but I declined both, on the ground that I did not consider myself as yet free of the craft of authorship. The truth is, I am unwilling to convert my literary amusements into mere matters of business; and I am afraid that, were I to set myself down to write for money, I would soon learn to consider them as such. Before I became a mason, I have spent whole days in constructing arches, and in building towers and houses; now, however, I seldom either build or hew, except when I cannot help it. It would be a sad matter were prose and verse to become but half as irksome to me as building and hewing. Besides, I have little need for money, and need not risk any of my happiness in striving to acquire it. I am nearly as poor and as rich as the old cynic, Diogenes, though, I trust, not so ill-natured. I am poor in worldly goods, rich in moderate desires. He who has lived contentedly on half a crown per week is by no means so much within the reach of fortune as thousands of the people who would not scruple to term him a very poor man.

"Accept my thanks for your excellent advice regarding the manner in which I ought to conduct myself with respect to the partisans of Inverness. . . . About a fortnight ago I saw an article in the ———, the matter of which declared that paper to have a very long list of subscribers, and the manner of which very satisfactorily proved that it ought to have a very short one. I took up the thing with all coolness, and perfectly free of party prejudice; I laid it down boiling with indignation. . . . . I found my friend, Mr. Carruthers, treated by him in a manner in which no gentleman ever treated any one; and you know, madam, it is much easier to forgive one's own enemy than the enemy of one's friend. . . . . I intend writing nothing but prose until I have improved my talent for this species of composition to its utmost of my capability. I am at present rather out of conceit with poetry; and, were it not for one circumstance, I would deem the publication of my little volume a subject of regret. That one is, the impulse which the coming in contact by its means with the public has given to my mind. Formerly my mind was slow and indolent; it is now comparatively roused into activity; and I am led to think that the much which is dull and tame in my printed poems is rather to be attributed to that apathetical indifference which, about two years ago, constituted my almost every-day mood, than to any want of native power. You smile at my conceit. Well, I have done so myself. Remember, however, that the species of conceit which I display on the present occasion is not quite that of the past. It plumes itself on an ability to produce, not upon anything produced already. . . . I begin to relish Spenser. . . .

"You inquire regarding my plans and prospects. The former are not complex, the latter are not gloomy. In the spring, summer, and autumn seasons I intend plying the mallet, that I may be independent; in the winter I purpose exercising the pen, that I may be amused, and (the truth will out) that I may be known. With independence, amusement, and a very small portion of celebrity, I trust to enjoy a competent share of happiness; and, with the assistance of God, to prove myself not quite unworthy the esteem of the few individuals whose characters resemble that of my present correspondent."

The Mr. Strahan referred to in the following letter was one of the many friends whom the publication of his poems procured him. Mr. Strahan was himself a writer of poetry; and it may be mentioned that it is a son of his whose name appears on the title-page of this biography. Furthermore, that it was on Miller's recommendation and advice that the publishing profession was chosen for the son of his friend, — Miller himself making the necessary arrangements with Messrs. Johnstone and Hunter of Edinburgh:" —

"CROMARTY, March 12, 1831.

"In the long, beautiful days of summer I have often pitied my friend Mr. Strahan, confined as he is by his profession to a dull, monotonous apartment. After flinging down my mallet to contemplate the glorious sunshine, poured out around me on the fields, woods, and mountains, when a light refreshing breeze, laden with the scents of the wild flowers, has come sweeping over me, or a sudden gush of melody has burst from a neighboring thicket, I have deemed myself the happiest of all mechanics. But mark the contrast; winter comes, and then Mr. Strahan's profession proves the better of the two. The thicket has still its music, for the blast howls through it, loud and continuous as the roar of the ocean; shower after shower comes beating against me, dashing my poor tangled tresses against my cheeks ; there is no solace in looking abroad, all is dull and dismal, — nature lies dead, and the very firmament is but a burial vault ; and thus I toil on, till a colder blast or a heavier shower sends me home half frozen, and somewhat less than half alive, to cower and chitter over the fire. Well, such is the balance of human life. Where are they that have no winter? . . . .

" You recommend to me the study of sculpture as a means of bettering my condition in life. Why, it can't be much bettered. 'Tis true I am not rich, — and yet, thanks to the industry of my father, should Lord J. Russell carry his motion, I shall have a voice in the legislation of my country. With books, which you so obligingly offer me, I am rather poorly provided ; but the great book of nature lies continually open before me, and were I to live to the age of Methusaleh, I would still have much of it to peruse. Oh, with what splendid passages are its pages filled ! "

The incident of Miss Smith's falling into the burn (of Eathie), alluded to in the next letter, occurred at one of those picnics of which Miller and his Cromarty friends were fond. Miss Smith, having fallen into the burn, was contemplated by Hugh with a placid interest which did not in the least prompt him to lend assistance. He was considerably bantered for his ungallant conduct. From the concluding portion of the letter it is evident that Miss Dunbar had pressed Miller to visit her.

" CROMARTY, March 12, 1833.

" You have been unwell for a long, long time, but now that you have recovered I may venture to say ' It was all for the best,' without, I trust, subjecting myself to the suspicion of being one of those cold, philosophic sort of people, — mere abstract intelligence, — who are so bravely employed in thinking that they have no time to feel. Indisposition is, to be sure, a sad thing in itself. Sad matter for the soul to be sitting in darkness, in the recesses of her poor shattered tenement, like Marius amid the ruins of Carthage ; to have at morning to breathe one's wishes in the language of the text, ' Would God it were evening !' and at evening, ' Would God it were morning !' But when we consider human life as a whole, and man as a creature that lives both in the past and the future, we see that even pain and sickness form parts of a beautiful and well-arranged system. Nay, I am convinced, paradoxical as the opinion may appear, that they add nearly as much to the sum of human happiness as they take from it. You, my dear madam, have been long very unwell, and now you have recovered, — recovered what? health? — nay, that would be but little, you had that some few months before, — have you not also recovered your youth? — the freshness, gayety, and the warm hopes of girlhood? Life palls upon us when our course through it lies, if I may so speak, on a smooth, level road, bounded by two straight walls, and we grow old in our spirits while we are yet young in years ; not so when the path goes winding over hills and valleys, with here a deep, broad stream which we must ford at the risk of being swept away, and there a beautiful meadow with its flowers and its birds. Every recovery one has from sickness is in some degree a return of one's youth, and I could almost endure to be many times sick for the sake of being many times young.

" Now that I have got into this train, I must give you the result of my speculations on character, of which you yourself (nay, do not start) are in some measure the subject. I have observed that you are one of that happy class of people who have the principle of immortality so strong within them that they never become old. The whole human race may be divided into two grand classes, but the one is to be reckoned by its tens, and the other by its millions. In the more numerous class, we see man the animal, the creature of corruption and decay ; in the other, man the child of eternity. The young of most animals are gay, sportive creatures, to whom life is enjoyment, — only think of the lamb and the kitten ; but the one becomes the stolid, ruminating sheep, the other a staid, demure puss, with a great deal of worldly wisdom, and powers of gravity altogether incalculable. Thus it is with the animal class of men. You may know their age as exactly by the state of their minds as that of a cow by the rings on her horns ; they are playful in youth, grave and staid when mature, stupid in old age ; their minds are so much of a piece with their bodies, that it needs no ordinary powers of faith to believe that they will not perish together. The people of the other class are animals, it is true, — the more the pity, — but the man preponderates in them over the animal. It is the part of them which neither dies nor becomes old, that gives their character its tone. We see the *earthy house* of one of this class falling into decay, and know that it must soon be altogether uninhabitable ; but then the tenant is still young, and all we think of the matter is, that when term day comes, he must just leave the falling tenement, and go somewhere else. Even so much as to dream of his perishing along with it would be preposterous. It is his house that is falling into decay, not he himself. You, my dear madam, are one of these young people, and I congratulate you on the fact ; I myself, perhaps, belong to them ; but in my case there is a sad circumstance which nearly balances this advantage. You very wisely became a young woman before you stood still ; I, on the other hand, grew up to be a boy some fifteen years ago, and a boy (don't tell) I have continued ever since. Can't help it, however. . . . How defend my conduct in the burn?

Very easily. Never was there young lady so wofully in danger of falling a martyr to a classical association. You remember the old mythological story of Venus springing from the waves of the sea. On seeing Miss Smith rising out of the stream, instead of thinking on the best means of extricating her, I could think of only the story. And I could not help that, you know! If Miss Smith, however, will but favor me by falling into the burn a second time, no association, however classical, shall come between me and my duty.

"I have been thinking of your 'little chamber in the wall,' with its bed and its stool, and find that it wants only the prophet; but a word in your ear, the prophet is not at all sure that he has yet succeeded in establishing the authenticity of his mission, and is disposed, until he has done so, to content himself with the modicum of honor which he receives in his own country. If my Traditions come out, I am vain enough to think I might venture in the strength of them as far as Forres; but to be pointed out in such a place merely as the author of a volume of prose rhyme would seriously injure my pride. You have now my secret. It is based on a weakness in my disposition, which I would not much like to unveil to everybody; but I know with whom I have to deal, — one too intimate with human nature, and too conversant with its better feelings, to be severe on what is wayward in the character of, honored and dear madam," etc.

Miss Dunbar is not disposed to put up with this excuse for refusing to visit her, and has expostulated on the subject. Miller now offers to go. His half-comic, half-savage remarks on the Cromarty Radicals are characteristic. The pamphlet mentioned I take to have been that on the Chapel Case, of which we have heard.

"I have been a very great blockhead; not so much for

raising the curtain, as for having anything behind it which were better concealed than seen. Instead, however, of apologizing in the ordinary way, I shall just raise it a little higher, and give you a full view of what you are yet only acquainted with in part. In a case like the present it is policy to be candid. Is it not partial views and half glimpses that convert bushes and stones into ghosts and witches?

"In the first place, then, it was no fear of being made a *lion* of, that kept me on this side the frith. I know you better than to fear that. I may indeed belong to the class *felis* in both your opinion and my own;—but then so does the common cat; besides, at the very best I am but what the schoolmen would term a *possible* lion, and it has long since been decided by the Angelical Doctor that an *existent* fly is better than even a *possible* angel. But though I had no fear on this head, I am a most foolish fellow, and there is a feeling—a morbid one, I suspect—that continually hangs about me that produced in this matter nearly the same effects as if I had. I must explain. You remember Addison's description of those trap-doors on the bridge of Mirza, through which the unfortunate passengers were continually dropping into the water? The minds of some men abound with such doors. Their judgments seem stately structures, if I may so speak, that connect the opposite regions of causes and effects, of means and ends; we see their purposes and resolves moving rapidly along the arches, and think they cannot fail of passing from the one extreme point to the other. Suddenly, however, they disappear in the midst, and leave their objects unattained. Or, to drop the allegory: How often are we surprised in even superior men by some unthought-of inconsistency that mars all their wisdom, some latent weakness that neutralizes all their powers! There is, my dear madam, a weakness, an inconsistency, a trap-door of this kind in the mind of the poor fellow who has now the honor of addressing you. Its appearances and modes of operation are as various as the circumstances in which it exhibits itself, but, for a general name, I believe I may term it diffidence. It torments me as much as conscience does some men. For instance: There are a few excellent people in Cromarty whose company I deem very agreeable, and whose friendship I value very highly, but whose thresholds without a special invitation I never cross. Why? Just because diffidence tells me that I am but a poor mechanic, regarded with a kind, perhaps, but still compassionate feeling, and that, if I but take the slightest commonest liberty of social intercourse, it is at the peril of being deemed forward and obtrusive. Well, I receive an invitation and accept it. I come in contact with persons whom I like very much; the better feelings are awakened within me, the intellectual machine is set a-working, and I communicate my ideas as they rise. 'You chattering blockhead,' says Diffidence, the moment I return home, 'what right, pray, had you to engross so much of the conversation to-night? You are a pretty fellow, to be sure, to set up for a Sir Oracle! Well, you had better take care next time.' Next time comes, and I am exceedingly taciturn. 'Pray, Mr. Block,' says Diffidence, the instant she catches me alone, 'what fiend tempted you to go and eat the lady's bread and butter to-night, when you had determined prepense not to tender her so much as a single idea in return? A handsome piece of furniture, truly, to be stuck up at the side of a tea-table. Perhaps, however, you were too good for your company, and wish to make them feel that you thought so.' But truce with the accusations of the witch; fifty pages would not contain the whole. Was not Diffidence the wife of that giant Despair, whom Mr. Greatheart slew when he demolished Castle Doubting? She, too, is said to have perished at the same time, but both must since have been resuscitated. I stand, however, in no fear of the husband, giant though he be ; but alas for the iron despotism of his lady !

"Need I say anything more on this head? Just one other sentence. Some of the concluding lines of my last were written indeed by me, but only as amanuensis to the giantess. And now that I have made a full disclosure, and constituted you my confessor, what penance are you to impose? I am just going to ask you whether I shall yet get leave to visit you some time in the leafy end of May ; and if you are very, very angry, and intend being very, very severe, it is in your power fully to avenge yourself by forbidding me to come at all. I often think of Forres, not much, indeed, comparatively at least, of the beauties of its scenery, or of its old castles and obelisks, though I am not the kind of person wholly to slight these, — I think of it as the home of some of my friends ; particularly as the home of her who has so kindly interested herself in my welfare, whose friendship I have deemed so much an honor, and found so much a happiness, and who in her warm-heartedness has held converse with me, not as the mere lady of birth and education who condescends to notice some poor, half-taught mechanic, but such as one intelligence holds with another of the same class. It is wonderful how numerous the analogies are which subsist between the intellectual and material worlds. You are acquainted with that principle of attraction which binds into one solid mass any amount of particles which have been pressed together until brought within the sphere of its influence, and that opposite principle which makes them repel one another when removed from out of this sphere by the least possible distance. And are there not similar principles operative in the respective states of mere acquaintanceship and friendship? Is there not repulsion in the one, attraction in the other? Nay, are they not both operative in even friendship itself? The friend who converses with one merely on paper, or in a mixed company, or under the influence of some such evil spirit as diffidence, is environed by an atmosphere very different from that which surrounds the friend to whom, when the pen is happily no longer of use, the world shut out, and the fiend dispossessed, one can open one's whole heart, and mingle thought with thought, and feeling with feeling. I trust that before the end of May I shall have availed myself so much of your kindness as to be fully within the influence of the better principle. But not one word of Altyre, — remember the giant's wife.

" We of Cromarty have narrowly missed losing our minister, and to the thinking part of us a shrewd loss it would have been. Mr. Stewart would have proved himself second to none, or I am much mistaken, in even the pulpit once occupied by Dr. Chalmers; but who, alas! could we have got to fill his? And I much suspect that, in less than a twelvemonth, he himself would not have found the amount of his happiness at all increased by the change. He has too little of the working-day world about him for the bustle of public life, and his mind, with all its powers, is not of the kind best fitted for a regular routine of business. It is said of the lion that, with all his immense strength and activity, he is a slow-paced and sluggish sort of animal, and that though on extraordinary occasions he can leap twenty feet at a bound, and carry off a buffalo with as much ease as a horse carries its rider, he can yet lie for whole days in his lair half asleep, half awake, too indolent to move head or limb. There is something of this disposition in Mr. Stewart; not that he wills to have it, but because he has been born with it. When fresh and in heart he can make amazing lion-like efforts; but he is no steam engine, and must be indulged with long breathing spaces in which to recover himself. With all his eccentricity he is an excellent sort of fellow, eloquent, pious, an original thinker, and singularly fortunate, if he but knew it, in both his friends and his enemies; a person of spirit, you know, would like to have the choosing of the one as certainly as that of the other; but Mr. Stewart somehow does not seem to be aware of this. It so happens that we are much infested in Cromarty by a kind of vermin called Radicals, and have not yet got an act of parliament for knocking them on the head. To Mr. Stewart they bear a decided antipathy; very naturally as blockheads they dislike him for his genius, and, being bad men, hate him as Shylock did Antonio, ' for he is a Christian;' and I am afraid the petty annoyances they contrive to cast in his way molest him at times more than they ought. He has weak nerves, lives retired, and has scarcely any turn for friendship, and so little hurts him; but I trust he will yet learn wholly to disregard them. I am a Whig, and yet they do me the honor of hating me nearly as heartily as they do him; but I am a thick-skinned, rough, shagged kind of animal, and as in all the *bickers* in which they have engaged me I have contrived somehow to get the laugh on my side, and could besides give the best of them a drubbing would they but choose to favor me with an opportunity, I have been let alone of late. You have seen my pamphlet. Is it not a piece of mortal ill-nature? Remember, however, that I am not to be judged with regard to it by the laws of the *Duello*. I had not to fight with a man of honor, but merely to horsewhip a low fellow who had insulted a party of ladies and a reverend gentleman. . . . .

"For my own part, though no one can surpass me in the esteem I entertain for the better sex, and though, perhaps, not naturally unsusceptible of the softer passion, I deem myself as much tied down to a life of celibacy as if I were a Romish priest. A refined taste and cultivated understanding I have vainly sought for in women of my own sphere; and though I have sometimes found both in those of another, I cannot seriously think of such as objects on which to fix a hope. No one of a superior station could become my wife without making a sacrifice which I could not permit in the woman I loved; I could not wrong her so much as to make her the wife of a poor mechanic. But friendship still remains for me. Some of the best of my species do not disdain to be connected to me by this tie; and with the help of God it is my purpose so to live that their kindness to me shall be no sacrifice."

The speculations on the philosophy of evil in the following letter are not without ingenuity, but we have already seen that Miss Fraser, the lady who accompanied Miss Smith in the walk described towards the close, could put the needle-point of her woman's wit and logic with rather startling effect into the prettily colored balloons which Miller used to fly upon that subject. It seems probable that she pressed him closely on this occasion, and that the compliments to her sex into which he launches may be viewed partly as a magnanimous tribute to her victory.

"CROMARTY, May 21, 1833.

"What exquisitely lovely evenings this month has given us! I have just been out among the woods enjoying one of the finest sunsets I ever witnessed, and a very pleasing flow of thought besides. The clown in Othello advises the musicians who were serenading his master to put up their pipes unless they could play a kind of music that could not be heard. The very best kind I am acquainted with has this peculiarity; and I have been delighted with it this evening. The trees all bursting into leaf, the sea, the distant hills, the sky glowing with crimson and orange, a little quiet town, — nay, the very heath and moss, and the shapeless blocks of stone that glimmered red to the light in the openings of the wood, — all seemed to me the chords of an immense instrument which had but to be awakened by the soul to yield it a sweet music. And I was so happy as to succeed in awakening them. I felt the tranquillity of the scene infused into my mind, and (I may hazard the expression) my thoughts and feelings as if beating time to the tones of it. The unknown author of ' Enthusiasm ' * has made an ingenious distinction between meditation and those more vigorous states of thought in which the cogitative faculties alone are active, and he has said that the former is more characteristic of the Asiatic cast of mind, the latter of the European. If the remark be a just one, I have been quite an Asiatic this evening, if, indeed, we may define meditation to be that state of the mind in which its better sentiments and its intellectual powers are active together though perhaps not in an equal degree ; these combining, or creating, or arranging, perhaps slowly and languidly, those looking on with intense delight, rejoicing in every idea, and loving every new or pleasing image with an overpowering love. Take, as illustrative of what I mean, the cogitations of a few minutes of this evening. I stood on the sweep of a grassy declivity sprinkled over with forest trees and bushes. Some of the former spring out of the higher edge of the bank, and interlace their boughs at a great height over my head ; some of them have fixed their roots so much farther down, that my eye is on a level with the cradle which the magpie has built for her young among their branches ; I look over the topmost twigs of a still

---

* Now so well known that it seems almost superfluous to name him, — Isaac Taylor.

lower tree. See there is the ash, with his long, massy arms, that shoot off from the trunk at such acute angles, and his dark, sooty blossoms spread over him as if he were mourning; and there is the elm, with his trunk gnarled and ridged like an Egyptian column, and his flake-like foliage laid on in strips that lie nearly parallel to the horizon; and there is the plane, with his dark-green leaves and dense heavy outline, like that of a thunder-cloud; and there, too, is the birch,—a tree evidently of the gentler sex, with her long flowing tresses falling down to her knee; there, also, is the lime, and the larch, and the beech, and the silver fir. What a combination of pleasing forms! See in that vista to the right, which appears so exquisitely beautiful, every outline is a wavy one, without any mixture of broken angles or straight lines, while in the darker recess beside it there is a harsher, stiffer assemblage of forms; it is full of cross lines and angles. But do not the deformities of that recess render the scene, considered as a whole, more perfect than it would be without them? Do they not enable me to appreciate what is exquisite in the rest of it? If there existed no such thing as deformity, we could have known nothing of beauty; just as if there was no such thing as sickness, health would not be a word in our vocabulary, or as if there were no such thing as shade or darkness, no one would ever have said, ' It is a good thing to behold the light.'

"And is it not true that the scene now spread out before me, with its many beauties and its few deformities, is a work of the Deity? that it was foreknown of him at a period when the very earth of which it forms so minute a part was but a portion of empty space in an infinitely extended vacuum; nay, that it was foreknown of him from all eternity, and that this his idea of it, as forming a portion of his infinite knowledge and coexistent with himself, may be regarded as forming, *with its apparent defects*, a part of himself, though he be *perfect* and *indefectible?* At least, is it not true that the sentiment of beauty and the sense of deformity, as they exist in the human mind, are effects of which he is the cause, that the scene before me is marked by traits that arouse this sentiment in me, and awaken this sense, and that the latter was given me that I might be conscious of possessing the former? And how do these principles bear on that great, I may add, inexplicable problem, the existence of evil, misery, folly, imperfection, in the works of an infinitely good, benevolent, wise, perfect God? May not evil be the shade with which good is contrasted, that it may be known as good, the sickness to which it is opposed as health, the deformity beside which it is shown forth as beauty? Nay, may it not be affirmed, on these principles, that the plan of the Deity would not have been a perfect one if it did not include imperfection, not a wise one if it admitted not of folly, nor a good one if evil did not form a part of it? Is there not something like this implied in the remarkable text which informs us that the weakness of God is mightier than the strength of men, and his foolishness more admirable than their wisdom? Such was the train of thought which passed through my mind, and the conclusion at which I arrived; and though, regarded as merely an intellectual process, it may, perhaps, be neither very striking nor of much value, as a matter which engaged my better sentiments, awakened my more pleasing feelings, and afforded me for the time much happiness, I found it to be valuable and truly good. . . .

" I had the happiness, a few evenings since, of falling in, in my usual walk, with our common friend, Miss Smith, accompanied by another young lady (by far the most intellectual of her companions), and had a long and very amusing conversation with them; so long, indeed, that at length the stars began to peep out at us, as if wondering what we were about. We differed and disputed and agreed, and then differed and disputed and agreed again. *We*, of the rougher sex, arrogate to ourselves the possession of minds of a larger size than we admit to have fallen to the share of the members of yours. True, indeed, we have not yet thought proper to produce the data on which we found the opinion, and are by far too strong to be compelled to it, but should we once seriously set about it, Cromarty would prove a desperate bad field for us. By much the greater half of the collective intellect of the town is vested in the ladies."

Before our next letter is written, the promised visit to Miss Dunbar has taken place. Immediately on returning to Cromarty, Miller had written to her, and intrusted the letter to a young lady, who lost it. This will sufficiently explain the opening paragraph. The rest needs no elucidation; but I know no letter of Miller's which does more honor either to his head or his heart. The brotherly walk home with the poor woman on whom society had so long frowned was intensely characteristic of Hugh. It would be pleasant to know how *she* was impressed by her companion.

"CROMARTY, July 24, 1833.

"Only think how unfortunate I have been! Your letter reached Cromarty on Sunday morning, but the poor fellow whose heart would have leaped within him at the sight of it was not there to bid it welcome. This is now Wednesday evening, and I have only just got home to the perusal. The loss of my letter is positively nothing, — at least, nothing in itself; but how vexatious it is to me to think for the last few days you must have entertained hard, bitter thoughts of me, — I have been careless, I have been indifferent.

But no; I will not permit myself to believe that I have suffered in your esteem. There is a faith and charity of friendship as certainly as of religion; a faith that is the evidence of the good things hoped for, a charity that believeth no evil; and where shall I look for these if not in you?

"I have, I believe, told you that I keep copies of the letters I write to all my better and more valued correspondents,—partly because, loving often to peruse the letters I receive from them, I have found that when the topics of the passing moment had escaped my memory, my own were necessary to me to render theirs intelligible; partly, too, because my letters furnish me with a history of my thoughts, my sentiments, my feelings; in short, enable me to prosecute the study of that most important of all the branches of philosophy,—the philosophy of one's own life. The loss of my unfortunate epistle is therefore virtually nothing but the loss of a little paper; you shall have every thought and every word of it in this long, ungainly sheet. Not that I deem it at all worth copying, but because what I said and felt when writing it is exactly what I have to say and what I feel now.

"Your truly welcome letter of the 2d of July found me buried up to my eyes amid books and manuscripts, in a little, old-fashioned room within which my great-grandfather, John Feddes, passed his honeymoon with Jean Gallie, in the good year 1698. I dare say you remember the story. He was a sincere but not a favored lover, for he was poor and red-haired, and as ugly and awkward as his great-grandson, who is said very much to resemble him; whereas Jean was the prettiest girl in the parish, and nearly the richest, and she had, besides, the handsomest fellow in the whole of it for her lover. Well, John saw her married to his rival, and then went out in a terrible passion a buccaneering to South America, where he wreaked his disappointment on the poor Spaniards, and filled a great box with doubloons. On his return to Cromarty he found Jean very poor and a widow; the man of her choice had been worthless and a spendthrift, and had only courted her for her money. John, who had never ceased to love her, liked her none the worse for her poverty; and, as she had now no lover but himself, she very wisely married him, though he was not only as ugly and red-haired as ever, but very much sunburnt to boot. And here they lived for about fifty years, exceedingly well pleased with each other to the last. My room is, as I have said, a little one; its small, dull-paned windows are half buried in the thatch, and there is no getting in at the door without making a very profound bow indeed; and yet, little and rude as it is, John Feddes has been as happy in it as ever Cæsar was. And I have been very happy in it too; never happier, however, than when perusing your kind, kind letter. You know I am quiet in all my feelings,— quiet in my very enthusiasm; but do not imagine that the stream is as shallow as it is noiseless. Do believe that there is both depth and power in at least those feelings of affectionate gratitude of which you yourself are the object.

"I had only left you for about half an hour, when the clouds began to lower on every side of me, as if sky and earth were coming together, and the rain to descend in torrents. The great forest of Darnaway appeared blue and dark, as if greeting the heavens with a scowl as angry as their own; and there was a low, long wreath of vapor that went creeping over it like a huge snake. And how the wind did roar! I thought, with Lear's fool, that 'twas truly 'a naughty night to swim in;' and when taking shelter for a few minutes under the arch of a bridge, I wished I could convert your books and the 'Superstitions' (can you forgive me a wish so unpoetical?) into a great loaf, and the arch into one of my Cromarty caves, that I might kindle a fire in it, and take up my lodgings for the night. I wish you had but seen the *locale* of Shakespeare's witch scene, as it frowned upon me in passing, with the old Castle of Inshoch, half enveloped in cloud and mist, standing sentry over it. The black, dismal morass, with its inky pool and its white *cannach*, that showed like tears on a hatchment, appeared still more black and dismal through the blue-gray tints of the storm, and the heavily laden clouds went rolling over it like waves of the sea. And then how the firs waved to the wind, and the few scattered trees swung their branches, and groaned and creaked; the thunder and the witches were alone wanting. You see, my dear madam, that though I might, and would, certainly have been happier in your snug-sheltered parlor at Forres than when exposed to a storm of wind and rain on the Hard-moor, my situation was not quite without its little balance of advantage. Bad as the day was, I would not now exchange my recollection of it for that of many better ones.

"I reached Fort George, dripping wet, a little before three o'clock, and found among the passengers who were waiting the ferry-boat, a woman of Cromarty,— a poor, disreputable thing, who, by making a false step in early life, lost caste, and drifted, in consequence, almost beyond the pale of society. We kept company all the rest of the way, and had a good deal of talk; and I found, what, indeed, I had often found before, that human nature, even when at its worst, has always something good in it. People often read the Scriptures amiss on this point, and think, despite of an often-repeated experience, that because our species is there represented as thoroughly separated from God, we can have no sincere regard for our neighbor, no true affection for our friends, no forgiveness for our enemies, — no

love, no tenderness, no pity. But we have all these, however, and this from nature; and these, and all the other
feelings which draw us out from ourselves and give us to
one another, are good. Both tables of the law were originally set up in the sanctuary of man's heart. When he fell
the first of these was broken into fragments, which were
raked together by guilt and terror, and formed into an uncouth idol named Superstition; but the second table, though
sorely rent and shattered, survived the concussion, and,
with its darkened and half-dilapidated inscriptions, holds
its place in the sanctuary still. But this is not quite what I
meant to say. I found that my fellow-traveller had an old,
bedridden mother, whom she labored to support; that she
kept her daughter at school, and that last year, on the
breaking out of the cholera, when a spirit of selfishness
seemed to pervade the whole country, and no one thought
of friend or neighbor, she had attended in his sickness a
relative, from whom she had formerly experienced some
little kindness. I have found that what are called the good
and bad of our species (from the circumstance, surely, of
their having their virtues and vices based on a nature radically the same) resemble each other much nearer, and have
much more in common, than the world chooses to allow.
The human God and human monster of common report,
when one comes in contact with them, and is enabled to
balance all their traits and qualities, prove to be nothing
better nor worse than mere men. For my own part, I have
often found the good, when I became thoroughly acquainted
with them, to be not much better than myself, and the bad
to be not much worse. This may, perhaps, be thought wild
doctrine; but I know it to be favorable to the exercise of
those charities which bind us to our species, and opposed
to that idolatry of our nature which prompts us to prostrate
ourselves before some poor, faulty thing like ourselves; and,

besides, did not He act upon it, who, though repeatedly accused of being the friend of publicans and sinners, never once rebutted the charge? I got home about six o'clock, without being nearly so much fatigued with my journey of thirty miles as when I had travelled it in the opposite direction; and my friends were all as glad to see me as if I had been away from them for a much longer period. I am, I believe, richer in true friends than any other person I know, and my only secret regarding them is the very simple one of being sincerely attached to them.

"I look back on my visit to Forres with great and unmixed pleasure. I really love my friends, and, indeed, mankind in general, all the better for it; it has added, too, to the stock of my ideas, and enriched the little mental *studio*, in which I have stored up my conceptions of the good and the beautiful, with a series of images superior to most of the others. I have read of a celebrated Italian master who was so exclusively a painter of landscape that he could not so much as introduce figures into his pieces. The scenes he portrayed seemed to be scenes of the infant world at the close of the fifth day's creation, ere there were animals on the plains or in the forests, or man had become a living soul. Now, this is not at all the way with my landscapes. There are a few figures in the foreground of every one of them, and the same figures too. You yourself I have introduced into every scene. Here you stand on the brink of a precipice, there on the verge of a stream, yonder amid the glades of a forest. Immediately on our return from the banks of the Findhorn, I was almost afraid that I had visited them to but little purpose. I had seen so very much, and my attention had been so fatigued, that my recollection of their many beautiful scenes resembled the reflection on a lake, whose surface is partially agitated by the wind. My mind might be compared to the apartments of a house that has just been taken possession of by a new tenant, when the pieces of furniture lie *higglety pigglety* on the floors, and we marvel how they can ever be so arranged as to leave room for anything else. But it is not so now. I have now a complete picture of the river, with all its rocks and its woods, its pools and its rapids, from where it sweeps through the meads of St. John to where it receives the waters of the Devy. The picture is rolled up in a recess of my mind like a web of tapestry, and, when I but will it, it unfolds scene after scene, until the whole is spread out. See, there are the meads, with the river playing with us at *bo-peep*, — now hiding itself among the bushes, now looking out and laughing as if at our attempts to discover it; and there is the heronry, with the large, gray, ghost-like herons sailing over their nests, that look like so many lawyers' wigs; and yonder is the little, fairy-like village of Sluie, inhabited, despite of its beauty, by people who have no more poetry in them than if they were confined to a hempen manufactory, and saw only walls of dingy brick and roofs of red tile.

" Observe now how suddenly the character of the scenery has changed. We have just left the district of secondary rock — of abrupt, sandstone cliffs and widely extended meadows — for that of gneiss and granite; the crags have become more rugged, the banks more invariably precipitous, the river more turbulent. Every trace of the labor and skill of man has disappeared; there are no impressions, not even the slightest, on the rocks, the stream, or the forest, of the refinement or civilization of the present age. The low country is all over stamped with these; we see them in the fields, the houses, the villages, the gardens. Here, on the contrary, Nature is still as much in her infancy as when the naked huntsman of two thousand years ago, his long beard whistling to the wind, and his breast and limbs stained blue, and tattooed with rude figures of the moon and the stars, first broke through the tangled underwood as he pursued the stag, and met the animal at bay on the steep edge of a yet unknown and nameless stream. But why unroll the whole web? I cannot add to the vividness of your impressions, but I can show you the distinctness of my own.

"My imagination had been busy for a whole month before I set out for Forres, in drawing pictures of all I was to be there brought acquainted with. I had a Findhorn of my own, and a Relugas, and a Churchyard of Altyre, and a Dr. Brande, and a Mr. Grant; and now I have both the real and the imaginary landscapes and portraits placed side by side, just like the two rainbows we saw side by side, a bright and a fainter, when returning from our excursion. But the real and imaginary scenes and images are, in many respects, strikingly dissimilar. You yourself, and you only, are altogether what I had conceived. Previous, indeed, to our meeting at Forres, some parts of my transcript of the character were defined by only faint outlines, and these outlines are now filled up; but, for the truth of my general conception of it, I appeal to the letter I wrote you in March last.

"I shall not be out of Cromarty (if I but live so long) for the next two months. But why write so hesitatingly on this subject, as if the devoting a few days to pleasure and to you, whatever my engagements, was to be regarded as a sacrifice? It is not probable that I shall be at all occupied at the time of your visit; but had I to travel fifty miles to meet with you, or to postpone the most pressing engagements, the balance of happiness and advantage would still be largely on my side, — and this, too, leaving gratitude altogether out of the question. I have been of late among *my* rocks and woods, and have explored all *my* caves, large and small, together with the burn of Eathie.

" Our sacrament here is just over. We have had at least three splendid discourses, — two from Mr. Fraser, Kirkhill, one from Mr. Stewart. The latter is the more powerful man, the former has the more logical head. Mr. Fraser is a reasoner only, and though nothing can be clearer or more conclusive than his arguments, the attention is apt to be fatigued by a discourse altogether argumentative, and too long for some relief; a sermon may thus be good in all its parts, and yet faulty as a whole. Mr. Stewart, on the other hand, is both a reasoner and a poet. He narrates, he describes, he reasons, he illustrates, with equal effect; he can sink into the familiar without being mean, and rise into the sublime almost without effort. In fine, Mr. Fraser is a limited monarch, and governs by the law; we find him continually appealing to it, and to our understandings; like true Whigs, we are nearly as much his judges as his subjects, and only submit to be governed by him so long as he is constitutional, and can produce the codes and precedents under which he acts. Mr. Stewart, on the contrary, is a despot. — we find he can do with us whatever he wills, and are such Tories as never to question his right. As for the law, he can either make a merit of judging by it, or transgress it with impunity. Forgive me so brief and imperfect a sketch of two of the most talented clergymen in the north of Scotland. I trust you have tendered my best thanks to Mr. Grant for his elegant and truly excellent discourse. He carried me with him from beginning to end. He had my full assent to the truth of all his remarks, and the justness of all his principles. — I felt all he wished me to feel, and saw all he intended I should see.

" I have regularly wound up my watch every night since I left you, and have begun to find out its various uses. One of these belongs to it exclusively, as an individual watch. Need I point out that one? "

Miss Dunbar had, with much difficulty, prevailed upon Miller to accept from her the present of a watch.

The following letter gives us a glimpse of the " voluntary controversy," at this time agitating Scotland ; an interesting hint, also, of that anti-patronage fervor which was to make Miller the champion of non-intrusion. The sternness of our friend's orthodoxy is to be noted ; " the Arminian " must be driven from his pulpit. Hugh Miller had no sympathy with Broad Churchism in any sense.

"CROMARTY, August 15, 1833.

" I was a very few days ago at MacFarquhar's Bed and the gypsies' cave, — the scene of my ' Boatman's Tale.' About four hundred yards to the west of the Bed there is a second cave, in a corner so wild and sequestered that it is scarcely visited, except, perhaps, by myself, once in a twelvemonth. The sides and roof are crusted over by green mould and white stalactites. It reminds me of a burial vault ; and I never visited it alone and in the evening without keeping a sharp lookout for the inhabitants. It has been haunted by evil spirits, it is said, time immemorial. There is no path to it, and so I am afraid you will find it inaccessible ; besides, to visit it by day, and with a party, is not at all the way of seeing it. Twilight and solitude, and a melancholy, imaginative mood can alone render it interesting. Well, it is night ; the moon has just risen out of the frith, the bolder features of the cliffs are partially relieved from the gloom of the deeper recesses, and a level stream of pale light has entered the wide mouth of the cavern, and falls on the dim, glimmering objects within. See how the dark roof arches over us, and how the columnar stalactites of the sides seem advancing towards us ; observe, too, how our shadows stretch inwards and mingle with the darkness ! What a theatre for the wild and the horrible! The floor is strewed over with what seem the fragments of human bones; and then that spectral-looking object within. — does it not move? Hear how the deep sullen roar of the sea awakens all the echoes of the place till they mutter from the deeper recesses, like the growling of a wild beast, and the wave seems calling over our heads! Nay, draw nearer to me. I tremble like a school-boy. Surely these are human bones scorched and blackened by fire, and gnawed by the teeth; and look yonder, is not that a skeleton reclining on the floor? See, the bony hand rests on the tattered fragments of a book. *He* was the last who perished; and, oh! with what feelings must he have opened that book after he had finished his horrible meal! You have now seen the cave, and more; but the *more* I am afraid you will deem rather a nightmare of the imagination than a dream. Am I not bound, however, to tell you all?

" Before leaving MacFarquhar's Bed, I had a delightful bathe among the rocks. There was a heavy sea tumbling ashore, bordering the whole coast with a fringe of foam. I shot out through the surf and reached the open sea; the waves were rising and falling around me; at one time I sunk into the hollow, the hills and rocks disappeared, and I saw only a valley of waters; anon I was lifted up on the ridge, and laid my hand on its white mane as I looked down on the shore. What would you not give to be able to swim? The exercise has its mischances, however. On landing I was dashed against a rock, and had to walk very softly for three days after, lest I should be asked whether I was not lame.

" Is it not a pleasant thing to lie, in a fine, clear day, on the sea-beach, amid the round polished pebbles and the pretty shells, and see through the half-shut eye the little waves dancing to the sun, and hear, as if we heard it not, their murmur on the shore? To be all alone, — shut out from the world, — the wide ocean stretching away for many a league before us, and a barrier of steep cliffs towering behind. There is, my dear madam, a kind of social solitude which fits us for society by training us both to think and to feel; or rather, I should say, in which we are *trained*, solitude being but the school, imagination and the social affections the teachers. Let me illustrate : I lie all alone on the sea-shore, but in imagination my friend is seated beside me, and so my thoughts and feelings are thrown into the conversational mould. My attention is alive to what is passing around me, my memory active, my reasoning faculties in operation, my fancy in full play; and all this because the conversation must be kept up. And thus friendship and solitude operate on my thoughts, as the waves operate on the pebbles which lie in heaps around me. There is a continual action, a ceaseless working, till the rude, unshapen ideas, like the broken fragments of rock, are rounded and polished, and display all their peculiarities of texture, and all their shades of color.

"After all — and I speak from experience — controversy, though often a necessary evil, is invariably a great one. Never in all my life did I sin so grievously against my neighbor and my own better feelings, as when battling about two years ago for my towns-folks and myself in the affair of the chapel, and this, though my own conscience, and the best people I knew, assured me I was in the right. . . .

"You must surely have admired, in the 'Paradise Lost,' that expansiveness of moral prospect (if I may so speak) which the poet has spread out before his readers. The work resembles a lofty range of terraces rising one above the other, and the grand object to be contemplated from each of these is the Fall. In our ascent upwards we first use the terrace of human nature, and turn towards the

object. It is too near, and too much on a level with us, to
be descried other than imperfectly. We see it only as a
thing of sin and suffering originating in a sceptical disobe-
dience and the wild impulses of a blind desire. We ascend
to the second terrace (it is the place of the fiends), and look
down ; the object appears in a clearer light, — we see it as
the result of deep, crooked design and a malice as artful as
profound. We then ascend to the top eminence ; it is
occupied by the throne of Deity ; the prospect spreads out
before us in all its completeness. We see the blind impulse
destined and directed by an unerring agent, — the little
crooked design forming part of a plan as extensive as 'tis
faultless, — infinite wisdom making use of folly as one of
its means, and infinite goodness effecting its purposes by
hatred and malevolence. But what, you ask, is all this to
the purpose ? Much. Let us try whether we cannot ascend
the several terraces, and catch a glimpse from each of them
of the question now agitating the Church. From the first
we see a scene of contention and uproar ; much good feeling lost and much bad argument found ; the Christian sunk
in the politician, and the peace of the Gospel swallowed up
amid the dissensions of the Churches. We reach the
second terrace, and the view begins to open. We see in
both parties the good and the bad linked together by a
common cause, and grown careless of that only true and
legitimate distinction which had hitherto held them apart ;
we see the infidel and the Christian dissenter united on the
one side, the cold-blooded hireling and the useful minister
on the other. Could the old deceiver have fallen on a more
ingenious stratagem for neutralizing the effects of Christianity than this of binding together the dead and the living ? Let us now ascend, but with becoming reverence, the
summit of the eminence. The view expands ; we see that
the effervescence below, however unconscious the discordant

elements which produce it, is tending to good, — to the purification of an excellent and venerable Church, which, however, like that of Pergamos, has its 'few things' that are evil. The whole structure is assailed, and the unsolid parts of it must fall. The good, not the wealthy or titled, must choose its teachers, — the hireling must resign his stipend, the Arminian quit his pulpit.

"In copying for me you cannot, as you truly observe, go far wrong. Our tastes may, perhaps, vary in some of their decisions, but they are evidently of the same family. Collins' beautiful Ode on the Superstitions of the Highlands I have seen, but not for the last ten years. I wished much for a copy of it when selecting matters for my Traditions; and I have still a volume of these to write; but really I must not put you to the drudgery of copying; it is worse than being chained at the oar. Tell Miss Grant how much I long to see her in Cromarty. If you visit me in my little room (I am not quite so nice on this point as cannie Elshy), she, I trust, will accompany you: and that you may see it in all its glorious confusion, I shall neither arrange the books nor mend the broken pane. Remember, 'tis I alone who am to be your Caliban during your stay in ' the island.'

> "'I'll show thee the best springs; I'll pluck thee berries;
> I'll fish for thee, and get thee wood enough.
> And I, with my long nails, will dig thee pignuts.
> Wilt thou go with me?'"

"CROMARTY, Oct. 29, 1833.

"The night has fallen, — a still, dreamy sort of night, faintly lighted up by the moon. About half an hour ago I was out among the woods; they were gloomy and ghostly, for twilight had begun to darken, and the trees are all in their winding-sheets of red or yellow, except where, in the more exposed corners of the wood, they stand like so many naked skeletons, stretching their bare, meagre arms towards the sky. I was in a rather low mood before going out, and there is little chance of one's recovering one's spirits by walking through a decaying wood in a cloudy evening of autumn. Mine sunk miserably. I remember that, some twelve years ago, I used often to wish that I could retire from the world altogether. I would have fain built myself a little rustic hut in the most secluded recess of some lonely valley, or in the depths of some solitary wood, or under the uninhabited precipices of some uninhabited shore; and in that hut would I have amused myself, as I fondly thought, with my books, and my pencil, and my pen; in digging my little garden and tending my few goats. I have pictured to myself the snugness and comfort of my little apartment in some boisterous night of winter, when the winds would be howling over my roof and the rains pattering on my casement, — trees creaking, streams dashing, waves roaring, and the whole heavens and the whole earth a scene of uproar and contention. Within all would be quietness, except that the flame would be rattling in the chimney, — throwing its cheerful reflection on my stool, my table, my little cupboard, my few books, and my bed. Every season was to have its own peculiar pleasures for me, and its own particular study: the phenomena of nature, the wisdom of the poet, the workings of my own mind, — each, all, of these, were to furnish me with employment. And thus I was to spend my days, until at length death, no very unwelcome visitor, would call in upon me, and my cabin would become my grave. Such was the dream of the boy, — of one who had but just begun to know life as it presents itself to the children of poverty and labor, and who was not aware that the irrational and inanimate worlds are much less interesting objects of study than the world of men; or that, by retiring into one's own mind, one may become more completely a hermit than by retiring into a desert. I was employed in thinking of all this in my walk to-night; in calling up the various circumstances of my dream, and in feeling, from an experience not a little strengthened by the depression of the moment, how very fallacious its promise of happiness. The best and strongest-minded of us, my dear madam, cannot always be happy in our own resources alone. We have all of us our hours and days of languor and melancholy, when we must look without ourselves for comfort. Seldom have I felt this more strongly than to-night, and never have I felt it without thinking gratefully and tenderly of my friend. I quitted the wood with its mournful-looking trees, and its heaps of withered leaves, and came home to write to you. . . .

"It seems Allan Cunningham, the Galloway stonemason, is engaged at present in preparing a new edition of Burns, with a memoir. He is desirous of procuring all the unpublished information which still exists regarding him, and as I once chanced to mention to Mr. Carruthers, with whom Cunningham is intimate, that the Mr. Russel whom the poet has brought so often and so conspicuously forward in his satirical poems, resided for several years as a schoolmaster in Cromarty, I was now applied to for all of his history I could glean from tradition. I wrote as requested, and produced a letter interesting for its facts. . . . . They may serve to show that Burns, in his quarrels with the evangelical clergy, might possibly have been less piqued with what was good in their religion than with what was bad in some of themselves, — an opinion not generally entertained; and that his stinging sarcasms were no chance arrows sent from a bow drawn at a venture, but true to character and fact. The descriptions of Russel in the satires, with the anecdotes of the latter which I have been able to collect, piece completely into one character.

"I am at present employed in the church-yard, and busily employed too, — for you must not suppose that I am always as idle as when you were here; on the contrary, there is perhaps scarcely a less indolent man in the country-side; though I love dearly to have the choosing of my own employment, and could never yet submit to be converted into a mere machine. I have at times, for weeks together, been performing the labor of almost two men, — writing nearly as much as men who only write, and hewing as much as men who only hew; but were the writing or hewing either to be imposed on me as a task, I would be miserable."

"CROMARTY, December 16, 1833.

"I have been low-spirited and unhappy. You remember the fine-looking young man, a cousin of mine, that Miss Reid pointed out to you when you were in Cromarty two years ago? He is dead. At the time I was enjoying so much in your company at Nigg, he was lying on a bed of sickness in a foreign land, with neither friend nor relative to smooth his pillow or speak him comfort. Poor Walter! His story is a melancholy one! He was long attached to a young girl of Cromarty, and in forming his little scheme of future happiness he had laid down his union with her as its very ground-work; but seeing, from the miserable depression of trade, little chance of providing for her in this country, he crossed the Atlantic in the hope that his exertions would secure for him in America what they had failed in procuring for him here. Alas, he has found only a grave! Poor fellow! He had a kind, warm heart, and all his acquaintances here regret him sincerely; what may not I? We grew up together from our mutual childhood as playmates and companions; and though for the last twelve years we were less in each other's company, for our pursuits were different, and mine led me to be much alone, we still continued to love and respect each other. You remember his appearance. He was a well-built man of six feet, but from his being so justly porportioned he did not seem so tall ; he had an iron constitution and great bodily strength, and when in Cromarty he used to expose himself with impunity to all the various hardships which, in this part of the country, spirited young men sometimes subject themselves to in quest of amusement. He has lain, in the season of the herring fishery, night after night, in an open boat on the Moray Frith, and watched with his gun for hours together, in the severest weather, for the otter and cormorant. Confiding in this strength of constitution without taking into account the difference of climate, he seems to have exposed himself in the same way among the woods and rivers of America. In crossing in a small vessel, late in September, one of the great lakes, he imprudently slept on deck during the night, and on landing was seized by a fever, which carried him off in about ten days. You will forgive me for dwelling so much on so melancholy a subject. I cannot get the poor fellow out of my sight.

"There are a few brief passages in his history that I know would interest you, were I but in the mood of telling them. About four years ago, when engaged in writing my letters on the herring fishery, I went out with him in a little boat to renew my acquaintance with the various phenomena of the frith, and rowed about twenty miles into the open sea. There came on a dismal night of wind and rain, and when, after folding myself in the sail, I had lain down and fallen asleep, the tossing of the boat was such that my covering was unrolled. fold after fold, until at length I lay exposed to the showers and the spray. I was awakened about midnight by Walter wrapping me up as

carefully as a mother would her child, and heard him remark to one of our companions that, come of himself what
might, he could not see Cousin Miller lie catching his death
in that way. 'The puir chield,' he added, 'is better at twa
three things than at taking care o' himsel'.' I cannot tell
you how often I think of this incident, or how very painful
the reflection that there should be no one to bestow on him
the care and attention which he could so lavish on another.

" Some eight years ago he resided for a twelvemonth or
two in Edinburgh. There was a sister of his father's who
had married and settled in Ayrshire well-nigh thirty years
before, and between whom and her relatives in the north
country there had been little intercourse from that period.
Walter, however, had often heard of his aunt, and that in
disposition, especially in her attachment to her friends, she
very much resembled himself: and so, setting out from
Edinburgh, he walked nearly a hundred miles to pay her a
visit. He reached the village in which she resided on the
evening of the second day, and, on being shown her house,
introduced himself to her as a person from Cromarty, who
had lately seen her brother. She started at the sound of
his voice. 'Can it be possible,' she asked, 'that you are a
son of his?' Walter smiled, and clasping her hand in both
his. 'I have taken a long walk,' he said, 'just to see you,
and get acquainted with my cousins and your husband.'
The poor woman was affected to tears.

" A fine-looking young woman, one of her daughters,
entered the apartment. 'Come here, Jessie,' said the
aunt, 'and see your cousin, whose kind heart has brought
him all the way from the north country to his friends in
Ayrshire.' Some one cried out in the next room: 'Bring
me to him, too, mother.' It was a poor little girl who had
been confined for years to her bed by an affection of the
spine. Walter had to sit beside her, and look over all her

playthings; and when he was going to rise she locked her arms round his neck, and held him fast till she fell asleep.

"A few days after he was invited with his Cousin Jessie to a country ball. Jessie, though attached to another to whom she was married shortly after, was yet as proud of him as if he were her lover. She introduced him to her little circle of friends, young women like herself; and Walter, who danced *par excellence*, and was a thorough adept in all the little arts of gallantry, was quite the Adonis of the evening. Some of the lads of the place, however, who were but ill pleased to see the handsome young man of the north more a favorite with their sweethearts than themselves, and carrying away all the luck of the ball, contrived to fasten a quarrel on him, and Walter, who was quite as ready in meeting an enemy as a friend, knocked one of them down. This took place in a kind of ante-room. In an instant he was attacked by four of the party at once, but leaping into a corner of the room, where he could keep them abreast of him, he found abundant employment for them all. I have never seen in a human arm so immense a structure of bone and sinew; his wrist used to remind me of the lower part of a horse's leg. He was fighting on at least equal terms with the four, when the sweetheart of Jessie, an active young fellow, drawn to the place by the noise of the fray, took part with him, and turned the tide in a twinkling. Ever after this night his cousins used to regard him as quite a prodigy. On the day he parted from them the poor little sick girl cried herself into a fever; and his aunt, ere she could take leave of him, walked with him for more than six miles, standing every few paces to bid him farewell, and then losing heart and going on a little further. Does not all this give you the idea of a man whom one could love very much?"

The rest of the letter is occupied chiefly with details

respecting Cousin Walter, which are given in the "Schools and Schoolmasters," one or two being added, which it is unnecessary to quote. Miller says that Walter was, like himself, "a Whig in principle, and a Tory in feeling, — a Tory, at least, as far as a profound respect for the great and the venerable can constitute one such." It is important to have this description of his relation to Whigism on the one hand, and to Toryism on the other, in his own words. It exactly corresponds to the fact.

He refers in the same letter to an offer of pecuniary assistance which Miss Dunbar has made him, with the same object as that of Miss Fraser. He firmly declines to accept it ; but, with chivalrous delicacy of feeling, half confesses that he may be carrying his assertion of independence too far, and begs her to pardon him the excess of a virtue to which he has owed much. " 'It is not given to man,' says your favorite Sir James Mackintosh, 'to rest in the proper medium.' And why? Because in the nature of things the principle that holds us aloof from one class of derelictions tends to precipitate us on another. We stand within a circle the whole circumference of which is evil, and cannot recede from any one point in it without approaching nearer to some other point. And if, in this way, the spirit which has been bestowed upon me to preserve me from all the little meannesses of solicitation, and to secure to me in my humble sphere that feeling of self-respect, without which no one can fulfil the duties of a man, or deserve the respect of others, should at times impel me towards the opposite extreme, and make me in some little degree jealous of even the kindness of a friend, will you not tolerate in me a weakness so necessarily, so inseparably connected with that species of strength which renders me, if anything does, in some measure worthy your friendship?"

Last of all, he glances at Cromarty politics, declaring

that he had narrowly escaped being made a Councillor in a late Burgh election, and had " fought as hard to get out of the way of preferment as most of his towns-people did to get in its way." Thus ends a letter as long as an ordinary essay. Before despatching his next to Miss Dunbar, he has learned from her that she is suffering under dangerous illness.

"CROMARTY, January 10, 1834.

" The feelings with which I perused your last letter were of a very different nature from those ever imparted to me by any of your former ones. Would that I could lighten you of but half your burden ! But, alas (how poor and in-sufficient are the friendships of earth) ! There are evils in which there can be no co-partners. How frequently do our better feelings seem bestowed upon us merely to teach us how very weak we are ; and how little else may it be in our power to give to those to whom we have already given our best affections. It is well, however, that there is one Friend who, more sincerely such than any other, is infinitely more powerful too. He is willing to bestow every good upon us, and quite as able as he is willing.

" You are going to Edinburgh, and will, I trust, soon return in stronger health and with brighter prospects. Do not suffer your spirits to droop. Regard the past as an earnest of the future, and cherish the invigorating hope that there may be yet many years of life and happiness before you. But there is a hope better and surer and more invig-orating still, that you do well to cherish. How cheering it is that our present little day, with its clouds and its storms and its momentary gleams of brief and imperfect sunshine, with its chill and troubled evening and its long and gloomy night, is but the prelude to a day placid and unchanging, in which our sun shall never be clouded and never go down ! The more my experience of life and of man, the deeper my conviction of the truth of Christianity. It is so entirely fitted to our nature and to our wants. I do not think it possible for us to form a thorough attachment to any except individuals of our own species; — we may have some little regard for inferior natures, and may bow before a *superior* with awe and adoration; but it is on a human breast only that we can, as it were, rest our whole souls; and what but human sympathies alone can meet and mingle with ours! The deist may bend before his God, but can he for a moment entertain the thought that there is aught of amity in the feeling with which he looks upwards, and the feeling with which that imaginary being looks down? He did not 'know what was in man' who first made such a religion. How well it is for us that there is so complete an adaptation, in this respect, between our nature and the nature of Him in whom we believe; that He whom we worship as God is also man, one whose tears burst out over the grave of a dead friend, and whose bosom supported the head of a living one; one who has endured sorrow and suffered pain; one who was born like ourselves, feared death as we fear it, and died as certainly as we must die! God grant, my dear madam, that we may have Him for our common friend! He loves us much better that we can love one another, and can sympathize with us more sincerely. But He can do more than love and sympathize, and we cannot. He can comfort and heal. The man who wept over the tomb of Lazarus, commanded as God that Lazarus should come forth, and the dead came. I know you will not be offended with me for indulging in this mood; I am light-hearted and foolish, and indulge in it too seldom; and yet there is surely nothing which should be so conducive to lightness of heart as the truths on which it dwells.

"When last in the parish of Nigg with John (Swanson), we ascended together the eminence from whence, two short months before, I had the pleasure, in your company, of looking over so wide and diversified a prospect. But oh, what a melancholy change has that brief period produced! You remember how the distant mountain seemed melting into the sky, and of a hue scarcely less transparent; how the patches of wood on the range of hills which rise towards the north, touched, and but barely touched, by the Midas-like hand of Autumn, seemed so many pieces of embroidery on a ground of purple; how the Frith of Cromarty lay in all its extent before us, — a huge mirror, over which two little silvery clouds were coquetting with their own shadows; how the *mirror frame* on either side was embossed with trees and fields and villages, — all enveloped in brightness and beauty; how the distant friths and the great sea beyond were sleeping beside their shores, as if, having sworn an eternal peace with them, they were soliciting confidence by showing how much they trusted; and how even the very rocks themselves, bold and rugged and abrupt as they are at all times, were so colored by the season, and so relieved by the sunshine, that their very savageness seemed but a sterner beauty! But why all this? A single recollection will do more for you than fifty such descriptions. You remember, then, that the scene was one of the most pleasing, — beautiful in all its parts, — sublime as a whole. When I last gazed on it I deemed it one of the dreariest I ever saw. All the higher grounds were covered with snow or enveloped in cloud; all the lower were dark as the surface of a morass. The woods, brown and sombre, seemed like the dark spots on the face of the moon, so many cavities scooped out of the sides of the hills. The sky was of a dull, leaden hue; the sea of a color approaching to black, except where edged along the shores with a broad fringe of foam. I could think of it only as a huge monster stretching its immense arms into the bowels of the land, and could liken it only to the Brahminical hieroglyphs of the terrible man-lion starting from its column, and tearing to pieces the blaspheming prince. Was not the scene a gloomy one? I did not then know you were unwell, or the contrast would have struck me still more forcibly. Your letter has tinged all my thoughts with sadness."

"CROMARTY, Feb. 14, 1834.

" I need hardly tell you that I never yet received a more truly welcome letter than your last; the very handwriting on the cover was worth a whole file of ordinary epistles. I trust I am not too sanguine when I anticipate for you many happy days in the future, days in which you will live, as in the past, not more for yourself than for your friends, and in which, enjoying all that is truly good in the present world, you will only occasionally be reminded that physical like moral evil has a tendency to destroy itself, and that there is a world in which evil, either physical or moral, can have no place. I often think of the truly noble sentiment expressed in your letter of the 8th January, and fully acquiesce in it. No one can think aright of the weakness of our nature, without seeing that there is much to fear; but then no one, on the other hand, can believe in the goodness of the Almighty without feeling that there is much also to hope.

" What shall I say of the warm interest you continue to take in the fate of my luckless History? nay, rather, what can I say when I think that that interest should be manifested at such a time? This much at least, that those philosophers who resolve all our affections into a principle of selfishness must have had little experience of true friendship. I am afraid you will render me quite a bankrupt by your kindnesses, that my gratitude will never be able to keep pace with them. Sir Thomas too! Whatever my fate may be in the future, it is not likely I shall ever forget that a gentleman so high in the political and literary world should have so honored me with his notice, and so interested himself in my behalf. So far, at least, as you and he are concerned, I find that my pride and my gratitude are mixed up into one sentiment; and though the better feeling is perhaps less pure in consequence of the alloy, it will, like everything else of value that is hardened by a baser mixture, be rendered all the more indestructible by it.

"I am engaged as busily at present with my second volume as if my first had already passed into a third edition, and I have got the larger half of it written, but in a style so like that of the former, that if the one sink, the other can have no chance of rising. I am not without hope of becoming a more skilful writer than I am at the present, but it must be in some department of literature in which I can employ my mind more than in my present walk. I often find it too narrow for me, and that, while I am gossiping over my old-wife stories, and dressing up little ideas in very common language, my more vigorous powers are standing idly by, perhaps pining away for lack of exercise. But I must complete the work at all risks, were it but for the sake of poor Cromarty, before I take up anything else. I am no hypocrite in literature, but an honest, right-hearted devotee, to whom composition is quite its own reward; and truly it would need. How many of my chapters, think you, will Professor Wilson read? Some of them are mortally heavy, and should he stumble on two or three of these, alas for my Traditions!

"The story of the shipwreck to which you allude is a truly affecting one, but you are only partially acquainted with the circumstances which render it such. The master was a fine young fellow barely turned of nineteen, who had just been promoted to the charge, and who, on quitting har-

bor on his last and unfortunate trip, shook his father heartily
by the hand, and assured him that neither he nor mother
might need want for anything now. It was the first voyage,
too. in the ill-fated vessel to the lad Junner, — a rough,
frank-hearted sailor, who, a few days before, had quitted,
under circumstances highly honorable to him, a smack, in
which he had sailed for several years. On coming down on
the preceding trip from London in very stormy weather, a
large, wood-freighted American ship. when passing within
a few hundred yards of the vessel in which he sailed, was
struck by a sudden squall and fairly upset. Thirteen of
the crew succeeded in clambering to the keel, where they
began to cry for assistance in tones so fearfully energetic
that the sounds have been ringing in the ears of some of the
smacksmen ever since. There was a high broken sea running at the time, but Junner, a thorough-bred seaman, convinced of the possibility of saving at least some of the poor
men, weared ship and bore down on the wreck, when the
master came on deck. and, pronouncing the attempt impracticable, ordered him to bear away. Junner remonstrated,
backed by our old friend Gilmour; nothing could be easier,
he said, than, by running under the lee of the foundered
vessel, to open up a communication with the men on the
keel. The master, however, a low fellow, who had got
charge of the smack only the voyage before, did not choose
to risk himself in the attempt, and the poor men on the
wreck were left to their fate. Before losing sight of them,
their number was lessened to eleven; and Junner, who,
had the rest of the crew backed him, would have rescued
them in spite of the master, vowed that he would never set
foot again in the same vessel with a wretch so unfeeling.
He accordingly engaged with the poor young master of the
' Oak,' and perished with him a few days after.

"I met in one of my walks, a few days after the disaster,

with a young lady, and our conversation happened to turn on it. ' I am sorry,' she said, ' for the master, poor young fellow! and for the wife and children of Junner; but he himself was so rude in his manners, and so ungrateful to the owners of the vessel in which he had sailed so long, that I cannot be sorry for him.' I saw that she had been misinformed regarding him, and set her right. But why relate so commonplace an incident as this? I will tell you why. I am placed at present in a rather unusual point of observation with respect to the two classes of society of which our little town, and indeed every other town, small or great, is composed. I see all that is passing among our tradesfolk and laborers, and know all their opinions; I see, too, much of what is passing among the people of a higher sphere, and have been acquainted with their opinions also. And what is the result? That there exists little good-will between them, and that their mutual suspicions and jealousies are effects, in the greater number of instances, of mistake and misconception. They are so divided that they never meet to compare notes; — a sad state of society, surely, in such times as the present, when popular opinion is so powerful and so conscious of its power. What wonder that the people of a whole country-side should interest themselves in the fate of such a man as poor Junner, or that they should feel indignant at those who could misrepresent his character in the way related! True, the misrepresentation could not have originated with those who would be hated and reviled for it, were the people to come to hear of it; the author is probably some mean little thing that has wriggled itself into the ear of one whose notice it would deem a bargain at any price, and which it has purchased at the cheap rate of betraying a few secrets, and telling a great many falsehoods. But the people would never think of asking who the author was.

They never distinguish between those who credit and those who invent; indeed, they are at too great a distance to make the distinction; and thus there are heart-burnings produced and jealousies fostered, which even in the present day destroy the better charities of society, and which must produce still sadder effects in the future. 'If,' says Lockhart, in his Life of Burns, ' the boundary-lines of society are observed with increasing strictness among us; if the various orders of men still day by day feel the chord of sympathy relaxing, — we may well lament over symptoms of a disease in the body politic which, if it goes on, must find sooner or later a fatal ending.' There is true philosophy in this remark; and it is not one of the most harmless consequences of such a state, that the higher orders should have so often to form their opinions of the lower on the data furnished by the eavesdropper and the tale-bearer. I need not tell you that during the week I passed at Forres I saw much that delighted me, but I have not yet told you what it was that delighted me most: just your manner of addressing the poor people whom you occasionally met by the way; the frank inquiry, the kind reply, the good-humored remark, the caress bestowed on the child, the compliment paid to the mother, — in short, the numberless proofs of this kind which you so unwittingly gave me that your sympathies crossed the broad line of demarcation and found human nature on the other side, inspired me with a respect for your character which no opposite course could have led me to entertain. I have often said to myself, Give me an aristocracy of Miss Dunbars, and we shall have no revolution for a century to come."

"Cromarty, March 29, 1834.

" You have returned to Forres. Would that it were under happier auspices and with brighter hopes! But I do trust that in the quiet of retirement, and amid all that constitutes home, you will find that there yet remains for you much of comfort and enjoyment. I cannot suffer myself to think that my friend is to be other than happy, and would fain believe what I so earnestly wish. There is a moral alchemy which can transmute the evils of life into blessings, and you are not unacquainted with the secret. Besides, it is wonderful how our bodies, and our minds too, accommodate themselves to the circumstances in which we are placed, and how, even amid much pain, and much unavoidable depression of spirits, enough of pleasure may be found to render life desirable. I would fain have something to build upon regarding you, — were it but the consideration how rest proves positive enjoyment to those who labor, and a cessation of pain positive happiness to those who suffer. I would fain find something to solace me in the story of the prisoner, who found his dungeon for the first few weeks so utterly dark that he could hardly distinguish day and night in it, but whose eye became so accustomed to the gloom that he could at length see the smallest insect creeping along the floor. But there is in reality only one source from whence comfort may be drawn, — the mercy of that God who does not afflict willingly, and whose goodness is equal to his power. . . .

"I spent two hours very agreeably a few nights ago on the wide tract of sand that in large spring-tides stretches beneath the town. The stream was one of the largest I ever saw; I could walk dry-shod over tracts of beach which, in ordinary ebbs, are covered by well-nigh five feet of water. The evening was cold and stormy, and yet half the children of the town were frolicking over the sands, — some gathering periwinkles or catching razor-fish, and not a few philosophizing, like myself, on a class of vegetables and animals so unlike the productions of either kingdom we were accus-

tomed to meet with on land. There is no study so universally a favorite as the study of natural history, and at no
age are people of the common order such minute observers
as in their childhood. One half the degree of attention bestowed by the boy on the wonders that surround him would
render the man a philosopher. Among the juvenile philosophers of the ebb I saw a little deaf boy watching with
much apparent interest a contest between a large *buckie* and
a young razor-fish. The *buckie* had inserted its proboscis
into the shell of the latter, and was pulling out the poor
tenant, who seemed incapable of any other mode of resist-
ance than the very inefficient one of rendering itself difficult
to be swallowed. I saw another little thing of about six
years turning over with a stick that strange-looking animal
which we term the sea-snail (naturalists have another name
for it), and admiring its uncouth conformation. By the way,
there is something singular about this animal which I have
never yet seen noticed, and which I must set myself more
minutely to examine. I remember that when sailing my
little ship, some eighteen years ago, I once or twice acci-
dentally set my foot on a sea-snail, and there exuded from
it, in consequence of the pressure, a blood-like liquor which
tinged the water with crimson for yards around. You know
the famous purple of the Tyrians — the finest and most
precious of all the ancient dyes — is said to have been ex-
tracted from some unknown species of fish. What if that
fish be the sea-snail! Would it not be rare good fun, think
you, to restore one of the lost inventions, and that solely
for the benefit of one's fair countrywomen? I do not know
whether you be acquainted with the animal. It is a reptile-
looking thing about four inches in length and two in breadth
when at the largest, of an oval shape, and furnished with
legs resembling those of a caterpillar magnified. The back
is of a dusky brown and covered with hair, which, when the

animal is alive, seems tinged with all the hues of the rainbow, but which fades into a dirty sand color when it is dead. I have observed that more unusual phenomena are to be seen in a large spring ebb than in twenty ordinary ones; for, though the water falls only a few feet lower, in these few almost all the plants and all the animals are uncommon. On ascending a high mountain in a tropical country, the botanist, after rising a certain height, finds it girded round with a broad strip of vegetation composed of the plants of a more temperate climate; he ascends, and finds in a second belt the trees and plants of still colder countries; anon he arrives at a third belt, then at a fourth, and at length, bordering on the line where all vegetation ceases, he meets with the mosses and lichens of Greenland and Nova Zembla. Something analogous to this may be seen on the wastes left uncovered by the ebb of such a spring tide as the last. First we pass over a sterile region of water-worn pebbles and gravel, and meet with neither animal nor vegetable life. Then we reach a strip of plants of a deep green color, some of them resembling tufts of hair, some of them broad-leaved, and of a texture exceedingly delicate. The small green crab and many-eyed star-fish are natives of this region. We then arrive at a strip, broader than the last, of brown furcated weeds, beneath which we find whole colonies of the black periwinkle, and the craw-fish buckie. A waste of sand succeeds, inhabited by several varieties of shell fish of the bivalve species, and sprinkled with tufts of long sea-grass and brown rope-weed. We find in it, besides, the sand-worm, the builder-worm, and the yellow-spined sea urchin. A stony region comes next, shaggy and rough with kelp-weed and smooth-stemmed tangle, and abounding with the cow-cockle, the brown, toad-like crab, and the large, strong-shelled buckie. Last of all, we find at the water's edge a forest of rough-stemmed tangles, the favorite resort of the red crab, the pink-colored sea urchin, the dwarf lobster, and the lump fish. But I perceive I am giving you rather an index than a description. Ever since I recollect myself I had a turn for the study of natural history, — not the natural history of books, but of the woods and the fields and the sea-shore. I was studying it all unwittingly, when my friends thought I was doing nothing, or worse ; and I now find that through my predilection for it I have learned more in the days I played truant than in those I attended the school. Who knows whether I may not yet turn my acquaintance with it to some account? I question whether Sir Thomas had any thought, twenty years ago, of coming before the public as the editor of a work on natural history.

" Lady Clare is going on with her improvements on her newly purchased property, and threw down, a few days ago, a little old house, which, with its low, serrated gable to the street, ran back, in what Professor Jameson calls the Flemish style, into the heart of the garden behind. And what of that? you may say. Not much to any one but me, but I have grieved for that little old house as for a friend. I have spent in it some of the happiest hours I ever spent anywhere. The front part of it was occupied by the shop of a house-painter, but in the upper part there was a little room which, during his apprenticeship, my poor, deceased friend, William Ross, used to call his own. He slept in it, and drew in it, and wrote in it, and took in it many a review of the past, and formed many a hope for the future. I saw his handwriting on the wall, in a much-admired quotation from Blair's Grave : —

> " ' Sure the last end
> Of the good man is peace ! How calm his exit !
> Night dews fall not more gently to the ground,
> Nor weary, worn-out winds expire so soft.'

I have heard him repeat the passage at a time when he little thought it was to be soon realized in himself. For the last fortnight I have been employed in writing a biographical sketch of him, which is to serve as one of the chapters of my second volume; and it will not, I trust, prove one of the least interesting. He has now been in his grave these six years, and yet my recollections of him are as fresh as if he died yesterday. I cannot forget him, and if I myself be ever known to the world, the world shall know why."

The last-mentioned intention Miller made good. A separate biographical sketch of Ross from his pen I have not, indeed, seen, and no second volume of Traditions was ever published; but he has immortalized his friend in the "Schools and Schoolmasters."

The letter of Mrs. Grant of Laggan, author of the once popular Letters from the Highlands, referred to by Miller in the letter which follows, was written to her friend Miss Dunbar, and contained a very favorable opinion of Miller: —

"CROMARTY, April 22, 1834.

"How shall I thank you for your elegant gift? I have already spent some hours in admiring it, and every time it catches my eye I can gaze on it with fresh interest. There are some faces which one never tires of looking at, — transparent sort of faces, through which we can see the soul, — and Sir James' is as decidedly one of this class as any I ever saw. Did you ever before see an expression so unequivocally indicative of the pure, good-tempered benevolence, which one cannot but love, blent with that calm but awful dignity of thought which one cannot but revere? One of the first political works I read with interest was Sir James' 'Vindiciæ Gallicæ.' As a piece of argument, it is superior to the exquisite volume of his opponent, and little, if at all, inferior to it as a piece of composition. The same year robbed us of Sir James Mackintosh and Sir Walter Scott. When shall another year find us with so much to lose? . . . .

" Speaking of faces, it will be found that those we can look longest at, and with most pleasure, bear the impression of the gentler and softer, rather than that of the more violent passions. I once saw a dead infant on whose placid features I could have gazed for hours together. They were so beautifully formed and reposed in so exquisite a tranquillity! The poor mother was weeping beside it; the father, though less subdued, had not less to contend with; the features of two or three relatives wore the downcast expression befitting the occasion; but there it lay, in the midst of sorrow and melancholy, the happiest-looking thing that death had ever passed over. There was an air of intelligence, too, about it which a masterly sculptor might, perhaps, have transferred to a piece of marble, but which was associated with feelings which no piece of marble could have awakened. Every one has observed how very intelligent children sometimes look; it has even been supposed, prettily enough, though fancifully enough, too, that infants, when they smile in their dreams, are conversing with beings of a better world (Professor Wilson has introduced the thought very happily into one of his shorter poems); and so natural is the supposition, that I have repeatedly heard it expressed by people who had borrowed it from no one. But the expression in the case I describe suggested thoughts which, equally interesting, had more of an air of truth about them, — thoughts of the new state into which what, in the language of earth, was termed the deceased infant, was newly born, and in which it might have already learned more than the wisest of those it had left behind.

" And now for an incident. When gazing on the sweet little face, footsteps were heard approaching the door, and the cloth was drawn over. The latch was raised, and a poor beggar woman, accompanied by a little girl and boy, the eldest not more than five years of age, half crossed the threshold and then stood; but, on seeing from the furniture, which was hung with white, and the appearance of the bed, that there was a corpse in the apartment, the woman dropped a few words in Gaelic, by way of apology for the interruption. She lingered, however, at the door, and I saw her eyes fill with tears. She was a widow, a native of the Western Highlands, which were visited that year by scarcity; and, to avoid starvation, she had travelled as a mendicant with her little family, which had consisted of three children, to the low country, but, in crossing the hills, a few days before, her youngest child had taken ill and died. She stated her simple story in a few words, and begged to be permitted to look at the dead infant. The face accordingly was again uncovered; but I want words to describe to you what followed, and yet the scene was one of the simplest possible. The poor woman, rather good-looking and young, though much worn, with nothing of the beggar in either her dress or expression, stood fronting the dead, her hands clasped on her breast, and the tears coursing down her cheeks. All the mother was roused in her; and the feelings of the other mother, reawakened by the excitement, were finding vent in a fresh burst of sorrow. Every one present, even the firmest of us, was affected; while the two Highland children, holding by the gown of their mother, were looking anxiously at the object of an interest so general, — the elder with more of curiosity, the younger with more of terror. Would that I were a painter!

"'It is sweet,' says an old poet, 'to be praised by one whom all the world conspires in praising.' Need I say with what feelings I perused the letter of Mrs. Grant, of Laggan? merely as a letter of hers, — as affording an instance of mind triumphing amid the decay of matter, — as furnishing a proof that the affection of a generous heart neither the chills nor shadows of old age can darken or impair. — I would have deemed it highly interesting and valuable; but to me it is all this and a great deal more. Every man is somebody to himself; but I have the good fortune, and I am not dull in appreciating it, of being somebody to myself and to Mrs. Grant, too. I have been a good deal in luck in the number and quality of the compliments paid me of late, but with one or two exceptions I think I can trace you either directly or indirectly in them all. First, my 'Stanzas on a Sun-Dial' appeared in 'Chambers' Edinburgh Journal,' prefaced by a note, in which they are designated as nervous and elegant, and the fact that the author should be a working mason questioned. Next they appeared in a Sussex paper, in which they are praised still more highly. — described, indeed, as ' marked by a refinement of thought, an elegance and propriety of language. that would do honor to the most accomplished poet of the day.' Where, think you, did they next appear? In a Newry paper, which was sent me by the editor, a man I never before heard of. He is extravagant in his commendations of the whole, and some of the lines he has printed in italics, as peculiarly felicitous. The stanzas then took the round — for they seem to have pleased the *Irishes* hugely — of well-nigh half the Hibernian periodical press. I was just recovering my modesty. which, after all these shocks, was, as you may think, in a bad enough state, when out came the second volume of Allan Cunningham's Burns. with the compliment which you have seen. To weigh against it. however, and keep me humble, I find he has compressed my letter into half its original bulk. and that more than half its brains have been squeezed out in the operation. But still there is a little sense left;

and the compliment is from Allan Cunningham. And now, last of all, and worth all the others put together, comes the letter of Mrs. Grant. But how, in sober fact, do I feel after all this? Grateful, I trust, and certainly much pleased, but not at all elated. I have myself to contend with, and myself to satisfy; it will be a long time, I am afraid, ere I shall be successful in so hard a contest, or succeed in pleasing so fastidious a critic; and yet, until that time comes, the approbation of others, however profound their judgment or exquisite their taste, will have the effect rather of showing me what I ought to be, than what I am. Is it not wonderful that the fancy of Mrs. Grant should be still so active, so engagingly playful? There is not less of it in her last brief epistle to you than in any of her earlier ones.

"If ever my Traditions get abroad they will be all the better for having stayed so long at home. And now, what shall I say of your last brief epistle? This much, at least, that were it ten times more brief, still I would value it as coming from you. At this time of day I need hardly tell you of the value I set on your letters, how fondly I treasure them up, or how often I peruse them; but I must not be selfish, and you will judge that I am not, when I say, do not for the future, till your health fully permits, give me more than half a sheet, and do not fill even that at one sitting. That God may be with you, to support and comfort, is the earnest wish, and, I trust, earnest prayer of," etc.

"Cromarty, May 8, 1834.

. . . . "There is a poor idiot boy in the neighborhood here who spends much of his time with me in the church-yard, and who, when I am writing in my little room, frequently creeps upstairs and squats himself beside me. I never yet saw any one of the class in whom intellect is so entirely wanting as in this poor thing. He cannot even count three; but he has a few simple instincts which seem given him to supply in part the want of the higher faculties, and (a still more important matter) some of the better affections of our nature, — love and compassion, and sorrow for the loss or absence of those who have been kind to him. It is interesting to find these so *rudely set;* they seem bestowed upon him to awaken a sympathy for him in the breasts of those to whom he attaches himself. He is present, sitting beside me, babbling in an uncouth, imperfect dialect, which I can only partially understand, about himself and me. I am to get leave to sleep with him, and he is to give me sugar and a dram, and two eggs. Only a few days ago he lost his father; but until the day of his funeral he could not be made to understand that he would have to part with him. He was sleeping, he said, and would be well when he awoke. When he saw the corpse placed in the coffin, however, and people gathering for the funeral, some faint idea of what had happened seemed to cross him, for he became silent and melancholy; and, stealing out of the house to where I was employed in the church-yard, he laid hold of me with an 'Oh, come, oh, come, — father sleeping, — no waken, — no waken at all, — oh, come!' I went with him and followed the funeral, partly to satisfy him, partly out of curiosity to see the workings of nature in a mind so uninformed and imperfect. He squatted down at the head of the grave, and watched, with an expression indescribably affecting, and in which grief, astonishment, and terror seemed equally blended. every motion of the sexton and the bearers; and when the grave was filled. and the sod placed over it. he seemed uncertain whether to return home or remain where he was. He is even now telling me that he is to keep part of his morning piece for his father, who is to come out of his grave to-morrow. I have remarked, though without well knowing on what principle to account for it, that the grief or affection of poor helpless things of this class has something in it which touches us more than the expression of similar feelings in persons possessed of an ordinary share of understanding. Perhaps we are more convinced of their sincerity, — perhaps struck by finding amid such miserable ruins of our nature a part, and that no unimportant one, so entire and unbroken, — a human heart so abstracted from a human understanding, as to remind us of the story of John Huss, whose heart remained unconsumed among his ashes; or, perhaps, as they stand so much in need of our protection, there is a natural provision made for them in our bosoms, on the same principle that there is a provision made for the helplessness of children in the affection of their mothers; and the interest taken in their uncouth expressions of affection may be but a natural effect of the principle. Whatever the cause, the feeling certainly exists, and some of our best writers have not disdained to appeal to it. The fool in Lear is not less true to his poor forlorn master than the most devoted of his nobles. It is Davie Gellatly whom Scott has described as moaning in the bitterness of regret amid the ruins of the Baron's mansion, and as faithful to him in his lowest extremity. It is Wamba, too, who of all Cedric's servants is readiest to lay down his life for him, like a faithful fool, and whose devoted attachment extorts tears from the stern old man, though he has none to shed over his own disasters, or the dead body of his friend.

"Mr. Stewart has just closed a course of sermons on the future return of the Jews to their own land, in which he has delighted the thinking part of us with many splendid bursts of eloquence, and an immense body of original thought. Some of his bolder opinions on the subject he rather hinted at than fully expressed. I have succeeded, however, in laying hold of a few of the more interesting of these. He seems to be decidedly of opinion that the Jews are reserved for the accomplishment of some great purpose in the moral government of the world. What, says he, if the spirit of infidelity, so dominant in the present age, and which seems to be sapping the foundations of every religion, true and false, should at length so thoroughly prevail that the Church and the Pagod and the Mosque should come to be involved in one general ruin, and every form of worship be banished from the earth; what if, when there survived, of all who had prayed to any Deity, only a few despised, disheartened followers of the cross, — when the great mass of the people in every country, amenable to no authority, without one tie of morality, or one belief of a future world of rewards and punishments, shall, with their mouths filled with denunciations against tyranny, be themselves the bloodiest and most despotic of tyrants; what if, at such a time, the Spirit of God should breathe upon the dry bones of Judah until, covered with flesh and sinew, and animated by the principle of life, they shall stand up among the nations, an exceeding great multitude, to testify through the miracle of the power and faithfulness of God, — and, converted themselves, be the grand and fully adequate means of the conversion of a world? Is there not something wonderfully expansive, and, at the same time, highly pleasing. in the thought? Take another in the same style. What if those differences which now divide the Christian world, — setting even good men in hostile opposition to each other, and destroying, in no slight degree, those charities which it is the part of religion to inculcate, — are to receive their final adjustment on the return of the Jews? It is to be no common outpouring of the Spirit which is to sweep away in that people the prejudices which, for a period of nearly twenty centuries, have shut them up

to an obstinate rejection of the Messiah; and when under
the influence of that outpouring they shall set themselves to
the study of the whole Scriptures, to fix their belief as a
Christian Church regarding those minor points on which
Christians at present disagree, there is little probability of
their being led into error, or that their decision shall not
influence the Churches of the Gentiles.

"I have been so fortunate of late as to procure the
perusal of a highly interesting piece of antiquity: the
Session Records of Cromarty during the Establishment of
Episcopacy. They commence in the year 1674, and terminate in 1688, the year of the Revolution. They are
written in an extremely old hand (which, however, I am
antiquary enough to decipher), and from this circumstance
have lain in the archives of the Session for at least the last
three generations unopened and unread. They furnish me
with a great mass of local history curiously stamped with the
peculiar manners of the age; with narratives of the little,
foolish bickerings and disputes of men whose sagacity we
look up to as very superior to our own; and stories long
since forgotten that at one period employed all the tongues
and all the ears of the place, for no better reason, I am
afraid, than that they exposed the weakness or wickedness
of an acquaintance or neighbor. Our great-great-grand-
fathers, I suspect, were not a whit wiser, or better, or happier than ourselves; and our great-great-grandmothers,
poor ladies, seem to have had quite the same passions as
their descendants, with as little ability to control them. I
see there are vices which, like passions, have their rise and
decline; and that we often deem an age more virtuous
than our own merely because it was wicked in a different
way. There were ladies of Cromarty in the good year
1680 'maist horrible cussers,' who accused one another of
being 'witches and witch-getts, with all their folk afore

them,' for generations untold; gentlemen who had to stand at the pillar for unlading the boats of a smuggler at ten o'clock on Sabbath night; 'maist scandalous reprobates' who got drunk on Sundays, and 'abused decent folk ganging till the kirk;' and 'ill-conditioned raggit loons who raisit ane disturbance and faught i' the scholars' loft' in the time of divine service. Were I not so engaged at present, I would draw up from the Session records of the parish a scheme of comparative morality of each succeeding generation for the last hundred and fifty years. The scheme would be at least a curious one, and might show, among other things, how little conducive the iron despotism of the reign of Charles was to the establishment of a high-toned morality among the people. Husbands and their wives do penance in the church in this reign for their domestic quarrels; boys are whipped by the beadle for returning from a journey on Sabbath; men are set in the jougs for charging elders of rather doubtful character with being drunk; boatmen are fined for crossing the ferry with a passenger during church time; and Presbyterian farmers are fined still more heavily for absenting themselves from church. Under a tyranny so intolerable the people seem to have been brutalized, and, in consequence, greatly increased in crime."

"CROMARTY, July 10, 1834.

"I would have written you long ere now, but I have been for the last fortnight in a rather unsettled mood and unable to fix my attention very strongly on anything. I have been looking at the world and the world's matters, at my friends and myself, through a darkened medium, and you will but too well comprehend the *wherefore* of the case when I tell you that my nerves have been affected. Addison was quite right when he remarked that the habit of looking on only the bright side of things is worth five hundred a year.

" My way home from you was divided between a very pleasant drive and one of the most disagreeable, tedious voyages you can think of. I was more than six hours on the frith, — and six such hours! — beating all the way right in the teeth of a strong wind and a heavy tumbling sea, with a sick female passenger who had thrown herself, in a paroxysm of nausea, on the floor of the little cabin, where she lay like a corpse, and a set of boatmen, who were too seriously employed in taking in reef after reef as the gale increased, to afford me any amusement. The fellows were too frightened either to make jokes or to understand them. I wish you had seen the expression with which one of them shook his head, and said he hoped we would get through, on my remarking to him that the wind was coming thick and thin like ill-made porridge, and how he shut his eyes and showed his teeth every time a heavier wave sent its spray half-way up the mast. Above all, I wish you had seen the hills of Culbin as they looked this day over the water. Some of the heavier blasts raised the sand in such dense clouds, that when the sun shone they seemed heightened by more than a thousand feet, and towered over the blue hills behind; but the outlines were faint and ill-defined, and, like the waves that were tumbling around us, they rose and fell with the wind. I got home about six o'clock.

" I would doubtlessly have derived more pleasure from my visit had I found you enjoying the health and spirits of the previous season; but it has not been without its pleasures. I have seen much that interested me, and experienced much kindness. There is comfort, too, in the conviction that my friend, though she has to suffer, can suffer patiently and well; and can indulge in the hope that even pain, as the dispensation of a benevolent God, who does not afflict willingly, must have its work of mercy to perform. How good a thing it is to be enabled to repose our trust upon him! . . .

"My imagination is still full of the wild sand-wastes of Culbin ; a scene so very unlike any I ever saw before, but which corresponds so entirely with all I had read and heard of the arid, wide-extended deserts of Africa and the East. I could almost fancy, when, standing in one of the larger hollows, I looked round me, and saw only hills of barren sand and heaps of gravel, with here and there a dingy rocky-looking flat which had once been vegetable soil, but which could no longer support vegetable life, — I could almost fancy that, having anticipated the flight of time by many centuries, I had arrived at the old age of creation, and witnessed the earth in its dotage."

"Cromarty, August 25, 1834.

"Do not deem me careless and ungrateful. Not one of your friends has thought more regarding you during the last four weeks than I have, though a hundred unlooked-for demands on my time, and (what proved much more harassing) a nervous indolence, which of late has hung much about me, prevented me from writing. Burns seems to have been quite in the right in deeming those disorders which we term *nervous*, diseases of the mind, though they perhaps rather depress our confidence in our powers than prostrate the powers themselves. 'I cannot reason,' says he, in one of his letters to Mrs. Dunlop, 'I cannot think; and but to you I would not venture to write anything above an order to a cobbler.' It is a singular enough fact, however, that the letter in which he says so is one of the finest he ever wrote.

"My time, I have said, has been much occupied of late:

I have been twice to Inverness, thrice at the burn of Craig-house, twice at the beds of bituminous shale, with their numerous and highly interesting animal remains, once all around the northern Sutor, and I know not how often on the hill of Cromarty and at the Doocot Cave. It is a sad thing to be unable to make a proper use of the important monosyllable *no*. My trips to Inverness, however, were solely on my own account, and in a few days I think I shall visit Tain on a similar errand. I have written within the last month more than twenty letters, some of them of considerable length. Withal, I have been employed in the church-yard, though of course not quite so regularly as if there had been no parties or no writing.

" Mr. Stewart is at present at Strathpeffer, in quest of health, and his place here is occupied by a relative of his own, a Mr. Robertson. He is a son of the late Prof. Robertson, of St. Andrews, and a truly fine fellow, — frank, open-hearted, talented, and well-read. He and I have been at Eathie together, and all over the hill. We have explored, too, the whole northern Sutor. There is much pleasure in coming in contact with an original thinker, and there may be much profit. In the present day the world of books is open to every one, but there are many thoughts which arise in one's mind which cannot be tested by anything we find in books. But the mind of an original thinker, when one is fortunate enough to meet with one, can be brought to bear on one's inner mysteries of thought, — he is a touchstone to try, a light to discover. I have felt this with regard to Mr. Robertson. In passing with him along the northern Sutor I could not help regretting that our expedition to it last year should have been so unlucky. Some of the caves are truly superb; one in particular, which perforates the base of a huge rocky promontory, I have not yet seen surpassed. It has three magnificent entrances, all terminating in one point, from whence a second cave shoots off still deeper into the recesses of the rock, and at the extremity of which noon is dark as midnight."

Mr. J. R. Robertson, referred to in terms so flattering in this letter, is now resident in London, and has kindly furnished me with the following vivid and interesting account of his intercourse with Hugh Miller : —

" In the summer of 1834 I went to Cromarty, intending to stay a few days, and then to pursue my wanderings through the north Highlands. Circumstances detained me upwards of two months. Almost immediately on my arrival, I was introduced to Hugh Miller, who was already a celebrity in his native town and neighborhood. He was tall and athletic, and had a large head, made to look huge by a rusty profusion of not very carefully remembered hair. His whiskers were not large, and represented red sandstone, his eyes gray and keen, his features spoke of intelligence and determination, and exposure to the sun had daubed him with freckles. He did not appear quite so tall as he was, owing to a slouch in his walk, and a tendency to carry his massive brow in the van, which gave him the semblance of stooping.

" He had before this time exhibited his wonderful powers of composition, and achieved a pretty wide local fame as a great student, a deep and original thinker, and a writer of articles in an Inverness paper, and of telling pamphlets on matters of interest to his town and country and the region round. I had not previously heard his name, and only by degrees became aware of the great pride his fellow-citizens took in him, and in what he was expected to do. A day or two after my arrival in Cromarty, I was walking past the church-yard, and saw a man with his coat off, busily chiselling a tombstone. Vaulting over the wall, I went towards him. Hugh raised himself, and after a few minutes' con-

versation put on his coat of hodden gray, and said he
would show me the caves on the northern shore of the
southern Sutor. As we passed the disused burying-ground
of a ruinous old chapel, he told me the story of the solitary
grave outside the boundary wall, where reposed the dust of
a man, who gave directions for his sepulture in this spot, as
it would give him the start of his companions or accusers
on the Day of Judgment, to be held on a neighboring elevation. Our path was by a well, about which he told a
legend. It was celebrated for the curing of some com-
plaints. The caves were rendered classical, also, by stories
of daring smugglers, and of other wild doings.

"During the eight or nine weeks I remained in Cromarty, Hugh and I walked over all the neighborhood. We
tried each other's strength in many ways, — leaping, vaulting, throwing heavy stones, climbing precipices, etc. He
took me to many of his haunts. He was very successful in
the search for geological specimens, and in breaking nodules. We discussed all the questions of the day. He was
very well acquainted with English literature, and had carefully studied translations of most of the celebrated foreign
classics, ancient and modern. He appeared to me to be
more of a practical philosopher than either distinctively
literary or abstractly scientific. He had made some good
water-color sketches, and practised poetry as well as prose.
His former poetry was far behind his poetic prose.
He was admired and wondered at by all classes of his
townsmen; and I met him at dinner and at evening parties
constantly. The questions daily put to me were, 'Isn't
Hugh Miller a wonderful man?' and 'Isn't he very humble?' I always acquiesced in the opinion that he was a
wonderful person, and dwelt so much on this that the inquiry as to his humility was generally forgotten. Had I
been pressed on that point, I should have answered, No.

He had great ability, and he knew it, and was determined that the world should one day know and acknowledge it. He was some five or six years older than I was, but in our short acquaintance we became mutually very frank. On one occasion, he spoke enthusiastically about a departed literary grandee, and used some expressions which led me to ask him whether he would like to be he. He turned on me a flash of indignant, almost contemptuous surprise, as if no living, thinking being, with a spark of soul or true ambition, could do other than desire to be that man. I said, ' But remember, Hugh, he is dead, and we have no evidence that he is with the Lord, nor are his writings calculated to save any souls, or to keep any souls in the right way.' He strode on doggedly with clenched fist, and then suddenly stopped and said, ' It would be well always to remember that.'

" The Rev. Alexander Stewart was the minister of the parish. His fame as a preacher was high. On my return to Edinburgh, I met Dr. Chalmers, and he asked me where I had been spending my summer. I said at Cromarty. ' Oh,' he exclaimed, ' Stewart is the best preacher in the Church of Scotland.' I replied, ' With one exception, I think so.' His retort was a most hilarious laugh. Hugh was an exceedingly attentive hearer, and a frequent associate of this gifted minister. He generally occupied the corner of a square pew in the front of the gallery of the parish church, opposite the pulpit; and as the sermon proceeded he might be seen to lean forward, and fix his keen eyes, from under their remarkable penthouses, on the face of the preacher, seeming not so much to hear the sermon as to penetrate, examine, and sift the man.

" He was always investigating, and, as we walked along, either by road or dry channel of mountain stream, or waded through the heather, he would suddenly interrupt our high argumentation on some recondite subject, by pulling out a stone from the ' dry ' dyke, to examine its geological character, or picking up a pebble from the bed of the rivulet, to note its travels from the distant upland, to which its native rock belonged; or, on the hill-side, he would find berries suitable for a very hungry man's lunch, and descant on the wild botany of the district; and when we swam, he would, whilst dressing, keep his eyes open to the movements of the dwellers in the deep, or amid the pools and crevices of the rocks. The cuttle-fish suggested opaque learnedness, which, far from enlightening others, only seemed to afford the possessor of so much inky knowledge a mode of escaping the detection of his weakness; and the large lobster, hurrying off with one big claw and a little one, suggested the self-sacrifice necessary to safety, taught us by a crustacean who could fling off his leg to save his life.

" Hugh had built a house for his mother and her second family, and he occupied a room and closet in the upper story; the closet was fast becoming a crowded museum of specimens of geology, botany, conchology, etc., and he had a good many books, hardly a library. He used to read passages of a book he was engaged in writing, and courted criticism, though now and then his eye flashed ominously, if the critic diverged into irreverent fun.

" To follow so daring a cragsman had for me the zest of danger, and he would sometimes heighten my terrors by indulgence in a practical humor bordering on malice. On one occasion, for example, we had to ascend almost perpendicularly from the sea-beach, which had become impassable by the advance of the tide during our explorations, — Hugh, of course, in advance, to show the way. The cliff was some one hundred and fifty or two hundred feet high. After mounting steadily to within twenty or thirty feet of the top, we arrived at a perfectly perpendicular wall of solid stone, to be scaled cat-fashion, by clinging successively to bits of clinging ivy. The situation was anything but pleasant, and Hugh suddenly startled me by saying, in what I believe to have been merely an assumed tone of doubt and concern: 'I can't get up any further.' To go down safely was impossible; even to look down at the creamy edge of the little waves beating the shore immediately beneath, would have made me giddy. I mastered my fears as well as I could, and replied: 'Never mind; hold on where you are, and I will climb over you and help you up.' He started off, and was in an instant on the top. I arrived almost at the same moment, and threw myself on the grass, panting out: 'Hugh, you deserve hanging at the very least.' He was always investigating, and for the moment may have forgotten that his curious inspection of my nervous system might have cost me my life. He seemed to me to have a stern pleasure in danger, — a pleasure, I confess. I was quite willing to forego, — and he tried to educate his companions by a little wholesome exposure and risk. He underrated his powers to please by agreeable manner and easy conversation, and chose to force admiration by his courage and energy.

" He affected (as I thought) indifference to gentlemanly appearance and fashionable manners, and adhered to a certain rusticity of aspect and style, — possibly because he dreaded failure in any effort to become perfectly polished. I at first wondered at him, then I was deeply interested in him, and finally I became much attached to him. As our acquaintance became more intimate, and our rambles longer and more numerous, I admired his powers and his information more and more; whilst his character, which seemed to me at one time harsh and even fierce and dangerous, dissolved into romantic heroism and almost feminine tenderness. I cannot pretend to have fathomed and mapped out

Hugh Miller's character thirty-five years ago, but I can recollect my sentiments towards him then, and what I attributed to him as the justification to myself of my admiration and affection. The soft, mellow radiance of piety and youthful domestic virtue which enveloped him filled my heart with an affection which has never grown cold."

In the letter to Miss Dunbar from which we took our last quotation, Miller spoke in a tone almost of sharpness of the infrequency of her letters, urging that it was dispiriting to write without any hope of reply, and adding, "Must I have to say of you what the children sitting in the market-place had to say of their companions : ' We have piped to you, and ye have not danced ; we have mourned, and ye have not lamented '?" This enables us to understand a passage in the following letter from Miss Dunbar to Miller. It is inserted here, not only because it displays the delicate intelligence and sterling worth of his correspondent, but because, through the eyes of this bright and gracious lady, we can see him with an authentic clearness and a revealing sympathy which even his own letters do not afford : —

"FORRES, September 19, 1834.

" I would as soon suspect you of murder or high treason as deem you careless or ungrateful. I only wonder that, embarked as you now are in an ocean of occupation and anxiety, you can give so much of your thought and time to me. And yet, differently situated as we are at this moment, it will be found that affection has nicely adjusted the balance between us. You are ceaselessly employed, asking of one minute the work of two, and anxious regarding the result of your scheme, hoping and fearing alternately, and yet you can devote time and thought to me. I, on the other hand, am suffering in constant and still increasing distress, — withdrawing myself as I best may from all worldly hopes and desires, and striving to fix my thoughts where they ought to rest; but you still have power to call them back. I think of you and of your present business, as involving your future fame and usefulness, with an interest, a pride, a solicitude, which I find no other human being or earthly scheme can now excite. Death can alone render my heart cold to you. Among many sad thoughts and regrets there is one peculiarly painful, — the thought that, confined as I am to a sick-room, I can aid you so little; nevertheless I do what I can.

"Both Mr. Grant and Dr. Brands happened to be with me when your parcel arrived. They enter warmly into your scheme, and the Miss Cummings of May not less warmly. You have stanch friends, too, in the Messrs. Andersons, who have anticipated us, I find, at Dunphail, with Major Cumming Bruce; and Sir Thomas, I doubt not, is active in Edinburgh. You seem to have started in a highly favorable time; but you must not tell me of a ' nervous indolence creeping over you,' — you who are so much the delight of all who know you. I must say your prospectus did not please me so much as I expected; you cannot do other than write well. but there are scores of your legends which I would have liked better. True, your reasoning is good and ingenious, but still it is reasoning. I often question whether your book will ever be in my hand; I fear not, but I shall go on wishing and thinking about it as though I were certain of living to see it.

"And so you have been on many excursions of late; why should a deathlike pang shoot across me at the thought? It will be a year on Friday next since I crossed over from Nairn to Cromarty. and you were not in the way, nor could be found for two hours. In the three weeks that followed, oh, how much I enjoyed! I can recall all our walks together, and all the topics on which we conversed. But why should such recollections disturb or distress me? You will be happy with other friends and favorites; oh, yes, yes, you will, I hope and wish it, — and you will bear me in mournful remembrance, though you will be nothing to me then. But I shall see you once more, — I may hold out for months yet; and as you have promised to come to see me, you will.

"But why, my friend, do you chide me for not writing you? I can feel the awkwardness of your situation as a correspondent, in writing letter after letter and receiving no reply; but it is God who has laid his chastening hand upon me, — do not reprove me, but let this be a testimony of my willingness to write. Oh, I have many things to say to you that I could say to none other, for I think that above all others you can put your ' soul in my soul's stead.' Keep my manuscript books carefully. I wish you had them all, and many other little things; but I know you will need no tokens to remember me by. How happy you would make me if you would call upon me in any way in which I could really serve you. How do you manage to live? You are not working much, and must, at a time like the present, have many little expenses: do you want money? I have enough and to spare, and I would injure no one by giving to you. Away with your high notions of what you deem independence, but which, I assure you, has more of alloy than of true metal in it. No proper feeling can be injured by an accommodation of the kind I propose. Now be not offended; if you are, I shall say you are yet unacquainted with my heart."

The following reply at once gushed from Hugh Miller's heart : —

"CROMARTY, September 25, 1834.

"How shall I thank you for your truly kind, truly excellent letter! My heart bounded to my lips, as opening it I exclaimed, 'From Miss Dunbar's own hand!' and I glanced my eyes over it with a hurried eagerness,—an intense impatience that seemed to begrudge the minutes which were to be spent in the slow process of perusal, and to desire that all its contents might be stamped upon my mind at once. Need I say how deeply I sympathize with you and how highly I esteem you? Often do my thoughts carry me to Forres; I seize the extended hand, and then draw in my chair beside you; and, though my heart sinks when I see how pale and thin you appear, I am again reassured by the expression of your eye and the calm placidity of the tones in which you address me. It is surely a good thing to be enabled to look forward through the clouds and darkness of our present state of being to the calm, sunny fields of the future; to be assured that the life which commenced as but yesterday, and whose events seem huddled together as if they were the occurrences of one short day, shall never, never terminate, but continue to go on, and on, and on, through the unreckoned and ever-succeeding periods of an eternity, whose further edge of boundary God himself cannot perceive. And is it not well, my dear madam, that as creatures possessed of so quenchless a vitality, our affection should be fixed on each other and on Him who occupies all the future and all the past? If we fix them on objects less enduring than themselves a day of final separation must come, and when they depart to their far country they must go forth wounded and widowed.—still, still looking back and halting by the way, wishing, and weeping, and longing, but wishing and weeping and longing in vain. How different must that journey prove to those whose hearts have been prepared to love their God, and whose affections have met and mingled with those of their fellows! They will go onward, assured of meeting with him; finding the stream of his brightness increasing the nearer they approach him; and, reckoning the amount of their successions of happiness by other periods of duration than those by which in the lower world we measure our days of languor and suffering, they shall say, 'Our God is with us, and we shall be joined by our friends early on the morrow.' Much as I sympathize with you and grieve for your sufferings, I find there is much regarding you from which to derive comfort.

"Forgive me the passage in my last by which I was so unfortunate as to give you pain. One is not always master of one's mood; and there are impatient, unthinking moods in which we say and write what afterwards we wish unsaid or unwritten. I merely meant to express how dispiriting a thing I felt it to be to write without the hope of receiving a reply; a sudden analogy came across me, and I embodied it without noting that it gave a cast of meaning to my words which the thought I meant them to convey did not bear. But I know you will not think harshly of me.

"For the last fortnight some of my very few leisure hours have been employed in collecting geological specimens for my kind friend, Mr. George Anderson, — one of the most thorough-bred geologists in the north of Scotland. By the way, I see from the newspapers that he has been highly complimented for his labors in this department, at the great scientific meeting at Edinburgh. Some of the specimens I have procured are exceedingly curious; they contain the petrified remains of animals that now no longer exist except in a fossil state, — bits of charcoal, pieces of wood, and nondescript substances which one can hardly refer to either the animal or vegetable world. Of the several animal tribes the very curious shell-fish termed the *cornu ammonis* abounds most; but, though at one period the most numerous of all the testaceous tribes of the country, it is now no longer to be found except as a fossil, deeply embedded in limestone or bituminous shale, and buried under huge hills of clay and gravel. There are grounds, indeed, for the belief that the race of man, and almost all the tribes of animals with which we are acquainted, have come into being since it ceased to exist; at least no remains of the living tribes have been found in the beds in which the cornu abounds. Like the nautilus, it was a sailing animal, and, though different in form, its structure seems to have been nearly the same. We find it partitioned in the same way by little cross walls, which divide the cavity within into a number of minute cells, by means of which and by a power it must have possessed of altering its gravity, by nearly vacating or occupying these to the full, it seems to have moved upwards or downwards at pleasure. The inner part of the shell seems, from the more perfect impressions of it which I have met with, to have been of a pearly lustre; the outer is ridged and furrowed with much regularity, and there is at least as much elegance in its general contour as in that of the Ionic volute, which it nearly resembles. But why so much beauty when there was no eye of man to see and admire? Does it not seem strange that the bays of our coasts should have been speckled by fleets of beautiful little animals, with their tiny sails spread to the wind and their pearly colors glancing to the sun, when there was no intelligent eye to look abroad and delight in their loveliness? Of all the sciences there is none which furnishes so many paradoxical facts and appearances as geology. . . .

"Mr. Stewart returned last week from Strathpeffer, in improved but still rather delicate health, and preached one half of the day last Sabbath. His discourse, though in a lower and more subdued tone than some of his more powerful ones, was truly beautiful, — full of exquisite sentiment and lovely description; and there was an air of tenderness about it which rarely characterizes his compositions. He spoke of the finely fibred and wonderfully complicated frame of man, of its liability to derangement, and its capacity of pain; of the weariness of sleepless nights and the heavy yet restless languor of tedious days. He spoke, too, of the solitude of suffering, — a solitude complete and unbroken even in the midst of society; of the gloom which to the sufferer seems to hang over all the present, and which deepens into thick darkness as he looks towards the future. And where, he asked, shall we look in such circumstances for comfort? Where but to Him who is thoroughly acquainted with our frame, — acquainted with it, not only as God the Creator of it, but also as man the inhabitant of it; not only as him who can look into all our sufferings, but as him who entered into them all; him of the lacerated hands and feet and the pierced side, — whose forehead was cinctured with thorns, and over whose back the ploughers have driven long furrows. Mr. Stewart's recent experience has not been without its use to him, — his sufferings have taught him the language of consolation.

"Accept my warmest thanks for your kind, generous offer. It would prove a poor return for your goodness, were I to chide you for what ought so thoroughly to awaken my gratitude. Believe, if I do not avail myself of what you so frankly tender me, it is out of no proud or improper feeling."

Mrs. Grant, of Laggan, suggested about this time to her friend, Miss Dunbar, with a view to Miller's advancement in life, that he might do the "blocking work" for a young sculptor "likely to rise to eminence." Mrs. Grant referred to "Allan Cunningham's success in doing the blocking work for Chantrey," by way of illustrating the promotion intended for Miller. On this Miss Dunbar wrote to Hugh: "I could not well take it on me to reply to what she suggests without a reference to yourself, though I dare say I anticipate your answer, and so I write. Pardon the terms she uses as applicable to you, and believe me, that neither in speaking nor writing of you have I expressed myself in a way to sanction them. I had honesty and delicacy enough not to assume the airs of a lady-patroness; I ever spoke of you as my friend, and as proud that you were such." In the same letter Miss Dunbar mentioned that Baron Hume, nephew to the historian, pronounced by Kemble "positively the first" critic of the day, had seen the prospectus of Miller's book. "He perused it," she adds, "with much interest and no little surprise, and states as his opinion that the writer excels in that classical style which many well-known writers of the present day, so far from attaining to, do not seem even to understand." Hugh, in his reply, speaks of Baron Hume before touching on Mrs. Grant's proposal.

"CROMARTY, October 25, 1834.

"Never was my little remnant of modesty in such danger as it has been exposed to by the critical remark of Baron Hume. But, if at all worthy of the compliment it conveys, I owe my merit chiefly to accident; to my having kept company with the older English writers, — the Addisons, Popes, and Robertsons of the last century,— at a time when I had no opportunity of becoming acquainted with the authors of the present time. And the tone of these earlier writers I have, I dare say, contrived in some measure to catch, just as in my spoken language I have caught the tone of our Cromarty Scotch.

"I am much gratified by the kind solicitude of Mrs. Grant; but you seem to have anticipated my reply to what she suggests. Though I have sometimes amused my leisure hours with sculpture, my best efforts in this department have been only half-efforts; I made them without either hope or care, and saw them balked without disappointment; and though, perhaps, rather a superior workman as workmen go, I have become such I hardly know how, and never think of my profession, except as fortunate in that it does not employ my mind, and that I can prosecute it in the open air. These are not the views of one destined to excel as a sculptor; and, as for a mason, I am well enough as I am. My ambition points in a different direction; and when the public shall have decided regarding my modicum of literary ability, should the editorship of some magazine or paper come my way, I shall cheerfully resign the mallet altogether; though till such an opportunity occurs I shall grip fast to its rough handle as my only hold of independence. Allan Cunningham's situation is considerably different from the one referred to by Mrs. Grant. Chantrey is not merely a sculptor; he is also a contractor on a large scale for sepulchral monuments, and employs many workmen; Allan is his foreman, and manages the under details of his business; were he merely a sculptor, the poet would hold only the place of one of the mechanics whom he superintends. Favor me, when you write Mrs. Grant, by tendering her my best thanks for her suggestion, and the interest she takes in my welfare, and oblige me by stating that I cannot avail myself of the former. But why, my dear madam, apologize for the terms she employs in speaking of me? Trust me, I am not one of those who repay with insolence the notice by which they are honored. The much kindness you have shown me, and the confidence you have reposed in me, have not yet made me forget our respective places in society ; and though no one entertains a more sincere love of independence, or more carefully avoids any imputation of meanness, it would not cost me a single blush were the whole world to know how much cause you have given me to be grateful."

CHAPTER XVI.

TWO LETTERS ON RELIGION.

THE two letters addressed to Mr. William Smith, Forres, are without question among the most important Miller ever wrote. They form a supplement to that portion of his spiritual history which embraced his period of indifference and semi-scepticism, and contain not only an explicit confession of faith, but a statement of that intellectual basis on which it was for him a necessity that his faith should rest. Reticent as he was in all that related to his soul's condition, — sensitively averse to the unveiling to human eyes of his spiritual experience, — he would probably never have written such letters, had not an occasion occurred which constrained him to overcome every scruple. A friend lay ill, perhaps unto death; it seemed possible to Hugh that he might minister to his spirit's health and his eternal salvation; and he yielded to the impulse of affection and the mandate of duty. The scheme of religion which he unfolds in the letters is that of simple acceptance of Christ for salvation, as he is offered in the Gospel.— acceptance with the heart as well as the head, acceptance with clear consciousness that the difficulties of the intellect cannot be wholly removed. The religion of Miller was to cling close to Christ, to die with Christ. to rise with Christ, to wear with him the crown of thorns, and to receive from him the crown of glory.

The idea formerly thrown out by Miller, that Christianity

suggests objections so many and so obvious that common sense would not have permitted its invention by man, receives in these letters its balance and counterpart in the hypothesis that the adaptation of Christianity to man's wants is so exquisite and its evidence so strong, that its obvious offences to mere human reason tend to prove that it is divine.

From a biographic point of view the letters have a special interest as showing the tenacity with which Miller retained thoughts which had once been deliberately accepted into his intellectual system. The illustration of the working of the atonement of Christ, given long subsequently in the " Schools and Schoolmasters," is but a slight expansion of that which he here lays before his friend, and the thesis maintained, that man can apprehend facts and results in God's universe, whether physical or spiritual, but not the constructive principles and processes by which they are brought about, is worked out in a chapter on the Discoverable and the Revealed in the " Testimony of the Rocks," which is perhaps the most valuable that Hugh Miller ever penned.

"CROMARTY, August 5, 1835.

" My dear William : — I need not tell you how famous Cromarty is for its hasty reports, or on how slender a foundation the imagination of the townsfolks sometimes contrives to build. I must needs tell you, however, for the circumstance forms my only apology for now writing you, that the last story current among us affected me more deeply than any of its class ever did before. On your late severe attack, your brother, the doctor, was called hastily to Forres, and the story went that you were dead. I never before knew how much I valued and esteemed you ; the thought, too, that one with whom I had so often conversed, and with whose mind I was so thoroughly acquainted, had passed the dark bourn which separates this world from the other, had something inexpressibly solemn and melancholy in it. I felt for the time that, disguise the fact as we may, the main business of this life consists in preparing for another, and conscience was not quite silent when I remembered that, though you and I had beaten together over many an interesting topic, the most interesting of all had been omitted. You remember the fable of the wise men who were permitted to make a three days' visit to the moon that they might report to our lower world regarding its plants and animals, and who, on their return, had to confess that they had squandered their time in drinking with gay young men and dancing with beautiful women, and had only remarked that the trees and sky of the planet, when seen casually through a window, very much resembled those of our own. Alas, for the application of this ingenious story!

"There are few men who do not at some time or other think seriously of the future state, or who have not formed some, at least, theoretic set of notions regarding the best mode of preparing for it. Man was born to anticipate a hereafter; he is a religious animal by the very constitution of his nature, and the thousand forms of superstition which still overspread the world and darken every page of its history are just so many proofs of this. It has often struck me that the infidel, when in his assaults on revelation he draws largely from this store of delusion, sadly mistakes his argument; every false religion which has sprung out of the nature of man shows us, not surely that there is no true religion, but that we stand in need of a true one; every mythologic folly and absurdity should convince us that we need an infallible guide. Regarded in this light the 'Shaster' and the 'Koran' are substantial proofs of how ill we could do without the Bible; and Paganism and Mahometism powerfully recommend Christianity. You, my dear William, to whom it has been given to possess an inquiring and reflecting mind, must have often thought of the final destinies of man; I myself have observed in you much of that respect for sacred things which is one of the characteristics of an ingenuous nature; but there is perhaps danger that your very ingenuity and acuteness might have led you into error. Christianity is emphatically termed the wisdom of God, but it is not on a first examination that a reasoning mind can arrive at the evidence of its being such; on the contrary, some of its main doctrines seem opposed to the more obvious principles of common sense; and this quite in the same way that, before the days of Newton, it would have seemed contrary to these principles to allege that the whiteness of light was occasioned by a combination of the most vivid colors, or that the planets were held in their orbits by the law which impelled a falling stone towards the ground. Now this is exactly what we might expect of the true religion. A religion made by rational men — many Deists, you know, were eminently such, and we may instance theirs — will be, like themselves, rational and easily understood; but this very facility is a conclusive proof that it had its origin in the mind of man. It is like all his other works, — like the clocks and watches and steam-engines of his construction, — easily understood, and easily imitated; but it is not thus with Christianity, nor is it thus with the great machine of the universe. Let us, my dear William, take a brief survey of some of the main doctrines of this religion; they concern us so nearly that it may be fatal to misunderstand them.

"The invariable reply of the apostles of our Saviour to that most important of all queries, 'What shall I do to be saved?' was, 'Believe in the Lord Jesus Christ.' Belief seems to be, if I may so speak, the main condition of man's acceptance; but belief in what or whom? in a person who is at once God and Man, and who thus, to the perfection of a Divine nature, adds the feelings of a human heart. Now there is something amazing in this, something which, for its exquisite fitness to our moral and sentient constitution, is worthy the conception of a God. Observe, my dear William, the false religions of the world, and you will find that they run into two opposite extremes. In the artificial religions which have been formed by the intellect of man, God is represented as a mere abstraction of wisdom and power. He is the Great First Cause of the philosopher, and it is scarcely more possible for the human heart to love him as such than it is for him to love any of the great second causes, such as the sun with its light and heat, or the law of gravitation. And hence the coldness and utter inefficacy of all such religions, whether known under the name of philosophical Deism or Socinian Christianity; they are totally unfitted to the nature of man. The religions of the other class are rather the offspring of passion than intellect; they arise in those obscure and remote ages when unenlightened man created his gods in his own image. What was Jupiter or his son Hercules, or what their companions in the court of Olympus, the Dianas, Venuses, or Minervas with which the old poets have brought us acquainted, but human creatures bearing the very mould and impression of their worshippers? And such deities could be loved and feared just in the way one human creature can love or fear another; the belief in them powerfully influenced the conduct, but their worship, as it originated in the darkened human heart, was a worship of impurity. Observe with what a truly godlike wisdom Christianity is formed to avoid the opposite extremes of these two classes, and how it yet embraces more than the philosophy of the one, and more than the warmth of the other: the object of our worship is at once God, the First Great Cause, and the man Jesus Christ, our brother.

"But not merely must we believe in Christ as God, but also as our Saviour; as the restorer of our moral nature, and our sacrifice or atonement. There are wonderful Janus-like mysteries here, — inexplicable in their one aspect as they regard God, though simple and easy in the other as they regard man. Perhaps an illustration from the human frame may serve to explain my meaning. Need I remind you, who are an anatomist, and acquainted with Paley to boot, of the admirable adaptation of the human frame to the various ends for which it was created, or how easy it is for a person of even ordinary capacity to be made to perceive this adaptation? Almost any one can see how fairly and beautifully the machine works, — but who, on the other hand, can conceive of the higher principles on which it is constructed? Who can know anything of the workings of the brain as the organ of thought, or of the operations of the nerves as the seats of feeling; of how the chyle is chosen by its thousand blind mouths, and every other fluid rejected; of how one gland should secrete a liquor so unlike that secreted by another, — of, in short, any of the thousand phenomena of our animal nature when we trace them towards their first cause? The working of the machine is simple, its construction we find to be inexplicably mysterious. Now it is thus with Christianity. No one can understand how the sufferings of the Saviour satisfy the justice of God, — that regards, if I may so speak, the construction of the scheme; but every one who examines may see how wonderfully these vicarious sufferings are suited to the nature and the wants of man, — for that regards its working. But it is not in the limits of so brief a composition as a letter that such a subject can be discussed.

" May I recommend to you, my dear William, to lay hold on this Saviour as the way, and the truth, and the life? He is willing and able to save to the uttermost all who trust in him. You suffer from pain and dejection; he suffered from pain and dejection also, and hence his wonderful fitness to be the God and Saviour of a race born to anguish and sorrow. Not only does he know our weaknesses as God, but he sympathizes in them as man. Forgive me the freedom with which I write you, — it is as a friend, — as one foolish and careless, and often so wrapped up in the dreams of life as to forget its real businesses, but also as one convinced that the Saviour can, through his Spirit, make wise unto salvation, and that to secure an interest in him is to possess a righteousness that is perfect, and to have every sin forgiven through an atonement that is complete. May I ask, my dear William, that when you address yourself to him, — and, oh, he is willing to hear and ready to help, — you will put up one petition for your affectionate friend, Hugh Miller."

" Cromarty, August 27, 1835.

" My dear William : — I have learned from your brother that you are still confined to your room. Believe me, I sympathize with you very sincerely; and it is in the hope of helping to enliven your solitude for at least a few brief minutes that I again avail myself of a leisure hour in which to write you. I know from experience that there is no solitude like that of a sick-chamber, — it wears away the poor remnant of spirits that indisposition spares to us; but it will not render the sense of this loneliness weightier to you to learn that an old friend, though also a powerless one, continues to regard you with sympathy and esteem. It is a better assurance, however, that He who is more thoroughly your friend than any one else, and who can sympathize with you more deeply, is possessed of a power that has no limits.

"Your brother hinted to me that you are not unwilling I should recur to the subject of my last. I feel, my dear William, that I am unworthy to approach a theme so sacred; I am also too little impressed with it, too little in love with it; but I know of its importance, and I believe in its truth. In one respect, too, we may be better fitted for conference with each other on the doctrines of religion than either of us would be with minds who had never doubted of them. I know you are not unacquainted with infidel objections,— you are familiar with some of the most insidious writings of Voltaire; I am intimate with these also, and with those of many a sceptic besides. And so, as we can approach our subject over nearly the same ground, it is surely not irrational to expect that it may present itself to us in nearly the same points of view.

"I think I remarked to you in my last letter that Christianity is no common-sense religion; were it such, it would have little in common with the other marvellous workings of Him who devised it, as these are shown in all he has made, and in his mode of governing all. But do not infer from this, as some infidels do, tacitly at least, that to the human comprehension the absurdities of false religions and the mysteries of Christianity are placed on a similar level. Between what cannot be understood because it has no meaning, and what cannot be understood because it surpasses the grasp of our minds, there not only obtains an infinite difference, but a difference fully cognizable by the human intellect. The scribblings of a child and the abstruser calculations of a Newton or La Place would not appear equally unmeaning to an attentive observer, however humble his powers; he could not but see now and then little breaks of sense in the mysteries of the one and wonderful effects produced by them, which would most effectually distinguish them from the nothingness of the other. And it is thus with Christianity. We get occasional glimpses of its meaning, and see instances of its power that may well enable us to distinguish between it and the ' Shaster 'and ' Koran.' Its adaptation to the nature of man is truly exquisite. There is a pretty story in Kames' ' Art of Thinking,' introduced by the philosopher for a very different purpose, which will in part enable us to conceive of this. Two men who fought in the wars of Queen Anne — the one a petty officer, the other a private soldier — had been friends and comrades for years, but, quarrelling on some unlucky love affair, they became bitter enemies. The officer made a natural though ungenerous use of his authority, in continually annoying and persecuting the other, whom he almost fretted into madness, and who was often heard to swear that he would die to be avenged on him. Both were men of known bravery, and on an occasion of some dangerous service, both were chosen to be of the party selected to attempt it. But the attempt was unsuccessful, and the officer was struck down by a ball in the retreat. ' Ah, and will you leave me here to perish?' he exclaimed, as his old companion rushed past him. The appeal was irresistible ; the poor injured man returned, and, raising his wounded enemy, he bore him off amid a storm of shot and shell. And he had just reached what seemed to be a place of safety, when he was struck by a chance ball and fell dead under his burden. But his fate seemed an enviable one compared with that of the wounded man. He rose, forgetful of his wound, and, tearing his hair, and flinging himself on the body, he burst out into the most heart-rending lamentations. For two days he refused all sustenance, still calling on his companion, and ever exclaiming, ' Hast thou died for me who treated thee so barbarously!' and he expired on the third, the victim of mingled grief and remorse. Do you not perceive, my dear William, that the principle which the story unfolds lies deep in our nature? Nothing so prostrates the pride of man or so stings him to the heart as a return of benefits for injuries, — of great good for great evil. In the expressive language of Scripture, it is heaping live coals on the head, and to blow up these to a tenfold intensity that the hardest heart may melt under them, it is necessary that the injured benefactor, instanced in the story, should die for his enemy. Need I attempt an application, or point out to you with what marvellous, God-like wisdom Christianity appeals to the principle described? 'Peradventure for a good man,' says the Apostle, 'some would even dare to die; but God commended his love towards us, in that, while we were yet sinners, Christ died for us.'

"I am sorry we should have missed so many opportunities of conversing on this subject; little can be done for it in the limits of a letter; and besides, in the course of conversation, doubts may be stated and cleared which, though they may weigh heavily on your mind, cannot be anticipated by mine. It must have struck you as something very mysterious in the scheme of Redemption that man, instead of having to trust to his own virtues for reward, and his own repentance for pardon, must look exclusively to the righteousness and atonement of the Saviour. And yet so important is this doctrine, that the scheme of Salvation is inefficient without it; for, for what other cause did the Saviour come into the world, or in what other sense could he be said to die for us? I have seen much of what may be called the working of this doctrine, and, unable as I am to comprehend it in the abstract, have admired its wonderful adaptation to the nature and wants of man. There is no place where its importance can be better appreciated than beside a death-bed. In the closing scene of life, man's boasted virtues become, in most instances, so intangible that they elude his grasp; and his sins, however little noted before, start up around him like so many threatening spectres, to call up all his remorse for the past and all his fears for the future. It is then that the scheme of Redemption appears worthy of the infinite wisdom and infinite goodness of a God; that the righteousness of Him, who ever went about doing good, appears an inexhaustible fund to which we may apply; that the agony in the garden, the mockeries and scourgings in the hall, the inconceivable sufferings and shame of the cross, array themselves on the side of mercy, and sum up efficacy enough to annihilate every sin. It is when every minor light of comfort is extinguished that the Saviour shines forth, and more than compensates for them all.

"So much for the fitness of this scheme. I have stated that, regarded in the abstract, it surpasses my comprehension; but do not suppose from this that it is more surrounded by difficulties than any of the many schemes of religion which men have opposed to it. The simplicity of most of these is but an apparent simplicity, complete in the eyes of the shallow thinker, but which entirely disappears when subjected to the gaze of a superior discernment. True, the difficulties of Christianity may be more strikingly apparent than those of philosophic religions, but it is only because God in his goodness, instead of confining it to the acute and the highly talented, has brought it down to the level of the whole race of man; and thus common capacities are brought in contact with truths of so lofty and abstruse a character that the greatest minds can but see their importance and consistency without being able to comprehend them. It is well, however, that the heart of the simplest can be made to feel their fitness; and that the excellence of doctrines too mighty to be grasped by the most capacious minds can be so appreciated by babes as to be made effectual to their salvation.

" After all our reasonings, my dear William, it is through the heart alone that we can lay hold of the Saviour; and to prepare the heart ' by working faith in it ' is the office of that Spirit which God giveth to all who ask it. Have you ever considered the doctrine of the Trinity, and the peculiar fitness which it gives to the character of God as a God of man? Perhaps the query is rather obscure; what I mean to express is this: One great proof of the wisdom of the Deity is derived from that exquisite adaptation of parts which obtains throughout creation. You have studied this in the human frame, and must have seen, in extending your view, that not more admirably are the parts of that frame fitted to each other than man as a whole is fitted to external nature. Now, by rising a little higher, and taking with you the Scripture character of a *triune* God, you will perceive that there is yet a third exquisite adaptation of the nature of man to the nature of the Deity, — what, indeed, we might expect, when we consider for what purpose and in whose image man was originally created. The subject far exceeds the limits to which I am restricted, but I must attempt giving you a brief outline of my meaning: In all true philosophy, God is regarded as the first *cause* of all things, and as *uncaused* himself. Necessarily, then, he must have existed from eternity, while everything else must have *begun to exist;* and, ere that beginning, he must have existed an eternity alone. But is this, his eternity of solitude, to be regarded as the womb of Deity, in which, though his *thoughts* might be employed (I am acquainted with only the language of earth), his affections lay dormant? Surely not. Who can think of a God of infinite goodness existing for an eternity without love? But love requires an object, and God existed alone. Yes;

but when we feel that the ill-conceived God of the philosopher must, so circumstanced, have been a solitary being, we know that the God of the Christian existed in the society of himself, — regarding the Son and the Spirit with an infinite love, and infinitely beloved by them. Is there not something wonderfully pleasing in this view of the character of God, — something that harmonizes with our nature and all its affections of love, friendship, brotherly affection, filial attachment, and paternal regard? And then to think that all the persons of the adorable Godhead are interested in us, and perform a part in our redemption! The Father willed that the Son should be sent, the Son became man and died for us, and by the Spirit is the sacrifice made effectual to us and our hearts prepared. It is surely no marvel that angels desire to look into a mystery so fraught with the wisdom and goodness of Deity.

" Permit me again, my dear William, to recommend to you Jesus Christ as the only Saviour. Open all your heart to him, for he is man and can sympathize in all its affections; trust yourself implicitly in him, for he is God, omnipotent to aid and unable to deceive. Faith can realize his presence, and there is happiness to be found in his society, when the full heart pours itself out before him, of which the world can form no conception. In life or in death, in health or in sickness, it is well to be able to lean one's self on him, as John did at the last supper, and to feel as it were the heart of his humanity beating under the broad buckler of his power. Whatever it may be your fate to encounter, — whether protracted, spirit-subduing indisposition, or that solemn and awful change so big with interest to the human heart, and so fitted to awaken its hopes and its fears; or whether you are to be again restored to the lesser cares and narrower prospects of the present life, — in whatever circumstances placed, or by whatever objects surrounded, you will find him to be an all-sufficient Saviour, and the friend that sticketh closer than a brother. Would that I were more worthy to recommend him to you, — more like himself; but I know you will forgive me the freedom with which I write, and that you will not associate with his infinite wisdom and purity any of the folly or the evil which attaches to, my dear William, your sincere and affectionate friend,

"HUGH MILLER."

CHAPTER XVII.

THERE are a few letters of a miscellaneous kind, some dated, some undated, written to various correspondents in the Journeyman period, which it will be as well to take in here. Two or three of them are addressed to Mr. Strahan, and one to Mr. Forsyth, containing Miller's "theory of the moral character of the people of Scotland." To these are added, first, the account, referred to in preceding letters, drawn up by Miller of "Black Russel," one of the "old-light" clergy satirized by Burns in the "Holy Fair;" secondly, a sample of those descriptive paragraphs contributed by Hugh to the "Inverness Courier;" and, thirdly, a letter to Mr. George Anderson, of Inverness, giving an account of the writer's scientific explorations, and interesting as containing the first allusion, made by Hugh Miller, in black and white, to the pterichthys. Allan Cunningham printed but half the sketch of Russel in his edition of Burns, and Miller thought that Allan had left out more than half its brains. The short description of the boat accident is in no respect to be distinguished from others of the same kind, but it characteristically exhibits the simplicity, compactness, and sincerity of style, on which, in preference to sentimental effusion, rhetorical ornament, or technical fine writing of any kind, Miller had learned to depend for effect.

412

FROM MR. JOHN STRAHAN.

"FORBES, Dec. 24, 1829.

"DEAR SIR: — It is with much pleasure I sit down to
avail myself of my good fortune in getting on the list of
your friends. Until a few days back I was but partially
acquainted with you as an author, and yet, from the little
knowledge I had of your great literary acquirements, I
certainly envied the few who shared most of your esteem,
and ranked highest in your regard. And when told lately
by Miss Dunbar (who, I rejoice to say, is our common
friend) that it was probable you might soon visit this quarter, I requested her, should you come to Forres, to introduce
me to you. She kindly agreed to do so; and from that
moment I began to anticipate the pleasure I should derive
from having the honor of pointing out to you the numerous
scenes and antiquities about Forres, which are, I imagine,
not unworthy of the eye of the poet. Were you to trace
the scenes in our neighborhood now rendered classic by the
author of the 'Wolf of Badenoch,' you would confess that
some of them are themselves poems, produced by the great
poet Nature in her holiest and happiest moods. But it is
to myself, and not to rural scenery, that I wish to refer
now. From what I have said you can conceive something
of the happy response my heart gave to the wish you expressed, that we might become friends: with my whole soul
I subscribe to your proposition. Friendship with me is not
merely a name; I hold it to be a sacred, and, as I have
often found it, a joy-giving reality. It is the groundwork
of all social pleasures, and the chief promoter of individual
happiness; and it is the more to be esteemed that it makes
its home alike in the heart of the laborer and of the lord, —
binding all congenial spirits together by its sweet and mysterious influences. I am deeply interested in your welfare,

and I feel sure that your industry will insure you success, and gain you a name among the authors of your country. It will give me great pleasure to see and know this. I am not a little proud of the opinion which you have expressed regarding my pieces; an encomium pronounced by one of your taste and judgment weighs against the censure of a thousand, who, in their ignorance, prattle of such matters."

TO MR. STRAHAN.

"This is not the first time I take up the pen to write to a poet. I had a friend, not many years ago, who also had learned the art unteachable, and whose heart was as warm as his imagination was active. He is now no more. Since his death the place he occupied in my affections has remained a blank; and part of the pleasure I derive from your kind letter arises from the hope of having that blank filled. The life of the friend I allude to was one of melancholy and disappointment. He possessed no ordinary powers; but from an unfortunate diffidence, which was, I believe, constitutional to him, he almost always despaired of attaining the object he pursued, when every other person who could judge of the matter deemed him just on the point of gaining it. The consequence was that he failed in almost everything he attempted, and that, though endowed with a fine genius for both painting and poetry, he gained not a modicum of celebrity in either. He died nearly two years ago; and were the existence and the hopes of man confined to the present world, it might be said of him, that, as he lived in it almost without enjoyment, so he quitted it without accomplishing anything. But the contrary was the fact, for in reality he achieved much. His name was William Ross, a name which you may repeat a thousand times and in a thousand places without awakening a single recollection of him who bore it. No sense of sacredness, no feeling of devotion, connected with either his genius or his worth, shall ever press on the minds of those who behold the nameless sod which covers his remains; and yet, though thus obscure, he has earned a loftier fame than that which the men of this earth can bestow. Through the grace of God, he had subdued his own spirit; he had striven against the ills of human life and human nature, and so far as these concerned himself he had overcome them; and as he had the merit of living without reproach, so he had the happiness of dying without fear. These, my dear sir, were achievements greater than any merely literary ones. and, you know, the fame awarded to such, God has described as bestowed by his own lips and those of the pure spirits of heaven. Forgive me this slight sketch of the character of your predecessor.

"Accept my thanks for the copy you have sent me of your interesting little book. What have the critics said of it? Upon mine they have delivered every possible variety of opinion. I am a man of genius, — I am a blockhead, — my name is to be at once illustrious and obscure. I do not intend writing verses for a long, long time. I purpose devoting myself entirely to prose; partly, perhaps, because the study is easier in itself, partly because I am of opinion that nature has fitted me to attain a considerable command of the pen in this department of composition. If ever I gain celebrity, it will be as a writer of prose."

TO THE SAME.

"My page of history, since I parted from you at Rosemarkie, occupies little space, and is by no means very brilliant. I have hewn tomb-stones, and sold such fame as the chisel affords, — and warranted to last a whole century,— at so much per letter. I have built houses during the day, and castles during the night. I have written pages, and have promised to write books, and I now find myself on the verge of my twenty-eighth year nearly as foolish, and quite as much without a rational aim in life, as when entering on my fourteenth.

.   .   .   .

"I have not yet written a single line in verse since the publication of my book, and I now flatter myself that my cure is radically complete. But, alas! there will be writers of bad verse in abundance, though I should never write any. In June last I was visited by a Highland versifier, who, after having blotted much good paper with miserable rhyme, determined on publication about two years ago, and he has been wandering over the country ever since in quest of subscribers and a patron. The terms are that half the money be paid him in advance, but as what he receives barely affords him sustenance, his day of publication is as far away as at the beginning. He is so far honest, however, as to prefer the fame of a poet to all the money in the world; and, from a conviction of this, I strive to do him a service, not by telling him that his verses were bad, for that would have been taking a wolf by the ears, but by assuring him that the person who could not write as well as Scott and Byron and Wordsworth had no chance of becoming popular, and so had better not write at all. 'Ah, craving your pardon,' said the poet, 'one may be very eminent without being quite at the top. You must surely allow that there is nature and originality in my pieces; possessed of nature and originality, it is impossible for me to fail. I will print four thousand copies of my work, and shall sell every one of them.' We have another poet in this part of the country, who has issued proposals for printing a metrical history of Joseph, consisting of twenty thousand lines."

TO THE SAME.

"SCHOOL-HOUSE OF NIGG, Sept. 5th, 1833.

"I send you, according to promise, a copy of my young friend's verses. They are, as I have already stated to you, quite her first attempt in metrical composition, with the exception, perhaps, of half-a-dozen stanzas, and, regarded as such, indicate, or I am somewhat mistaken, considerable powers of thought and expression, a delicate sense of the beautiful, and much of what metaphysicians term the conceptive faculty. It is wonderful with what facility some happily constituted minds acquire an ability of wielding all their powers, contrasted with the much labor it costs others, though of no inferior order, to attain a very limited command of these. There are *winged* spirits which can reach at a single flight the higher pinnacles of art. I have read of a common mechanic, who, after watching for a few hours a copperplate engraver when at work, bought a plate of copper from him, and, going home. produced a masterpiece. There is a similar story told of West, the painter. How different the progress of other minds! They can but *climb* upwards; and, resting in succession on every one of the thousand ledges which lie between the summit and the plain below, gain only half a footstep at each advance. How many miserable lines did I not write before I became sufficiently skilful to produce merely tolerable ones! Favor me at your earliest opportunity with your critical opinion, and write it in such a way, though freely and with sincerity, that I may show your letter to the fair authoress, with whom I am sufficiently intimate to know that she has too much good sense to be offended with truths, however severe, which tend to her improvement. I dare say I ought not to tell you, for fear of biasing your judgment, that you are much a favorite with her, and that when you

27

waited on her at Forres it was less on my account, the ostensible reason, than in consequence of an interest awakened in her on your own. I trust that, in your present season of leisure, you will occasionally think of me, and that your interesting autobiographical memoir is still incomplete. Shall I return you the first part, or have you recovered your own copy of it?"

The lines enclosed to Mr. Strahan were addressed by Miss Fraser to her friend Miss Smith, on the occasion of the departure of the latter from this country for America: —

> " Bella, we part; between us two
>   A desert ocean soon shall lie;
> From childhood's home and love you go,
>   The stranger's love and home to try.
>
> " Oh! it is hard to sunder us,
>   So tenderly, so closely twined,
> From all that's dear to turn the eyes,
>   And leave the spirit's joys behind.
>
> " Yet droop not, love, nor shed the tear
>   Of anguish or of dark despair;
> Bleak may the distant scene appear,
>   Yet many a sweet flower blossoms there;
>
> " And images, now painful, when
>   Time's softening hand has swept their lines,
> Shall be the fairest, loveliest then,
>   That in your memory's mirror shines.
>
> " Thus when Columbia's setting sun
>   Across the shadowed forest gleams;
> And rainbows, fading one by one,
>   Uncolored leave the foamy streams;
>
> " In fancy still you'll wander o'er
>   The pine-clad hill that walls the deep;
> And hear the dashing billows roar,
>   And see them scale the rocky steep,

" While that sun, sinking in the west,
   Rests on Ben Wyvis' distant brow,
And woos the ocean's rugged breast
   To golden smiles and gentle flow.

" 'Twere but to wrong a faithful heart
   If I should say, remember me;
Affection will, I know, impart
   Fidelity to memory.

" But earthly friendship at its best
   Is but a fragile, feeble thing;
Powerless to soothe the sorrowing breast,
   From ill our bitter drop to wring.

" Oh, then, my Bella! may you find
   The heavenly Comforter your Friend;
'Tis his the broken heart to bind,
   For heaviness he praise can send."

TO MR. ISAAC FORSYTH.

" States, like individuals, decay as they advance in years, and they at length expire. Their progress from youth to age includes two extremes and a medium. But in one respect bodies politic differ from bodies natural; for in the several members of the former there may be different degrees of age. In this country there are districts peopled by men who have not yet reached the medium line, and there are others whose inhabitants have gone beyond it. Of the former kind are the Highland districts; of the latter are the greater number of those of the Lowlands, especially such of these as contain large towns. But it is only among the lower classes that the differences of the several stages are discernible; for the people in the upper walks of society bear almost the same character all over the kingdom. And it is, perhaps, only by an observer who is placed on the same level with the former, and who, from this circumstance, becomes intimately acquainted with their manners, habits, and modes of thought, that at least the minuter differences can be discerned. By such a person, however, if the theory be a just one, a tour through Scotland may be regarded, not merely as a journey through various places, but also as an extended existence through different ages.

" Each situation in life, regarded as a point of observation, has advantages peculiar to itself, by commanding a view of certain objects which cannot be so happily studied from any other point; but the situations of the middle and higher classes of society have been so repeatedly occupied by skilful observers, that their fields of view present not a single object which has not already been examined and described. This is not yet the case with the lower points of observation. The gentleman philosopher who writes upon character will, if he desires to attain originality, have, perhaps, to become a mere theorist, or to set himself to unfold hidden principles and motives; but how different would the case be with a philosophical gypsy, could we imagine such a person! His range of observation, however contracted, would be perfectly new; and to attain originality he would have only to describe. I reckon that one of the advantages of my place in society (it would require to have some, for the disadvantages incident to it are somewhat numerous) that it commands a wide and diversified prospect of the latter description.

" This part of the country contains a rich and as yet unexplored mine of tradition; but some of the stories are of too wild and fantastic a character for furnishing a suitable basis for a prose tale; and the great bulk of them, though they might prove interesting when wrought up together, are too simple and too naked of both detail and description to stand alone. They resemble some of the

minuter flowers, that scarcely appear beautiful until bound
up in a nosegay.

" Conversation to me proves generally an imperfect
medium for the conveyance of thought; and I expressed
myself rather loosely in what I said when in your company
in Cromarty regarding the assistance which, in detailing
these traditions, my memory derives from my imagination.
Imagination frequently assists me in giving a something
like life to narratives which were before dead. It draws
landscapes, too, around the figures to which tradition has
introduced me, and sometimes furnishes these figures with
the language of dialogue. This, however, was not at all
what I at that time had meant to state; but I may, perhaps, be more happy in conveying my meaning by the
pen. The faculty of my mind which was first developed
was imagination, and the development was neither partial
nor gradual. Before I had attained my fifth year I had
become the inhabitant of two distinct worlds, the true and
the ideal; and the images of the latter appeared to me
scarcely less tangible or less clearly defined than those of
the former. My mind presented me with a vivid picture
of every incident of which I was told. This faculty was
productive, in some instances, of consequences of a rather
ludicrous cast. As early as the period referred to I was
one day sitting beside my mother, listening with great
attention to a recital with which she was entertaining a
neighbor of some of the circumstances connected with my
birth, — such as a singular dream my father had concerning me, an unusual conformation of head which the midwife observed in me. and which she deemed indicative of
idiotism, and the details of the christening. According to
custom, my imagination presented me at the time with
pictures of all I heard described. Well, about eighteen
years after, by one of those sudden freaks of memory

which are not very easily explained, even on the associative principle, these pictures were again brought before me ; and, as I did not at first remember anything of the narrative which had produced them, sadly was I puzzled to account for the recollection. And, after thinking on the subject for a few days, I had a narrow escape from becoming one of the most singular of metaphysicians, by being enabled to unravel the whole circumstances of the matter as related. I have also two several recollections of spectres, which would render me a firm believer in apparitions, could I not account for them in this way, as the creatures of an imagination which had attained an unusual and even morbid strength at a time when the other mental faculties were scarcely at all unfolded."

TO MR. CARRUTHERS.

"CROMARTY, Oct. 22, 1833.

" The last of Mr. Russel's scholars, unfortunately for your request, died last year. But I dare say I shall be able, notwithstanding, to furnish you with as much information regarding him as your friend, Mr. Cunningham, may choose to avail himself of. Do not, however, I pray you, insert any of it in your paper.

" It is now somewhat more than seventy years since John Russel, a native, as I have heard, of Moray, and at that time a probationer of divinity, was appointed to the parish school of Cromarty. He was a large, robust, dark-complexioned man, imperturbably grave, and with a sullen expression seated in the deep folds of his forehead, that boded the urchins of the place little good. And in a few months he had acquired for himself the character of being by far the most rigid disciplinarian in the county. He was, I believe, a good, conscientious man, but unfortunate in a harsh and violent temper, and in sometimes mistaking the dictates of that temper for those of duty. Never, certainly, was schoolmaster more feared and hated by his pupils; and with fear and hatred did many of them continue to regard him long after they had become men and women. I have heard of a lady who, unexpectedly seeing him, many years after she had quitted his school, in the pulpit of one of the south country churches, was so overcome by sudden terror, that she fainted away; and of another of his scholars, named M'Glasher, who, on returning home to Cromarty from some of the colonies, a robust fellow of six feet, solaced himself by the way with thoughts of the hearty drubbing with which he was to clear off all his old scores with the dominie. But ere his return the dominie had quitted the parish. There was a poor boy named Skinner among Russel's scholars who, as was customary in Scottish schools of the period, blew the horn for gathering the pupils, and kept both the catalogue and the key; and who in return was educated by the master and received some little gratuity from the boys besides. Unluckily, on one occasion the key dropped out of his pocket; and when school-time came, the irascible dominie had to burst open the door with his foot. He raged at the boy with a fury so insane, and beat him with such relentless severity, that the other boys, plucking up heart in the extremity of the case, rose on him in a mass, and tore the poor fellow out of his hands. And such, it is said, was the impression made on the mind of the latter, that, though he quitted the school shortly after and plied the profession of a fisherman, until he died, an old man, he was never seen, in all his life from that day, disengaged for a single moment without melancholily thrusting his hand into the key pocket. One other anecdote illustrative of Mr. Russel's temper. He was passing along the streets of Cromarty on

a coarse, wintry day some seventy years ago, with his head
half buried in his breast, for the day was one of wind and
rain from the sea, when he came violently in contact with a
thatcher's ladder which had been left sloping from the roof
of one of the houses, half-way across the street. A much
less matter would have been sufficient to awaken the wrath
of Russel. He sprung at the ladder with the ferocity of a
tiger, and, dashing it down on the pavement, broke with his
powerful fist every one of the steps before he quitted it.
He was schoolmaster in Cromarty for about twelve years,
and for at least the last six of these was not a little popular
as a preacher. His manner was strong and energetic; and
the natural severity of his temper seems to have been more
than genius to him when expatiating, which he did often, on
the miseries of the wicked in a future state. I have seen
one of the sermons in print; it is a controversial one,
written in a bold, rough style, and by no means very inferior as a piece of argument; but he was evidently a person
rather to be listened to than read. He was quite as rigid
in church matters, it is said, as in those at the school, but
with no very marked success. He contrived to flog some
of his boys into very tolerable scholars; but though he set
himself, in Cromarty, so much against the practice of Sabbath walking that he used to take his stand every Sunday
evening in one of the avenues which leads from the town,
and turn back the walkers by the shoulders, after he had first
shaken them by the breast, the practice, out of the sheer
wrongheadedness of the people, became more popular than
before. He was called from the school of Cromarty to a
chapel of ease in Kilmarnock, and there came in contact
with Burns. I do not know that he is the hero of the
'Calf,' but he cuts a rare figure in the 'Holy Fair' (see
stanzas 21 and 22), in the 'Ordination' (see stanzas 2
and 13), in the 'Kirk's Alarm' (see stanza 5), and in the

'Twa Herds,' one of whom (see stanza 3) was the worthy Russel. The poet must have regarded the rugged preacher of the north as no common antagonist; for against none of all his other clerical opponents has he opened so powerful a battery.

"I have an uncle in Cromarty, now an elderly man, who, when residing in Glasgow in the year 1792, walked about ten miles into the country to attend a sacrament at which the learned Mr. Russel was to officiate, and which proved to be quite such a one as Burns has described in his 'Holy Fair.' There were excellent sermons to be heard from the tent, and excellent drink to be had in an alehouse scarcely a hundred yards away; and between the tent and the alehouse were the people divided, according to their tastes and characters. A young man preached in the early part of the day; his discourse was a long one, and ere it had come to a close the mirth of the neighboring topers, which became louder the more deeply they drank, had begun to annoy the congregation. Mr. Russel was standing beside the tent. At every fresh burst of sound he would raise himself on tiptoe, look first with a portentous expression of countenance towards the alehouse, and then at the clergyman, who, at length concluding his part of the service, yielded him his place. He laid aside the book, and, without psalm or prayer, or any of the usual preliminaries, launched at once into a powerful extempore address directed over the heads of the people at the alehouse. My uncle has often assured me he never in his life heard anything half so energetic. His ears absolutely tingled, as the preacher thundered out, in a voice almost superhuman, his solemn and terrible denunciations. Every sound of revelry ceased in a moment; and the bacchanals, half-drunk, as most of them were, were so thoroughly cowed as to be fain to steal out through a back window. Mr. Russel, before his death, which took place about twenty years ago, was one of the ministers of Stirling. A Cromarty man, a soldier in a Highland regiment, when stationed in the castle of that place, had got involved one day in some street quarrel, and was swearing furiously, when a tall, gaunt old man in black came and pulled him out of the crowd. ' Wretched creature that ye are,' said the old man; ' come along with me.' He drew him into a quiet corner, and began to expostulate with him on his profanity in a style to which the soldier, an intelligent, though by no means a steady man, could not but listen. Mr. Russel, for it was no other than he, seemed much pleased with the attention he paid him; and, on learning where he had come from, and the name of his parents, exclaimed, with much feeling: ' Waes me that your father's son should be a blackguard soldier on the street of Stirling! But come awa'.' He brought him home with him, and added to the much good advice he had given him an excellent dinner. The temper of the preacher seems to have softened a good deal as he became old, and he grew much a favorite with the more serious part of his congregation. He was, I doubt not, with all his defects of temper, an honest, pious man; and had he lived in the days of Renwick and Cargill, or, a century earlier, in the days of Knox and Wishart, he might have been a useful one. But he was unlucky in the age in which he lived, in his temper, and in coming in contact with as hard-headed people as himself."

WRITTEN FOR THE " INVERNESS COURIER."

" CROMARTY, May 29, 1830.

" On Monday, the 24th instant, a Cromarty boat, which had gone with the passengers from Invergordon to Wick, left the latter port on her return, about five o'clock in the evening. The crew consisted of three seamen, two of whom were brothers; and there were also on board a native of Tain, John Ross, who had taken his passage with them to Cromarty, together with his wife and six children; in all, eleven persons. There was a light breeze from the north, accompanied by a moderate swell, and, with both sails stretched to the mast-head, the boat swept for about five hours at an easy rate along the shore. At ten o'clock she was nearly opposite the Castle of Dunbeath. About this time Alexander Skinner, now the sole survivor of the eleven, became drowsy, and, quitting the stern of the boat, where the helmsman (Andrew Johnston) and the passengers were, he went ahead of the mainsail, and lay down to sleep. His last recollection of this period is, that the helmsman and Ross were engaged in conversation. He was awakened about an hour after by a tremendous shock, and a huge wave which broke over him. On starting up, he ascertained that the boat had run upon a ledge of rock, detached from the shore, which was to be seen through the dim twilight about thirty yards distant. The scene that follows baffles description. The boat hung fast by the midships; a heavy sea was tumbling round her, and breaking over her; the children were screaming, and the boatmen shouting for assistance. A pinnacle of the ledge was only partially covered by the surf, and, as it promised, for at least a few minutes, a less precarious lodgment than that which the boat afforded, — for she now began to break up, — the crew and the passengers removed to it. Alas! the tide was rising; and, melancholy to relate, in about half an hour some of the children were washed away by the surf. One of the boatmen, David Johnston, could swim a little; and, stripping off his clothes, he leaped into the water, and reached the shore. The survivor (Skinner), though he could not swim, sprang after him, and his struggling, assisted by the heave of the sea, brought him into shallow water, where he found footing. The boatman who had first reached the land, recognizing, amid the heart-rending cries of the sufferers on the rock, the voice of his brother, returned to his assistance; but, in the attempt to bring him ashore, the latter was drowned; and he himself was so exhausted with fatigue and cold, that he expired in the fields, into which he had gone, after his second landing, in quest of shelter and assistance. Skinner pressed onwards, and came up to an inhabited house; but the inmates, deeming him some deranged person, — an opinion which, it is probable, his state of mind at the time almost justified, — denied him admittance. In consequence of this mistake, a considerable space elapsed before men who could render assistance were apprized of the disaster; and, when they at length arrived, they found exertion unavailing, for there remained no object to call it forth. The rock was buried beneath the waves, and three, whom Skinner had left clinging to it with all the energy of despair, had perished. Four of the bodies have since been found, besides that of the boatman who died in the fields. It is supposed that the accident was occasioned by the pilot having fallen asleep at the helm, as the spot where it took place is considerably out of the course which the boat ought to have pursued. It is not a little remarkable that since the middle of autumn last a greater number of the inhabitants of Cromarty have perished by sea than for the thirty years preceding."

TO MR. GEORGE ANDERSON.

"CROMARTY, Sept. 15, 1834.

"Whatever may be the value of my specimens, — and I am afraid they are very rarely of any, — my discoveries almost always turn out discoveries at second hand. I see it is a great matter to be acquainted with what has been done by others. I have spent week after week in arriving at a knowledge of facts which I could have acquired in a few minutes from the pages of a geological catechism, had I but known that I might have looked for it there. I have formed theories, too, at some little expense of thought, only to find that some more fortunate speculatist had built them up much more neatly, and long before. Sir Thomas D. Lauder, for instance, has anticipated my theory of the formation of the great Caledonian valley, and Mr. Murchison my hypothesis regarding the erection of the Sutors. This is all by way of preface to what I have to say of a little discovery I have lately made, which may, in the same way, be no discovery at all.

The *lias* beds, which appear at Eathie and Shandwick, form evidently parts of a continuous ridge, which stretches between these places in a line nearly parallel to that of the coast ; and they must have formed the superior strata of the great secondary basin of this part of the country at the period the granitic rock of the Sutors was forced through. But where, I have frequently asked myself, am I to look for the remains of similar strata on the northern and western sides of these rocks ? or am I to infer that they rose at the extreme edge of the *lias*, thus merely throwing it off towards the south and east. from the sandstone on which it had rested ? I conceived of the *lias* strata as of ice on a pond ; a wedge forced through it in the centre would break up its continuity, and derange its position on two sides, — the two sides of the wedge, — whereas a wedge forced through it at its edge would merely separate it from the bank, and derange its horizontal position on only one side. The great thickness of the *lias* at Eathie seems, however, to militate against this latter supposition, — the wedge must have been forced through a central part of the pond ; and for several years past I have been examining, in my rambles, the various ravines on the western and northern sides of the Sutors. and the rocks laid bare by the sea within the bay, in the hope of meeting with the *lias*. I have at length found, not it. but something equally curious. Rather more than half a mile east of the town the granitic rock is bounded, as you are aware, by a thick bed of breccia ; then there occurs a small vein of limestone, and then alternate strata of coarse red and yellowish sandstone, with here and there a vein of stratified clay, containing nodules of a calcareous stone, prettily variegated with red and yellow. From the breccia to the bed of sandstone nearest the town, there is rather more than a hundred yards ; and, from the almost vertical position of the strata, we have merely to pass along their edges to gain an acquaintance with them, which could only be acquired, were their position horizontal, by sinking a shaft nearly a hundred yards in depth. I used to conceive of this advantage by the ease I found in running my eye over books arranged on the shelves of a library, contrasted with the trouble I had in taking them up one after one when they were packed in a chest.

" For several hundred yards nearer the town the beach is so covered with shingle and stones, that we see no more of the strata till we reach a small bay, only a very little beyond the bounds of the borough, where we find beds of a stratified, grayish claystone, lying, as nearly as can be judged from their broken state, in an angle of about twenty with the horizon. From the extent of nearly vertical strata which intervene between them and the granite rock, and their comparatively slight inclination from the horizontal, I was led to think that they must originally have occupied a very superior place, and that their situation, with regard to the opening between the Sutors, must have preserved them from the derangement of the other strata. Under these impressions, I have of late examined them very minutely. As nearly as I can judge from the little of them which appears above the sand, they are separated from each other by thin bands, of a grayish indurated sandstone, and thickly interspersed by flattened nodules of an elliptical or circular form. On breaking these nodules across, I found them to be composed of either an imperfect limestone, or indurated clay; and saw that in the centre of each there was a broken line of deep black, in the direction of which they separated more easily than in any other. I have split up several hundreds of them, in the expectation of identifying their contents with the remains at Eathie, but they seem to belong to a formation altogether different. I find none of the chambered univalves, no bivalves, no belemnites, but abundance of fish; some scaled like the haddock, some roughened like the dog-fish, or shark. Some of the nodules are sprinkled over with small, irregular patches, somewhat resembling scales; in others there are confused masses of a bituminous-looking substance. In some, unmixed with the scales, I can trace what seem to have been the bones of fish; in others, what appears to have been wood; and in one specimen, which I unfortunately spoiled in the breaking, there were the remains of what seemed to have been a toad, or frog. I have kept for you four of the best specimens I could find, and shall send them when I have procured a few more for you from the beds at Eathie. Owing to the prevalence of sand and clay in the nodules, the remains are very imperfect; they seem, too, to have been subjected to great pressure. I find that the purer the limestone, the more entire the shells, or fish, which it contains. But I am afraid you will deem all this mere tediousness. The entire province of geology is a *terra incognita* to me, and I do not know whether I am now describing to you a part of it with which every geologist is acquainted, or a part known to only myself."

END OF VOL. I.